FOX in the FOOTLIGHTS

A Novel by

E.F. Winters

2025 Kenspeckle Production LLC

Copyright © 1-14991115531
by E.F.Winters All rights reserved.

Published in the United States by Kenspeckle Productions LLC
Distributed by IngramSpark and
Lightning Source as Print on Demand

Library of Congress Cataloging-in-Publications Data
E.F.Winters & Kenspeckle Productions
ISBN 978-1-940531-07-6

Printed in the United States of America

Cover Art by E.F. Winter

Cover design: by E.F.Winters & J.L.Winters

Edited by: J.L. Winters

Also by E.F. Winters:

MEMELOOSE: The Island of the Dead
First in category winner
Somerset Awards
Chanticleer Writing Competition

SHARKS AND MINNOWS
Book One of the
Jolie Chronicles

GHOSTS in the GRAVEYARD
Book Two of the
Jolie Chronicles

CATCH the DRAGON'S TAIL
Book Three of the
Jolie Chronicles

THE PEOPLE'S GIFT
SIGNEY'S BEAR

Watch for:

EBULON
Book One of
The Keepers of the Truths

FOX in the FOOTLIGHTS

Kenspeckle
Productions, LLC

THE FOX and the FOOTLIGHTS

PROLOGUE:

"I am invisible.

I must be because people look right through me and do not see me.

I am invisible even when I am in the room, standing right there. Right here. I understand it is not scientific, but my experience remains.

I have become a dust mote floating in the stale, silent air.

If the sun would only come out, I could dance on a beam of light, capturing a glance from a passing eye, seen, if only for a moment.

If the sun would come out, I could look to see if I have a shadow.

Having a shadow proves you have substance and therefore exist, doesn't it?

But it does not prove that I matter...to anyone.

If my grandmother were alive, she would pirouette the drapes back, fling the windows open, and sing in the sun, but there has been no sunlight in this house since the day she took to her bed.

Her in-laws snip and stretch pity onto their long faces, pretending they are not relieved to be rid of this embarrassing connection to the unconventional Drakes, but I see their lies.

Children know.

A gray skin of dust reveals the molting half-efforts the staff now expend toward the care of my grandmother's house.

Wriggling their fingers, they measure the size of their pockets against the size of coveted objects; treasures my family has collected over generations of their uncommon lives.

In pity-soaked whispers, they mumble pretentious promises for prayers that will never be spoken, condescension underwriting the triumph over my misfortune that they secretly hug to their breasts.

"I knew it. I told you." The housekeeper uses her self-declared prescience to justify her resentment. "Responsible adults do not drag their families to the wilds of the world. You don't move around like that unless you have something to hide."

Prologue

"Good people stay put." The cook pecks at the housekeeper's secrets like seed corn

"No one could believe it when Mister Abott married an actress!" The gossip's mouth twists in disdain. "The woman may as well have been a gypsy, or a circus freak."

The housekeeper had been with my grandmother for forty years.

I have known these people most of my life, but I never knew their hearts, nor they mine, because I am invisible.

Act One, Scene One: March 1863, Wallack's Theater, 844 Broadway, New York, New York.

When I was deposited on the curb outside Wallack's Theater in New York City, I was a boy teetering on the edge of a growth spurt that would tease at the man I would become. It was a drizzly afternoon, and the driver of the hired hackney reined his horse in alongside the red-block building, waiting impatiently for me and my single bag to depart his cab. My feet had barely touched the pavement when he drove away, but I expected no less. His services had been arranged and prepaid by our family solicitor, and he could no more hope for a generous tip through better attention, nor have any fear of receiving a lesser sum due to poor service, certainly not to a person like myself, half-grown, of modest income, with no position or family connections.

You could be forgiven for wondering how a stranger would possibly know such intimate details, and I would be forced to confess I do not know. I can only say that it happens. All the time. Whenever I am newly introduced, I am measured and dismissed. I tell myself it is my age, my small size, my plain face, but I suspect invisibility. Still, it is possible that it is due to something else about myself that I do not yet understand.

The low sky dripped a sorrowful rain, gray and cloud-filtered; it hunched over a working-class neighborhood striving to pass as something better. The theater occupied half the block of Broadway between Twelfth and Thirteenth Streets, the other half given over to Gibson's Glass and Architectural Specialties. The perimeter of the building along Broadway had been sectioned into shop spaces. Green canvas awnings were attached above the street-level shop windows, but they had not been pulled out today, leaving the shops looking like gentlemen who had gone out without their hats.

Manhattan was a new city as cities went, as were all the settled spaces of North America in 1863. During my ride from the train station, I had seen only new and newer buildings, all built to present the growing city as it hoped to become. Young, vibrant, and more than a little impulsive, New York was old enough to know it wanted to be *something* and brash enough to have the energy to race toward whatever that something might be, but lacked the wisdom to consider the cost of its ambitions, or so said the folk of Ohio.

Though Broadway and its attendant walkways were wider than the streets of Cincinnati or the ones I remembered from my childhood in London's West End, the five and six-story buildings on either side meant the sun only reached the pavement at midday, imposing a false twilight long before the sun set over the Hudson and the streetlights were lit.

I waited at the curb, clutching my bag as much for its familiarity as to keep its contents from being soaked through, expecting at any moment that someone would come through the wrought iron gate guarding the theater's entrance and take charge of me.

I am not an orphan, I reminded myself. Though my grandmother's in-laws, the Lowdons, had tried to attach that label to me, I refused to accept it.

When my mother was first informed by my father's colleagues that he had died while surveying with them in the California desert, I acted as I had in his presence, retreating to my bedroom and wrapping myself in invisibility.

I should have felt bad. I should have felt devastated. But I did not. It was unnatural. *You are unnatural,* I told myself.

I looked to my mother, as a child will, checking for clues from the person who helps them understand what is expected, and how to navigate human emotion. She was not devastated either. Maybe there was something wrong with both of us, or maybe the wrongness was not ours, but his. Johnathan Becket would never have admitted to any wrongness. He was, in his view, perfect.

He had been a desperate academic, self-involved and driven, like most men of the era. His single-minded pursuit of new discoveries and the attending recognition he so longed for left only crumbs and splinters for his wife and child to pick through. Even when he was home, he was not there. He was not part of the family my mother and I created between us. His person and the life he led were adjacent but separate. Johnathan Becket expected that we would feel honored at the privilege of being spectators to his career. And so, I marked his death. I was not affected by it.

But the early years and fears of a child's life leave a strong imprint, and the unspoken relief of my father's removal from our lives did not end the habit of mistrust and caution ingrained in my character due to his heavy hand and belittling nature.

When, some months later, my mother put me on the ship in New San Diego bound for New York and eventually my final destination in Cincinnati, she promised she would join me soon. Loving the freedom of the western wilds of California, exploring the shorelines and woodlands with my only friend, Matias, I had not wanted to leave. Unable to understand why I must go when she was staying, confused and bereft, I watched her small, stoic figure shrink to the size of a doll, then a sparrow, as the ship's sails were hoisted and took us out of the bay.

I watched for her every day since, scanning every river dock, wagon, or train station along the way as I and the lieutenant who accompanied me traveled the long months to my banishment in Ohio.

Grandmother Manon had done her best to make me feel at home, but I never abandoned the habit of lurking at windows, watching the street, and hoping. I went through the mail, studying the postmarks, clinging to the belief that, despite the growing term of our separation, my mother would return, and when she did, everything would miraculously become as perfect as pudding and a book by the fire on a cold winter night.

Once committed, I can be most stubborn.

By the time my grandmother gave in to age and illness, Leonara Marchand Becket had been declared missing and presumed dead.

But presumption is not certainty, not to a child. However invisible I was to the rest of the world, my mother saw me, and despite the flaws hidden behind my plain appearance, she loved me.

And now I had come to New York.

My great aunt's name on the posters outside Wallack's Theater was written twice as large as the title of the play she was performing in. In nearly equal-sized lettering, it was announced that this production of *MacBeth* would be lit by gas and limelight.

Even here in the United States, currently not so united, Aunt Bernadette's talents were in demand, and Lady MacBeth was one of her most acclaimed roles. Despite her Ludlow in-laws' disapproval, or maybe because of it, Grandma Manon had stubbornly displayed daguerreotypes of her younger sister on her grand piano. My grandmother was not a shy person, and her sister Bernadette had toured to accolades in Europe and been recognized in her native Great Britain with the honorific of a "Dame" of the realm. The Ludlows were "normal' people: bankers, lawyers, architects.

My mother and I had lived at Aunt Bernadette's West End townhouse several times during my early childhood, including a year when my father traveled in the Middle East. My memories of my great aunt, therefore, were a toddler's: swaths of midnight skirts sweeping by my head, rife with the scent of Christmas: citrus, cedar, and cinnamon.

Though Bernadette Drake's name frequently appeared in newspapers and journals alongside famous and influential persons, I had never read or heard any reference linking her to a husband or children. Unlike her elder sister, Bernadette had chosen a career unencumbered by family. A fact that gave me pause. I had held deep affection for my grandmother, Manon, but sisters were just as likely to be wildly different in disposition as they were to be alike, and I could not think that Dame Drake's avocation would give her the time or interest to raise a great-nephew she had not seen in a dozen years. Aunt Bernie was doubtless accepting my guardianship out of filial duty, nothing more. What use could such a widely celebrated actress have for an invisible boy? Unfortunately for her, she was my only provably living relative. Still, alongside my anxiety, I nurtured a spark of hope that my aunt would be more prone to kindness than cruelty, both because I had read David Copperfield more than once and because of what it would mean for my circumstances and my future.

All of these considerations, which I had been weeding and hoeing like a prize winning garden, raised questions about how my aunt would oversee the final years of my life before I entered adulthood— whether that oversight would be near-at-hand, or merely by paying for an education at some distant academic institution where I would be forcibly polished-off before being released into the world to make my way.

Frankly, a future predicated on being abandoned to the tortures of boarding school bullies without any hope of escaping other children, whom I knew to be the worst and most vengeful beings alive, terrified me. My previous forays into mass adolescent warehousing had been a disaster that ended in my leaving within months of having been deposited there, never to return.

With the traditional childhood path of boarding school closed and bolted behind me, I had grown up being educated by my mother and traveling with my parents, dragged along to discussions and lectures given by the intellectuals representing the scientific institutions and academic societies my father wished to be connected to. But while my mental appetites had been fed, any experience of my peers remained blank pages that I felt no urgency to fill, enjoying the eternal possibility of their fragile, ivory emptiness. That is, until I found and lost my friend, Matias, in New San Diego. The losing part of the experience had been very painful and caused me to swear off the indulgence of friendship, renewing my belief that all I required of life was that it leave me alone with my books, gadgets, and drawing materials.

It had not cooperated.

Standing outside Wallack's theater, one hour ticked by, then two. With the shadow of the buildings opposite the theater now encroaching on my position, I began to reconsider my situation.

The day was waning, and no one had come to collect me. A situation that did nothing to lessen the concerns I nurtured over my welcome, which I feared foreshadowed my future inclusion in my aunt's household, or more likely, the lack of it. However, I could not merely stand in the rain all night, like a forgotten lamb bleating on the hillside. New York City was not known for its shepherd population. So, strengthening my resolve, I approached the gate barring the theatre doors and peered through the vertical slats like a prisoner on the wrong side of freedom.

As I stepped away, considering whether to look for an alternate entrance or make inquiries at one of the shops, a slip of a girl in a fine, charcoal gray wool cloak approached, pulled the gate aside, and side-stepped her broomstick frame through the narrow opening before returning the gate to its closed position. Embarrassed by my own timidity at not having tried the gate myself, I waited until she was well inside before following.

A young man arrived at the gate just before me.

"After you." He smiled, holding it open. He looked closer to twenty than twenty-five, his winsome smile making him seem young and vulnerable while his confident manner hinted at more seasoning. I felt a twinge of envy at such a young person possessing this wealth of confidence, allowing him to navigate the world undaunted by the fear of other people's judgment. But then he was quite handsome, sea green eyes peeking out from behind a fall of ash blonde hair that brushed a high cheekbone, teasing an interrupted view of features that could have been the model for an angel or a pagan god. People of such natural beauty experience the world differently from the rest of us.

"You are here to see…?" he prompted me. I looked at him dumbly. "The stage manager, Woolrich, perhaps?" he kindly attempted to help me overcome my awkwardness. Dressed in the standard wool overcoat and trousers that were the fashion for a middle-class man not involved in physical labor, I discerned that, despite his physical beauty, he was not a gentleman.

"I am here to see my aunt," I stuttered. "I have just arrived and was instructed to meet her here." The young man's blond eyebrows arched, silently indicating the question he was too polite to voice. "My aunt, Bernie—uh, Bernadette Drake." I indicated a nearby poster.

Recognition lit the young man's comely face. "Lady Drake?"

"Yes," I confirmed. "I am her nephew, Christopher Becket— well, great nephew. She is my great aunt."

"Yes, that is the way those things usually work," he teased. "She is a lady who has certainly earned the label 'great', but in the future you might wish to leave that bit off. Actresses, even legends like Lady Bernadette, can be sensitive about their age." He winked as if we now had a special secret, making me wish we did. Invisible people do not make casual friends, or any friends really, outside of favorite books.

"Pleased to meet you, Master Becket. I am Gilbert Collmeyer--an actor with the company. Come." Collmeyer led me past the grated gates and through the doors.

The warmth of a well-tended fire that reaches out to you as you approach it melted the shiver from my skin, beckoning me to cross the threshold. But there was no fire inside. There was no source of physical warmth at all. My guide was going on without me, and I hurried to catch up.

Everything inside was red or gold, including the plush carpeting, its lush texture giving our gaits elegance through the genteel hush it lent our footsteps.

Gas sconces decorated the walls of the lobby, a dozen chandeliers hanging from the punched tin ceiling. When lit, the gaslight's glow would be reflected many times over in the large plate-glass mirrors on the walls, but the lights were dark now, and the miserly amount of daylight that had followed us in struggled to cast even a spark in the gold-embossed wallpaper.

"This way." The young man pulled aside a heavy, red velvet curtain, inviting me to exit the lobby and enter a new, cavernous cathedral.

Three tiers of balconies leaned in anticipation toward rows of green velvet upholstered seats striping the main floor. Private viewing boxes held court on the second and third levels on either side of what could only be the stage, an area defined by an ornate frame as tall as a four-story building. It was decorated with swirls and masks expressing joy and sorrow.

"Lady Drake will be in Wardrobe now, but you can wait here." The young actor strolled down the declining aisle toward the stage.

"Where?" I asked, flummoxed by the hundreds of choices on this floor alone.

"Anywhere," he tossed the word back over his shoulder before disappearing to the left of the staging area.

I placed my bag in the seat beside me and sat, prepared to wait.

No one came.

Men walked onto the staging area, going about their tasks, humming or muttering according to their nature, then vanished back into the hidden world beyond.

My stomach rumbled and pinched. I had run out of the scant provisions and pocket change the Lowdons had sent with me for the journey and was now beyond hungry, but I dared not leave and risk missing my aunt's summons. Though whether running out of funds was due to my elder's ignorance of inflated costs because of the war, or whether it was due to my naive spending, I could not say, but the outcome was the same. I had little money, no notion of what costs were in New York City, and I was afraid to venture away from where I was expected.

I continued to sit, equally ignoring my predicament and being ignored.

The train had not stopped, but we knew it had been boarded; the sounds of gunfire, shrieks of terror, and deadfall thumps were moving slowly toward our car.

"Do not try to fight," Lieutenant Lewis cautioned the frightened passengers. "If you do not attack them, they will most probably leave you to travel on in safety. They are after money, not lives." He turned to me.

"Get down between the seats next to the outside wall and stay quiet, even if they threaten or injure me, Christopher. Whatever happens, just stay on the train and show your ticket to the conductor when he asks. Your grandmother will be waiting for you in Cincinnati."

I nodded and slid off the seat, scuttling back against the wall. Lieutenant Lewis moved away to an empty seat as far from any of the other passengers as he could without leaving the car.

The train robbers entered our car, their boots thumping against the wooden floorboards, their long rifles rattling like winter tree limbs as they scratched the sides of the passenger benches. My vision shrank to the small space in front of the bench I huddled beside, tracking the robber's progress by the sound of their footsteps until a pair of worn, gray boots, the leather cracked with clotted clay, stood at the end of the aisle before me.

"Where's them that sat here?" the robber demanded in a strong Southern drawl. My bag was on the seat, and Lieutenant Lewis's was on the shelf above.

The robber scanned the bench and its surroundings. He would see me. He must. I was right there on the floor.

But he did not. For I was invisible.

From forward in the car, Lieutenant Lewis spoke, drawing the robber's attention away from where I huddled, hidden by my insignificance.

A thunderous blast ricocheted off the passenger's horrified screams. A dull thud followed.

From beneath the seat to my left, I watched as the spark of Lieutenant Lewis's life sighed from his body, his lifeless eyes staring at the me he could not see.

A cat meowed, and I awakened in Wallack's Theater. I had fallen asleep.

The sound of another person moving about among the seats reminded me where I was, and I opened my eyes to see a black cat on the floor beside me, its hair lighter at the roots, its yellow eyes intensely focused on my own.

Eyes…. My mind rolled back to the dream of the final leg of my journey from California to Cincinnati, so often replayed. Had Lieutenant Lewis's dead eyes held forgiveness or accusation for the boy for whom he had sacrificed his life? The answer changed from day to day depending on how I felt. Was there a more permanent truth beyond my interpretation? If so, I did not know how to find it, but whatever Lieutenant Lewis's thoughts might have been, I blamed myself, and the guilt stayed with me, added to my collection.

The curtain at the front of the stage at Wallack's was closed now, hiding the secret preparations on the other side. A boy, somewhat younger than myself and Irish, if his red hair and freely freckled face were any indication, kept looking toward me from different parts of the vaulted hall as he swept between the seat rows. Finally, deciding that I was not going to do the right thing and leave, he approached.

"Beg your pardon, young Sir, but you are too early for the show. Is that your seat there you're sittin' in?"

I knew nothing about the theater, aside from the fact that it existed, and was absolutely confounded by the idea that the seats here had owners. Cincinnati was not so cosmopolitan as to have a theater, and the Lowdons would not have attended one if it did. The primitive New San Diego was far from such cultural ambitions, and I had been too young when my mother and I lived in London to have any awareness of anything of a theatrical nature. So, despite being a Drake on my mother's side, I was ignorant of the most basic facts regarding the theater and embarrassed to find myself occupying a seat that belonged to someone else. Deciding that the less I said, the better I could hide my ignorance, I said nothing.

"If it's not yours, you'll have to move," the boy declared with a scowl. "Let me see your ticket." He stretched out his hand.

"I don't have a ticket," I confessed, my cheeks burning.

"Then you got to leave."

"I cannot leave." Hopelessness grasped at my coattails.

"You can't be in here without a ticket. That's the rules."

"But I am meeting my aunt," I attempted to justify my continued presence. "She works here."

"Then your aunt should know better than to tell you to wait for her in the house," the boy scolded officiously.

I frowned. Again, I did not know much, but I knew the difference between a house and a theater, and this was the latter, not the former.

"Who is your aunt?" my tormentor demanded. "One of the seamstresses? A dresser? Tell me her name and I'll fetch her so she can tell you where to go."

"Bernadette Drake," I replied.

The boy paled, his freckles standing out like orange paint marks on new white paper. "You're not having me on, are you?" I shook my head, apparently convincingly, because he did not question my honesty a second time. "Beg pardon, but Lady Bernadette will be getting ready for the show now, and no one's to bother her when she's preparing, not even young Mister Wallack."

"Then what am I to do?" I demanded, struggling to keep the weep of desperation from my voice.

The boy shrugged. "Sit here until someone comes for you or wants your seat. You might have to move, but it's mid-week, there's sure to be some seats open." He left, leaving me once again alone to wait.

If I had not been accustomed to being invisible, I might have felt some slight at my treatment. I had traveled a long distance, I was very tired, and ravenously hungry, but if some newborn version of resentment was attempting to slither into existence within my breast, I was prepared to deny its existence, just as my own was being denied.

"You are alright," the rich tones of a woman's voice curled up like a kitten nestling into my ear. "He's in shock but not injured," she informed the train passengers behind her.

E.F. Winters

My eyes were so heavy I could not open them even the width of a knitting thread, my body too drained to move.

"Such a brave boy." A soft hand touched my cheek, then a whisper-breeze of moving skirts cooled my feverish skin.

She had left.

When I awoke again, I was still in the theater, but I could still smell the woman's perfume—my mother's perfume, hanging in the air. I looked about for her, my heart banging inside my chest, but all around me were only strangers.

While I had nodded off, the theater had begun to fill; middle-class couples, a few men in uniforms that were not uniform in style but seemed chosen to celebrate some shared cultural heritage. I moved my bag from the seat beside me to the floor, hoping to be less conspicuous, but if those around me saw me at all, they took no note.

The private boxes were the last to be occupied; a higher degree of wealth, better tailoring, and a greater confluence of gemstones worn by the womenfolk making a visual brag of elevated position and influence.

Since rediscovering patriotism with the attack on Fort Sumter in April of 1861, New York had allied with the Union, its leadership reluctantly backtracking from the January announcement by its city council that New York City was seceding from the United States and declaring itself a neutral city-state open for business to all parties during the conflict to come. Though the theater attendees around me conversed in lowered voices, snatches of conversation drifted to me, more than one gentleman voicing disappointment that the city had not held to its decision to secede, because now it was embroiled in an unpopular war led by an incompetent, backwoods bumpkin of a president.

He meant Abraham Lincoln.

I was very uncomfortable with this. Cincinnati had its share of differing points of view on the sixteenth president, but publicly declaring disloyalty to our government's leader would not have been acceptable. It seemed even worse for New York's population to complain. Their city had reaped so many benefits through Union contracts that a new social class had been created.

Cincinnati, being a region settled predominantly by pacifist farmers from Prussia, was directly across the Ohio River from slave holding Confederate territory and had therefore witnessed decades of abuse to enslaved populations. They were, however, a pragmatic people and understood that ideals made for interesting discussions, but purchased neither seed nor plow. While New England and the uniquely American intellectuals it produced went about proudly declaring their democratic superiority and freedom from static European notions, the new Midwest American was focused on a future that gave their families land and the generational sustainability that came with it. Philosophical debates about human rights, justice, and equality aside, words that had drawn them across an ocean to seek a new life, Midwesterners recognized that those who looked, thought, and prayed like them were more likely to come to their aid, vote like them, and fight beside them, while people who did not share their nation of origin, or skin color—were an uncomfortable unknown. Furthermore, the enslaved, namely black, brown, and red people, presented a barrier to the dreams that had brought the immigrants to this new land. Slavery might be discussed, but in the end, was dismissed as "someone else's problem".

I had thought the Lowdon's entitled attitudes in the face of the misery of our enslaved neighbors and the native people I had known in California were an aberrant family trait. I had not understood it to be a general opinion within our young country, and I slunk down into my seat, a sense of unease settling in my chest.

"I think that's P.T. Barnum," a woman in the row in front of me pointed to a box on the right. She was dressed up for the theater, though I would not have said she was "well-dressed," her taste called to question by the mismatched colors and overdone decorations of bodice and bonnet.

I stretched up and to my left so I could see over the box's low wall, craning to catch a glimpse of the famous showman. He had company, but all I could see of that person was the top of their head and a curl of smoke lazily twirling above it.

"That must be the Little General, Tom Thumb, with him," the woman suggested. Others in the rows joined my awkward craning posture.

The party taking up the opposite box arrived, the menfolk speaking loudly and making a show of themselves.

"And that would be Mayor Fernando Wood and his new bride," the overdressed woman added, self-important in the attention she was gaining. Apparently, viewing the audience before the stage performance was as much a draw as viewing the play itself.

"He's not a mayor anymore," her male companion grumbled.

"No, he's a *senator* now," his wife responded stiffly, picking at the lace and glittering braid on her bodice. "Which is even more important."

"What he wants is to be king of New York City, but we've had enough of kings in this country. For god's sake, Bridey, sit down." The man squinted at the box. "The woman with him is not old enough to be his wife. She must be his daughter."

"She is his *third* wife," Bridey explained haughtily. "She is said to be very young."

"Yes. Young enough to be his daughter," her husband repeated.

Fernando Wood was a man of slight build, like me, only old. Whereas I still had the possibility of growing out of my uncommon thinness, Wood's years were beyond that. The newspapers described him as handsome, but I could not see it. In my opinion, he had the crafty look of a weasel without the piquant charm. His nose and cheekbones were skeletal. The skin on his face clung to the bones beneath as if no muscle or flesh cushioned the connection, and his eyes were sunken and troublingly close together, which only accentuated his dead-man appearance. It was not a face that inspired trust, and I wondered how such a person could have risen to a position of power in a system where people voted for their leaders, presumably because of the very characteristics this man did not look to possess. Wood stood beside the outer balustrade of his box, looking across the audience, conspicuously taking in the box opposite his own. P.T. Barnum smiled and nodded, and Wood returned a marginally polite gesture of greeting.

"There is no need to be polite to the scoundrel, P.T.," Barnum's unseen friend spoke from below the box's edge. "The man is a traitor and an ass. Lincoln should have locked him up two years ago."

"Hush, Charles. There is no need to be rude," Barnum whispered loudly enough that those of us on the floor below could hear. "This is a public theater, not the deck of your steamship, and we are here to see a play, not make a spectacle of ourselves."

"Speak for yourself." General Tom Thumb stood up on his chair and looked over the balcony wall. "My condolences on your recent nuptials, Missus Wood," he raised his voice, bowing gallantly to the young bride across the way. "Have you met your new husband's children yet? They would be about your age. Perhaps you went to school together? That would be awkward." He glared at Wood, adding, "For any decent man that is."

Barnum hid a laugh in his handkerchief before shrugging apologetically to Wood as if to bemoan that there was no controlling his friend.

"A tiny man with a tiny brain," Wood dismissed the erstwhile Tom Thumb to his companions.

"A bigger man than you!" The celebrated performer puddled the bulge of his penis in his hand as if weighing it, winking at young Mrs. Wood as he did. She blushed fiercely. "I would help you out, Madam, but I am newly married myself and thus reformed from my wild ways."

The men on the main floor in earshot laughed, their womenfolk tittering behind their hands. I had read of the phenomenon of Tom Thumb's popularity with women. He had been feted by royalty across Europe and paraded through cities where women lined the streets just to get a look at him.

"Charles, sit down." Barnum's tone was that of a parent reining in an errant child. Tom Thumb allowed Barnum to distract him and get him seated.

When the room was stuffed like a plump pigeon, the grand chandelier was drawn up into a recessed area in the ceiling, dimming the light over the seats below. As the slothful curtain slowly folded open, revealing a staged woodland, the audience's conversations stuttered then stopped.

E.F. Winters

The dark, mossy ground, rife with rough rock and unseen evils, oozed shadows that reached across the footlights toward us, the forest branches rattling in dry cackles expressed from tree limbs by a breeze that surely must have been captured out-of-doors and magically transported to the stage. Limelight moonbeams cross-hatched the tree's murky greenery and spilled onto the painted backdrop. Our communal breath catching in our throats, human instinct cautioned that there was danger here that reason could not push aside. Somewhere outside this woodland realm, light and hope remained, but they would not be found here.

The three witches who open the play rose from the moss-blanketed ground, confirming the audience's suspicions that bad things lurked in these woods.

"When shall we three meet again in thunder, lightning, or in rain?" The first lines broke the spell of silence that the opening of the curtain and slow dawning of the lights had cast.

"When the hurly-burly's done, when the battle's lost and won." Costumed as if they had grown from the moss and bark, like toadstools, the witches spoke their future-telling phrases like throaty grackles impersonating human voices.

When my aunt made her entrance as the lady of the castle, I understood why my family had so rarely seen her. In truth, had anyone? The woman was a sorceress of the stage, a being of light and dark, charm and torment, an artist at the height of her craft, manipulating her admirers on both sides of the footlights with coy smiles and the flash of her mocking eyes, just as Macbeth's lady manipulated her husband to the doom of his house.

I had read the words of Shakespeare on the flat pages of books, but seeing the work in performance was a revelation. Bernadette Drake did not mimic or pretend. She simply *was*. She did not play a role; she breathed it, speaking the words of the character as if she were that person. It was true of most of the actors in Wallack's company who endeavored not merely to mouth the Bard's words but spoke them as if they tumbled out, crumbling and distorted by the desires and pain of their own hearts. I had never understood the lines or the thoughts so well until I heard them uttered from the stage by the characters for whom they were written--to whom they rightly belonged, spoken by actors of skill and nobility.

The music of the master playwright's phrases affected each of us in the audience in personal ways, bending and twisting our emotions like a conductor mutes and swells his orchestra.

Where are you, Mother? Where did you go?" my scalded heart responded like flat champagne. "Y*ou said you would follow. Whatever could keep you so long?*

"Death," a voice whispered from the deep recesses of my mind.

I shut my ears, pushing the possibility away. *"I need you. I am lost in the dark and need somewhere to belong…a family."* I thought of the many times my mother's hand had helped me crawl out of a corner and find my feet after retreating to avoid my father's temper. That woman would never abandon her son to the struggle of surviving on his own. She knew how raw my wounds were--how timid my nature. Something had happened—something unexpected.

"Tis the eye of childhood that fears the painted devil," Lady MacBeth's voice from the stage covered and cloaked her audience like a coastal fog.

Though the story being played out on the stage was not my own, the words being spoken shed echoes of my own cowardice coating me in their dust, wisdom whispering to my heart that it was time I wriggled from my cocoon of fear and the crushing grip of grief, and faced the world as it was; grand, uncertain, cruel; marked by darkness and light, grief and joy. The performance before me shouted that it was up to each of us to turn from the darkness; a choice we faced anew every day, with every challenge, amidst every joy or sorrow, whether choosing acts of loyal friendship or reaping the punishment of betrayal, understanding that though the view from the heights was rapturous, descent was equally part of the journey.

Wrapped in the theater's dark, forgiving embrace, I wept silently.

It was a shock when the lines ended, and the stage lights dimmed. The curtain closed as the chandelier above slowly lowered, severing the spell the performance had cast, returning us each to the ruin of our everyday lives. It was a waking so painful I could barely breathe.

"It cannot be over," I gasped.

"No, dear. It is only the interval," Bridey turned to reassure me as she rose from her seat. "It is quite a long play, but Lady Drake is divine, isn't she?" I nodded silently, unable to find words. Her husband looked as if he had just woken from a nap, but he roused himself to escort his wife out of the seating area.

I stood as well. Not wanting to carry my bag, but also not wanting to leave it, I merely slid out of the row to the aisle to stretch my legs.

The curtains covering the entries to the lobby had been drawn back by silent ushers. I caught a glimpse of the Irish boy who had requested my ticket. The theater's front doors had been thrown open so the audience could spill out onto the sidewalk. Menfolk stood outside in groups, smoking and passing monogrammed flasks between them. Their female companions conversed in the foyer with women of their acquaintance or, if they lacked social connections, stood awkwardly against the gold-embossed walls, waiting. Invisibility was not solely my domain. The affliction erased from view any person considered less because of gender, age, skin color, wealth, or the lack of it, and any state of perceived differentness, from a crooked nose to a gimpy limp.

I watched as Senator Wood's box emptied, presumably to join the appropriate groups on the street or in the lobby. Across the way in Barnum's box, a new twirl of smoke rose from below the balcony wall. The Drakes were not the only performers who avoided mingling with the public.

When the interval break was over, people resumed their seats, but Wood's party did not return; his box conspicuously empty for the second half of the play.

Released from the spell of the actor's performances, I turned my attention to the activities of those who spoke no scripted lines but instead supported the actor's efforts by creating the illusions of the environments that clothed and colored those lines through the arts of light and design.

On each side of the great picture frame inside which the performance's visuals were played out were wooden towers, their platforms accessed by ladders. Men and boys of varying ages climbed these ladders, the youngest among them younger than myself. All were of small build, surefooted, and nimble, climbing up and down the towers like seasoned sailors navigating a sailing vessel's mast. Four of them, two on each side, settled onto seats surrounded by huge reflectors, glass bottles, branches, and fabrics used to create the illusion of the moonlit forest, the torchlit castle, and all the somber shadows required of the play's dark theme. A third pair of stagehands on each tower used their weight to work wooden planks like pumps, filling and emptying the bladders that controlled the gas for the limelights.

When the performance continued, I studied how the stage lighting focused the audience's attention to the illusions the master controller wished us to see, and away from those he did not want us to notice, effectively capturing our attention and holding it within the theater's space. In this masterful reflection of machinations, much like Lady MacBeth's own, the imprisoned beams of light murdered the existence of the outside world, holding the audience-witnesses hostage just as the murderous lady held her guests hostage, spending their lives like breadcrumbs tossed upon the water to sink or be devoured as fate willed.

I had overheard friends of my grandmother speak of the transformative effects of theater, how the best of it could touch the soul, and had scoffed at their overly dramatic declarations, but I was not scoffing now. It had been my ignorance and folly that kept me from understanding, my mind unable to imagine the masterful illusions brought to bear in a truly skilled company of theatricians. I felt changed.

All of us, hundreds of people gathered together in the darkness, had shared—even been part of something miraculous, and it had bound us together. We had entered the theater sanctuary as separate individuals, our thoughts clouded by the petty details of politics and self-interest, the will of others more powerful than the whispers of our own hearts, then Shakespeare's tragedy had come to life, cautioning us to beware of petty ambitions and fearful inner voices so susceptible to collusion with humans' worst instincts. None could look away. None could stop their ears or close off their hearts. Not if they had the courage to stay. I looked up to the box that Fernando Wood had vacated. Some hearts could not bear to be opened. Some minds could not bear to have the Truth revealed. Mine would not be among them, I vowed. By the time the curtain closed on the final line of the performance, I was in love.

The actors presented themselves to the audience's thunderous applause. Slapping my hands together until my palms stung, I felt more alive than I ever had, blood careening through my veins, my

E.F. Winters

heart dancing and drumming, wild in my chest. The world was not as I had believed. It was not dire, drear, and dimly lit like the plodding Lowdon's insisted. It was *this*. And actors were not thieves and cheats; they were mortals raised to the stature of gods, endowed with the ability to paint humanity as who they could and should be if only they would hold themselves to the highest standards and become their best selves. My view of the world had been transformed, and I, along with it. Here, in this hallowed place, dust motes danced nightly in colored cascades of light not only seen but celebrated.

Act One, Scene Two

Act One, Scene Two: Wallack's Theater that same night

The audience rose slowly from their seats, testing their voices as they left to pursue the activities they had planned for the rest of the evening. Could anyone actually go home to bed now? I felt like swimming the English Channel or racing over the heaths and hills of Scotland to win a kingdom like the characters in the play. I longed to ride a horse, swing a sword, wear a kilt, and shout brave poetry to my enemies. I had profound pity for those who had never experienced such a transformative moment, chained to the drudgery of a life without depth of feeling, robbed of any hope that their lives might become better.

My attention returned to the silent crew climbing down from the towers. Anonymous and unapplauded, they wore workman's clothing in dark hues that allowed them to do their jobs without drawing the audience's attention. Invisible by design, their skills were imperative to the performance experience. Oh, how I wanted to do what they did, assisting in the magic, watching the actors' work night after night. Would it always be like this? That would be a human-created magic.

Exhausted and dizzy from hunger, my thoughts moved with magnetic confluence to my mother. She had attended the theater many times. She had worked as an actress in London before she married my father. She knew the theater world. She had been part of it, and she had never shared anything about it with me.

She walked away because of you, I told myself. She could not fulfill my father's demands, or my needs, and perform nightly.

The patrons had left. The stage curtain opened back up, the lights and their shadows, the actors and their poetry, gone. Workmen swept and mopped the floor, removing whatever recipe had been used to simulate blood along with the dried leaves and bits of moss. More workmen moved furniture and walls, trees, rocks, bushes, and a stairway to the sides, leaving the bare boards of the playing area open; a chessboard waiting for the next game.

And still no one came to collect me.

An older man with thinning, graying hair dressed in the dark stage workmen's clothes carried in a stand from which hung a single lantern. He was placing it on the stage when another man entered. Taller than the first, the second man wore a heavy black cloak with a capelet, a dark scarf concealing the lower half of his face. They came together in the center of the stage and began a discussion I could not hear even in the enhanced acoustics of the theater, but dressed as they were, I was sure they were not actors. The taller man's top hat was pulled low, covering his hair, forehead, and brows, hiding his features. Both men had a wariness that might have been due to their surroundings or because of some distrust they had of each other. They paused when a stagehand finishing his business came close, not continuing until he left.

With a swirl of black wool, the taller man removed himself from the stage, exiting to the unlit recesses beyond.

"You can turn it off, Giddy," the shorter man called out to someone unseen. The general lighting on the staging area was cut out. Looking out over the empty seats, the man noted my presence before making his exit, walking with an odd, rolling gait.

Moments later, he came out of the curtained-off doorway that Gil Collmeyer had entered earlier. Had that only been hours ago? It felt much longer.

"I am sorry," I apologized as he approached. The show was over, and I was not supposed to be here, seeing the mundane efforts behind the magic. I rose and offered my hand. "I am Christopher Becket, Dame Drake's nephew."

"Kit Becket, Leonora's boy?" I nodded, surprised that this rough-looking man smelling of fuels and sulfur knew my mother's given name and was using it rather than referring to her as Missus Becket, as was proper between strangers.

"I have only just arrived," I went on. "Before the play, I mean, which was wonderful. I fear my aunt has forgotten I was scheduled to arrive today. I have been here quite some time, and she has not yet seen me." The wiry fellow scratched his gray head, screwing up his face as if this helped him think.

"Come with me, son. If we hurry, we should just be able to catch her." He walked away, making me think of pirates walking the deck of a sailing vessel. "I was sorry to hear about your mother." The words strained to stay together, struggling to push past his thick gray bristle-brush mustache. "But I wouldn't give up hope. People have a way of turning up, especially you Drakes." He ducked through the curtained side archway that led out of the audience area, and I followed.

The hallway on the other side was as dark and close as a tomb, and I slowed my steps while my eyes adjusted. Outside of the audience's sight, the wooden bones of the building were unclad. The lobby's pomp and glamour were the first layer of the theater's illusions. There were no gas lights here, only kerosene lanterns hung at intervals along the wall, their yellow light slivering dramatic shadows that slipped and slid among the angled edges of the structures that were stored near the stage: castle walls, stone stairways, high turrets, and garden archways.

Stacked in the corners were furnishings from every age of man, and some so whimsical they could not have been created by an orderly universe, but must represent the abodes of otherworldly beings, fauns and fairies, or the Gods and Goddesses of an ancient world. Stepping beyond the curtain that separated the outside world of the audience from the inner temple of magic where the theater's illusions were created, I felt I had stepped away from my old life into a new world.

During my travels as a child, I had been privileged to visit great cathedrals and village churches, and was therefore not unaccustomed to the otherworldly effects the architects and masons of old had incorporated into their designs, but though I had felt the intended awe of those places, I had never felt such an uplifting of my spirit as I experienced in this building, and I wanted to know all of its secrets.

I followed my spare, lath-legged guide down a set of stairs, then another, continuing through ever-narrowing hallways, each more poorly lit and increasingly unfinished. We passed door after door bearing signs that labeled the use of the room behind them: wardrobe, props, and names of actors I did not recognize.

A door up ahead opened, and the black cat I had met before in the seating area bolted from it, running down the hall as if it had seen a mouse and it was eager to stretch its body, tooth, and claw. The leak of light stabbed the darkness, outlining a man, tall and dark-clothed. Was it the same man I had seen onstage? He swept by without acknowledging me or the short man he had just been speaking to upstairs.

We stopped before the door the mystery man had just exited. The initials BD were painted on it in gold lettering. A note nailed below read: *"Think before you knock. Knock before you enter, or save us both the bother and go away."* My guide's eyes smiled, though his mouth seemed not to know how.

"Being prickly keeps the worst of the bores and fawners away, but most of the time her bark is worse than her bite." He knocked. "Bernie?"

"Go away. I am too weary to preside over The Idiot's Court tonight."

"This idiot bears an uncanny resemblance to your brother Albaugh and claims to have the same blood, poor lad. He says his name is Kit Becket, and you are expecting him."

There was a flustered command from the Grande Dame, and the door opened a crack. The comely, caramel-colored girl I had seen going into the theater earlier peeked out.

"For God's sakes, Idabelle, open the door," my aunt's rich contralto chided her.

"You're in it now, young Kit." The old man saluted me as if I were about to be buried at sea. "I'm Wixx, by the way. In case she forgets you again and you need something." His rolling gait took him back down the dark tunnel of a hallway.

"Come in, boy. It's no use standing about out there; someone might think I am taking callers, which I am not." The red-brown-haired maid, her position now made clear by the white-bibbed apron over her black wool dress, opened the door just wide enough for me to squeeze through.

My aunt sat at a much-abused dressing table. A large, chipped and pocked mirror hung on the wall above it, a row of candles lined up across its lower edge, illuminating a collection of small glass pots I presumed were the face paints used by actors to accentuate their features or create illusions.

Kerosene lamps were attached to the freshly papered walls of the small room. A dressing-screen, an armoire, two travel trunks functioning as small closets, two chairs, the one my aunt occupied at her dressing table, and an upholstered wingback, presumably for more distinguished guests, filled the room, making space a premium.

The raven-haired beauty I knew from my grandmother's daguerreotypes was still present in this more mature version of Bernadette Drake, but seeing her close-up after watching her on stage was like viewing a painted portrait near enough to make out the half-erased pencil lines behind the bold strokes of oil paint. I noted the family resemblance between my aunt and my grandmother, the long, haughty nose, bow lips, and striking gray eyes; a pair of winter ponds glinting under the moonlight. A soft silvering of Bernadette's dark hair had infiltrated the fine tendrils around her face, proclaiming that at least most of Lady MacBeth's abundant hair was her own.

"Well, now that you're here, let me have a look at you." She took that familiarity.

On or off the stage, my great aunt's legendary charisma remained undiluted, but what struck me most truthfully was the shadow of sadness betrayed in the lightly drawn age lines visible in her resting face as she examined my not-quite-grown one, comparing it to the toddler's face she once knew. She was a clear-eyed woman who had seen the world's beauty and its ugliness but kept on despite the pain both had given her. The moment of vulnerability slid away like water off taffeta, replaced by a mask of sharp intelligence and unforgiving certainty. "Wixx is right. You do resemble my brother, Albaugh, when he was young. All Drake, barely a hint of Becket in you, except for that cowlick."

"My mother was a Marchand," I pointed out, feeling compelled to defend her in her absence.

Aunt Bernadette raised one eyebrow. "Barely," she drawled in her perfect Queen's English. "She also favors her Drake blood. Say what you like about Sir Francis's pirating escapades and using his dashing looks to manipulate old Queen Gloriana, the Drake heritage is a strong one." She examined me as if viewing me through a magnifying glass, able to expand the most hidden corners of myself, sniffing out secrets in places I had not yet dared to look. "Bloodlines are fascinating, don't you think, Christopher?"

"I have not studied that science," I admitted. "Though I do love uncovering secrets and am very interested in the sciences, and books of all types."

"An expected outcome. Johnathan Becket was an arrogant boor unless you were talking about botany or geography, but he and your mother did like their books. I do hope you did not inherit any Becket boorishness."

For a moment, I felt very small and very much wished to be invisible. My aunt's face registered surprise, then swiftly covered.

"I hope not, Aunt, but I can hardly be an impartial judge," I replied, the excitement of the evening and the lack of food making me uncharacteristically bold. "I must leave the boorishness for others to decide, perhaps yourself, if that is your habit." Predatory eyes scrutinized me as if deciding whether such a runt of a youth was worth the trouble of biting or if I might be allowed to scurry off, saved for another day. "I do hope you will give me time to learn something about where I am and what is expected of me before you pass such a judgment," I went on, bravely—or perhaps foolishly. "I do not feel I have quite got my feet under me since mother disappeared and then Grandmother died. I missed you at the funeral." Pain sprinted across my aunt's face. Perhaps I did harbor a sliver of resentment at being ignored.

"Touche'." She bowed her head toward me as if we were friendly enemies and I had just bested her. I hoped that it was not to be our dynamic. "I am sorry you had to deal with Manon's death alone, nephew. The Lowdons and I are…estranged. And I am very sorry about…" She seemed about to address my mother's disappearance, but suddenly pivoted, "not making myself available to meet you earlier." The phrase was delivered with a hint of emotion as if she were struggling to keep her feelings under control, unable to speak of painful memories. Whether her delivery was honest or she was using her acting skills, I could not be certain. "Forgive me. I should have made arrangements. But no harm done. You are here now." She turned back to her mirror and began removing darker bits of makeup. "You saw the show?"

"I did. It was wonderful—especially your parts."

She eyed me coolly, through the mirror's reflection, immune to my flattery, and taking it for that. "And have you seen many plays before, in Cincinnati, or California, or wherever your parents have been hiding out?"

That she thought my parents were hiding struck me as an odd statement, but I was not normally of a rebellious nature. I looked down at my shoes, certain I had already said too much. I was hungry, my temper testy, but I was at this woman's mercy, and it would do me no good to get on her wrong side.

"This is the first time I have seen a play, Ma'am," I admitted.

"Then you can hardly be much of a judge, can you?"

"No." I reached for an appearance of contrition, a simulation I had mastered in dealing with my father. "But I would like to see a good many more," I perked up hopefully. "Perhaps then I could learn to be."

Her mouth twisted up on one side. "Just what the theatre needs, another critic," she scoffed, scanning her dressing table. "Idabelle, where are my red kid gloves? I was sure I left them on the edge of the dressing table." The maid began to search. "Are you a good student, Christopher?" my aunt turned her attention back to me.

"I believe so," I ventured the small boast, dreading the logical follow-up about what boarding school I would be attending. Well-bred male children all attended boarding schools.

"And what subjects do you favor?"

"I can barely choose," I answered enthusiastically, now on ground where I had confidence. "I enjoy figuring things out and am very interested in new inventions like Breguet and Bourseul's electric voice telegraph, and Humphrey Davy's electric lights."

"Don't you mean Edison's lights?"

"No." I frowned. "Thomas Edison did not invent the electric light. He merely put Davy's discovery to commercial use." The shadow of a smile played at the corners of my aunt's painted lips.

"You are very eager to rush progress, nephew. Why, New York theaters are only just figuring out gas and limelight."

"And the effects are astounding," I raved. "Can you show me how it is done, Aunt?"

"Me? Oh, God no. You must ask Wixx about all that." She changed the subject. "Have you dined?"

"Not today," I admitted.

"You have not eaten all day?" My aunt looked shocked.

"Nor yesterday," I admitted, embarrassed, as if the fault was my own. "The provisions the Lowdons sent with me ran out...and the money." A cloud darkened my aunt's face, giving me a taste of how terrible the storm of her displeasure could be.

"That damn family," she said under her breath. "As if they do not know how many meals a boy might be expected to eat traveling from Cincinnati to New York and could not spare enough to make certain he did not go hungry." She sighed. "And I have been no better, ignoring your arrival and feeding you nothing but Shakespeare and illusions." She studied me again. "And yet you do not offer me a cross word." She turned to her lady's maid. "Go along ahead, Idabelle, and tell Begam Dweeti to prepare a late supper for Master Christopher. After, you may stay at the house and retire. I will do my own hair tonight." She began to weave the long locks into a single braid, locating pins to fix it into a bun at the nape of her neck.

"Beg pardon, Mum," Idabelle spoke up, "But I believe tonight is Begam Dweeti's night off."

"Oh dear. Then you and Kit had best take the carriage and drop by Pfaff's on the way home. I will have Wixx get me a cab."

"A cab, Madam? Tonight? But…" My aunt cut off the girl's protest with a sharp look.

"I will be fine, Ida. Tell Weaver he can collect me as arranged. Forget about the gloves. They will turn up." She addressed me again. "You and I will speak further tomorrow."

"You are not coming with us, Aunt?" I asked.

"No. The play may be over, but the most important performance of the night is only about to begin. There is no need to wait up, Idy. I am likely to be so late that it will be early."

"Mister Wixx will accompany you then, Madam?" Idabelle asked her mistress.

"Stop fretting. I will be perfectly safe."

"Yes, Madam." The girl gathered her cloak and began to lift my bag.

"No need for that, Miss." I stopped her, taking it up myself.

"I will see you tomorrow, Kit." I could feel my aunt's intense gaze following Idabelle and me as we left.

There were similarities in the Drake sisters' looks and their builds, though it was hard to tell a female's true shape with all the tortures fashion compelled them to wear, but my hope that my great aunt's personality might be akin to her sister's had faded like the theater's lights. The Drake sisters were nothing alike.

Act One, Scene Three: Pfaff's Pub, 647 Broadway, New York City, later that night.

As my aunt's carriage traveled through the city, Idabelle explained that Wallack's relocation was part of a trend to create a new entertainment district north of the tenements and expanding commercial districts of Lower Manhattan. "New money" was pushing North of the original Dutch settlements to Union Square and areas surrounding the newly created Central Park, building homes in areas previously considered the countryside. Reluctantly, old-money Knickerbockers, long entrenched in their Lower Manhattan brownstones, were following.

As the carriage drove south along Broadway, the Astor Hotel's blue granite walls gleamed white under the glow of the streetlamps that lined the curb. Women in full hoop skirts, ruffle-petaled peonies floating on gaslight beams, glided in and out of doors modeled after European palaces. In some cases, they were the doors of the palaces, shipped across the Atlantic. Cincinnati had nothing so ethereal.

"It is a beautiful city at night," I commented as we passed.

Idabelle sniffed. "And two miles south, the streets are as dark as tombs, and the poor are stacked in bug-infested tenements with no windows, no clean water, and one overflowing privy in a muddy back lot to serve multiple buildings. It's a travesty, and some of those fine gentlemen dining at the Astor are their landlords, including Astor himself. The expense of adding these lovely gaslights was justified because it would reduce crime, but the lights were installed on the streets where the wealthy have businesses and attend entertainments, not on the tenement streets where crime is king. New York intends to become not only the hub of commerce and banking in North America, but the most influential city in the world, leaders of finance, and arbiters of taste, despite Europe's insistence that we have none."

Idabelle was a young woman of strong opinions, particularly for a person in service. I wondered where she had been schooled to gain such radical ideas.

I nodded as if I knew something about what she was saying, but I was a stranger to New York and its brand of poverty. Still, having lived in New San Diego alongside the mixed cultures of the Southwest, I imagined I knew something of poverty's challenges.

"On this continent, *we* are the immigrants," I said, hoping to earn her respect by showing I was not shallow and dull-witted, nor blinded by prejudice. She raised one eyebrow, a gesture so like Aunt Bernadette's that I was startled by the resemblance.

"Be careful to whom you voice your opinions, Master Becket. New York is a town divided, an in-between place: geographically Northern, but only marginally supportive of Mister Lincoln and his war. Manhattan has a long history of trade and commercial ties with the South.

The population of the North End of Staten Island is largely Abolitionists who support the Union, but many of their neighbors are plantation owners with summer homes on the island who have remained year-round because their homes are now battlefields. We are not truly in the Union here, Master Becket," she mused.

"My aunt is a performer, Miss Idabelle. Not a politician."

Idabelle held up a cautioning finger. "Your aunt is a public figure, and her standing in society helps fill theatre seats. Americans are still moon eyed over everything upper-class and British. As long as Lady Drake remains neutral, which, as a British citizen, is not that difficult, she may claim to have no interest in American politics, and New York society will remain open to her. If she were a man, particularly a single man of means, she might be forgiven by a hostess for holding strong opinions, but a woman would not be forgiven. Your aunt keeps her private opinions private, and she will expect you to do the same."

I wondered what sort of opportunities Aunt Bernadette valued so highly that she was willing to be a hypocrite to protect them. Such an investment in one's image seemed crassly commercial. I might have asked, but the carriage turned right and pulled up before a six-story building. We had arrived at our destination.

A sign declared the establishment to be "Coleman House Hotel". Rows of small windows like rectangular gemstones strung in a bracelet defined each story. I stepped out to help Idabelle to the curb, looking for the pub my aunt had mentioned, but aside from the modest hotel, which appeared to be closed and shuttered for the night, there was no evidence of any public eatery. Idabelle, however, left the carriage without hesitation, descending into a suspicious-looking opening in the pavement.

I hesitated. What kind of place had we been sent to? Why would a proprietor keep their location so secret that they did not even provide a sign, unless their business involved something unscrupulous? I was reminded of the salty comments and pursed lip scowls of the Lowdons whenever Aunt Bernadette's name was mentioned. Was I, an inconvenient relative, being sold to crew on a sailing vessel? It did seem a rather Dickensian twist, but I had read a number of maritime novels where such things happened to young boys and had been fond of joining my mother watching for ships sailing along the Pacific Coast, imagining they were pirate ships. Until my mother resurfaced, no one, outside our family solicitor, would question my disappearance. By then, I could be buried at sea, my bones being nibbled on by fish. I vowed to write to our solicitor first thing in the morning and begin a regular correspondence as a safety measure against the uncertainties this new life presented.

I followed Idabelle down the steps connected like a rippled tongue to the hole in the street, trying not to let my imagination run amok with how like the experience was to walking through the throat of some underground beast and failing utterly. My imaginings were quickly dispelled as Idabelle opened a carved wooden door hidden from view at the street level, and light and the roar of life spilled out, kicking shadow and suspicion up the stairs behind us.

"Wait here," Idabelle commanded. She really was not like a servant at all.

Crossing the room with sprite-like efficiency, she was greeted by ready smiles and nods from the wait staff. This young woman was well known and liked here.

"Papa Pfaff," she hailed a short, balding man with bushy eyebrows. "Lady Drake asks if you might provide a dinner that we could take back to the house?"

"Ah, Ida, my belle!" the man greeted the young woman warmly. "And where is our dear Dame tonight?"

I did not hear Idabelle's reply, but Pfaff looked my way, leaving me to understand that some explanation for my presence had been given. My cheeks flamed, and I tried to look elsewhere, uncomfortable with being the subject of attention. The attention stopped, Pfaff seeming to lose sight and interest in me as he turned to other tasks.

Relieved, I wrapped myself in the comfort of my invisible nature and began to casually wander the eatery, exploring it.

The vaulted ceiling was surprisingly high considering the pub's cave-like location, but unlike the descriptions I had heard of the rathskeller-style pubs and beer gardens of Cincinnati, there were no heavy trestle tables here. Pfaff had adopted a Parisian café style, scattering intimate round tables about the pub's wood plank floor, with one exception: a rectangular table at the back wall. The bar was beautifully carved, oiled, and polished to shine. Glass bottles with many different colored labels stood at attention on the shelves, which I took to indicate the bar was well-stocked.

The scraping of chairs against the wood floor provided low base tones contrasting pleasantly with the high tinkling notes of crystal glassware and the mid-tones of heavy crockery and copper mugs, all stitched together by the buzz of conversation, most of it coming from the back table.

Curious, I moved closer.

A unique collection of voluble men and a few women--most dressed with more flair than fashion, jaunty scarves, dashes of surprising pocket handkerchiefs, a pin, or other jewelry--were engaged in lively debate, their passion spicing the air as much as the aromas that wafted from the kitchen, which were decidedly not sauerkraut and sausage. The delicious smells mingled with hoppy beers and spiced liquors, liquifying my hunger. My stomach moaned in anticipation of the meal to come, its impatient gurgling forgotten as the proprietor approached, his hand outstretched.

A warm smile belied the annoyance of the bushy eyebrows, which grew so close together that they formed an eternal scowl, as if the lower half of Pfaff's face was mismatched with an upper half borrowed from a menacing twin.

"Master Drake. I am so pleased to make your acquaintance." Pfaff shook my hand.

"I am a Becket, actually," I corrected him. "My grandmother's maiden name was Drake, but there have been several marriages since."

"Of course. Nevertheless, a Drake by blood and bloodline will tell." He winked at me. "Idabelle says you have come to live with our dear Dame."

"I have only just arrived. We have not yet spoken about the specifics of the arrangement," I replied cautiously.

"But of course you will stay. You must take up the Noble Cause. I have no doubt you will be of great assistance to your aunt's efforts. We are all very fond of our dear Bernie. Her work is an inspiration." He winked again.

I nodded, attempting to appear agreeable, but I had no idea what cause the man was alluding to, or if I was destined to be connected to my aunt in any way aside from her paying for boarding school.

"Pfaff!" A boisterous man at the back table hailed the proprietor. "Ada has had a letter from Walt in Washington. He indicated a stunning brunette, one of the most beautiful women I had ever seen. "Come join us. And bring more wine!"

"On my way, Henry," Pfaff responded readily.

The animated group at the long table listened to their friend's letter in respectful silence before reverting to their habit of multiple, overlapping conversations. As Pfaff left, I edged closer, hoping I would not be noticed and thought rude.

"Walt is right," the second female in the group was speaking. "I went to a meeting of the Knights of the Golden Circle last week—it was perverse curiosity," she dismissed her motives, her voice a warm, slow-drip contralto. She was middle-aged, extraordinarily dressed in the tailcoat and tie of a gentleman, her dark hair pulled back and pinned up to complete her masculine look. The precision of her diction, like the pinging of a crystal goblet, made me wonder if she was an actor or orator. "The Copperheads, for do not fool yourselves, that is who the Golden Circle Knights are aligned with, not only mean to maintain slavery but expand it across the entire Southern half of North America all the way to the West Coast." Her declaration ignited several side conversations.

"These Golden Circle men seem confident that once the South has won a few more battles, Europe and the rest of the world will jump in to support them since everyone wants their cotton and tobacco, and that New York will join their Confederate America."

"Fernando Wood cannot still believe..." a Quaker gentleman sitting among them started.

"He does," the masculine costumed woman interrupted. "He was there, still declaring the city would split with Lincoln."

"Be careful, Charlotte," the man Pfaff had called "Henry" cautioned the woman. "Wood and his friends have spies everywhere, and they are not above violence."

"Yes, be careful, Miss Cushman," a handsome silver-haired man reiterated the advice. "Your political views and perverted lifestyle could put you on their list of dangerous persons." He grinned impishly.

"My perverted lifestyle is none of their business," the woman, now identified to me as the famous actress Charlotte Cushman, replied. "You are just jealous that I can hold hands with my paramour in public and you cannot because society sees nothing wrong with a close friendship between women. They cannot be having sex. No one has a penis."

I blushed, but the group roared, drawing the attention of the other clientele in the pub, who looked over with curiosity and some longing. The back table at Pfaff's was the place to be, and everyone wished to be there, myself included, though I confess I did not understand the joke, only that it had something to do with the intimate activities that women might engage in in private.

"And now we have circled back to where we started," Henry claimed. "Which is the question of whether there are things that are indisputably wrong, for everyone, everywhere, or whether those ideas of morality are merely societal constructs."

"What is right or wrong varies by culture and time." The silver-haired gentleman slung his arm around the shoulders of the handsome young man beside him. "We see our love as beautiful. Others view it as a deadly sin. I know I cannot change their minds, and they are not going to change mine, so they drink at the Metropolitan and we drink here." He kissed the young man beside him soundly on the lips, and the table hurrahed.

This unquestioning acceptance of the male couple was rather a shock to me, though a refreshing one. I had never given much thought to intimate behaviors. In fact, I had never thought much about the fairer sex at all, as I had never found them to be that fair. My body's visceral reaction to Gilbert Collmeyer's astounding beauty, however, had indicated a maturation of preferences I had suspected since my friendship with Matias in California. Matias and I had not only explored the wilds of the West Coast but had spent a few shy sessions exploring the wilds of each other. Apparently, my interests had nothing to do with heaving bosoms or ruffled skirts, aside from the pure aesthetics of good lines and interesting design.

"Surely, no one is taking these Golden Circle men seriously?" the Quaker demanded incredulously. "I met this Bickley once. He seemed the worst sort of con man."

"Con or not, anyone connected to cotton or tobacco, be it banks or individuals, whose finances have been negatively affected by Emancipation and the Union's embargo, is listening," Henry stated. "And many are supporting Bickley's plan for the cause."

"You mean supporting Bickley's bar tab, don't you, Clay?" another man harumphed. "The Confederacy will never see a dime of what is 'donated' to the effort through Bickley."

"Then the scoundrel is doing us a favor," the silver-haired gentleman insisted.

A dark-haired fellow with a serious countenance who had been listening but not contributing now spoke, "This is exactly why we must support President Lincoln. *His* war is *our* war. He understands how dangerous these people's twisted ideologies are."

"And he would have had my support, Edwin, if he had not started trampling free speech and closing newspapers," Henry Clay declared. This support of journalism helped me connect the man to where I had seen the name "Henry Clay" before. He was the editor of Harper's Weekly. I glanced around the table, wondering who else I should recognize. The stunning russet-haired woman, Ada, who had read the letter, gestured broadly as she spoke, as if she were conducting the conversation.

None of them were common people. They were dressed with panache, even flamboyance, flouting a demand for attention that fed their egos, and they seemed comfortable with this.

"Don't worry, Booth, Lincoln's legacy will survive his mistakes. As long as he wins the war, no one will care how many laws he broke to do it. History is a whore, accepting the thrust of any pen, then lying about how good it was." Charlotte Cushman's comment sparked another round of laughter.

The Quaker wiped his eyes. "Miss Cushman, you should take up light comedy. You would be brilliant."

"I am always brilliant," Cushman countered flippantly.

I had never been of a political nature; I was more interested in how gadgets went together than how governments did, but it was interesting to me how readily these people spoke their minds, expecting their friends, whether by agreement or argument, to help them fine-tune their ideas as they all worked toward some undefined greater understanding. New York went to the plays they were in; the nation read the books and articles they wrote. They were molding public opinion; opinions I saw now were formed and polished here at Pfaff's.

The man, Edwin, returned to his support of the Union president. "However, Lincoln is judged as a politician; he is a decent man, trying to keep these United States and democracy alive."

"I know you are Lincoln's friend, Booth..."

I made another connection: the dark, silent man was Edwin Booth. The Booth family, Edwin, Junius, and John Wilkes, was one of the three leading families of the American Theatre with a legacy rivaling my aunt's in Great Britain.

The conversation began to jump around so quickly that I could not see who spoke or follow the separate conversations, and I shifted my position to find Charlotte Cushman scrutinizing me.

Frozen like a rabbit under a wolf's targeting stare, I waited. She was a handsome woman, her eyes bright with intelligence, not pretty in the fleeting canary-in-a-gilded-cage manner of so many actresses. Charlotte Cushman had an American nose, Germanic and broad at the tip, and an exceedingly square head, her face ending in a squared-off jaw. I could only see her upper body, but what I could see gave me the impression of a person of strength. I wondered if, when she stood, she would be tall.

Ada's laughter broke Cushman's concentration, and she turned her attention away from me.

"Lincoln is a good man surrounded by incompetents, Miss Clare," Edwin Booth was still trying to excuse his hero's faults.

"Incompetence or greed, Edwin?" Ada Clare challenged. "His administration nearly lost this fight before it began, with all its hasty contracts, and the profit skimming those contractors employed." Ada Clare was, as I had noted before, a very comely woman. I knew her by name as a writer and sometimes actress who had spent some years in Cincinnati when she had been married to a Jewish man there. It was possible she had even visited my grandmother, Manon, but if I had been introduced, it would have been brief. I would not have remained for the visit, preferring my books to company.

"It is astounding how many old Knickerbocker Republicans who were facing financial ruin before the war were suddenly drenched in bank notes," Charlotte Cushman commented sourly.

"And now, they will be rich for generations," Henry Clay pointed out.

The silver-haired gentleman shook his head. "And George Opdyke and his friends have the audacity to moan about how badly the war is going after what they did."

"But Opdyke is the mayor, isn't he?" the man's paramour asked innocently.

The elder man twined a tendril of his lover's hair around his finger. "Yes, but honest men do not become Mayor of New York City, my dear."

The Quaker nodded. "The United States paid a high price for our freedom from the tyranny of British rule. It is hard to watch these Masters of Commerce just replace them. They are as self-serving and avaricious as King George ever was."

"I miss Walt." Ada Clare sighed. "Where is our Great Gray Poet when we need him? Those soldiers he's tending have no idea how we suffer without him here to nurse our wounded souls."

"To Walt." Glasses were raised in a moment of remembrance, of futility nesting in their breasts.

"I am leaving mid-week, on assignment," a young man who had sat listening and not spoken previously announced. "I've been hired to cover the war from Washington."

Henry clapped the young man on the back. "Good man, Ned. Write honestly. Let people know the truth of what is happening."

"I'll try, but I'm not writing for Harper's, Henry. I'll have an editor to answer to, and it won't be you."

"Emma and I have decided to return to Italy as well," Charlotte Cushman announced.

Ada wilted. "No, Char. Not you too."

"She's been commissioned to sculpt a fountain for Central Park, 'The Angel of the Waters' or some such thing. She has asked me to model for it, but she needs creative space without the distractions of this awful war to do the work."

"If everyone keeps leaving, there won't be anyone interesting left in the city." Ada pouted. "Who will come to my Sunday salons?"

I wished I could say something to give them hope, these brilliant minds, but I was only a youth struggling toward adulthood, confused, alone, and at the moment very hungry.

"Bernie is staying," Henry Clay said. "And Gerald, and James." He nodded to the silver-haired gentleman and his lover.

"I'm staying," Mark announced. "I've accepted management of the National Theatre."

"Mark Smith, how very clever of you," Ada Clare congratulated him.

"But it's hardly fair to you." Charlotte frowned. "The timing couldn't be worse. With this war, half the theaters in the city have closed and there's no place worth touring anymore."

"There's the North," Booth suggested.

Gerald harrumphed. "Northern cities barely tolerate theater or theater folk."

Cushman made a face. "Damn Puritans. At least in the South, they treat us like people, not whores and thieves about to steal the silver."

"Don't romanticize them, Charlotte," Gerald grunted. "If they had known us for who we really are, our Southern hosts would have been just as happy to tar and feather us."

"Everyone knows who you really are, Gerald," Mark teased. "And they love you anyway. Ford has approached Laura Keene about touring *Our American Cousin* to his theatres." Several people at the table groaned.

"My God, what is the theatre coming to?"

"We can't all make a career of doing Caesar and King Lear, like Edwin." Mark sighed. "We have bills to pay, and that means sometimes we have to do *Meg Merillies*."

"May the theater gods forgive us," Booth moaned theatrically.

Mark shrugged. "When times are hard, people want to laugh. Laughter sells tickets."

"So do tits," Gerald pointed out. "But we leave that sort of entertainment to the Bowery."

Mark grinned. "I don't know, you should see the new costume designs I just received from my London designer for *Midsummer Night's Dream.*"

Cushman raised her eyebrows. "Tits?"

"Tits on fairies. We will have some of the finest tits in the city."

"All hail the fairies." Cushman raised her glass. "I'd pay to see that--those." Everyone laughed.

"*You* won't be here. *You* are leaving," Mark pretended offense. "I do expect it will significantly increase ticket sales to our soldiers on leave, however, which will help make it profitable, which is why the Knickerbockers hired me."

"Is there a part for me?" Ada asked. "I could play Titania, the queen of the fairies." She threw her scarf around her neck dramatically.

"He'll have to see your tits," Cushman warned her.

"He already has." Ada fluttered her eyelashes.

"You can see mine." Gerald's lover, the young James, opened his shirt, revealing his nipples. He cupped them from beneath to cheers and laughter.

"Walt will be sorry he missed that," Cushman joked. And just like that, the merriment died, reality shoving its way back in, the wine gone, their hearts heavy.

"I miss him so much." Ada Clare looked around the table, her eyes sparkling with tears. "If more of you are going to leave, and this is our last night all together, we should make it memorable."

"Yes. Papa Pfaff, bring more wine!" Mark hailed Pfaff. "We must give our wanderers a good sendoff."

"It doesn't need to be good wine, Papa P," Cushman added. "None of us is sober enough to know the difference anymore."

The friends laughed.

And then Idabelle found me.

"Ah, there you are. I didn't see you. It will only be a minute more. The kitchen is just packing up your dinner. You've been listening in on The Bees…"

"No!" I protested.

"Don't be silly, of course you have--you and everyone else in the place. That's why they come, you know, hoping for a chance to rub elbows with the brilliant, free-thinking Bohemians who sit at the infamous 'back table'. You have to pass Papa Pfaff's special standards to get seated there," she informed me. "Outsiders call it a pub, but it is really a cathedral for ideas. The greatest, most inventive minds in America have made their way here at one time or another. They come to meet other minds and talents like themselves. There's no place like it, outside of Paris, and France does not have audacious American thinkers like we do: Emerson, Whitman, Thoreau, Clay, Cushman, and Clare. But be careful, Master Kit." Her brown eyes twinkled; the seriousness that made her seem so much older burned away by an unexpected mischief. "The Bees are a terrible influence. They will corrupt you." I suspected her warning had come too late.

And that was why Pfaff's had a hidden entrance and no sign. Here, women could dress however it suited them, speak their opinions with confidence, and be welcomed. Here, men were not afraid to listen to women friends or to follow their hearts in the face of society's disapproval and openly display affection for each other. A particular kind of non-exclusive exclusivity reigned at Pfaff's. The currency here was not dollars, it was creativity, intelligence, and a person's willingness to reveal a pregnancy of ideas not yet fully developed or birthed.

Papa Pfaff did not need a sign because he knew that the spirits who hungered for what he served here would find their way.

"It's hard on them, the war," Idabelle interrupted my thoughts. "They believed so strongly that this new democracy was the beginning of a model of enlightened government that would spread around the world: equality and freedom for all. Now, they worry it will not survive the decade, and they cannot bear to watch it die. So, they're scattering; Paris, Amsterdam, Rome—anyplace the war is not. Of course, most of them don't know what it's like to be in a battle, except maybe Walt Whitman, who is in Washington volunteering at a military hospital. Have you read his poetry book 'Leaves of Grass'?"

I pretended mock-horror. "Poetry? Oh no, that would be far too scandalous for the Lowdons. They're Presbyterians, not Episcopalians."

Idabelle gave me another one of her extraordinary smiles. "So, you were not sent away so much as you escaped?"

"Exactly."

"You should read Whitman," she advised me. "His poetry is fresh and bold. Your aunt has a copy. She will be glad to let you borrow it."

Out of the corner of my eye, I saw movement from the kitchen. Expecting the delivery of my dinner, I turned my head. The mystery man I had seen at the theater was striding out of Pfaff's kitchen, scarf up, hat down as before. I had not recovered from my surprise before he exited out a back door.

A male waiter brought out a basket, the dishes inside covered by white linen.

"Thank you, Gunther." I followed Idabelle back to the carriage, taking the basket from her while she climbed in before handing it back. She rapped on the ceiling to let the driver know we were settled. "Home, please, Weaver." The cab stuttered into motion.

"Miss Ida, I just saw a man," I began, uncertainly. "A man I also saw at the theater speaking to that man, Wixx. The same man was coming out of Aunt Bernadette's dressing room..."

"The theater is a small world, Kit," Ida interrupted me. "Everybody knows everybody, but there are circles within those circles. The Bees are one, but there are others."

"Is this man a friend of my aunt's, then?" I tried to draw her out.

"I cannot say," Idabelle replied. "If Dame Drake wants you to know something, Master Christopher, she will tell you."

Ida's attempt to dismiss the mysterious man's existence, for that was what I took it to be, made me even more suspicious, which, with my curious nature, meant I was more interested than ever. But I had only just discovered the theater and barely had a taste of it. I could not risk my aunt deciding I was an inconvenience and banishing me. I took a portion of Ida's advice and did not speak of it further. I would pretend I had not seen anything strange, but I knew that I had.

E.F. Winters

Act One, Scene Four: Drake House, Sixty-One Third St., Washington Square, New York City, later that night

The carriage retraced its journey for a few blocks, going north on Broadway before turning onto a tree-lined street of brownstone row-houses built around a small park. It was an older neighborhood, reminding me of what Idabelle had said about the old New York families clinging to their brownstone neighborhoods. Aunt Bernadette was not a Knickerbocker, but she had owned this house on Washington Square for some years.

My aunt's driver stopped the carriage mid-block in front of a four-story townhouse with marble stairs leading to a small portico, a decorative wrought iron fence at its foot. The curved archway on the portico was a common design element among the houses in the row. Bernie's has double doors with black iron hinges, hasps, and pulls. The main difference between it and its neighbors was that it was lit at this late hour, and the others were dark.

Idabelle climbed out, addressing the driver, "Thank you, and goodnight, Weaver." Once I, too, was outside the carriage, I tried to hand the dinner basket from Pfaff's back to her. Pulling her hands away, she pointed me to the front door.

"Ring. Burke will let you in." She went through the low gate and down the stairs to the servant's entrance to the right.

The carriage pulled away, and once again, I was on my own.

Would this place be my home now, I wondered, looking over the townhouse's facade. Or was this just another stop along my way? I had been tugged along with the luggage through Europe, visiting the universities of Great Britain and the Americas, a satellite caught in the sphere of Johnathan Becket's gravity. While my father pursued his interests in lectures at New England universities, my mother and I visited my grandmother in Cincinnati. Our last home together, one my father barely set foot in, had been the rented, New England saltbox shipped around the Horn by New San Diego's over-confident developer. I missed it every day that I spent in Cincinnati.

Act One, Scene Four

San Diego, New and Old, was an isolated community wedged between the Pacific Ocean and the great Southwestern deserts. Out of necessity, its inhabitants were close-knit. They relied on each other because there was no one else. If a person possessed a useful skill, they were quickly folded into the community. My mother, being well educated, was as capable of teaching someone to read or balance an account ledger as she was in assisting the local midwife.

We lived in the little saltbox, enjoying the freedom of a life outside the strictures of society's many rules, for close to three years, when the Union government decided a military presence was needed on the Southern Coast of California, specifically San Diego Bay. Local talk was that a vote by California's governing body had led to a decision to divide the state into two parts, the Southern portion leaning Confederate, but when the proposition got to Washington, it had been filed in a bottom drawer and never seen again. Unwilling to risk the Confederacy gaining a port on the Pacific Coast, Lincoln's Administration decided to install a fort on the bay, a presence meant to quell the increase of Confederate privateers intercepting gold and silver shipments from San Francisco. The government usurped the failing developers' overambitious plans for New San Diego and began to build a military garrison in the lower city.

Along with its arrogance, the Army brought smallpox.

When my mother was informed that my father's survey team had been attacked by Yaya warriors and he had been killed, she arranged our exit to Cincinnati. I knew Cincinnati from our many visits, and I much preferred life in California, exploring and hunting with Matias, but when the smallpox epidemic hit, my mother ignored my pleas to stay and sent me away in the care of an officer, the hapless Lieutenant Lewis of my nightmares. Lewis was being recalled to Washington, D.C., and agreed to accompany me, my mother promising that she would follow soon.

It was the only promise I had known her not to keep.

The breeze off the Hudson River shivered the tree branches above me. The storm had passed, stars winking down from a freshly cleared sky, the smell of new grass, and spring leaves reminding me that life eternally renewed itself wherever you were. I lifted my face, letting the breeze slide over my skin.

"Please come back," I whispered, hoping somehow, wherever she was, my mother would hear me. I missed her, not only for herself, but selfishly for the sense of safety and confidence her presence gave me. I was a better person when she was with me. At only seventeen, I knew that I should be more grown-up; my intellect was that of an old man, my soul, a child's. I was trying, but I was a cake pulled too soon from the oven, caved in and hollow in the middle, and the world I faced alone was so much more chaotic and confusing than I had imagined, believing, as a child will, that outside of my father's tempers, everything was whole, and once I grew beyond his power, I would miraculously be whole too.

The doorknob on the door at the top of the townhouse's stairs snicked open, and a slender, brown-skinned man descended. A stately fellow, with an elegant bearing, he reminded me of a wild stag balancing a great crown of antlers. It was well past midnight, but not a wrinkle marred his perfectly pressed presence. Not a hair, either salt or pepper, was out of place.

"Master Becket, I am Burke, at your service." Though his skin was light brown, the lanternlight revealed the light-colored eyes that named him mixed race. "I run your aunt's household," he explained, inviting me into the circle of his calm. "I have been with her for many years. You probably do not remember; you were very young, but I was there in London when you and your mother lived with Lady Drake. I fear you have had a long and difficult journey. Please, let me assist you.". He took both basket and bag from my weary arms. It was a small gesture, but gratitude rinsed away my exhaustion like spring water poured through cheesecloth, and I felt my shoulders relax.

I gave one last look up and down the street, hoping my mother would appear, then followed my aunt's butler into her house.

The dining room Burke showed me into was longer than wide, with the tall ceilings that people who aspired to a higher social status demanded. Tall, narrow windows facing the midnight park were set against rich mahogany paneling and framed by heavy burgundy drapes.

Not wanting to be a bother, I encouraged Burke not to stay up, but he kindly dismissed my suggestion.

"It is not my habit to retire until Lady Drake has returned for the night," he demurred before leaving, waiting around the corner in the

Act One, Scene Four

foyer while I ate. It was an oddity of our culture how it isolated people through class and differences, so much so that it was acceptable for a respected elder to wait on a young man of dubious position. Ida was right. The Bees would corrupt me.

There were many things askew with the world, and I envied The Bees their community of intelligence, living by norms they created, based on rules they defined, disregarding, even shattering what they considered to be false, Puritanical, or Old-World feudal boundaries. Might I live like that someday? Could I find a life where I was accepted with all my oddities? Or make one. My mother, my grandmother, and Matias were the only people with whom I had ever felt accepted, and they were all gone--I hoped not forever, but their absence meant I could not ask any of them the questions weighing on my mind.

I sated my hunger by the light of a single beeswax taper, my only other company the plate of eggs, bacon, and the most amazing savory pancakes I had ever tasted.

Candlelight tickled the faceted surfaces of the crystal drops hanging from the unlit chandelier, making them twinkle like fading early morning stars. The meal was very good, or I was very hungry, or perhaps both were true in some measure. When I was finished, Burke reappeared. Handing me a second taper, he led me up two flights of stairs to a guest bedroom, which he was careful not to call that, a kindness I believe he hoped would soothe the newness of my situation and encourage attachment.

He asked me if I required anything else or needed assistance disrobing, a suggestion that terrified me as a young person still experiencing the physical changes of a young man. I quickly assured him that I was accustomed to taking care of my own dressing and undressing and needed nothing more than a place to rest my head.

"Very good, Master Christopher." He retreated, adding quietly, "And welcome to your new home." The door softly closed.

I should have fallen asleep as soon as my head touched the pillow, which was exceedingly soft and smelled of lavender and citrus, a favorite among Drake women, I supposed, due to its familiarity. But I lay in the dark, staring at the ceiling, watching the play of moonlight casting shadows from the trees outside, and trying to release the tensions that I had been wearing like a second skin. After some time, I noted that the pillow felt damp, the feathers clumping together in lumps that poked my cheek. A tear or two might have slipped out along with my tensions.

I was still half awake when I heard a carriage galloping down the street. It pulled up at the curb outside my aunt's house.

Rising from the bed, I tiptoed to the window, a half-height affair in a row of third-story windows with hooded arches tying them by design to the arch over the front entry. As I approached the window, an elderly woman was alighting from the carriage, assisted by a slender man swathed in a greatcoat, a tall hat, and a muffler. I could not see him well enough to be certain he was the same man I had seen earlier, only well enough to wonder. His frame was the same, and he was dressed as the other man had been, though that had little significance since men's fashion dictated that all gentlemen don the same basic costume: a morning coat, frock coat, or tailcoat, as suited the occasion, with a greatcoat if weather required it, and a hat. None of the identifying details a gentleman might use to set themselves apart in this uniform were visible in the darkness or from this distance.

The woman, who should be my aunt as the carriage and driver were unquestionably hers, was moving with a cautious effort that indicated an injury. Wary of being seen, she sent a cautious glance darting along the line of houses. Surely, this was Aunt Bernadette? The height was right, but the costume was entirely wrong. Mismatched, apparently unwashed, her clothing poorly mended, the woman I watched was dressed like a lower-class working woman, a charwoman or factory worker.

She leaned in to speak more intimately with the man I thought was my mystery man, but whether this intimacy was symptomatic of the late hour or the secret nature of their conversation, I could only speculate. Rude though it was, I did just that. They whispered, even on a deserted street in the middle of the night, because they were cautious of the consequences of their secrets being overheard.

The woman ended the conversation, limping toward the front door below and to the right of my position. A light appeared, presumably held by Burke. I caught a quick glimpse of the woman before she passed below my window and confirmed she was Aunt Bernadette.

Act One, Scene Four

In disguise. Her hair and clothing had been altered, but as she paused on the landing, the charwoman bearing vanished, replaced by Lady Drake's own imperious, straight-backed posture. For a flicker of a bird's wing tip, I saw an exceedingly little man, his legs as thin as twigs, his body round as an apple, standing beside her. I blinked, but he did not vanish. His costume was as tailored as a gentleman's, but the colors were as boisterous as a circus tent. The moment my mind registered this oddity, the figure was gone, or perhaps it had never been there, merely an illusion made by a knee, and the toe of a shoe, and some moving fabric.

What had Aunt Bernadette been doing in the wee hours of the morning, disguised by poverty? I recalled Idabelle's concern when my aunt first offered us the carriage in her dressing room and her inquiry about whether Wixx would remain with my aunt, then my aunt's sharp reply. A skin-crawling worm of certainty wriggled from my gut to my brain. There were activities happening in this household that were being concealed from the light of day.

The cab rolled away, the lantern light on the porch cut off, and my long-legged mystery man swept across the street, his coat furling in a gust of wind off the river before being swallowed into the park's greenery.

Moments later, he reappeared on the open lawn beyond the woodsy edge of the park, the moonlight dripping like rain onto the tops of his shoulders…the top of his hat.

As if responding to a stage cue, a second man stepped from the shrubby shadows and moved forward, furtive, cautious. The mystery man stepped back. Pulling a small object from his inner coat pocket, he pointed it at the intruder. The second man stopped, gestures accompanying some explanation I could not hear, but tracked through the intensity of gusts of steam puffing from his mouth. The two figures moved cautiously closer until they were near enough that the second man was able to pass something drawn from his inside coat pocket to the mystery man. The transaction accomplished, the second man was reabsorbed by the greenery. The mystery man paused, scanning the banks of windows facing the park on all four sides. When he reached the window where I stood, he stopped.

E.F. Winters

I gasped, holding my breath, the frozen blood in my veins preventing me from moving away.

He stared at my window so long that I was sure he saw me, as if I held the one flare of light in all those dark windows, but though my white nightshirt glowed in the moonlight, my face was hidden in shadow, my candle snuffed out hours ago. As long as I did not move, he might suspect that he was being watched, but he could not know.

"I am not here. You see nothing, because there is nothing to see," I chanted under my breath.

As if responding to my child's spell, the mysterious man spun and marched off across the moonlit lawn to the North. But his adventure was not over.

Two new shadows extracted themselves from the tree line, followed by a third, then a fourth; burly men all, dressed in rough working-man's clothing, unkempt hair, and crumpled caps. Again, my mystery man reached into his pocket. This time, a small revolver's silver surface blinked as he moved the weapon slowly from mark to mark, pausing at each man before moving to the next. But the men who had come from the trees had their own weapons: clubs, knives, and a single handgun. Both groups waited to see who would move first, planning the arch and order of deadly movements to come. Or maybe I was giving the thugs too much credit. They did not look like thinking men. Maybe they were just waiting, like a boulder would, because it is incapable of doing anything else unless it is pushed by an outside force. Even when it falls, a boulder has no strategy. It devastates everything along its path, even itself, pieces chipping off until at the bottom it is crushed by its own freefall.

Once again, lantern light flared on the porch below me. The metallic click of a rifle being cocked ricocheted across the square, bouncing off the brownstone facades of the rowhouses.

"There is nothing here for you but trouble." Burke's baritone turned heads. "I have a Henry Repeating Rifle, and I am quite a good shot. I can put at least one bullet in each of you before you can make cover. So, whatever you were promised for your work here tonight, it is time to ask yourselves if it is worth dying for, because I was trained in war. Which means I was trained to kill."

Act One, Scene Four

Two of the roughs were backing up, their companions shouting for them to stop. They did not, the puffs of their breath spreading and floating away.

A carriage hurtled around the western corner of the park, drawing the remaining men's attention as the horses raced to the middle of the block. When I looked back at the green, the tree-thugs were gone. My gaze shifted again. My mystery man was gone. I shifted again. The carriage was shuddering over the cobblestones, iron horseshoes sparking as the animals scratched and slipped, turning onto Broadway.

And the park was empty.

The lantern below was snuffed out. The door closed.

Everything returned to midnight quiet, as if nothing had happened.

And maybe it hadn't. Maybe it had all been a dream, like the one I had about the attack on the train when Lieutenant Lewis was killed. It had been a terrible thing, but I had lived, and that was all you could say about it. But the mind is a strange thing. Sometimes it scrambles our fears and worries, putting them back together in new ways.

This felt different.

Movement in the park again caught my eye. The same little blue-skinned man I had imagined seeing beside my aunt now stood in the park, his nut-round eyes glowering at me in my window. As I stared back, trying to sort out what I was seeing, he disappeared. He did not walk across the green or run away. He simply vanished.

Shivering in my nightshirt, I wrapped my arms around myself, but there was no comfort in it. The tree branch shadows on the ceiling were suddenly more devilish, jerking and shuddering, an ominous evil. Teeth chattering, I scrambled back into bed, burrowing beneath the bedclothes as if the blankets could provide sanctuary as I had imagined when I was little.

What had I stumbled into? In New San Diego, after learning that privateers were pirates with government licenses, I had scoured the Pacific Ocean's horizon, longing to see a real pirate ship, but I had never wanted to be a pirate, throwing myself into the storms of life.

And yet, here you are, abandoned to those storms, fear slapped me. *She knew there was something wrong with you;* the fingers of my insecurities crept over my shoulders, stabbing and twisting like

E.F. Winters

corkscrews into my heart. *She only pretended to love you, but who would love you? Your father never did. You were a mistake, and now that Johnathan Becket is gone, Leonie Marchand can be free, herself again...as long as she stays away from you. She sent you to live with these strange people whom she has not seen in years. What kind of mother would do that?*

What if my mother never comes back? What if she never meant to keep her promise, and I am left here to deal with whatever this is, alone?

Hidden beneath the covers, I bit my lip hard, wiping away the hot tears splashing down my cheeks, and tried to shove my fears away. *It isn't true. My imagination is just playing tricks on me. My mother loves me.*

I just needed to sleep.

Closing my eyes, I awaited unconsciousness.

After too long, it came, a brittle, edgy thing, but I embraced it. Maybe tomorrow my mother will return.

Act One, Scene Five: Drake House, Washington Square, the Next Morning.

Waking the next morning, I had just taken my first conscious breath when I felt my heart contract.

How long would it be before I stopped expecting my mother's presence to be the first thing that pierced my awareness each day? Wherever we traveled, she was my North Star.

In a rush of adrenaline, I remembered my situation, realizing I had slept later than was polite and probably already made a poor impression on my aunt and her household.

I dressed quickly in a clean, if wrinkled, shirt, splashed cold water from the basin onto my face, and smoothed my hair with damp hands. Studying myself in the mirror above the basin, I viewed the boy that others saw: a young person of no remarkable features, the slender frame of a half-grown youth, brown hair, blond lashes, and brows framing almost blue eyes. My hair was too straight, my chin too pointed, my lips too full. A few gingerbread freckles speckled my nose. It was a face comprised so entirely of "almosts" it defied notice. My grandmother had insisted that when I smiled, which she claimed I did not do often enough, my appearance became rather charming. But grandmothers are notoriously prejudiced in favor of their grandchildren and not to be trusted on the subject of their good looks. Possessing neither charm nor grace, I was utterly dismissible.

I felt a stab of envy remembering the Greek-god beauty of the young actor, Gilbert Collmeyer, which took my thoughts to Pfaff's and silver-haired Gerald and his lover, James. There was no reason a person like Gil Collmeyer would take notice of me, or smile at me like Gerald had smiled at James, or kiss me.

Before yesterday, romantic entanglements had been outside my thoughts, my mind occupied by books and inventions. But the encounter at Pfaff's had given me a view of a world I had not encountered outside the works of ancient Greek philosophers. Even among the straight-laced Lowdons, there had been bachelor uncles and spinster aunts lurking at the edges of society. Until now, I had never asked myself why they might have chosen an unmarried life. Yesterday gave me a clue. They had chosen to live their lives on their own terms rather than live a lie. A single existence was preferable to a life of lies.

I repeated my ablutions, then started down the stairs. It was my plan that if anyone asked how I had slept, I would say, "Very well," and insist I had been so exhausted that I slept like a stone, concealing what I had witnessed outside my window.

The dining room felt as awkward and abandoned as I did—no clinking crockery, no singing of silver tines, no harmonious morning greetings.

Following the smell of coffee and fresh bread, I located the servant's stairs and ventured down.

"Hello? Is anybody there?" I called out as I reached the bottom step, landing on a smooth stonework floor.

A matronly East Indian woman with round, deep-set eyes, her glossy black hair pulled back into a severe bun, stretched her head out from a broad archway down the hall that accessed a large, open kitchen.

"Good morning, I am Christopher Becket," I introduced myself as I approached. There were two wooden tables, one for cooking, one with chairs around it for the staff to eat at. "Lady Drake is my aunt."

"Of course, Master Becket," the woman replied, her English heavily accented. "We were expecting you. The others are not up yet. They keep late hours because of our mistresses' theater schedule. They will eat later, but I am happy to prepare something for you now. A young man requires regular meals, which may be a challenge in this household. But whenever you are hungry, just come to the kitchen, and we will find you something. Now, what would you like this morning?"

It was a surprising offer. People did not go out of their way for invisible boys, and I was not accustomed to having my needs catered to.

"I do not wish to put you to any trouble, Ma'am," I said politely.

"They call me Begam Dweeti, or Missus Dweeti here. And it is never any trouble for me to cook. It is my job and my pleasure. I must make my own breakfast before the others rise anyway, and it is no more effort to cook for two. Now tell me, what do you think of eggs?"

"We are acquainted, and seem to get along," I replied, smiling.

"English or American style?" Though she tried not to reveal her own judgment, her nostrils flared like she had smelled something spoiled when she mentioned American-style eggs. Even more uncertain what to expect from a dish I had thought of as simple and uncomplicated, I went with the least committed choice.

"I am not particular." I shrugged.

"Well, we will have to change that," Missus Dweeti declared. "When it comes to food, one should always be particular. You have traveled, I am told. Have you had Indian spiced breakfast eggs?" I shook my head to indicate I had not. "Are you feeling adventurous this morning, Master Kit, or would you prefer something familiar this day?" Her eyes wanted to be friends, but her smile kept secrets.

"An adventure," I stated, wondering what devilish spirit had come over me.

Missus Dweeti began grinding herbs and cracking eggs, adding leftover rice and vegetables to the dish before setting pieces of the soft, white flatbread that had been perfuming the air on the side of each plate. Soon, the kitchen was filled with the most wonderful fragrances. The final dish kept every promise they had made. I had eaten every bite, along with a second helping and several pads of the bread she called "Na'an," before Burke joined us.

I was so afraid he would see through my pretended ignorance that I could barely look at the rifle-wielding butler, but I stuck to my plan, hoping he would interpret my reluctance as a lack of confidence in a shy boy thrust into new surroundings.

Watching Burke and Missus Dweeti navigate the kitchen, I could see they had worked together for some years. There was a rhythm between them that only came from people who knew each other's habits and preferences well. Recalling what Burke had said about remembering my mother, I ventured to inquire how long Missus Dweeti had been in my aunt's household.

"Begam Dweeti came to live with us some years after your mother left the household to marry Mister Becket," Burke answered. "She had only just entered service with us when your father went to the Middle East, and your mother stayed with us again. If my memory serves me, you turned three that year."

"Missus Leonara was a very pretty lady." Dweeti nodded approvingly. "Very English."

Apparently, Missus Dweeti also doubled as the head housekeeper, as she persuaded me over breakfast to bring down the soiled clothing from my travels so she could launder them. I had just deposited my bundle when my aunt appeared in the kitchen wearing an eggplant-colored satin dressing gown. I was quite surprised at her joining us. It would never have happened in the household of the very class-conscious Lowdons.

"Dweetie, where is Frostine?" On seeing me, my aunt stopped abruptly. "Oh." She pulled the edges of her dressing wrap together, concealing her nightdress. "Good morning, nephew." She noted the used plates on the kitchen table. "You have eaten."

"I have, thank you, Aunt."

"Good. Then you may come talk to me while I have my breakfast."

Dweeti grinned. "He likes the spice, Madam."

"Well, that will certainly simplify meals. Bring me whatever you have made, please, Dweeti. It smells wonderful."

"Yes, Madam." Dweeti winked at me. "Madam likes the spice too."

I sat on one side of the formal dining room table, my aunt sitting at the near end, eating the same rice, egg, and vegetable dish I had enjoyed.

Despite the half-night of fretful sleep and two good meals, I remained worried, fearing I walked the edge of dangerous events, a state I had occupied twenty-three hours a day since my grandmother's death. My hope that my new guardian's home would provide a safe haven, like Manon's had been, had been utterly shattered by last night's hugger-muggery. Every corner of the house seemed to be teasing secrets, whispers rippling the air like heat waves just out of my hearing. Had there been hidden meaning embedded in that casual comment between Aunt Bernie and her butler? Had I caught a clandestine glance between Dweetie and her husband? I analyzed every twitch. Was that finger wiggle a secret hand signal?

Passing by the parlor, I had seen a daguerreotype of the three Drake women on the mantel: Aunt Bernadette, Manon, and my mother, Leonara, with a toddler, me, sitting on Manon's lap.

I remembered my aunt's West End townhouse, the Persian carpet beneath my chubby legs, the voices of my mother and Bernie in the next room.

"I will see the assignment through, Bernie," my mother was saying. "I promise."

"And what about the child? I want you to finish—it is important, Leonie, but if Johnathan is leaving the country again, who will look after the child when you must go out?"

"Burke can look after him."

"Burke is not a nanny. He needs to be looking after you, to keep you safe, not changing nappies," my aunt argued. "Damn your husband for dropping this on you. It should be him looking after the child. It is his baby."

There was a long silence before my mother said, "I do not want to leave Johnathan alone with Kit." Another silence. "He's not good with the boy. He's not patient."

"What are you not telling me, Leonie?" Bernie's voice was a slow, steady threat.

"I will make arrangements," my mother declared. "I'm not giving up our work, but expecting any sort of interaction from Johnathan is unrealistic."

"Very well. We can sort out the rest of it later, but do not think I will forget this conversation. I will not. Lord Byron's man will expect you at eleven. I will come by after the show and check to make sure everything went all right."

"It will be fine," my mother assured her. "I will be fine. I gave birth. I did not lose my mind."

"The two seem strangely close in nature," Bernie quipped.

My mother came into my view, lifting me to her hip and exiting the room, and the memory ended, but it was strange remembering what I had forgotten. Had there always been odd goings-on swirling around our lives? Had I discarded certain memories as childish imaginings, telling myself I had not observed a secret finger code? Where had I even come up with that thought? My mother and I had never played such games. I suddenly had flashes of strange late-night visitors and blood being washed off the kitchen floor.

I had lived in proximity to strange happenings for years. As a baby and never much more, I had been allowed to view and be present at discussions I could not understand…then. But I was older now; an outsider in a household that held to its secrets like family heirlooms.

Instinct told me that if I wanted a home here, I should conceal the insights of my memories and say nothing of my suspicions.

"So, you have met the staff, except for the new girl, Frostine," my aunt began. "She helps Begam Dweeti with the house chores. I suppose you did not properly meet Weaver last night. Weaver drives for us and fixes things. So, if something is broken, don't try to repair it yourself. Ask Weaver, or his feelings may be hurt. Everyone needs to feel useful. You will not meet my brother, Albaugh, your great-uncle, for a week or two. He is away at a conference.

"Now tell me about yourself, Christopher. You were hardly more than an infant the last time I saw you—not even a person yet, really. What should I know about you? What have I missed?" Aunt Bernadette eyed me over her spiced eggs and rice.

"Fourteen years," I answered in the most literal manner.

"Oh dear." She sighed. "Whatever was your mother thinking, sending you off to the Lowdons. Horrible people."

"Mother did not send me to the Lowdons," I corrected her. "She sent me to her mother's, your sister's."

"Yes, quite right. And Manon's dying was not part of the plan, nor was it your mother's."

"My mother is not dead," I said before I could stop myself. "She is missing. There is no proof of anything else." To my surprise, Bernie neither mocked me nor argued the point.

"No, there is not." She pushed back from the table. "You should rest, get settled, and clean up. Be certain you do all three," she commanded brusquely. "Make a list of any personal items you need and give it to Burke, or if you prefer to choose for yourself, he can take you shopping. You will need new clothes. What you are wearing simply will not do. I cannot have my nephew walking around New York looking like a ragamuffin. Now, I have a fitting at Worths this morning." She dabbed her linen napkin at her lips. "We open *School for Scandal* next month, and I am in need of new costumes. I am too old to play Lady Teasel now. There is nothing sadder than an aging actress refusing to move on to mature roles." She rose. "After I am done at Worth's, I have a luncheon, followed by a session at Sarony's Studio for a new daguerreotype." She started to leave the room to go upstairs and dress.

"Oh, and while I am thinking of it," she stopped herself. "What would you say to leaving the surname Becket behind and being introduced as my nephew, Christopher, or Kit Drake?" My mouth fell open, my jaw unable to hold up my bottom lip. "It would be easier if we did not always have to explain your situation and your parents' misfortunes. Such tales of familial tragedy destroy any possibility of interesting conversation, and sharing them either feeds the imaginations of thrill seekers and the curious or makes one the subject of pity. Either inevitably leads to questions that are no one else's business. I see no benefit in any of that. But, of course, the decision is up to you."

I remembered the poorly played pity I faced after news of my mother's disappearance became public, and could well imagine the deadly effect it would have on new acquaintances here. I imagined Gil Collmeyer listening politely to my story, then forever after avoiding me as a person to be pitied.

"Also, there is an actor—and I am using the term very generously, a dreadful man, by the name of Beckett, though he spells his name with two ts, and I would not want people to assume an inconvenient connection between you and him. I understand changing your name may feel like I am asking you to lose a part of your identity," she went on, "or dishonoring your parents' memory, and I assure you that is not my intention, but we must call you something, and once we have started down the Becket road, we are committed. If we are to make a change, and you are to belong to the Drakes in everyone's minds, it must be here at the beginning."

"Kit Drake, not Kit Becket?" I asked foolishly.

"It is not a lie. You are a Drake on your mother's side, and it is not unusual for a ward to take the name of their guardian. Introducing you as a Drake will instantly associate you with me whenever we go about the city's social circles, sidestepping any awkward explanations. We do not need to make a legal change. There may come a time when you no longer wish to be associated with the Drake name, and if that were to happen, it would be very simple to return to using your legal surname, a sort of clean slate. Think about it and let me know before we go to the theater tonight."

Christopher Becket wanted to lock himself in a closet, but Kit Drake rather liked the idea. Aunt Bernadette wished me to take her name--to be associated with her. It was a great encouragement. She planned to include me at social events. My head spun. Being connected to her would elevate my social status. Perhaps some of the dust of her charisma would settle about my shoulders, thrusting me forward in people's minds. I had already witnessed the phenomenon at the theater. But did changing my name make it seem like I was ashamed of my parents?

Not your mother, I realized. Drake was not her legal surname, but it was very much a part of who she was. She had used it as her stage name in London before she married my father and gave up the stage. Being known as a Drake was a chance to reinvent myself in a new, bolder image.

With my brain full of possibilities, all I managed to blurt out was, "I am going to the theater with you?"

"You did say you wanted to learn more about it, did you not?" Aunt Bernadette replied.

"I did."

"Good. Wixx can teach you." She and her purple dressing gown swished up the stairs.

This will change nothing. You will still be you, an inner voice reminded me. *You will still fall short of people's expectations.*

Maybe. But maybe in that brief moment when I am first introduced, I can make a better first impression. It was a chance, and I would take it. Christopher Becket would become Kit Drake.

Act One: Scene Six: Wallack's Theater, New York City.

Wallack's theater was a world apart from the city. Each time I stepped inside, I felt it.

"Theater people use a different language," Darragh, the Irish usher I met the first day, explained. Being the company members closest to my age, Darragh and "young" Giddy, who was a lighting stagehand like I hoped to become, had taken on the project of teaching me about the theater. "Where the audience sits is called 'the house'." Which explained the confusion he and I experienced when he confronted me about not having a ticket.

"And in the theater, that is *stage right*, and that is *stage left*," Young Giddy took over the tutorial, pointing to the opposite sides of the stage from the norms every English speaker in the world uses. "We all change our left and right to match the actor's left and right as they stand on the stage facing the house, so no one gets confused." I was already confused. "The stage directions seem backward to you right now because we're standing in the house," Giddy clarified.

"There is also a house right and a house left," Darragh went on. I wondered if they were putting me on.

"And then there's upstage and downstage," Giddy continued. "Upstage is to the back, and downstage is up front, by the footlights. My grandad explained to me that those directions came from way back when the stages were often raked, or sloped, toward the audience with the back raised so all the dying parts played on the boards, the stage's floor, could be seen by the poor folk who paid a penny to stand in front of the stage to watch the play."

"They were called *groundlings*," Darragh interjected cheerfully.

Giddy glowered at being interrupted. "Anyway, it's important in the theater that you know the right words to call things. You don't want to get it wrong, especially around Wixx."

"You have to know what folks are talking about."

"And this is how we all talk."

I frowned. "So, the lighting people still refer to the left and right as if they were actors standing facing the audience?"

"The house." Giddy corrected me.

"Even though the towers are outside the stage's picture frame in the house?" My friends nodded.

"If it's about what's on the stage, we use stage directions," Giddy insisted with all the seriousness of a school tutor, though I doubted he had ever spent a day in a classroom. Both Giddys, young and old, worked at Wallacks, their pay going to support a large extended family that lived in a small house in Lower Manhattan. "It's just the way it is." I had been hearing that phrase a lot.

The theater not only had its own language, it had its own superstitions.

We three boys were cleaning lenses by the stage right tower when the black cat came sauntering by. I was about to shoo it off when Darraugh stopped me.

"Leave it be. That's Kindle-cat. It lives here."

"I've seen it here before. I figured it was just a stray." I eyed the saucy minx as it was eyeing us, as if judging our efforts.

"No, it's our cat, but it is wild. You can't touch it."

"It don't much like people," Giddy cautioned. "But it's good luck for a theatre to have a cat."

I frowned. "Black cats are bad luck."

"Not in the theater."

"And also, it eats rats and the like. So that's good."

"Aye. So, don't be giving in to its tricks and feeding it," Darragh warned me. "It has a job to do, and it needs to stay hungry to do it."

There was a lot to learn in the theater.

But people at Wallack's seemed happy in their work, whether their tools were a needle and thread, or paint, hammers, lights, or lines. Though the actors were the ones the audience saw and admired, the company recognized that each of them had a part to play, on or off stage, and it took everyone to create true theater magic. The Costume Designer needed to respect the seamstresses who took their drawings and cut and sewed them into clothing. The actors needed to respect the designer and the seamstresses who made their costumes fit and flatter while allowing for whatever movements were required for their role. Seams came undone or had to be let out or taken in as an actor's waist expanded or contracted. A costume that was too tight could tear during a fight scene. A costume that slipped off a woman's shoulder was a distraction for actors and audience. A pocket might be needed where one had not been designed.

The sets had to be not only beautiful but supportive of the action of the play and safe for actors and stagehands, whether the lights were up or out. A raw nail could slice a hand or rip a costume.

It was a close-knit group working with a common vision to build something wondrous from nothing but words on paper. Though no one would allow any disparagement of "the Words".

But whatever challenges a production faced, there was a cardinal rule: everything had to be ready by eight o'clock when the curtain went up.

Wallack's new theater had a number of innovations. With the advent of gaslighting came the challenge of adding heat to a building that got close and stuffy when filled with people. And then there was the problem of exhaust from the gas. In the early days of gas lighting, audiences fainted, poisoned by the fumes. Theaters quickly closed and refitted with fans and ventilation systems.

Wallacks benefited from other theaters' missteps and built a ventilation system of tubes and fans alongside the flybridge, and narrow boardwalks, 'the grid' that crisscrossed the high spaces above the deck, or 'boards', where the actors performed.

The theater's true ceiling was high above the boards where painted canvas 'drops', several stories tall, were 'flown' in and out of the stage area by stagehands using a rope and pulley counterweight system and rigging. Wixx's rolling gait was not a singular trait among stagehands. Many of them were plucked from a sailing life working tall ships. With them, they brought a series of tie-offs, knots, and understanding of best practices now commonly used and part of the theater lexicon; the pin-rail, the deck, rigging, and the flybridge, often shortened to merely 'the fly'.

When the show was over and the stage cleared, the 'ghost light' was brought to the stage and lit. It would stay on until the stage was set up for the next show. With the strange-angled sets tucked away in the wings and pushed up against the back wall like the oversized blocks of a troll child, the stage was a different space; rustic, barnlike, rough-sawn posts supporting hand-planed beams mounted over unfinished wide-plank floors sanded smooth by the soles of actors' shoes.

Theaters ran shows from Tuesday through Saturday nights, sometimes adding a trendy new Sunday matinee if the show appealed to a daytime audience. *Macbeth* did not. So, Sundays and Mondays we were 'dark'. This was the case across the city.

The Company took its traditions and the business of educating the next generation seriously. Always eager to lend a hand, and with nowhere else I needed to be, I learned to sew hems and re-attach buttons while "Needle Maggie" shared memories of the famous, the infamous, and those who had passed through Wallack's without becoming either. I found adventure in exploring the forest of costumes hung from poles and chains attached to the ceiling in Wardrobe, and wonder royal raiments heavy with glass gemstones and metallic braid.

I learned to paint and spatter sets, using techniques to make paint look like rock or brick or water, or sky. When Mister Clare, who had come from London to design for Wallack's, discovered I had an interest in design, he encouraged me to look at his sketches and ask questions. I also examined the gadgetry and machines being used for lighting, and here Wixx humored me, taking the time to look at my "improved" designs. My unofficial internship resulted in the best outcome I could imagine. When the stage right, light tower boy quit, I was offered a position. I had officially joined the company.

Deeply enamored of my newfound love, I declared loudly and often that every man, woman, and child should attend. Hearing my declaration, Wixx's ocean-hued eyes studied me from behind weathered folds of skin pushed against them like the wind-sculpted ripples on sand dunes. The gasman had an unhurried, languid way, as if his timekeeper was not a metronome marking swift seconds but instead was measured by the gentle sway of a below-deck hammock moving in the rhythm of the sea's swells.

"There is entertainment and then there is Theater," he said, his voice reminding me of a retreating ocean wave sifting through beach gravel. "If you're going to work in the trade, you'll want to understand the difference." A special language, its own superstitions: theater people had their own way of looking at things as well.

I was accompanying Wixx as he closed down the theater and set the ghost light when I asked him, "Why does the ghost light change everything?"

Wixx chuckled. "There are as many stories about why we leave a ghost light on stage as there are theaters. Most of its superstition, but there's a safety angle to it, too. It's fearsome dark in here when everything is shut down."

"But why does the building change, Wixx?" I prodded. "When the ghost light is on, the stage looks so old, like a deserted barn, or an abandoned church that's been left to crumble." I moved my foot over the smooth deck planks. The wood had the sheen of a gray pearl where the actor's feet had sanded it for many years—more years than Wallacks had existed in this place.

"It is in a theater's nature to change, looking like different places," Wixx half answered.

"But what is its true nature? The rustic wooden building, or the gilded hall?"

Kindle appeared from the darkness and, quite to my surprise, walked across the stage and began rubbing against my legs. I picked the cat up and it let me, its purr rumbling warmth into my chest as I cuddled it in my arms. It looked over at Wixx as if it too was waiting for the answer.

The old gasman worked his lips, poking them out and folding them in, like words were trying to come out, but he was keeping them prisoner. He studied the stage sculpted in the chiaroscuro of a shadow born of a single light.

"I see what the theater lets me see. Not everyone sees the same thing." It was an odd reply, but he did not try to put me off or tell me I was imagining things. "I wouldn't say anything about it to others, though. They might not understand and think you're a bit, you know, strange."

I was strange, but I did not think it was a secret; my fixation with gadgets, my obsession with learning everything to do with the theater marked me as an oddity, but people here did not seem to mind.

"People are threatened by uncertainty," Wixx extended his explanation. "They need to believe that what they see is what everyone sees, and that because everyone agrees what they see, it must be real. If they can touch it, that's proof.

"But that's not the nature of theater. A theater is about illusion. We make things you can't touch but that look real--things that can as easily float away as burrow deep inside you. Make-believe has been given a bad name by religion and such, but it is not a bad thing to make someone believe in the possibility of experiencing something that's inspiring rather than mundane. We are bogged down by the heaviness of an existence we are told is the single reality we will ever have and that we must all believe in. Make-believe is the antidote to plodding through life trying to survive religion's insistence that until we die, we cannot expect better, and all our hopes rest with the afterlife.

"It's the theater's job to suspend false certainty in a way that common folk can accept, so they can experience new ideas and feelings, and see greater possibilities for their lives."

Kindle struggled in my arms, and he leaped to Wixx. He cradled the cat in one curled arm, petting it with the other hand.

I followed him as he carried Kindle off stage, headed for the stage door where Bernie would be waiting with the carriage.

"I didn't think you liked cats," I commented.

"This is not a cat." He scratched Kindle under the chin. "It's a spirit in a cat's body."

As I followed Wixx and Kindle into the next circle of light that we would snuff into darkness, I glanced back over my shoulder. The stage shadows were gamboling in the ghost light's moonlit twilight, dancing and strutting, bowing and spinning. A cat who was a spirit? Who was I to disbelieve? I was too new to know this world.

Act One, Scene Seven-Wallack's Theater, NYC.

Watching *MacBeth* five nights a week, I began to notice small differences in the actor's performances. Sometimes it was an improvement in delivery, sometimes not. Performers endured bad nights when an actor felt 'off' and declared dissatisfaction with their performances, but there were other nights an actor felt on fire, their performances inspired. The most skilled performed with consistency, delivering more of the latter and less of the former. I was soon familiar enough with the play and how the director, Mister Wallack the younger, expected it to run, to notice when an actor 'went up' and forgot a line, their fellow theatricians covering for them, or the actor doing their best to make up lines in the Shakespearean style until a colleague could feed them a true line and get things back on course.

There were actors whose solid, even brilliant, performances night after night revealed great skill beyond natural talent, Aunt Bernadette and Edwin Forest, the actor who played opposite my aunt in the title role of *MacBeth*, a famous theatrician whom Charlotte Cushman had referred to when she mentioned the Astor Opera House and the Forrest-Macready riots that killed a dozen people and closed that theater. It had all been about which actor's performance was better, the native Forrest, or the British Macready.

There were also actors of lesser talent whom people did not riot over, the evidence not merely in the actor's struggles with their lines, but in the lack of depth and emotional range expressed in their roles. I understood Mister Lester one night when I overheard him mutter, "Forrest was right; when they are too inept and lazy to carry packages or clerk in a store, they think they can be actors. God preserve us."

The Wallack's Company had been founded by James William Wallack, now known as Wallack Senior. The Wallack family had pulled together a forward-thinking ensemble of solid actors of skill rather than relying on expensive big-name guest performers, though they invited headliner guests in major roles from time to time, and they had a few in the company, like Aunt Bernadette. The company's commitment to moving away from the old style of acting, where performers posed dramatically at the edge of the stage near the footlights wearing garish makeup so their features could be seen in the poor light and droning lines, embracing instead a naturalistic style that utilized the advantages of gas and limelights, was key. The ability to utilize the depth of a stage due to improved lighting meant that sets were more inventive and more usable, rather than relying on the backdrops of old. This allowed an actor's makeup to be less tortured and grotesque and for their expressions of emotion to be truer. But as happens with the evolution of any art form, new skills meant change. Realism required a unique skill set, and not all older performers were accepting of change.

Despite Lester Wallack's repeated directions and notes, Old Giddy Gasper continued to stubbornly deliver his lines in a series of overly dramatic poses, shouting phrases in a sing-song rhythm, with bawdy side bits added, often breaking the fourth wall, which was the invisible "wall" where the audience sat, and playing directly to them. This was considered a terrible sin, unless the style and direction of the work specifically called for it. Mister Lester, having envisioned and directed this production of *MacBeth* in a "natural" style, made Old Gideon's performance stand out in the worst way. He had been "talked to" about it more than once, and in truth, his antics had only been tolerated this long because of his long association with the Wallack family. But though he had temporarily toned down his performance after receiving Mister Lester's notes, he always reverted to his old habits, which resulted in snickers from the audience where snickers were not meant to be. Some people, finding his improvised "bits" too offensive, had been seen leaving the theater mid-play.

I was working on oiling the pivots on the stage right tower's reflecting mirrors when I overheard Mister Lester confronting the old guiser yet again.

"You cannot continue like this," Lester warned Old Giddy. "*We* cannot continue like this."

Old Giddy pretended surprise, as if he had not expected this, the white sclera visible all around his eyes. Even in real life, Old Gideon tended to the overblown and melodramatic.

"What are you saying? Speak plainly, Lester," he said defensively, which was how he reacted to anyone anytime they gave him a suggestion, performance-related or not.

"I'm saying that if you cannot adjust your delivery so it matches the rest of the cast's, we will need to make a change."

Giddy looked down his nose at the younger man over whom he towered by a good head. "What kind of change?" Mister Lester's expression said most eloquently what he did not wish to verbalize. "I have been acting since before you were born," Old Giddy declared. "Your father and I trod the boards together as pages in *Henry the Fourth*. My name has been filling houses for decades." The man donned swagger like an overcoat. "Audiences love me and what I do."

"Twenty years ago, they did, Giddy, but things have changed; styles have changed. Look, I could retain you as a Walking Gentleman," Lester threw the man a bone. Giddy had been a working actor since childhood. He had not made a fortune, but he had made a living, and he had an extended family to support.

"A 'Walking Gentleman'?" He was horrified. A 'walking' lady or gentleman were a human prop. No skills were required, except not to scratch anything embarrassing, or fiddle and draw the audience's attention. They spoke no lines.

"Audiences are becoming more sophisticated. They expect to see a certain style and caliber of performance, and that's what we want. We are teaching them the difference between legitimate theatre, vaudeville tripe, and burlesque, Gid, and *MacBeth* is a serious drama, not a farce."

"And in a few weeks, you will open the *School for Scandal*." And then farce would be the name of the game.

"Mugging to the audience and breaking the fourth wall will still not be acceptable, unless it is built into the blocking and direction." Giddy raised a single bushy eyebrow, silently questioning Mister Lester's statement. "How can I trust you to do what I ask in *that* show if you won't do it now in *this* one? If audiences are laughing in the wrong places for the wrong reasons, we owe it to them and the play to address the problem."

"And I am the problem?" Giddy's eyes narrowed as his lower lip thrust out in an arrogant pout.

"Leering and thrusting for cheap laughs is the problem. Wallack's has invested in making theater attendance respectable so men feel comfortable bringing their wives and children to see our plays, so that we can fill houses, keep the lights on, and pay salaries. What you are doing goes against those efforts. And I am not just talking about this show, Gilly, or Wallack's. The old poser style of acting is dead. Soon, there won't be a theater company in the country that will tolerate that sort of posing and mugging. It belongs in a burly house, not in a theater. It doesn't fit the material. It's not real. It's not natural."

"Acting is not *natural*," Gideon proclaimed haughtily. "If all an actor had to do was be 'natural', anyone could do it. If audiences wanted *natural*, they would stay home and listen to their wives, but they don't. They come to the theater to see us pull faces and fart when they wish they could but don't dare. They don't want to see lords and ladies acting n*aturally*. They want to see the highborn embarrassed; red blood, juicy gore, and sex they can smell from their seats."

Mister Lester shook his head. "That's not the audience we want here. Our goal is to perform good plays for people who think beyond their next beer and brawl."

"There's nothing wrong with a beer and a brawl," Old Giddy grumped.

"In a pub, not in the theater," Mister Lester disagreed. "Not in *my* theater."

"This is that high-born bitch, Lady Drake's doing, isn't it?" he sneered at Bernie's name. "Her and her immoral friends, bed hopping and buggering each other, pretending their asses don't stink. People can't just go to the theater for a night of fun anymore; no, we need to make people *think*. Bugger that. They might as well go to church. Do you know how many immigrants are getting off the boats every week in this city, Lester? Thousands."

"And they're broke. They're not going to the theater."

"They don't go to *your* theater, but they manage to scrape a few coins together to go to shows at The Bowery. If they make fifty cents, they spend fifteen of it on a few pints and a show."

"Taking the food right out of their kid's mouth," Lester countered, losing his temper. Everyone who had been working onstage had subtly disappeared, but I was stuck. If I climbed down the tower now, I would have to walk right by the two arguing men.

"Real folk have had enough of the high and snooty telling them they don't matter, that they don't know how to behave, and they aren't good enough. That's why they left where they were and came here. Your father understands that. Does he even know about this? About me? I can't believe he agreed to this."

"I have my father's full confidence."

Old Giddy harumphed.

"I believe in what we're doing here," Lester declared. "That's why I brought Mister Clare from England to design incredible sets and had gas and limelights installed in the new building. That's why Clare worked with Wixx to make the staging for this show look not only real, but better than real. We're nurturing an ensemble of true artists here, Gideon, actors who do superlative work, but it's based on a vision: *my* vision, and this is my decision to make. I have asked you to change your performance. I have offered you tutoring…"

"I don't need acting lessons," Gideon snarled. "I have been an actor for decades. Do you understand what that means?"

"I do," Lester replied. "I am a Wallack, and the Wallacks, the Jeffersons, and the Booths are the most recognized theatrical families in America. I grew up with that legacy, and I intend to honor it."

Gideon's cheek muscles worked beneath the skin, his jaw jutting in and out." You're going to run this company into the ground. You'll lose everything William built."

"I do not agree, but these are my choices to make."

"I could black my face and go to work at The Bowery in *Uncle Tom's Happy Cabin* anytime," Gideon boasted. "Daddy Rice would be thrilled to have me."

"And if that's the sort of acting you want to do, perhaps you should take him up on the offer."

"The *sort of acting*? You feckin' snob." Giddy's chin went up. "It's clear my talents and experience are not valued here. I quit." He spun on his heels and stomped off.

I scurried down from the tower.

"Does he mean it, Mister Lester? Is he going? Now?" I asked, breathless at witnessing this horrific turn of events. How would the play go on?

Lester ran his hand through his hair. "Yes. I think he does."

"But we have a show tonight. Who will play Malcolm?" I imagined the fallout that would play out in the next several hours. Lester turned to me, a look of recognition dawning on his face.

"You're Lady Bernie's nephew, aren't you?"

"Yes, Sir."

"Do you know Mister Collmeyer?" I nodded. "Do you know where he is?"

"I can find him," I vowed.

"Tell him I need to see him right away. He's going on as Malcolm tonight." Lester strode away to his office. My mind spun, all excitement and anxiety. Of all the people in the company who might have been given the task of delivering this news to Gil, it was going to be me. It was a pivotal moment for an actor: his first big role, an important role: Malcolm, in the Scottish play. (I learned quickly not to say the play's title while inside a theater, due to the superstition theater folk held that it was bad luck to do so.) Whether he was a success or a failure, this was something he would remember for the rest of his life, and I would be part of it.

I ran to find Gil.

"Try the roof." A stagehand pointed me toward the stairs.

I took the first two stories two treads at a time, startling Kindle, who skittered away and hid, but by the fourth, my breathing was labored, and I was forced to slow to a more reasonable pace.

"Gil!" I called out as the young man was about to step out of the doorway to the left on the sixth floor.

"Drake? What are you doing up here, my friend?" I wished that he did not see me that way, but I was grateful that he saw me. Sometimes we sat on the catwalk and ate lunch together, sharing company gossip or just talking about nothing. His casual friendship, given out of his own kindness, was a gift. Now I could give him something in return. "Come with me while I have a smoke," he invited me.

"There's no time for that," I informed him between gasps. "Mister Lester wants to see you, right away."

"Now?" Gil looked perplexed.

"Yes, now!" I exploded. "Old Giddy has quit, and you are to go on as Malcolm tonight!"

Gil stared at me, or maybe it was not me, and he was just staring, seeing nothing, but he was struggling to grasp the meaning of my words. Mister Lester probably should not have sent an invisible boy to deliver such an important message, but at Wallack's, I was becoming more visible every day.

"Malcolm? Tonight?" Gil said at last, his voice very small.

"Yes," I confirmed.

"But it's after three o'clock. The curtain is in less than five hours. I'll need to go over the lines and the blocking. I have to be fitted for wardrobe."

"Mister Lester is waiting downstairs," I reminded him.

"Right." He started down the stairs. "Malcolm..." He stopped suddenly. "Does Ginny know?"

Ginevra Wellbelove was the company's ingenue, a gold and pink rosebud of a girl whose beauty equaled Gil's own. I felt a stab of jealousy. Of course, his first thought was of impressing Ginny. She was everything a young man would want: golden hair, pretty face, pink lips, perfect skin. The fact that Ginevra Wellbelove, a self-chosen stage name that said it all, was ambitious, manipulative, and extremely aware that the sand of her youth was running through the hourglass of time, and when it was gone, so would be any leverage she had for snagging a wealthy husband, but this was beyond Gil Collmeyer's generous nature to see. Ginny was balancing caution with capriciousness, courted by several eligible young men of New York Society. It would not matter if Gil were playing Hamlet himself; he did not have the right last name or the money to have a chance with Ginny.

Secretly, I was glad. Gil was not only beautiful, he was a genuinely kind person—too good for Ginny Wellbelove. And, of course, I was desperately in love with him, though I worked hard to hide it.

"No, of course, Ginny doesn't know. No one knows," I informed my friend. "Technically, you don't know yet because Mister Lester hasn't told you. Go see him!"

"Right." Gil started down the stairs again.

Once Gil had been officially informed of his new status, he began to think of the many details that needed to be taken care of before the curtain went up at eight o'clock.

"Bloody hell, who will take *my* role?"

Mister Lester frowned. "What about young Giddy?"

"God no." Gil shook his head. "He's a stagehand, not an actor. Will he even stay on now that you've sacked his grandfather?"

"I did not sack his grandfather; Old Gideon quit. But I honestly don't know what young Giddy will do in the face of that," Mister Lester admitted. "I haven't made a general announcement yet, and I certainly haven't had time to ask the bellows boy about his plans."

Young Giddy loved his job. He loved Wallacks. I did not think he would want to leave, but Scottish families were clannish, and though the family needed the money, they might force him to leave if they felt staying was being disloyal to his grandfather.

Lester's glance fell on me. I could tell what he was thinking.

"I am not an actor either, Mister Lester," I protested.

"But you are a Drake. It's in your blood. The role is small, only a few lines. All you have to do is speak loud enough that the audience can hear you. The rest of the time, you just stand there holding the king's standard. You can hold a pole, can't you?"

Actors dreamed of getting a part. Invisible boys did not. People here did not know Kit Becket, the invisible boy who heard the house's whispers, marked its haunted halls, and peered through the darkness to suck the secrets from its shadows, consumed with unraveling the mysteries around him. They only knew Kit Drake, the helpful lad who was happy to be living with his aunt and going to the theater where people liked him. But there Gil stood, looking like a sculpted angel, his beautiful blue eyes hopeful, pleading with me to take this one last worry off his shoulders. I would do anything for him.

"I can. I will," I promised, ignoring the queasiness in my stomach.

"You'll be fine, Kit. Just forget about the audience," Gil advised me. "Focus on what is happening on the stage."

"And don't fidget," Mister Lester added.

"What am I doing?" Gil moaned as if everything had suddenly become too real. "I can't do this. I've never played a major role. I won't even have had one rehearsal."

"If there are any scenes you want to run, just tell me. We'll make the time, Gil. But I want you to listen to me now and know that what I'm saying to you is the truth. If you could not do this, I would not be asking. I would not have given you this role. There are probably four men in the city who have done Malcolm before. But I don't want them. I don't want another overacting poser. I want *you*, Gil. I want your youth and your promise. You know what I'm looking for, and even though you don't realize it, you know these lines. You have been at every rehearsal and every show."

Gil nodded. "I *should* know them. I *used* to know them, Mister Lester, but right now I can't think of how one of those speeches starts."

"When you hear the cue, you will." He put a hand on Gil's shoulder, looking him in the eyes. "I want tonight to go so smoothly the audience doesn't even realize there's been a change."

"Unless they've seen the show before," Gil said. "Old Giddy and I look nothing alike. He's old enough to be my grandfather."

"But that's what makes this so brilliant, don't you see?" Lester encouraged Gil. "Companies are always casting this role with some middle-aged or older actor, someone who didn't get the lead but has experience, so they throw them Malcolm like a bone to assuage their egos. But you are young and fresh, closer to the age I believe Malcolm would have been, and should be played. Self-doubt and remorse are eating the dead king's son alive, so he tries to hide from his responsibilities, drinking and bedding every woman in sight." Lester started guiding Gil to the hall that led to Wardrobe. "I know what you're going through. I was an actor. The dread of how you will be judged, and the knowledge that you're not ready, because how could you be, you haven't had one rehearsal? It's terrifying, but just know the company is all here for you, Gil. They're not going to judge you. We are here to support you, grateful that you are willing to take this chance and save this performance. I don't want you to try and play it like Old Giddy or anyone else you've seen do the role. Play it like *you* feel it, with all the complex feelings stirring inside you right now, the confusion, pride, fear, and hope. That unspoken belief that you just might be great at this, that's locked in a battle with the fear that you will fail miserably. That's Malcolm. That's the key to him. You will bring a nobility to his transformation that an actor like Gideon could never understand." Gil groaned, and Lester chuckled. "And at the end, when he finally overcomes his fears and embraces his role as the future king of Scotland, tormented and heroic? It is going to be brilliant."

Terror and inspiration battled over the landscape of Gil's handsome face. Mister Lester was right. It was fascinating to watch.

"But what if they don't like it? What if they don't like *me*?" his voice cracked.

Lester and I exchanged looks. "Didn't you hear me? They're going to love you."

"Especially the ladies," I added. Lester nodded.

"Especially the ladies, but whatever they do, flutter their fans, giggle, make eyes at you…"

"They'll lean forward so you can look down their bodices," I added. "I see them do that to Forrest all the time."

"Whatever they do, stay in character. Do not break the fourth wall. While you are onstage, ignore the very existence of any woman in the audience."

"Or on the stage," I interrupted again, thinking of Ginny Wellbelove.

"It will make them mad for you." Lester grinned. "Now, go get ready."

Gilbert Collmeyer's performance that night was a triumph. Mine was almost adequate. I held my spear and spoke my lines, terrified I would make a mistake and 'go up', but I made it through the play, speaking the lines clearly, though without inspiration. Strangely, though, each time I spoke, my fellow actors looked confused, searching the stage for the source of the lines, as if I had been missing entirely and a prompter had been forced to read my lines from the wings.

As soon as the torture of performing was over, I hurried back to the walking men's dressing room to divest myself of the mismatched costume that had been pulled together to fit my small frame. Kindle and Aunt Bernadette were both waiting for me.

"What happened?" My aunt forced the words past jaws closed so tight they might have required butter to be opened.

"Nothing." I frowned. "I said my lines just as I was supposed to."

"You were meant to say them onstage."

My perplexed frown remained. "I stood exactly where Mister Lester showed me." The cat stopped paying attention to us and began washing its paws. It occurred to me that the other actors pretending not to see me could be a hazing ritual for new actors, but if so, it was an American tradition because Bernie did not seem to know anything about it.

"There is no shame in having stage fright your first turn, Kit," she said. The words might have been meant to reassure me, but it wasn't working. Bernadette Drake was a prickly woman, but despite not wanting to, I had stepped in. I had done my best.

"I take no pride in giving a dull performance," I retorted, chin up. "And I will not say I was not frightened by the experience, but I am no liar, Aunt. I was in my place, onstage, as directed." The cat stopped its ablutions, came up to me, and began to rub its sleek body against my legs, looking up at me, its yellow eyes full of mischief. If I had been a mouse, I would have been shivering in my gray fur coat, but not being an option for dinner, the cat's playful attention did make me feel better.

"Upstaged by a cat," Bernie harrumphed. She studied my face like I had written a confession there, but there was nothing to confess. "Nerves can affect things strangely," she admitted. "And there were certainly plenty of those onstage tonight. Tomorrow will be better."

"I have to do it again?" I groaned. I loved the theater. I did not love acting. I was happy on a tower moving glass jars, leaves, or twigs in front of the lights. I was happy sitting beside Wixx on the gas panel, watching him dial just the right amount of fuel to the right light, watching when he cut the gases off fast or dimmed them slowly, controlling the audience's mood.

"You committed to this," Bernie replied. "No one told you you had to. You took it on of your own accord. Now, you must see it through. Drakes keep their promises. So, until Mister Lester finds a replacement, you will do the part…onstage."

Act One, Scene Eight: The Metropolitan Hotel, NYC, April 1863.

There was a rhythm to Aunt Bernie's household, and though I worked to find my beats within it, I felt I was in a play where everyone else knew their part while I stumbled around, ignorant of whether I was in a supporting role, cast as the comic fool, or merely a 'Walking Gentleman' likely to be gone from the stage before the second act.

If I rose early, I breakfasted with Begam Dweeti. Sometimes Burke joined us. If I slept late, I broke my fast with Aunt Bernie, joined by Idabelle, though Idy often left early to help at the Colored Children's Asylum. I helped Weaver with the horses, assisted Dweetie in the garden, and in the afternoon, Aunt Bernie and I went to the theater.

It was Kit Drake's face I put on each morning; a useful lad who never caused trouble or asked uncomfortable questions, but Kit Becket was still there, hiding, building suspicions around Bernadette Drake, who he was convinced was a conglomerate of segmented selves who shuffled her bags of secrets around so she could present whichever one was best suited for a particular event. He was not a loud boy, but he was persistent, and he kept his fears and suspicions tucked beneath the pillow where they were easily at hand in case he needed them.

"We will be lunching at the Metropolitan today, you and I," Aunt Bernie announced one morning.

The question that came immediately to mind was "why"? Kit Drake stuffed the question before it could get out, fearing he would not like the answer. That, and he did not want to seem cheeky. He had become comfortable with the routines of life at Drake House. This was not part of the routine, and that made Kit Becket sit up straight and pay attention. *Something is going on. Something is happening.*

"The tailor's order has arrived?" Bernie asked.

"Yesterday afternoon, after we left for the theater," I replied.

"Good. Burke will know what is appropriate for you to wear."

That was good, because I certainly did not.

I worried about that unasked "why" all morning. Why was Aunt Bernadette taking me out to lunch at all when Dweetie served a perfectly good lunch at the house? Did she plan to announce she was sending me away to school or an apprenticeship, or some other inscrutable plan? Had the maid, Frostine, discovered the fear hidden under my pillow?

Burke presented my newly acquired clothes, all organized neatly in the armoire in my room: four jackets: a sturdy brown for daily wear, a fine worsted morning coat, a black tailcoat for formal evening occasions, and a brilliant deep blue cutaway that looked like it belonged on stage, not on my thin frame. The pairing options were three pairs of tapered wool trousers, black for the tailcoat, a black and gray stripe, and charcoal gray, suitable for both business and more formal occasions where a tailcoat was not required. There were also three pairs of sturdier trousers: a dark brown, and two shades of gray, tailored in the block cut still worn by workingmen and men who did not follow fashion and had therefore not adopted the new slimmer lines that showed off a man's figure if he had one.

There were also half a dozen white or ivory shirts in varying weights of linen, silk, and cotton hung beside these jackets and trousers with two sets of detachable collars and cuffs set out on the shelf above them, along with three silk ties, a blue, a green, and a black one. A heavy black wool overcoat with a velvet collar hung on the far right, and a hatbox sat on the armoire's floor.

I had never seen such an array of clothing for a man. Burke pulled out the leg of one pair of heavy, brown, wool trousers.

"On a frame such as yours, I feared the boxy cut of workman's clothes would make you look like a child who had raided his grandfather's closet. So, I had your clothes for theater workdays tailored a bit narrower to suit your lean frame."

I was astounded. "Thank you, Burke. But there are too many. I will never wear all of them."

He smiled knowingly. "This is New York, Master Kit. Upper-class men dress fashionably. What you have here are different types of clothing for different occasions. Your aunt is a Dame of the British Realm. She has a place in society and a reputation to uphold. How you look and comport yourself reflects on her, so she will not have you dressed poorly, particularly when you are out in the city socially. Now, what costume shall I have Dweetie prepare for you?"

"That one?" I pointed hesitantly to the deep blue jacket, my attention drawn by the fantastic color.

Burke shook his head. "A stylish choice. You have an eye for quality and style, but that suit is not the correct choice for this occasion. The wearer of that coat is demanding to be noticed. On this occasion, your first venture into New York's social circles, the better strategy is for you to blend in. It will put less pressure on you." He drew out the plain gray morning coat that looked like every other businessman's. "You will not stand out in this, but your wardrobe will be recognized as being of quality." He indicated the narrower lapels and fitted waist. "The Metropolitan is one of the most fashionable dining establishments in the city, but the primary reason people patronize it is its reputation as a place where persons of power and influence socialize and make connections with others like themselves and those who wish to become one of them. Government contracts require patronage, and many officials in a position to offer such patronage may be found lunching at the Metropolitan." He chose a tapered pair of gray pants and a snowy white shirt, adding them to the items he draped over his forearm. "I will take these to Begam Dweeti."

"Thank you, Burke."

As midday approached, I dressed and joined my aunt. She looked me over.

"You will do." She gave me a curt nod, then breezed out the front door and into the waiting carriage with me in her wake.

"Do not look so nervous," she advised me as we exited the carriage at our destination. "Stay focused within yourself and do not look around at the room or any one person. Remember, you are the most important person in the room."

"But I am not." I stopped, horrified.

"But you are. You are with me." She punctuated the look she gave me with such an exquisite, arrogantly raised eyebrow that I had to stop myself from bending into a courtly bow before her. "You know how Mister Warren moves when he's playing King Duncan?" I nodded, trying not to get sick and befoul the marble steps as we ascended to the hotel's colonnaded porch. "Think about moving like that. Imagine it is a game, and you are trying to make Begam Dweeti laugh."

"But Aunt…" I began my protest. She stopped me.

"Women." She pointed to herself. "Are not allowed in the Metropolitan's dining room unless they are accompanied by a respectable, male family member. That would be you." She dipped her head toward me.

"No one is going to believe…"

"They will if you do." She took my arm. "Now, head up, chest out, back straight. When the Maitre'd asks, we have reservations under your name, Christopher Drake. We are leaving the wings, about to enter onto the stage, and now…we are on." We entered the hotel lobby.

I did my best to copy the strange combination of condescension and deference I saw gentlemen at the theatre use toward their female companions. I could not hope to emulate the complexities, but putting on an attitude of aloofness, which is very akin to shyness, I could handle. I added my longing for privacy, sucked in my cheeks, thrust up my nose, and added a judgmental sneer as if to my delicate senses everything smelled "off". We were barely seated at our table when I apologized again.

"I am sorry, Aunt. I am completely unsuited for this. You should have asked Gil."

"Take a breath and calm yourself, nephew. Being visibly upset in public shows a lack of breeding, even in this heathen country," Bernie replied pleasantly. "You may or may not be an actor, Kit, but you have a gift for mimicry. Anyone at Wallack's would have known exactly who you were imitating. And you are incorrect about being the wrong person. You are the perfect person. Gil Collmeyer is not one of us." I was about to protest her class prejudice when she continued. "What I mean is, he is not a Drake. Mister Collmeyer is gaining attention with audiences and the press because he is refreshing in his new role and exceedingly handsome. Which is exactly why he would be wrong for today's luncheon. He would have drawn attention. I, however, am respectable enough to be accepted here, but familiar enough not to be noted, and I expect you to pass unnoticed. You seem to have a knack for it. By tomorrow, no one will remember if we were here today or last week." She flashed me a rare, mischievous smile.

Though I had spent the morning hours imagining different scenarios around the possible topics of conversation my aunt might have planned for this luncheon: my imminent departure to boarding school, my apprenticeship to some sea captain, or that I was to be chained to a desk in a dusty bank vault adding and subtracting figures until I was as withered and moldy as a winter squash come March, none of those conversations appeared. We ate in silence, accompanied by the soft sibilants and long vowels of our neighbor's Southern accents.

"Emancipation, ha! That's like telling a rabbit they're free to leave the warren. 'Hey, you rabbits, you're free now, Ol' Billy goat Lincoln said so. Go on, leave!" The potbellied man at the table to my right made a shooing motion. "They're slaves. They have no skills. They have never had to fend for themselves. When the weather turns in the fall, they'll come crawling back to the plantations begging for a meal and a roof over their heads."

Bernie's spoon paused halfway to her lips.

"Your face, my thane, is as a book which men may read," she cautioned me. Chastised, I looked down at my plate, hooding my eyes. "It is such a pleasure to enjoy a quiet lunch, don't you think, nephew?" Her voice was rich, her elocution perfect. "So many people feel the need to fill silence with idle chatter. I appreciate you allowing me to focus on my own thoughts." Her words did and did not say what she meant, but I believed I understood her instructions: she had not come here for the food, and she was not here to talk. She was here to listen.

"Damn Yankees have no right to tell another country what it can and can't do," the potbellied man declared. The mutton chops on his florid, vein-riddled face looked like dark moss stuck to his cheeks, left out in the humid southland forest to mold and in need of scraping. "Abe Lincoln is a jumped-up, uneducated, backwoods boobie." He enjoyed being the center of attention, and neither he nor his companions saw any shame in his distressing characterization of America's President.

Bernie continued to placidly eat her lunch. I followed suit.

Lincoln's first declaration of martial law in Baltimore--right after his inauguration--had been a hot point of discussion in Cincinnati. As the transfer hub for all North-South or East-West bound trains, Baltimore was a strategic point the Union could not afford to lose. It was also the site of the first attempt on his life. Baltimore had not voted for him.

Act One, Scene Eight

Further controversy followed when, as Southern states seceded, Lincoln's administration began spending hundreds of thousands of tax dollars on weapons and gear to outfit an army to fight for the Union, none of it approved by Congress, all of it supplying a war that was not legal under the laws of the country. Throughout his campaign, Abraham Lincoln claimed he was not an Abolitionist. When Southern states began to secede, he continued to insist that he fought only to preserve the Union and democracy, not to end slavery, but the recent Emancipation Proclamation made him a liar. Two years into a war that everyone thought would be over in a few months, Lincoln still had not found a general who could win the conflict for him. A great many young men paid the price.

"Northerners are lily livered traitors entirely without honor," one of our neighboring diners declared heatedly. "They've always been cowards."

"That's why Lee's going to win this war for us." The potbellied man raised his glass. Several tables of men followed suit.

My heart was banging like a carpenter trying to race the first snow of winter.

"They are Confederate Rebels, Aunt," I whispered to Bernie, leaning over my soup.

"Just eat your lunch, Kit," she counseled me between ladylike sips of her soup. "And do not let your imagination run away with you." She smiled and dabbed her lips with her napkin as the next course was served. I did as I was bidden, gulping down panic with each bite.

"Before those damned Wide-Awakes started marching, I never knew a Northerner who fought back over anything," one of the speaker's tablemates agreed.

The grass-roots Wide Awake movement changed a lot of people's ideas about Northern and Midwestern folk being too bookish and pacifistic to stand up for their ideals. Which seemed foolish to me since the American Revolution was started in New England by New Englanders. I had been fascinated by the Wide Awake movement and read everything written about them in Cincinnati as more groups popped up like corn across the Northern industrial states and the Midwestern farm country: young men, and sometimes women, who felt the old, gray beards in charge of the country and their equally old fashioned ways of thinking needed to make way for new, more

E.F. Winters

forward-thinking leadership that better represented our changing country. Wide Awake marches had been purposefully peaceful, though a few situations had arisen where they were attacked by Southern sympathizers. The movement had built a reputation on a theatrical parade with members wearing prescribed hats and dark cloaks and carrying a special torch invented by a founding member. Their popularity had increased very swiftly, swelling their numbers across the country, except in the South, frightening the Southern states, who quickly claimed the Wide Awakes were planning to storm the Southern states. Propaganda painted a picture of fiery-eyed Yankees raping and pillaging their way across the South, which encouraged anti-Northern sentiment. There was more than a little shock, however, that the Yankees found they had backbones.

Though barely acknowledged by the Republican Presidential hopeful, Abraham Lincoln, the Wide Awake movement was widely credited for the unknown Illinois woodsman winning the Presidency.

"It isn't their own the Yankees are sending into battle," a man at the table growled. "It's these damn Irish immigrants. The Yankees grab them right off the boats before they've had a breath of free American air, offer them citizenship and a signing bonus if they go soldiering for the Union. The poor fools don't know what they're fighting for until it's too late. They don't understand the strings attached to those Yankee dollars. If they did, they'd spit in those recruiters' eyes, tell 'em to go to hell, and head South."

"The Irish can fight, though," someone declared.

"They can," the man with the potbelly agreed. "Hell, my great-grandfather came from County Cork, and I tell you, if the Confederacy had a port those immigrants could come into, they'd be fighting for us."

"They still could fight for us," a younger man sitting near the end of the table spoke for the first time. "The Irish have no love for the black man."

The potbellied man's smile was menacing. "The right push at the right moment, is that what you're suggesting, Bickley? Bring New York back into the fold?"

"What do you mean *back*? It never left." The men at the table nodded and chuckled in agreement.

Act One, Scene Eight

The man addressed as Bickley had thin, mean lips, his eyes hungry. His cuff links and jeweled tie tack were gaudy and not of good quality. Burke would have deemed him "not well put together," suggesting his appearance made him dismissible in high society circles, but this was a circle of plantation men, glad-handers and hopefuls, not political leaders or society.

"The effort failed because Wood was over-confident and ill-informed," Bickley sneered. "He didn't share his plans with us; he just went off on his own, half-cocked. If he had included us, the Golden Circle could have advised him on what to do to be successful. We could have helped him with timing. We have people who understand these things." Bernie's next bite paused halfway to her subtly stained lips. Bickley's inference about secret influencers had piqued her interest. "Wood's ego cost all of us," he finished.

I remembered Charlotte Cushman commenting on this Golden Circle, devout Anti-Abolitionists, loyal to the Confederacy but not officially connected to Jefferson Davis and his government. The Golden Circle was entirely a private enterprise.

"Which is why he is no longer mayor," one of the gentlemen at the table pointed out.

"And now we have Opdyke." There were noises of disgust.

"Who is afraid to decide anything?" Bickley's smile was all pretense and brittle greed; a burning banknote already burned to ash, ready to fall apart at the stir of a breath.

"You tell your Golden Circle Knights and their friends we're with them, Bickley, but they need to act," the speaker had a heavy Georgia drawl.

"They will act when the time is right," Bickley assured the group.

Aunt Bernadette had been sitting with her eyes cast down at her plate, but she now raised her head, scanning the neighboring table to identify the different speakers, covering the motion with a napkin dab. It was a genteel and relaxed gesture, but her eyes were as dark as a sea storm.

I had considered the effect of her displeasure within the company and her own household, but I had never considered the effect such a woman might be capable of on a broader scale. But women did not wield power in the United States, least of all actresses. Lady

Bernadette Drake, however, was not just any woman. What she was defied definition.

"This war's cost me, and now Lincoln's claiming my property isn't mine, telling my slaves they're free? That isn't legal. Black people, free or not, got no rights. Why are the Yankees fighting for them? I've given the cause my support." He pointed at the thick envelope on the table. "But we've got to get shipping lanes to England back. The Union's embargo is killing me."

"That's being worked on," Bickley assured them.

"No more fancy dancing like that damned Erlanger Bond fiasco," the portly Rebel fussed. "If I can't provide my British purchasing agents with cotton, they're going to go elsewhere."

"Where else could they go?" Bickley portentously pulled a cigar from his inside coat pocket, bit off the end, and lit it. "No other market can supply what the American South can, even in the middle of a war. And this war will not last forever. When we win, plantations will stretch across the entire Southern portion of the North American continent and the nearby islands. The British are not going to offend Southern planters." Bickley was so smooth—so slick, his hair heavy with oil and flat against his head, the oil dripping onto his face so it was shiny with it.

"And what about San Diego?" someone asked. "Have we taken it?"

My ears perked up.

"It's being worked on."

"But we…"

"It is being worked on," Bickley repeated, annoyed. "This is not about one plantation, Sir," he chided the plantation owner. "We have made oaths and agreed to risk everything we have to win for our Great Cause, knowing that if we lose, we will lose everything, even to our treasured way of life."

"These people, or the person, you say 'knows things', Bickley, have they said we will win this war?"

"Her sons fight for us," Bickley sidestepped a direct reply. "Do you think she would allow that if she saw us losing? We control Vicksburg and the Mississippi. We are kings in our own countries." The puff of cigar smoke Bickley blew out drifted over the tables. "And we are going to win, gentlemen. It is simply a matter of time. Now, if you will excuse me." Bickley stood, picked up the packet on the table, and slid it into his vest. "As always, thank you for your goodwill. Good day, gentlemen."

My mind was treading water, desperate not to drown in the currents of what I had just heard. As soon as they had cleared, we rose and began to exit the dining room.

"May I ask you a question, Aunt?"

Bernie indicated her assent.

"Why did we come here?"

"To have luncheon. You enjoyed it, I hope?"

"I felt out of place," I admitted. "Didn't you?"

"I never feel out of place. I know too well who I am to be affected by those around me." It was a very British upper-class attitude. "Perhaps next time we lunch, we can go to Del Monico's. They have a new offering. Something they call a steak dinner. It features a very large cut of beef served nearly raw, I understand." Bernie searched the street outside the hotel for Weaver.

"Did you know those men would be here?" I asked as she raised her hand to get Weaver's attention.

"Everyone knows that the Metropolitan is favored by secessionists."

"They were very free with their opinions."

"Free Speech is in the American Constitution."

"As if that mattered," I muttered. Bernie frowned. "I overheard The Bees talking about how Lincoln was closing newspapers that did not write favorably about him. That is not Free Speech."

"Henry Clay's words, no doubt, but Henry does not understand why those papers had to be shut down, and it is far more complicated than free speech." She gave me a quizzical look. "Odd that The Bees spoke so freely before a stranger."

I shrugged. "They didn't notice me."

The air went still, everything suddenly sharpened, every sound flattened into a tiny blade poised to strike.

"Like the night Gil Collmeyer was promoted to Malcolm," Bernie noted with the calm of a snake about to strike. "Uncanny. It is as if you were invisible."

It was almost an accusation, almost a casual remark, but between the almost and certainty, something else lingered, something she saw, and I did not. I wriggled inside my new clothes, a specimen squelched between two pieces of glass and slid under my aunt's microscopic eye. She began to pull on her gloves, leaving the Pandora's box before us unlatched but unopened.

"You are what, sixteen?"

"I am nearly eighteen," I corrected her.

"Of course. You were born in 1845 when Idabelle…." She did not finish "No one at 'almost eighteen' is comfortable anywhere."

"I am comfortable at the theater."

"Then I suggest you keep reminding yourself that all the world is a stage."

"I'm not comfortable onstage," I reminded her. "I am terrified there."

Bernie's stormy eyes pinned me. "We cannot all stand safely in the wings, Kit. If everyone did that, there would be no show. There are things we can do to make our world a better place, and things we cannot change and must simply be accepted. It is important we understand the difference because each of us must do what we can based on our talents and abilities."

Bernie owed nothing to the fledgling nation that had rebelled against her homeland, unable to hold itself together for a hundred years. American Democracy was a toddler, misstepping its way through history.

She opened her parasol. "Weaver will take you home. I believe I will walk."

As Weaver collected me, a boy approached Bernie and handed her a message. She read it quickly, her face becoming concerned.

"Weaver, collect me at the hospital in an hour," she informed her driver. "I have just received word that a friend has been grievously injured." The way she said the word 'injured' implied it was a polite choice of words, but not the most honest one. She struck out, her manner brusque and distracted.

My aunt had a purpose in going to The Metropolitan. She meant for us to be seated near those Rebels. She wanted to hear what they had to say. I did not know that purpose, but Kit Becket was determined to find out.

Act One, Scene Nine: Wallack's Theater April 1863.

I paused before entering the stage door, as was my ritual; a conscious crossing of the threshold between the mundane outer world to the magical theater world. Wallack's was my place; the place where I did not have to think about the problems scrambling my brain; my confusion about who I was, worrying about my missing mother, and the chaos trampling the country. At the theater, all of that faded, like the dimming of the houselights as the stage lights rose, drawing our attention to a human story; *the* human story.

When I opened the stage door, Kindle was sitting just inside as if the cat was waiting for me. The cat's piquant black face had one splotch of pink on its otherwise black nose.

"Hello, you." I bent down, running a hand over its black fur. Though the rest of the cast and crew found the cat prickly, running away if anyone came too close, it had taken a liking to me. Its back arched toward my hand, its tail twitching, and it began to purr. "If you come up to the fly bridge at lunch, I might have something for you." I put my finger to my lips to indicate this was our secret. The company was not supposed to feed the cat, but I was sure everyone did it. It seemed wise to secure the good luck mascot's goodwill, just in case. Kindle knew everything about us here at Wallack's, witnessing every misstep, every triumph, every act of compassion or disloyalty. You could see it in the cat's yellow eyes, the way it studied us, as if it were figuring out how human life worked.

"Good afternoon, Miss Wellbelove," Gil Collmeyer greeted Ginny as she passed Gil and me backstage. His good looks and youthful virility had transformed the character of Malcolm in our production of *MacBeth*, changing a self-absorbed, irresponsible profligate to a dynamic young leader whom audiences were confident would make a most excellent king; an Arthur if you will, and they loved him. Especially the ladies, though looking out over the house from my perch on the stage right tower, I had seen more than one male audience member's face transformed by longing for the handsome actor. Gil's social status, inside and outside the company, was on the rise.

"Good afternoon," Ginny responded, self-contained and cool as always.

Gil deflated like a punched-down loaf of dough. Despite my jealousy of his interest in Ginny, I hated seeing my friend so miserable.

"I am sorry, Gil. When *The School for Scandal* opens, you will be a featured player and she will have to notice you," I assured him. He sighed.

"No. There is no point fooling myself. She will ignore me just as before. Ginevra Wellbelove's sole purpose in getting into the theatre was to find a rich husband. As soon as her engagement to Teddy De Laurent is announced, she will leave the company, and we will only see her in pictures in the society pages of newspapers."

I made a face. "Why would anyone want to leave the theater to get married?" I realized that was exactly the choice both my mother and grandmother had made, though I assured myself their reasoning was different than Ginny Wellbelove's.

"It is hardly fair for us to judge her," the ever-kind Gil defended the young woman. "We are men and have a man's options. We can't truly understand the challenges a single woman without a family name faces, especially one as lovely as Ginny. There are few avenues open to her."

"Aunt Bernadette does well enough," I pointed out. "And Charlotte Cushman, Laura Keene, Sarah Bernhardt."

"All women of extraordinary talent and intelligence," Gil pointed out. "Ginny cannot stand among them. She is merely pretty. And pretty does not last. She knows that she must secure herself a future while she can."

"She is a fool not to see you are a much better option than Teddy De Laurent," I tried to cheer my friend. "He is a nincompoop, without a brain; an egotistical, self-important ass. Do you think the De Laurent family will allow him to marry her? An actress? She will have invested her entire attention and reputation in him, and then the whole thing will blow up. There are plenty of other pretty girls swooning over you, Gil. Some even have some kindness in their heart and a thought in their heads."

He sighed wistfully. "You know nothing of love, Kit."

I did not disagree with him, nor did I confess my feelings. Gil thought of me as a child still, and a friend. The first of those, time would change. The second, I was unwilling to risk an affection I recognized he would never return. Gil was wired as most men were. I was not.

We headed for the fly bridge, the territory of stagehands, where Gil and I often ate our lunches together, our legs dangling a story and a half above the boards below, watching people below without them knowing. Actors might play to the balconies, but they rarely looked directly above them. As we sat, an older gentleman entered at the back of the house.

"How now, you secret, black and midnight hags!" the fusty Brit greeted two other men he joined. I recognized Mark Smith, one of The Bees, from Pfaff's. There was another man who stood with his back toward the stage, so I could not see his face. Something about him struck me as familiar. I had seen him before: my mystery man.

"Do you see that man at the back of the theater?" I asked Gil.

"Fitz-Royal or Mark Smith?" Gil said. "Smith is the new manager of The National."

"No. The third man."

Gil's expression turned grim. "No, and neither do you." He leaned toward me. My breath caught, my heart jump-started like a racehorse. He was so close. I pulled back to make space between us so I could breathe. "You are young, impressionable, Kit," he whispered confidentially. "And new to the city. You need to be careful who you socialize with. I would hate to see you get into trouble."

"Trouble?" I laughed off his concerns, catching my breath. "What kind of trouble could I get into?"

"The fact that you have to ask shows how unaware you are of the dangers and pitfalls surrounding you." Kit Becket, the acolyte of mysteries and puzzle solving, was paying decided attention. "First of all, that 'man' is not a man, it is Charlotte Cushman." Gil's nose wrinkled in disgust. "She is always dressing up and going about town pretending she is a gentleman."

I was still trying to straighten out the bend in my mind created by the idea that my "mystery man" might be Charlotte Cushman. What had she and Aunt Bernie been doing that night? What had she passed to the other man in the park?

"What would people say if a man did that?" Gil's words brought me back.

I frowned. "Men do it all the time."

"No. What would they say if a man dressed up as a woman and flounced around town, like Cushman does? She holds hands with her women friends in public as if it is nothing."

"It is nothing," I exclaimed. "And in Shakespeare's time, most young actors with a handsome face, like yourself, played women's roles until they were bearded. Sarah Bernhardt is famous for playing breeches roles: Hamlet and Romeo."

"That is not the same." Gil frowned. "People are talking, Kit. They say your aunt keeps strange company."

"What people?" I demanded.

"I don't know; *people,*" he sidestepped answering. "It's not me saying these things. You know I adore Lady Drake. We all do."

It was a disingenuous statement. If everybody loved my aunt, who was saying these things?

"Well, I hope you told them they're balmy."

"Come now, Kit, you must admit your aunt is strangely mysterious." I was admitting nothing.

"She is British. We are private," I defended Bernie, though I too found her mysterious, which was quite telling since I lived with her.

Gil gave me a look. "You are not British, Kit."

"Half of me is. My father was British. I was born in London and spent many of my formative years there. Being half something gives you the advantage of belonging to two worlds."

"Or none at all, since both will find you suspicious and different," Gil deflated my argument.

I tore off a piece of Dweetie's flatbread. When we went to the theater early, Dweetie packed me lunch, knowing I preferred to remain at Wallack's rather than dine out.

"How can people think Aunt Bernadette is mysterious?" I grumbled after swallowing. "She is on stage most nights, then out in society. She is the most public person I know," I lied. Gil might be a good actor, but he was a terrible judge of character. After all, he was in love with Ginny Wellbelove, and she was no one's description of a nice person. I agreed that Bernie's activities outside the theater were suspicious, and our luncheon at The Metropolitan had only sprinkled salt on the mysteries surrounding her, but I was not going to feed gossip about my aunt. Gil's warning awakened the natural instinct within me to protect my family.

"Do you think your aunt is looking for a husband?" Gil asked, taking a bite of a slightly wrinkled late-season apple. "Some women do that when they feel the need to retire from the stage." I almost choked on the bite of dahl.

"God, no!" I managed to swallow. The thought of my aggressively independent, British aunt suffering as a "good wife" to some American businessman or politician was laughable. "And she does not need to retire from the stage. She is an actress in her prime."

Gil chewed. "She's not trying to arrange a match for you then, is she?" he tried again. "All those upper-crust folk are wild for titles these days."

I cringed. "No. And if she were thinking something so daft, she would not be looking at an American. And just so you know, being a Dame is like an honorary knighthood except for women. It is not an inheritable title."

"So, you will not be Lord Christopher Drake?'

"Never," I assured him, a bit annoyed at American suppositions.

"And that's why everyone thinks it's so odd, all this going out to dinners and parties with these rich folk, plantation owners, and politicians with questionable ethics. She doesn't even *like* people. No one in the company has ever been invited to her house, except maybe Mister Lester. She just isn't friendly."

Gil had a point. Bernie had associates, not friends. Her household was a contained circle; no outsiders allowed. I knew, because I had lived there for weeks, and I still felt like an outsider. Whatever was going on at the Drake house, I was not allowed to know about. Bernie met people outside of her home. She did not invite them in.

Because parties are like luncheons, Kit Becket's suspicious mindset offered an answer: *The social events she attends are to gather information.* And she would not hold parties in her home because of what might be revealed if someone were to poke around.

"Of course she has friends," I blurted out to cover the awkward lapse created by my remuneration. "She is just very selective." Even as my tongue tossed off the last syllable, I realized my mistake. Gil rose, and the pain of this judgment of him reflected on his handsome face. "I am sorry, Gil. I did not mean that like it sounded."

"It is not for you to apologize," he replied with his usual generosity, a touch of sardonic wishing things were not as they were on his face. "I am under no illusions that I have risen high enough to be included in Lady Bernadette's social circle. Whatever her motivations are, though, Kit, you would do well to steer clear of some of these 'friends' of hers," he thrust his chin toward Charlotte Cushman. "Excuse me. Maggie requires me for a fitting." He gathered his jacket and walked back along the catwalk to where it connected with the staircase to the roof.

I sat bereft, feeling my social ineptitude keenly, when out of the corner of my eye I caught an apparition gliding toward me among the rigging ropes. The air stirred and caught up the dust, two golden eyes glaring beyond me. Above them, perched on nothing but the dust swirls, was a thin prop crown used for rehearsals. It had gone missing the week before I arrived, its loss shared by the prop people when several other items, too, had gone missing. The thefts were being attributed to the theater's "ghost".

Red gloved hands, one holding a wooden prop dagger, reached out toward me, "When the hurly-burly's done, with the battle lost is won…." The sounds were garbled, a cat-like hiss with soft-lipped efforts at enunciation that were merely an impression of formed syllables. "If he is your enemy, so is he mine," the rasping hiss sounded as if the words were being pressed through a rusty metal strainer. Were they words?

"Gil is not my enemy," I protested, taken aback, though I cannot say what demon or spirit I might be protecting my friend from.

"But he is not your friend." The prop crown, gloves, and a wooden dagger fell to the boards of the narrow walkway with a clunk and a clatter, the dust falling with them, leaving only the objects and Kindle. My heart beat slowed. All was well. I had imagined it.

I retrieved the red kid gloves. "These are Aunt Bernie's." I looked at the cat. It looked back, giving no sign of guilt. "What have you been doing, you naughty kitty?"

The cat's mouth curled on one side before he turned slowly and sauntered off, hips slinking, tail undulating like a rope-snake rising from a fakir's basket.

I picked the objects up and went downstairs, placing the crown and dagger in a corner where they would be found, but not so easily as to raise questions of why they were missed before. Bernie's gloves, I took to her dressing room, pushing them into the crevice between the cushion and the body of the wingback chair. I could not explain Kindle's actions or how the cat had collected the items, and Kit Drake decided it was best to avoid trying. They had been returned, and that was an end to it.

Entering the stage right wing, I found Mark Smith with a handful of loose pages standing opposite the old Brit I had observed enter the theater earlier. Able to see him in greater detail, the cut and material of his clothes declared the elderly man as a person of wealth. This impression was strengthened by his elegant comfort with the Queen's English.

"I recently retrieved a case of bourbon I purchased in another state. I bought and paid for it." He held himself like a poser of the old theater. "It was clearly my property. No one questioned my right to take it home with me, and no one started a war over it." Breaking out of character, he turned to my aunt. "I understand the statement is making a point about retrieving slaves from non-slave states, Bernie, but it would be difficult to fit the anecdote into a conversation."

"Not the right conversation, Cyril," my aunt disagreed. Noticing me, she ended the discussion. "Thank you, gentlemen. That is all for today."

"I was sorry to hear about Archibald Musgrove's passing," Smith addressed my aunt. Cyril blanched. "Musgrove is dead?"

"Yes." Bernie nodded. "A few days ago."

"How? Why? He was only a courier," Cyril had quickly gone from calm gentleman to fanatically afraid.

"The city is a dangerous place these days, Cyril," Smith said. "Spies are everywhere. We should all watch ourselves. You carry a sidearm? A pistol?"

Cyril was horrified. "Of course not. I am a British gentleman and a lord, not a brawling brute."

Bernie placed a dainty hand on his arm to calm him. "All the same, you should be careful, Cyril. This is America, not Britain. Some of these people are barely civilized. I will see you both in a few days." She turned her attention to me as the two men departed.

"Who is Archibald Musgrove?"

"An acquaintance. He delivers papers for some of us from time to time."

"And he was killed?"

"No one said he was killed. He met with an accident. New York is a city. Such things happen here, war or not," Bernie tried to divert my attention away from Musgrove's demise. "What is on your mind, Christopher?"

I was disturbed not only by Archibald Musgrove's "accidental" death, but by my aunt's obvious wish to move my attention away from it, but she dug her heels in and was unlikely to reveal more.

"I was wondering if I might invite a guest to dine with us?"

She frowned. "Who?"

"Gil Collmeyer."

"I did not realize your acquaintance had come so far."

"I believe we are becoming true friends, but it is hard when all we can get is a moment here and there between our duties here." I did not say I hoped the invitation would quell gossip. There was an expectation by people who were private that by being so, they would not be exposed to gossip, and I did not wish to reveal Gil's role in my new understanding, or risk that it would drive a wedge between him and my aunt and damage his career opportunities.

"I will consult my calendar," Bernie's reply took me by surprise.

"You do not have to be there…" My aunt's steely look stopped me. If someone came into her home, of course, she would be there.

"We will look for a suitable night. Most nights, except Sunday, would be acceptable. Sundays are Ada Clare's salons. A Monday evening when the theater is dark would give you time to dine and visit without being rushed. You can discuss the menu with Dweeti."

Gil and another actor, Ethan Mickleburgh, began practicing theatrical sword fighting, and we watched the actors' feint and parry.

"Have you trained with pistols?" Bernie asked me.

"No, Aunt."

"Boxing?" I shook my head, no.

"Sword, saber, foil?"

"None of those. I am sorry."

"Surprising. Your mother was an avid fencer in her youth. She won quite a few competitions."

"I did not know. I found an old sword in the back of a closet at Grandma Manon's," I shared. "She did tell me it was mother's, but I never saw her use it. I suppose Father did not approve of her taking part in such an unwomanly activity."

"Becket was intolerant of anything that took attention away from him. I am sorry, Kit," she apologized. "He was your father. I should not speak badly of him. I have always had a great fondness for your mother, and I did not think he treated her as she deserved."

"He and I were not close," I let her know her apology was unnecessary.

"No, I don't suppose. You are a perceptive young person and would have seen him for who he was. He would have hated that. I have dealt with more than a few of his sort in my time. That and the laws of our times, which would rob me of all my property and independence, are why I am not married."

Had my mother understood how completely Johnathan Becket would demand she be subsumed within their marriage? Had she nursed unvoiced embers of resentment? If so, she never brought it to her son's attention, but then she did not have to. In time, I saw it on my own.

I changed the subject. "Mother did give me a few archery lessons," I shared hopefully.

"Impractical unless you're visiting an estate in Scotland or playing Robin of the Hood, which I assume you have no plans to do, given your reaction to your first experience onstage. Have you ever been in any kind of a fight?"

I hesitated. When I was six, I tried to intervene between my father and mother during one of his tempers, but that was private, not the sort of thing well-bred individuals divulged, nor did I believe it was the kind of fight my aunt was inquiring about.

"None that I won," I gave her an honest, if incomplete, answer.

"I will do something about that. Musgrove's accident has reminded me of my duties as your guardian to educate you in all aspects of being a proper British gentleman. Burke is an excellent marksman and quite capable of teaching you to shoot. Weaver could teach you boxing and hand-to-hand combat, and Mister Mickleburgh's instruction of Mister Collmeyer has been acceptable." She nodded toward Gil and Ethan Mickleburgh. "I think he could be enticed into adding you to his tutoring schedule."

"But, as I have said, Aunt, I have no intention of being an actor," I protested the idea of training for stage combat, though the possibility of spending more time with Gil was appealing. "And I have no interest in fighting anyone."

A raised eyebrow preluded Bernie's retort. "But they may have an interest in fighting you. A gentleman knows how to defend himself and those whom they are accompanying. It is expected." Her tone indicated that this term of study was not up for discussion.

Act One, Scene Ten: The Astor Hotel, Broadway between Vesey and Barclay Streets, NYC.

"But why must I go, Aunt?" I caught my reflection in the long, oval mirror hung above the mahogany console table in the foyer. Dressed in the formal tailcoat complete with a top hat, the greatcoat with the velvet collar cupping my lower face, and a delicious white silk scarf tumbling like a winter waterfall from beneath my chin, my pale coloring a handsome contrast to the darkness of the costume, I looked like someone else. I wished I were, but perhaps, as long as Kit Becket did not come along tonight, being Kit Drake would be enough.

"You are a single male who has joined my household," my aunt explained. "It is expected,"

It was the second time in as many days she used that phrase, making it clear her expectations of my role here had changed. Comfortable invisibility would not be allowed. Those days were over.

"I thought the Drake reputation was that we did not do what was *expected*," I observed that on occasion, a bit of drollness or wit might soften stubborn stances.

"We do not *embrace* others' expectations. We exploit other people's adherence to them for our purposes," she retorted.

"Which tonight are what exactly?" I asked, worrying I was in for another of her "there is nothing going on" slight-of-hand sessions.

"For you? To enjoy yourself and have a good time." She tucked a strand of brown hair behind my ear, an uncommonly familiar physical gesture that warmed my heart even as it sent off Kit Becket's alarms. "You need a haircut, nephew. Remind me to have Burke get you an appointment at that barber's shop on Bond Street. The barber there has suitable skill." Her tone changed. "This is only a party, Kit, not a performance--not for you anyway. So, meet people, listen a lot, and speak little. And if you do find yourself unavoidably caught in conversation, ask them about themselves. People love to talk about their own lives, imagining they are interesting, even though most are as boring as dirt, but once you get them started, you will barely have to say anything. If you must reply to a question about yourself, or more likely about me, reveal as little as possible," she cautioned. "Americans believe they have the right to know everything about other people's lives, but these people are not our friends and most decidedly not family. You owe them nothing. Who we are is none of their business. Remember that." I nodded. "And if you start feeling overwhelmed or uncomfortable, find a quiet corner. You are not required to be on display here. That is my job."

New York was a city of trade, newness, and dreams. So many dreams bruising and abrading each other that a complicated sifting of which would rise and which would be crushed was required. Much of that sifting occurred at society's parties.

It was also a city of secrets and pretense, situations and people appearing to be one thing while, after some scrutiny, it was found they were something else entirely. With a million souls and growing, the Dutch Knickerbocker families of Old New York were being overwhelmed by the flood of newcomers. Before the war, the old Dutch families had lived in the certainty that they knew whose word could be trusted and whose could not. Now every transaction was a gamble. The rampant fraud and embezzlement of the early war years were an embarrassment, but when a man's worth was measured by his bank account, and wartime contracts had the potential to give a family a place in society for generations, what man could be trusted to put his country first? The answer was not many.

The Knickerbocker's answer to this dilemma of trust was to build a social wall between old money and new and not allow new money into their long-established circles, though arguably the fox had already raided the hen house. Of course, there were exceptions, particularly those who were titled. Dame Bernadette Drake was an icon. I was merely her nephew.

The hotel staff at the Astor House Hotel removed my overcoat and Aunt Bernadette's cape, and she leaned into me.

"You are new. That will make you interesting, briefly. Shyness may be forgiven. Boorishness will not. But don't fret over winning their opinions. They are, after all, only Americans. We don't really care what they think." She turned to take in the room. "Stay near me as long as you are able." She donned her most charming smile and sailed into the room, the feathers in her elaborate coiffure sweeping back like black irises in a stiff spring breeze.

"They are a conquered people," a very British accent caught my attention.

"But they are not," an American disagreed. "They are our allies. We have made agreements with them."

We were passing a group of gentlemen engaged in something more akin to a lively debate than casual conversation. I recognized my aunt's friends, Mark Smith and Cyril Fitz-Royale, among them. Both were dressed in evening dress, which meant tailcoats and cravats, or, for the more fashionable, the newer accessory, the tie.

"You mean like the agreement the Northern states had with the Southern states to respect their borders? Cyril-Fitz-Royale sniffed in a perfect affectation of upper-crust British arrogance. "I bought a case of whiskey a few weeks ago. It was a legal purchase. There was no question it was my property. When I returned home, no one started a war over it."

I nearly stumbled over my own feet. These were the same words Fitz-Royale had been reading from pages a few days ago at Wallacks.

"You cannot equate a case of whiskey to human beings," Smith declared, as if he were hearing Fitz-Royale's words for the first time.

"Admit it, gentlemen," another man inserted his opinion into the scripted conversation. "This conflict has nothing to do with states' rights or individual rights over property. This is a war based on Abraham Lincoln's political ambition."

I was looking to Bernie to gauge her reaction when our hostess, Missus Livingston, appeared.

"Please, Gentlemen. Surely, you do not wish to damage your hostess's reputation by discussing politics at a party," she admonished them graciously.

The men muttered apologies, casting looks back over their shoulders to say that the discussion was not over, merely delayed.

"Lord Fitz-Royale, may I escort you to an introduction to our former first lady, Julia Gardner-Tyler? Be forewarned, she insists on being addressed as 'Missus Ex-President Tyler'. Such a charming conceit." Missus Livingston's polished laugh sang like crystal.

I hurried to catch up with my aunt, who had continued, ignoring the conversation she had a hand in creating.

The little blue man trailed in her wake.

I stopped, blinked, then blinked again, before finding my mind blank, unable to remember what oddity had stopped my progress by stealing my attention.

"Lady Drake, such a pleasure to see you," Fernando Wood greeted her as she closed in.

"Congressman Wood, where is your friend, Mister Bickley? You are so close. I was sure he would be here tonight." She eyed the behemoth of a man beside Wood but did not acknowledge him.

Wood's expression darkened. "Mister Bickley is not in the Livingston's circle."

"What a shame," my aunt twisted the social hatpin she was poking at the congressman. "Well, I am sure you could remedy that." Her delivery inferred she was aware Wood did not wish to be connected in these people's minds with the ubiquitous Bickley. I wondered whether P.T. Barnum and General Tom Thumb were in the Livingston's acquaintance and might have been invited.

"May I present my nephew, Christopher Drake?" my aunt continued, returning to social protocols.

"I would be delighted." Wood turned his rodent-eyed attention to me.

"Congressman Fernando Wood, this is my nephew, Christopher Drake," she gave the formal introduction. "Christopher, this is Congressman Fernando Wood, and his companion…? My apologies, Sir. I do not recall the name you were using when last we met." Bernie's choice of words was odd, but Wood's companion looked more amused than offended, and I realized I was observing a chess game that had been played out over many years.

Her opponent inclined his head. "Hieronymous Undergrove." His eyes looked to a point on the left, halfway down my aunt's skirts, an unpleasant twist of his lips briefly indicating disgust. I followed his eyes to find the little blue man once again hovering near my aunt.

The queen of secrets.

The blue man scowled insolently up at Undergrove.

Memories of old stories where humans made dire deals with otherworldly folk to gain unnatural talents leaped to mind. Bernie was extraordinarily gifted and as charismatic as the angels, whom humans were said to gravitate to in instant bondage. But in all these stories, enthrallment had devastating consequences, including an unfulfilled longing for that magical world beyond the veil from whence the enthralled human, now returned, found themselves banished. This creature, for whatever reason, seemed to have abandoned the fey world for the high life of New York City, attached to my Aunt Bernadette.

"Of course. A polite pretense, Mister Undergrove. I never forget." Bernie offered the bear of a man her hand. "It is a gift of my family lineage, but it has been a turn or two since we met. I take it you are newly arrived in the United States? I did not know your family had an interest in America's affairs."

"An intriguing experiment, democracy. Such a strange ideal; 'all men are created equal'." Undergrove looked at the rich socialites ebbing and flowing around them. "An ideal entirely built of words, without the actions or policies to make it true. Such a magnificent hypocrisy is most certainly doomed. Don't you think?"

I thought Bernie's polite smile was going to give the man frostbite, except that he looked to have an uncommonly heated nature, his face ruddy, a sheen of sweat that he was often required to wipe, marking every pockmark and scar on his rough skin.

Bernie turned her attention back to Wood; the sharp tension transformed into a treacherous politeness, the consistency of a thick treacle. "Christopher has recently come to live with me in New York," she informed Wood.

"I am pleased to meet you, Master Drake." Wood took my hand in the most tentative manner, giving his wrist a small twist and releasing my hand as if dropping a used handkerchief. I had thought weasel before. I revised my opinion to an eel with no bones.

"The honor is mine." The polite reply felt like swallowing porcupine quills. I glanced at Undergrove, whom I had not been introduced to. I did not know what to think of this magma-rock person with the dead reptilian eyes of a serpent, but Wood, though I had only seen him once at the theater that first night, I disliked firmly, without reason. So desperate was the congressman's hunger for information that if Bernie had not been beside me, I feared he would have thrown me down on the marble floor and sliced me open just to reveal any secrets he might find there. Why he had this reaction to me, I could not say. Being visible was proving less desirable than I had hoped.

Upholding the social forms, however, Wood acted as if he were unaware of my dislike.

"This must be quite a night for you, Master Drake," he said, trying to be charming, but only succeeding in showing himself to be a two-faced, lying scoundrel. "Out in society for the first time with your enchanting aunt."

"Yes, Sir." I wished I could wipe the sweaty slime of his hand off my own. Gratefully, the mountain, Undergrove, was not inclined to follow the manly ritual of shaking hands to size each other up. I had already sized him up, and, for his part, after looking me over, he had already dismissed me.

"Congressman Wood is one of the men responsible for approving Central Park," Bernie complimented Wood, who inclined his head in acknowledgment. "My nephew is very interested in the sciences and engineering."

"No draft for you then. You do not plan on continuing the Drake Theater legacy?" Wood inquired. Though he presumably spoke to me, his weasel eyes did not look at me, charting my aunt's every move and glance, as if she were a ship he needed to catch and he feared would escape him. It was not my secrets he salivated for; it was Lady Drake's. Wood's interest in me was merely a pretense to know more about my aunt. He was not in need of another wife yet, and he could not possibly have believed Aunt Bernadette would have an interest in a liaison with him. So, why was he so interested in information about her?

"I am no actor, Sir," I replied to Wood. "Though I do have an interest in the mechanics of theater lighting." I hoped this fit Aunt Bernadette's guidelines for seeming *interested,* but not *interesting.*

"It is wise of you to steer clear of that profession. It is a dangerous and inauspicious line of work, populated by deviants and pretenders who are eternally in need of funds. Hardly a respectable profession for a young man of promise." I was shocked he spoke so in my aunt's presence, but she was pretending her attention was elsewhere. This was, after all, a game. "The brilliant actor, Edwin Forrest, has said: 'Whenever a young man is incapable of learning a trade, is too incompetent to be a porter, too lazy to beg, and too timid to steal, he takes to the stage thinking he will make his living as an actor. Which only proves the fool's idiocy.' Wood laughed at the witticism, though it was entirely borrowed. I had already heard an abridged version from Mister Lester. "We have several fine educational institutions," Wood addressed my aunt. "I can provide your nephew with introductions if you wish. I am in a position to be of great assistance to your young man as he seeks his fortune, Lady Drake, and I would welcome the opportunity to do you a service."

"Then I would be in your debt," Bernie pointed out, her inflection inferring recognition of a courtesy while her words proclaimed that she realized the outcome and would never so expose herself. "I am sure a great many young men have found themselves in new circumstances due to your advice," she finished. The double meaning of the statement was clear if Wood had the wit to recognize it. He did not, but Undergrove did, letting go a full, boisterous laugh in recognition of how subtly my aunt had bested Wood. The congressman's intellect was so far below the level of the game being played that he had no clue what had just occurred or why his companion was laughing.

"Have you seen our illustrious former first lady?" Bernie asked Wood, returning to the social forms that were within his grasp. "I am most anxious to make her acquaintance. It is said that, though she is a woman, because of her former connections in Washington, she has a superb grasp of politics. I expect she is a fascinating conversationalist."

"I have not yet seen her. Perhaps she has not yet come down," Wood replied vaguely, his eyes shifting around the room, noting groups and individuals he wished to speak to who were vastly more useful to him than my aunt and me. He had made his offer of patronage and plied Bernie with opportunities during which he would have greater access to her person, but we had accepted neither, which put us in the category of "not immediately useful". We were taking up time he could better spend on others.

"It was a pleasure to meet you, Congressman, Mister Undergrove." I took Bernie by the arm and moved her away. "He had other business, and I thought it better to end the interview rather than to leave with an impression of awkwardness."

"A sound decision," my aunt gave her approval.

"What was that with his friend, Undergrove? Did you know him from before?"

"Stay away from Hieronymous Undergrove," my aunt snapped. "He is friend to no man, and Wood is a fool to believe he is. Undergrove is dangerous, Kit, and not to be trifled with." It seemed to me that trifling with him was exactly what she had been doing, but then who was I to judge?

"And Wood?" I asked, hoping to get Aunt Bernadette's take on Wood's grotesque efforts to wheedle information from me.

"Wood thinks himself important because Heironymous feeds that belief. Without Undergrove, Fernando Wood is just another petty politician, but do not underestimate his determination. Even a fool may be dangerous. Remember, whatever Wood knows, Undergrove knows, and therefore so do his allies."

"His allies?"

"Copperheads, Southern sympathizers and the like." She had paused most tellingly before answering. I did not think that Copperheads were the "allies" she had been referring to.

"What are they so set on knowing?" I asked, hoping this would encourage her to reveal her true concerns.

"Everything about me and what I do," Bernie replied automatically before stopping herself. "Do not let him know you are hiding things from him, Kit, but tell him nothing."

We moved through the room, the scents of many perfumes infusing the air. Everywhere my eyes were met by the shimmer of polished fabrics, the sparkle of precious stones, and the bounce of upswept curls dangling like vines against pale necks. The men glittered less, but were no less well turned-out, their tailcoats and creamy cravats making each a lord.

My aunt continued to introduce me, names and persons I had read about or heard of, given face and form, their manner hinting at their character. Some stood up to the impressions the papers had given; others fell short, often on something as trivial as the tone of their voice, or the kindness of their attention. There were so many people confined by such complex layers of etiquette that a person could not possibly know anyone by meeting them at such a party. The rules governing the event did not allow for anything more than the briefest encounter, and I saw how easy it was to judge a person too quickly. I was doing it myself.

"San Francisco audiences were most challenging, but of course, eventually I won them over." My attention was caught again by Cyril Fitz-Royale's very proper and well-trained voice. He was holding court, a Lord of the British realm, who also happened to be a middling-level actor. Bernie and I moved forward. "Of course, talent, skill, and Shakespeare's words win over ignorance every time," the Englishman went on. "But the boorish, caveman attitudes on exhibit there were absolutely appalling. I could not leave the place quickly enough." He paused for a sip of champagne.

The crowd parted as we drew near.

"You will find New York audiences much more sophisticated, Lord Cyril." My aunt kissed Fitz-Royale on both cheeks in the European fashion. "Though it is still decidedly not London."

"How have you survived, my dear lady?" Fitz-Royale looked down his long, patrician nose at her. "And this ape of a man, Lincoln? How did such a lout come to lead a country?" He turned to the crowd. "Perhaps when this little experiment in democracy is over, you can beg Queen Victoria to bring you back into the fold."

Fitz-Royale's audience turned to stone as if they had seen a basilisk. Suggesting that America rejoin the British Empire was a sure way to unite Confederate and Union sides. He had badly misjudged, and his audience dissipated swiftly, tumbling him from a personage of esteem to a British buffoon. I almost felt sorry for him. Almost. He was a British male of the upper class, so accustomed to privilege that he could not understand the challenges those less privileged had to overcome to gain positions of influence and ease. My aunt and grandmother had worked hard to create reputations of talent and respectability as actors, rescuing the family name from the shame of piracy and betrayal associated with it since the Elizabethan age when Sir Francis Drake sailed the seas, attacking and stealing Spanish silver for his queen, betrayed fellow courtiers to the politics of court, and obediently answered his aging queen's summons to her bed whenever she crooked her arthritic finger.

"I am sorry, Bernie," Fitz-Royale apologized. "I was getting to the part you wanted me to say. I was just warming them up. I am not built for this sort of intrigue."

"It is of no consequence, Cyril. It is a large party. There are always other ears. Just think of it like a dress rehearsal." She removed his nearly empty champagne glass from his hand, replacing it with a full one. "You know how it is, if things go badly on dress rehearsal, opening night is sure to be a success." She aimed him toward a new group and gently pushed him forward. "Control your expressions, nephew," she cautioned me. "To beguile the time, you must look like the time." Like so many actors, she often quoted The Bard.

"The man is an ass," I complained.

"The man is useful," she corrected me. "We all play many parts. There is an art to choosing the right actor for the right audience." She looked around. "I need to find our visiting celebrity, Missus Gardner-Tyler."

"Missus Ex-President Tyler," I corrected my aunt. "Missus Livingston says her guest insists everyone call her by that title."

Bernie rolled her eyes to the ceiling. "The hubris of celebrity."

The main doors from the street opened, and a man in the meticulous uniform of a Mexican military officer entered. Stopping at the threshold, every head turned his way, an intake of breath accompanying the rise of bosoms swelling like the tide. The gentlemen in the room blinked and twitched in instinctive mammalian jealousy.

The newcomer was exceedingly handsome, his curling hair a deep ebony, his skin the tanned leather tone of a man who has spent much of his life outdoors. A jaunty spot of beard pointed like an unnecessary arrow toward generous lips. He was a remarkable specimen of manhood.

Upon seeing my aunt, the gentleman's lips burst into a smile akin to an alpine peak's at dawn's kiss. He slid across the floor; liquid silver spilled from a smelting cup, and Bernie's arm slipped from mine. My aunt rather fell more toward him than walked. Clasping her gloved hand, he pressed his lips to it, not a courtesy but a prelude to private, intimate passion.

Bernie glowed.

"Mind my expressions indeed," I muttered. Abandoned to a room of strangers, I spied doors to a side room and made my escape.

It took a moment for my senses to recover from the brightness of the room I had just left, with its white and silver striped wallpaper, fluted columns, and glass ceiling, and adjust to the hushed-plush darkness of the empty room. The lush green carpet and heavy velvet drapes of the adjoining room had cut off the cacophony of conversation and practiced laughter with the finality of a neck meeting a guillotine. It was only faintly lit, the drapes drawn open, the gas street lanterns along Broadway marching North past the hotel. On the other side of Broadway, tiny pearl buds added texture to the branches of the trees in City Hall Park. The fountain in that courtyard, illuminated by the gas streetlamps, shot plumes of water into the night air, and I thought about Charlotte Cushman being used as the model to sculpt an angel for a fountain that would sit in Central Park for generations. Few would remember who the model had been, but one of The Bees would be immortalized in bronze.

An air of masculine solidity characterized this new room, a dropped cove ceiling giving the space an intimacy that the high, glass ceiling on the other side of the door could not achieve. Carved walnut panels retained the sturdy strength of the trees they were cut from. Metal sconces resembling tapers hung on the walls, a nod to comforts of the past, declaring that within these walls, tradition had value.

Leather chairs and sofas were pulled into groupings in the center of the room, while billiards and card tables filled in around the edges.

"If you are planning on doing something embarrassing, you should know you're not alone." The voice came from a high-backed chair facing the manorial fireplace.

"Too late," I muttered. I came around the side of the chair to find General Tom Thumb sitting at the front edge, his back military straight, his arms resting confidently on the chair's arms. His tailcoat was perfectly tailored to his size and dimensions, his boots made of the finest leather; noticeable because in his current position, his feet did not reach the floor.

"Of course, if what you're planning is really imaginative, I might join you. Charles Stratton," he introduced himself using his true name, not his alter-ego entertainment character. "Sit, won't you?" He pointed to a nearby footstool.

"Christopher Drake, Lady Bernadette Drake's nephew," I offered.

"Yes, Leonara's son. I can see that." Stratton offered a hand. I stretched my own out to take it.

"I am new in town," I added.

"No one would doubt it." A sardonic smirk softened the blunt comment. "And what do you make of The Livingston's little gathering?"

"It is…well attended," I prevaricated.

"A reply that says nothing and reveals less. Bravo. You may be good at this after all. I would not have thought it, Master Becket." It made sense that if he knew who my mother was, he also knew my true surname. "Don't worry." He flipped his hand with the panache of an actor. "Lots of people use different names; performers, murderers, con men, thieves."

"And which are you, General Tom Thumb?" I asked.

"Most of those at different times in my life. I will leave you to guess which and when, but all of them are more interesting than merely being a nephew, though being Bernadette Drake's nephew could make you a bit more interesting. I would wager you have a good story or two about your aunt if you could be coerced to share."

"I do not, and will not," I proclaimed firmly.

"Good lad. I am intrigued, however, that our dear Dame chose you as her protector against the passions of her past. Not an elderly duena, or a handsome rival, but a boy."

"I am nearly eighteen," I defended my manhood.

Stratton grimaced. "And that 'nearly' says it all. And how goes the fight, Master Drake? Has General Miramon arrived? Have you seen him in all his glory?"

He could only be speaking of one man, the stately foreign military officer who had swept up my aunt and all the other ladies' attentions.

"I have, but I assure you, my aunt is in no need of a protector, Mister Stratton," I declared. "I have never known her to be weak-willed."

"And you do not know her like I do. Well," he deftly slipped off the front of the chair, catching up a cane leaning on the far side. "You cannot serve your purpose from here. We must rejoin the party. Do try to keep up." He made his way to the door in a series of practiced dance steps. Reaching up to the brass knob, he tossed open the door and strutted through.

People turned to look as Stratton bowed and danced his way through the crowd like a gnome through a forest of frost-flocked trees. The partygoers smiled and bowed to him in return. For a few minutes, the false smiles pressed and starched onto their faces bloomed into sincere joy. Stratton had utterly charmed them.

Making for a stairway to his right, he led me to an elevated mezzanine that overlooked the foyer.

"Ah, and there he is: The Past," he commented. "General Miguel Miramon, former president of Mexico, now reduced to Representative of Emperor Maximilian--dare we call it 'democracy?' Perhaps it is better if we call it what it is; a bonbon to stop Napoleon's baby brother's whining. Max has always been a tedious young man. But such a lengthy title for an old friend is awkward. I will simply call our guest 'Miguel'. I'd love to hate him, but it would ruin our friendship." Stratton smirked. He was quite irrepressible, the sort of person who got himself, and those with him, into a good deal of trouble.

I liked him.

"I'm here to protect Aunt Bernie from *him*?" I made a distressed face. I was not so naïve as to believe that none of the stories of my aunt's liaisons had merit, but there was no blame in me for her if she wished to revisit a youthful affair with this man. My crush, the blond Adonis, Gil, was the most handsome man who ever lived, but Miguel Miramon's dark, swarthy version would, in his youth, have rivaled it.

"Tonight, every woman in this room wishes she were Bernadette Drake," Stratton mused. "Except that one." He pointed to ex-President Tyler's widow. "Her interests lie elsewhere."

"And where is that?" I asked, feeling that was what was expected of me.

"A very good question," Stratton muttered, watching the young widow. Julia Gardiner Tyler had been quite young when she married President Tyler, but she was middle-aged now. Unlike the other ladies, Julia Garner-Tyler did not make social rounds. She sat, stationary, while others came to pay her court. "She retains a lot of political currency for a widow," Stratton shared. "She was not the First Lady for long. Tyler was the Vice President when William Henry Harrison died in office. Julia Gardner's family was Old New York, but the

Tylers are an old plantation family, and Julia embraced southern ways like she was born to them. Her husband was a great supporter of states' rights and slavery. Missus Tyler claims she is only a mother now with a mother's concerns, but both her sons fight for the Confederacy, and she regularly travels back and forth between the Tyler plantation and her family's Staten Island estate, and both sides just stand back and wave her through. Who is going to say no to a recently widowed ex-president's wife? But if anyone thinks she is just a mother, they are fools."

Stratton returned his attention to Aunt Bernadette and Miguel Mirmon. "But the former Julia Gardner is the only woman in the room not interested in General Miguel Miramon," Stratton suggested. "Bored women who did what their families expected and married for money and a respectable old name, and now find themselves and their dreams unrecognizable, alone with their wealth, while their husbands dally with horses, whores, and mistresses. They will go home tonight to their stuffy mansions and imagine they are Bernie, taking this prince among men to their beds. Tomorrow, every upstairs maid will need to change the sheets. "It is only a sin if it becomes public." Stratton watched Bernie and Miramon talking together, the silent language spoken by their eyes and bodies bordering on scandalous.

"'And thus, the whirligig of time brings his revenges'," the little man quoted *Twelfth Night*. "Actors." He chuckled. "Forgive us. It is a sad side effect of the trade; our heads are so filled with the clever words of others that we struggle to deliver a unique thought of our own." He turned back to watching Bernie and Miguel. "They might have made a fine couple if they had been different people, but as you can see, they are themselves; beautiful, ambitious, and utterly self-absorbed. They met in Prussia while she and I were there performing in *A Midsummer Night's Dream*. It was a grand time, full houses every night, standing ovations, and partying with royals. We lived in a house near the palace that some lord had granted us the use of. Bernie and Miguel's affair was a casual dalliance then, based entirely on sexual attraction. They both bedded others, but on nights we ended up under the same roof, the three of us stayed up until dawn, slept until noon, then got up and did it all over again. It was glorious.

"Years later, they met again in Spain, but on that trip, I was in New York, so it was just the two of them. And that is when things became too serious and began to sour."

I did not know what Stratton meant by 'things'; the relationship, politics, either might tear apart two people with international careers tossed together by the whims of history.

Aunt Bernadette lifted her closed fan, touching a single finger to its tip.

"Oh, very coy," Stratton commented. "She is telling him that she is willing to renew their friendship but not their *relationship*." My aunt rested her fan on her closed lips. "Because she does not trust him. Ouch. That must have hurt. I am sorry, Miguel, my friend, but what did you expect, she is, after all, only an actress and is not obliged to give you the loyalty of a wife."

I frowned. "You are making that up."

Stratton's expression was all sincere innocence. "I'm not. Honestly."

"How could you possibly know that?" I demanded. "Did Mister Barnum teach you to read lips along with singing and dancing?"

"Not lips; fans," Stratton replied. "Watch your aunt's fan. It's a language; subtle…nuanced, but each movement has a meaning."

"The Language of The Fan, like in *School for Scandal*?" I asked. "I thought that was just the actor's stage business."

"Stage business based on reality, Master Christopher. See how she opens her fan wide, then closes it?" That means, '*Wait for me*'. Now she's twirling the fan in her left hand, which means 'we *are being watched*.' Which, of course, they are, not only by us. The whole room is watching them, though they pretend not to."

"It's not a secret language if everyone knows about it," I objected.

"*Everyone* doesn't know about it, certainly not in America. But people who have lived at a European court for any time know it, and of course, theater folk. Oh, look, Miguel is very persuasive. He knows Bernie's weaknesses." Stratton's eyes took on a devilish glint. "There is no foreplay like a good flirt. You can almost taste the skin, the breasts swelling over the bodice's lace edge. The mere glimpse of a finely turned ankle sends the mind creeping up the calf to the thigh, imagining stroking your way to that final sensuous prize. The stalking, the capture, the release." He exhaled gustily. "There is nothing like it."

I thought of how Gil had taken my breath away when I first met him—how he still did when the light caught his face or the silhouette of his body in a certain way. There was a perfection in such moments. But it was an artistic one. Aside from romantic notions about kissing and touching, the logistics of conducting a romance with the kind of person I was interested in was a mystery. I had seen horses and dogs couple, male to female, but had no idea how coupling in other combinations might be accomplished. When I returned from my thoughts, Charles Stratton was lying in wait for me.

"So that is the way of it, eh?"

I kept my face as blank as possible so as not to reveal myself, but it was a pointless effort at deception. Fans were not all Stratton was able to read.

"Don't worry, Master Christopher, freaks don't tell on other freaks. It's a strict code among us. I could say that I am sorry for you, but I won't. You see, I believe that though our differences make our lives more complicated, they also have the potential to make them more meaningful and eminently more interesting. The trick is to turn the complications into strengths."

Two broad doors across the room, twins to the ones behind which I had found Charles Stratton, were opened by hotel staff in livery, revealing an elegant dining room. The crowd began to pair up and go through.

General Miramon had my aunt on his arm and was not allowing any change of partners, whatever our host's plans might have been.

"Ah, Missus Livingston is beckoning you over, Christopher."

My throat went dry. "Why?"

"So you can be paired up with a lady to escort through to dinner."

"Why?" I squeaked.

"Stop worrying, she won't have paired you with some battleaxe who will chop you into splinters. I believe she intends your partner to be that plump little mouse over there." Stratton subtly indicated a plain girl, frosted and swirled into a ruffled pink cupcake of a dress. She looked as awkward as I felt. "Just escort her in for dinner," Stratton prodded me. "You are both young and relatively unimportant, so your places will be at the low end of the table. Acceptable dinner conversation is fashion, the weather, the theater…"

"The theater is *not* unimportant," I protested.

"Oh my God, you are a Drake. Do not get into the social politics of theater. Joe Jefferson's *Rip Van Winkle* is safe, or whether Edwin Booth or his brother John Wilkes is the better *Hamlet*…"

"I haven't seen any of those," I wailed. "What about the new *A Midsummer Night's Dream*?"

"The one that shows fairy tits? Absolutely not. But when it opens, we should go. Oh, right, you are among the 'confirmed bachelor set.' Well, male fairies have tits too."

I frowned uncertainly. My fantasies were of an esoteric nature, examining the male form like Da Vinci's David; Gil's head, eyes, lips, mouth, my mind moved down the body, shoulders…buttocks. It was a longer list than I had been conscious of. Nipples were not very exciting, but a firmly muscled chest could be a heart stopper.

I got through dinner with little embarrassment as the young woman beside me, a Miss Marion Anthon, was exceedingly talkative and excited by her first grown-up party, though, as she informed me, she was too young to be officially "out". We were the only two young people at the gathering, and though our temperaments were opposite, no one could have known how well our minds matched. We quickly forgot about anyone else at the table and the rules of propriety for a dinner party. We never got around to discussing the weather.

"I wish I could be in the theater," Miss Anthon declared wistfully. "But of course, that is not possible because then I couldn't marry my secret sweetheart, Styvie. We have grown up together, you see. Styvie is absolutely devoted to me, but he would never be allowed to marry an actress. He is a Fish, you see." My confusion at this statement must have shown on my face because she laughed out loud, snorting in a horsey, unladylike manner, only bringing her merriment under control when disapproving eyes were turned her way. "Not a fish like you eat, silly. Styvie's from the family of Hamilton Fish, and he's a Livingston on the other side, full-on Knickerbockers all around. So, you see, my having any sort of career is out of the question. The only distractions I will be allowed will be leading New York society and giving marvelous parties."

"I am certain any party you give will be wonderful, Miss Anthon," I said politely.

"Please call me Mamie," she pleaded. "I know it is not entirely proper since we have only just met, but it feels so stodgy calling each other miss this and master that. Who cares about those old rules? We are young. Life should be wonderful and full of surprises, don't you think, Christopher? May I call you Christopher?"

"Of course, Mamie. I think, however, that you will find that if it is your goal to rid society of its rules, you will find them quite set against you. Their rules are designed to avoid surprises, as surprises tend to lead to embarrassment and embarrassment is to be avoided at all costs."

"And that is why we all live like we're in a box, afraid to try anything new," Mamie bemoaned the status quo that gripped New York's Old Guard. "I am going to marry Styvie, but I am not going to live in a box."

"Small chance of that." I smiled. "Unless you undergo an extreme change of character once you take your vows."

"Styvie would not stand for it," Miss Anthon declared. "He agrees with me that as people of social influence, it is our responsibility to bring the old families into the modern age."

"And just how do you propose doing that, Miss Mamie?"

"By throwing the best, most unique, and refreshing parties anyone has ever seen, of course."

I had hoped for something of more substance, but though we were not far apart in age, I recognized that our experiences of the world were very far apart.

"I am sure there is a place for entertainment for entertainment's sake," I chose my words carefully. "But I am not sure that parties can effectively change the world. I do believe entertainment can be a tool for change. I have seen audiences so moved that I believe them changed, but it was because they found some deeper meaning in the performance—something profound."

Mamie made a face. "People get all dressed up just to be given lessons like they are at school? How dreadful. If that's what happens in a theater, I will never set foot in one. You are quite a moody fellow, aren't you, Christopher? What I mean is, you think about things."

"I do," I admitted.

"But just thinking about things is not enough. There has to be doing as well. Without doing, all that thinking is just a waste of time."

I smiled. Though I sensed I had been scolded, she was right. I thought…a lot. I thought, and stewed, and suspected, and scribbled my thoughts down, but I had never 'done' anything about what I thought was important.

"Mamie Anthon, you are a terrible fraud," I told her. She blinked in astonishment. "I don't mean that as an insult. I think you are the most astonishing young woman I have ever met. I suspect that you, and that chaotic brain of yours, must be secretly thinking all the time."

"Me?" Mamie's eyes opened wide in surprise. "Oh no. I am quite stupid and beastly uneducated. Everyone says so. Papa had to send my tutors away, you know. I couldn't understand half of what they said, and the other half? Well, to be truthful, I just didn't care. Why should I learn about some old Greek stories? They aren't even history, they're just myths. We have myths right here in America. Wouldn't it make more sense for me to learn those? My tutors kept insisting it was important I know about the Greeks and Romans because that was the cradle of civilization, but the Iroquois Confederacy has organized government here in North America at least as far back as those old Romans, and they treat each other much better—especially women. The Romans were awful to women. Why, if someone treated me like that, Styvie would have to challenge them to a duel. I think that American students should be studying American history, like the Iroquois, and things that have happened here. Why should I, or any child, study a culture from halfway around the world that we don't care a jot about?"

I used my napkin to hide a chuckle. "I can't imagine that opinion sat well with your tutors."

"It did not." She grinned. "But Styvie loved hearing about it. Thinking of me standing up to those old fuddy-duddies made him laugh."

"Well, your Styvie is clearly a man of good taste who is ahead of his time," I complimented her beau. "Having opinions of your own does not make you stupid, though, Mamie. It makes you a unique and original thinker. Ask someone to get you a book by Ralph Waldo Emerson. Or better yet, have Styvie take you to a lecture by Emerson the next time he is in the city." Mamie's eyebrows came together in a deep frown. "I'm not trying to trick you, Miss Mamie. I think you would genuinely be interested in what Mister Emerson says about being an individual in the face of others trying to make you fit into someone else's mold, and the singular perspective of American born people who have grown up with a different view of people's rights because of exactly what you said; the influence of The Iroquois Confederacy and our Native neighbors. Emerson encourages people to be self-reliant and think for themselves, rather than just accept things the way they used to be, as if that is the right and only way."

"Truly, Christopher? You're not having me on?"

"Truly, Mamie. Seeing past the way things are and being courageous enough to take on unraveling them to discover a better world requires a special kind of bravery. I wish I had it."

"You think I'm like that?" Mamie giggled. "No one sees it that way."

I smiled. "I think if you widen your circle, you will find there are a great many people who do. Just ask your friend, Styvie."

Mrs. Livingstone rose, signaling that the women were retreating to an adjacent room that would function like a private home's drawing room. The men would retreat to their own space and talk about men's things. Mamie reluctantly rose with them. She was not Missus Stuyvesant Fish yet, and for now, she still had to play by the old rules. As she left, I wondered what would happen when this hurricane of a girl was unleashed on New York Society. Would it ever be the same?

I was startled by a hand touching my shoulder.

"Forget about Miss Anthon, Drake. You are with us now," Fernando Wood's thin voice grated in my ear. I looked for Mister Undergrove but did not see him. "She is taken anyway, though I cannot imagine what young Stuyvesant sees in her, but in this town, even the nephew of a British Dame cannot compete with a Stuyvesant-Fish." Though Wood only admitted to being a Peace Democrat, whose political goal was to end the war, anyone who read the Herald could see that the party's proposal that the Confederate states be allowed to rejoin the Union without penalty and with emancipation rolled back so that all slaves were returned to their masters revealed their true agenda. Though Wood publicly denied it, he remained aligned with the Confederacy, believing New York could still regain independent status. He made his case as an independent city-state, New York could keep the import taxes it collects at New York ports. Washington was never going to let New York go. Eighty percent of the Federal Budget came from those port taxes.

Congressman Wood maneuvered me into the stream of menfolk meandering into the room where I had met Charles Stratton. "The women go to 'the salon' to gossip, talk fashion, and reorganize society to their liking, and we men enjoy an after-dinner drink and a smoke."

My voice leaped up an octave. "Alone?"

"No, together."

"Where is Mister Undergrove?" My voice betrayed my nerves by adding a squeak to my words.

"Oh, he is around somewhere. He will find us when he is done with his business," Wood dismissed my concern. "Now, you must tell me all your aunt's secrets."

That was exactly what I must not do.

"If my aunt has secrets beyond those she shares with her dressmaker, Congressman Wood, I am unaware of them." I tried to smile pleasantly, imagining Gil Collmeyer's face superimposed on my own. "And if I were to ferret them out, they would no longer be secrets."

The dark room now hummed with the low notes of male conversation and the burble of brandy, bourbon, and whisky being poured. Wood handed me a glass.

"Tennessee whiskey. Bottom's up." He modeled tossing the alcohol back. "It's the best way to get started. After the first one, it gets easier."

He was right, the first drink burned all the way down, lighting a fire in my stomach, but the second went down easier. I might even have tasted something beyond the bright bite of the spirits.

"I can see that you are a good lad—a smart lad." Wood assumed I would be susceptible to the flattery of being noticed by an older man of importance. Bernie was right. He was a fool. "Does your aunt ever speak to you of politics and the country's situation, the war between the states, and such?" he asked.

"Never." I tried not to let my annoyance at his blatant questioning show, but he was too focused on his agenda to notice. His goal was to ply me with enough alcohol to gain my confidence and loosen my tongue.

"I find Lady Drake an enigma," he prompted me, eyeing my glass to decide if it was time to refill it.

"A common complaint of Americans about the British," I replied.

"But beyond a natural reserve, she is rather a secretive person, isn't she?" Wood's weasel-face tried to look friendly but only managed acquisitive. I too was learning to read faces. "It makes one wonder if she has something to hide…some skeleton in the family closet, or perhaps a secret life? Help me get to know her better, Drake. Does your aunt have hobbies? Does she enjoy a particular type of art? Does the quilt or weave perhaps? What does she do outside the theater? She must have friends, and people she corresponds with?"

"I do not know the answer to any of these things. Public people have private lives, Congressman," I replied cautiously. "But that does not mean shadows haunt them. The whole of New York is aware you have been married multiple times, but I am confident you would counter that they do not know the intimate details of those marriages, or why you chose each bride."

Wood accepted my conversational pivot, though he scowled at my reference to his controversial marriages. "It just seems strange for such an attractive woman—and an actress at that, to attend so many events unattended." As if being an actress was still tantamount to being a prostitute. I wanted to punch him, but I knew my aunt would not have wanted me to make that impression on my first night in society.

"As I reside with my aunt, and am a member of her household, I expect that her attending events alone will not be a problem in the future," I replied, hoping I was not being overbold in making the statement.

"What is her business at these gatherings?"

"Business? There is no business, Congressman. Parties are simply a way for my aunt to unwind after a performance."

"Nothing more?"

I downed my drink, beginning to enjoy the burn before answering. "I think you have spent too much time in Washington, among the spies and politicians, Sir. If you are not careful, New York Society will label you a terrible bore and a gossip, and you will become persona non grata, and not…be… invited." Tipsy, I tapped his chest once for each word of warning.

"And what about you, young Drake? With no man in the household to offer you guidance, how do you plan to make your way?" It was a resentful challenge, harkening back to what he had considered to be his generous offer of patronage on his part. "Your aunt cannot possibly assist or advise you." He snorted. "She is an actress and a woman. Hell, she can't even vote."

"Neither can I," I pointed out.

"A situation you will grow out of. She will not."

"Respectfully, Sir, my aunt is a British citizen. Even if she were a man, she would not be eligible to vote in this country."

"I am aware. It is all her infernal dabbling, I wonder at her efforts to influence others using her name, her fame, and her…other talents." He had me. I had no idea what he was referring to as "other talents," and I dared not ask. I remembered advice Bernie had given me once regarding my shyness: "Adopt a pleasant, bland expression, and they will assume you agree with them. People like to believe those around them agree with them. They will not notice you did not actually say anything."

"I agree. Women are a mystery." I clapped him on the back. "My aunt is no exception. Your offer to help me is most kind, and I am grateful." I smiled. Foolishly drunk, but not foolish enough to fall into Wood's trap.

He scrutinized me, his eyes seeking chinks in the armor of etiquette I had reverted to. I took another drink of whiskey and tried to maintain my friendly expression of calculated disinterested interest.

"You are drunk," Wood complained.

I looked at the glass in my hand. "Am I? Well, that is the usual outcome of drinking, and it should not come as a surprise to you who have been filling my glass." Getting me to an inebriated state had certainly been his intention, but I did not think the strategy had played out according to his plan.

"When you are ready to become your own man and not a satellite of your aunt, come see me." He snaked his way to the window, where a smoking circle of his confederates had formed. I hid my relief by taking another sip of whiskey, glad to be rid of him, and losing a blissful struggle with the effects of drinking whiskey straight.

There were many different factions forming in this room of men. I tried to discern the method of their sorting. The obvious one was wealth; there was something to that, and power was its partner, but most of the men in the room were wealthy or pretended to be.

Age? Yes. There were a number of old and older collections of men, and one corner where a handful of young dandies were entertaining each other at the expense of some of them. I recognized their stripe from my brief sojourn at boarding school: a mean-spirited pack of wild dogs targeting those they perceived to be weaker than themselves. They saw no danger in belittling these older gentlemen in their suits and cravats. In the final months of university, they were overly confident in their male superiority, mistakenly importing the measurements of a player on a football field to this room. But while the Ivy League athletes had status on the ball fields of their universities, in a bank or boardroom, these older men held the positions of high status.

Several of the older gentlemen studied the young, sniggering faces, with a brief muttering following. One of the younger among the elders extricated himself, hurrying over to pull a younger version of himself away from the sniggerers. I suspected it was too late. The damage was done, and one day soon, after graduation, when these young athletes began to make the rounds looking for a position among their father's friends, the mocking dandies would find themselves sitting across a desk from one of these older gentlemen and would realize their mistake.

"It seems strange to me that Abolitionists abhor slavery but turn a blind eye to the plight of the Irish worker." Cyril Fitz-Royale's voice brought me out of the footballer's drama. "I have seen slave quarters more comfortable than the run-down tenements the landlords in this city rent to immigrants," Fitz-Royal jibed.

"And yet the Irish cannot wait to leave their homeland." I did not recognize the speaker, a Methodist or Presbyterian minister from the look of him.

"They're not given a lot of choice," Fitz-Royale argued. "With the passage of the Poverty Act, it costs an Irish landlord less to ship his tenants off to America in steerage than it does to pay the tax for keeping them on the land they have worked for generations." Were these Fitz-Royale's thoughts, I wondered, or something he had been prompted to say under my aunt's tutelage?

"Wages are intolerable," another man grumbled. "What happened to the grateful immigrant glad to earn a penny?"

"Come, gentlemen, we cannot solve Britain's problems of inequity," Mark Smith tried to turn the conversation. His presence was not surprising. If there were a prescribed conversation, it would take at least two participants to maintain the intended direction: a protagonist and an antagonist. Which was which would be open to interpretation and an individual's politics. "That's why our ancestors left England," Smith stated. "To start over…"

"And become the new lords of the land," Wood joked. There was polite laughter.

I moved slowly to the edge of the room and the chair where Charles Stratton sat, smoking a cigar, his feet sticking out over the seat's edge.

"'So many daggers in men's smiles'," he mused. "That one, Wood, may 'smile and smile and still be a villain'. And have you met Wood's shadow, Mister Undergrove? An odious creature. I cannot with any conscience call him a human being, as I am not sure he is one."

"What else could he be?"

"What indeed," Stratton replied mysteriously. Not for the first time, I thought Charles Stratton knew more than he admitted, perhaps even what kind of creature the little blue man who followed my aunt was. Boarding school might only be marginally better than living among the lost souls of the mental institution on Blackwell's Island, but I was in no hurry for either. "I am surprised at Mark Smith," Stratton continued. "He just took over management at The National. He can't afford to offend the Knickerbockers. They have always been inconsistent in their support of the Abolitionist cause. New York is a complicated city. The Old Guard have always had money, though they abhor the flaunting of it, but they are not so much cruel on purpose as by tradition. This new money that's risen on the back of the war, though? Now there are some vicious bastards. They rose from nothing, and for them, there will never be enough. Notions of right or wrong don't enter their thoughts.

"Was it your aunt who backed this little show?" Stratton asked. My mouth went dry. "Of course, you can't answer. I should not have asked." He took a drink from his glass, then began to pour a second glass from a decanter sitting on the table beside him.

"I think I have had enough," I deferred.

"We all have to get drunk for the first time. Best to do it on the good stuff in good company. This, my young friend, is a very expensive, very smooth bourbon."

"I've been drinking whiskey," I confessed.

"With Wood. Two mistakes you will never make again." He handed me the glass. "Don't worry, I'm here with you."

"That's why I'm worried," I countered.

"You're learning." Stratton raised his glass to me before drinking. "You made it through dinner unscathed, I see."

"My companion made it very easy."

"Companion, singular? What about the person on the other side?" I grimaced. "The etiquette, Master Drake, is that you divide your attention between both your dinner companions. In the first half of the meal, you converse with the person on your right, and in the second half, you talk to the person on your left. This etiquette may be allowed to slip if the guest on one side falls asleep or dribbles soup down their chin, but outside of that, it is considered a breach of etiquette. Since you and Miss Anthon are very young, however, you will probably be forgiven." He made the sign of the cross before me as if offering a blessing, having granted me absolution.

"I am not Catholic," I informed him.

"Neither am I, but any religion where I can sin, then pay someone to remove that sin, seems worth paying some attention to. I pay generously for my clean conscience."

The political drama of the smoking circle had not stopped.

"American businessmen are leveraging the poverty of these new Irish arrivals to keep wages low. Then they go further, fanning the flames of prejudice against free black men," the man of the cloth said, speaking rather stridently. I was not the only one feeling the effects of the Livingston's good alcohol.

"And that is the Right-Reverend Beecher," Stratton identified the man. "The father of Harriet Beecher Stowe, author of *Uncle Tom's Cabin*...

"I know who Harriet Beecher Stowe is; I am not a cretin," I countered.

"No. Of course not. You are a Drake. Famous as pirates and royal fornicators, not brutes." Miguel Miramon entered the room. "Now, where the hell has he been, and what's he been up to?"

Locating his host, Miramon crossed to Livingston and the two spoke privately at the side of the room before leaving together. Undergrove appeared from I do not know where and followed them out. "I don't like the look of that," Stratton declared. "Do not let your aunt put you in a carriage and send you home alone tonight, Christopher. She will be very displeased with you both tomorrow morning if you do."

Act One, Scene Eleven: The Streets of New York, Later that evening.

"You are not coming home with me?" I asked Bernie as we stood at the main door waiting for the carriage. It should not have been a surprise. I had been warned.

"The business of the night remains unfinished," she muttered, distracted.

"What shall I tell Burke?" I demanded. "He will worry. He always does. They all do. *We* all do."

"It is not your place to tell Burke anything." She looked at me as if I had insulted her. "But you may tell him not to wait up for me."

"You know he will stay up anyway. Whatever it is you are about to do, you should not do it, Aunt," I cautioned her. "Think about the consequences." Which is what I should have been doing, but Kit Drake was drunkenly ignoring Kit Becket's plea to stop talking.

My aunt eyed me coldly. "I am supportive of you having opinions of your own, Christopher. It is the sign of a thinking person, but you should not mistake that for permission to inflict those opinions on me. I have handled my affairs for a good many years now and expect to continue doing so unfettered by male relatives."

"Mister Stratton said if you went with the General and did not come home, you would be angry with yourself and with me," I tried to justify my interference.

"Charlie Stratton should keep his advice to himself," Bernie turned on me sharply. "How dare he use you to try and manipulate my behavior. I am no wayward girl. I do what must be done as I always have, though I have found little joy in it. Others who swore the same oaths as I abandoned them to chase their own happiness, leaving me to carry the family burden alone." She closed her eyes, a look of pain washing over her face. When she opened them, there was such pleading in her eyes that I staggered back a step.

"You speak in riddles, Aunt," I managed to say hoarsely. "I am sorry for whatever pain you have endured. You have placed great value on your reputation. Are you certain that whatever you plan is worth the risk?"

The frost on the planes of my aunt's face was hard sculpted. "Go home, nephew. These matters are beyond your ken."

I sighed. "I know, 'we will speak of this in the morning'."

"No," she stopped me. "We will never speak of this, not ever again." She waited for my agreement. Every part of me felt numb…every part except my curiosity.

I walked slowly through the Astor's main doors and dutifully got into the carriage, but as it pulled away from the curb, I opened the door on the far side and jumped out. I watched as Weaver drove the empty carriage North up Broadway.

The Livingston's party was ending, but even at this hour, Astor House was busy, as it was the fashion in New York to dine late, stay up even later, and take breakfast with those companions who survived the full term of the night's adventures beside you. That was when the upper class, half-dizzy with alcohol, formed relationships.

When I returned inside, I could see neither my aunt nor the general, but on my second scan of the foyer, I located Miramon being approached by our host.

Livingston took the General aside, then they left, turning to the right inside the Astor House Exchange, a gentleman's bar. To the casual observer, they might have been two men continuing a conversation started at dinner, but I was no casual observer. I was Kit Becket, treasure hunter, pushing my shovel deep to uncover secrets. When Mamie Anthon accused me of thinking and analyzing the world without acting, she had struck a chord. I needed to stop thinking about my troubles and do something about them. I was not sure which Kit, Becket, or Drake had the upper hand in deciding this. Perhaps they were finally united in this decision.

Men's formal evening wear was not only the uniform of gentlemen, but also the uniform of upscale members of the Astor Hotel's help. I walked boldly over to the bar, picked up a white towel, and followed Livingston and Miramon into a back hallway.

I had already lost sight of them, but moving down the hallways and peering into each side door, I saw them when they reappeared in the hall. They were joined by a black man, a woman, and a child wearing working people's travel clothes. The man was leaning so heavily on Miramon and Livingston that it would have been more accurate to say they were carrying him. They guided the family through the back hallways of the hotel, passing staff who noted them, but did not stop them. Until one did.

"What are you doing here?" a snooty Maitre'd demanded.

"Helping these people," Livingston replied. If he had told the man who he was, the head waiter would have immediately changed his tone, but since Livingstone did not do that, I could only deduce that our host was involved in some activity where he did not wish his identity known. The Maitre'd eyed Miramon, clearly a foreigner, then set his gaze on the refugee family. His lip curled.

"What are *they* doing here?"

"As I said, we are helping them." Livingston was trying to be patient, but he kept looking down the hallway. He was displeased with the inconvenience of the maitre d's questions and the delay they were causing.

"Helping them do what?" the Maitre'd demanded. "Guests are not allowed in this part of the hotel," he glanced from Livingston to Miramon. "And these people are clearly not guests."

I hurried forward. "It is fine, Monsieur. They are just leaving," I improvised an explanation. "The Livingston party is still lingering in the foyer, and the decision was made that it would be better to help this man out the back, rather than having to answer uncomfortable questions to the Livingstons and their guests about his disease." The Maitre'd's hand instantly flew up to cover his nose and mouth, and I pressed by, signaling Livingston and Miramon to follow me before the waiter recovered. "Hurry," I whispered with some urgency.

We were just exiting the delivery door in the back of the hotel when my aunt joined us, flushed and out of breath.

"Did you…?" Miramon whispered to her. She shook her head.

"Thank you, Lady Drake," Livingston greeted her. "Your young man here was most helpful." Bernie looked at me with surprise, quickly veiled.

"*This* we will talk about later," she whispered for my ears only. Weaver drove the Drake carriage into the service drive, and Bernie scooped the child up into her arms. The carriage stopped where the stairs from the first level reached street level, and those from the lower level came up to do the same.

Quickly settling the child inside, my aunt held the door as the woman in the party scrambled in, moving over to accommodate the gentle placement of the injured man.

"Thank you, both," Livingston shook Bernie and Miramon's hands. "When the timing fell apart and everything escalated, I was not sure what to do, but clearly you did. Thank you, truly." Bernie climbed inside and closed the carriage door before poking her head out the window to address me.

"You can find your way home?"

"Of course."

"I will see him there," Miramon offered. Bernie nodded, then rapped on the carriage to tell Weaver to drive on. He cracked his whip over the team's heads, and they raced East on Barclay, turning left up Broadway. Livingston and Miramon watched the carriage make the turn, then went back inside.

"A drink for you, General?" Livingston offered. "I could certainly use one." Miramon nodded.

I was not invited. But I was not *not* invited. An assumption had been made that, as I was now under Miramon's care, I was included in any activity involving the leftover menfolk.

"This was not part of our plan for the evening, I assure you," Livingston addressed us. "It was kind of you both to jump in so discreetly." He addressed himself to Miramon. "My apologies to you and Lady Drake for any inconvenience."

"The lady and I have exchanged our goodbyes. I am booked for passage back to Mexico tomorrow morning," Miramon replied. "I wish your friends a safe journey and much happiness. Gaining freedom is fraught with challenges. As hard as it is to gain, holding onto it may prove even more difficult."

"The law of the country says that all men are free now," Livingston commented.

"We have these same ideals in my own country--a large part of which is now your country, but as I am sure you know, Mister Livingston, free and equal are not the same things."

"The birth and growth of new ideas seems to require stages of imperfection, General. You were the president of Mexico, and now you are a member of this new puppet Emperor's cabinet."

"The Mexican people voted. They chose, even if other nations do not understand their choices."

"Or even if they choose poorly?" Livingston shook his head.

"We were peaceful neighbors for many years, Mister Livingston. We gave up many resources and much land when we signed for peace with your country to end the fighting. I believe the Mexican people hope France will treat them more fairly than the United States did."

"Democracy is a fragile thing. To get an entire nation to share one vision is complicated," Livingston ceded.

"I respectfully disagree, Sir. I believe that Democracy is like our peasant women: strong, with a slow, long-burning resilience. They carry life for nine months, working the fields, cooking, and keeping home and family together. I know of no man who could serve with such grace. So, I do not think Democracy is fragile. I think it is like those peasant women; strong, long suffering, but resilient--never giving up."

"I would like to believe that, General. Some days I do." Livingston tossed back the rest of his drink and rose. "But less and less it seems. Safe travels, Sir."

Miramon and I left the Exchange, making our way to the foyer where he would hire a cab. Charles Stratton found us first.

"You are still here, Master Christopher?" he greeted me. "Miguel." He and Miramon embraced, Miramon bending low to manage the awkwardness of a very tall man embracing a very short one. "So, this is goodbye again?"

"It is, my friend," Miramon replied.

"Bernie's carriage has left already?"

"She had another commitment. I said I would see the young man home," Miramon explained.

"But you are staying here, aren't you? There is no need for you to go back out, Miguel. You have a long journey ahead of you. I can see young Drake here home to his aunt's. It is no trouble. It is on my way." Miramon turned to me for my reaction.

"It is fine, General," I assured him. "Mister Stratton is an old family friend."

"I am aware." Miramon smiled wryly. "I will bid you both a goodnight then, and farewell." He bowed before turning away.

"A good man," Stratton mused. "A beautiful man. Sadly, those who are given great gifts often meet a tragic end. We used to blame jealous Gods. Now, we can only blame ourselves." He sighed before turning to me. "Should I ask how you and he came to still be here after Bernie has left?"

"No. Thanks to you, Aunt Bernie is now mad at both of us," I informed Stratton.

"I've been in trouble with Bernie half the time we've known each other. The storm will pass." He sighed. "It has been quite a night." He looked around at the empty lobby.

"It has," I responded without elaborating. He did not press me.

"My carriage is outside." Stratton gestured toward the door.

It was near dawn when Bernie came home. I knew because, unable to sleep, I was wandering the house's upper stories, avoiding Burke, who had fallen asleep in the parlor downstairs, waiting for her to come home. But Weaver did not drop my aunt off at the front of the house, driving around to the back. And she was not alone.

Miramon stepped out, turning back to catch Bernie up in his arms, crushing her to him in a passionate kiss. Her hair was disheveled, the remnants of her elaborate coiffure tumbling about her face and shoulders, her evening gown only marginally fastened up beneath her cloak.

Despite my attempts to thwart their liaison, I felt like cheering. She had done it. Despite all of society's judgments and jealousies, she had stolen a night of love and tenderness for herself.

I witnessed the lover's true goodbye as they shared one final kiss, releasing each other slowly before Miramon climbed back into the carriage and Weaver drove the General away to the docks, where he would board his ship for Mexico.

Before I turned away, I spied the little man in the striped pants sitting on the eaves of the carriage house. He was eating strawberries.

Act One, Scene Twelve: Wallack's Theater.

My worries over Aunt Bernadette's reaction to my part on the night of the Livingston party lingered in the back of my mind, but days passed, then a week, and nothing was said. Bernie declared that we would never speak of it, but that did not mean she would not react to it. Had I proven myself trustworthy or too independent and not compliant enough for my aunt's taste? Would I be banished and sent away now? I waited…and then forgot about it.

Kindle and I had a new game: cat and boy. Which was akin to cat and mouse minus the threat of being eaten. There was some eating involved because I felt compelled to reward the rascal's cleverness for discovering I was following it. I understood this was a questionable practice tantamount to encouraging sneaky behavior, but as Kindle was not a child and I was not its parent, I decided to just please myself and the cat. Regardless of the opinion of the rest of the company, Kindle was a very nice cat.

In pursuit of this game, I began to experience instances of icy air, my arms going all goose-fleshy, the hair standing up at the nape of my neck, and an increasing number of visits from the swirly apparition I had encountered up on the flybridge, often, just before Kindle joined me.

"Theaters are haunted," Young Giddy assured me with an air of great wisdom. "Everyone knows that. Well, everyone who is in the theater."

"But how can it be haunted? Wallack's is a new theater, Gid," I protested. "No one has died here."

"Maybe it was built over an Indian graveyard. Manhattan Island was full of Indians before the Dutch came," Giddy replied, easily convincing himself of this story's truth. I was not so gullible and decided to ask people who might know something about the building site because they were with the company when the new theater was being constructed.

E.F. Winters

I tried Wixx first, sailors being known to be superstitious, but if he knew anything unusual about the new building's site, he was too loyal to encourage rumors that might affect ticket sales.

My next attempt was with Maggie Walsh. Needle Maggie had worked as a seamstress for Wallacks since its early days under old Mister Wallack and knew a good story or three. But besides being a repository of anecdotes about the famous and infamous of the New York theater, Maggie was originally from Yorkshire and was well versed in old-country lore.

"Every theater has its spirits. Surely you know that, Master Kit. Why would you ask such a thing?" She said, not looking up from her work.

"Because Wallacks is a new theater. No one has died here. No one who worked here has died since it opened. I asked."

Maggie looked at me and shook her head as if I was being a dense dumbkin. "You've felt the emotions whipped up during a performance. They are strong energies. When the audience leaves, some of those energies go with the people, whooshing out the door into the world, but most of it stays right here, soaking into the woodwork and the stage drapes, lurking in the corners, until it's grown enough to have the confidence to come out and be seen." Her voice was soft, lyrical, and intimate, the fireside voice of a storyteller. "Spirits don't show themselves to everyone, though; they are particular. They may only show themselves to a special few, maybe a crew or cast member whose nature is a bit fay, or someone it has developed a connection with due to a kindness. Sometimes a spirit just gets caught by a hapless observer who is walking through the theater. But Wallack's theater spirit is, as you have said, quite new. It is only just feeling its way into being."

Oh yes, Maggie Walsh was a good storyteller.

"I can see you think I'm weaving you a tale when you're asking me for truth." She pursed her lips. "It's not my way to tell an untruth. You should know that by now. What you're thinking is an insult to me and our friendship." She kept sewing. There was always something needing mending, taking in, or being let out.

"I'm not saying I don't believe you, Maggie…"

"You're not saying it, but you are thinking it. I can see it on your face." She poked her needle into the material with unusual gusto. "Pay me no mind, Master Drake. I'm just a foolish old woman who likes to tell stories. I just thought since you were already claiming to see it…"

"See what?" I asked. "What am I seeing, Maggie?" She looked up from her work.

"You tell me."

I did not know what to call what I was seeing: swirly smoke apparitions with a penchant for theatrical costumes, a blue hobgoblin that trailed my aunt. Like anyone, I tried to dismiss seeing these things or explain them away with weak excuses. But they were getting clearer, longer, and happening more often. Worse, I was remembering. In lightning-flash images, I was having memories of the blue-skinned hobgoblin that went back to when I was a baby and my mother and I were living at Aunt Bernie's in London. My experience with the theater spirit was a new development. My interactions with the blue man were not. Would understanding one help me understand the other? If they were connected, how?

I knew by asking, I risked becoming one of Maggie's stories: a tale about a promising young stagehand from a famous family whose mind cracked when he began seeing things, ending what might have been a promising career, but my world was cracking apart like an egg. Still, both Kits in me needed to know. I took a breath and dove in.

"A week ago, a swirling smoke apparition with yellow eyes came at me up on the fly bridge," I confessed. "It wore a prop crown and held a prop dagger in a pair of red kid gloves, and it quoted a line from The Scottish Play—well, it tried. It kind of hissed the words, like it didn't know how to talk. I've seen it several times since, though not with the same items. I returned those. Currently, its preference is for fans, ribbons, and bits of lace."

"Items from the new production," Maggie mused.

"Exactly. The apparitions only appear when I am alone up on the bridge. Sometimes it turns out to just be Kindle. So, why is Wallack's haunted, and why am I seeing its ghost?"

Maggie shook her head. "That you will have to ask the spirit."

I decided to try something else. "Why would a spirit steal props and bits of costuming material?"

"It would only be stealing if it had no intention of giving the item back."

"But it's not giving them back. I am picking them up after it drops them and secretly returning them," I pointed out.

"So, you have an understanding with the spirit. Which answers your first question. It drops them, and you put them back."

"That's pretty sophisticated thinking for a spirit that plays dress-up, don't you think, Maggie?"

"Small, props…"

"And costumes…"

Maggie stopped me. "Not costumes. No costume has ever gone missing from Wardrobe."

"Are you sure?"

She pointed toward a saucer on the floor in the corner with a bit of cream sticking to the sides.

"You're feeding Kindle."

"I'm feeding the theater spirit," she corrected me. "It's a common practice in the old world, feeding the fairies. It shows respect. Scoff if ya' like, but we have no missing items here in Wardrobe."

"But the red kid gloves…?"

"Those were not costume pieces. Those were an actor's personal property." She was right. The gloves were Bernie's. "I told you, Kit, this is a young spirit—older than a baiern now, but still young. With each play we put on here, the spirit learns things and grows up a little bit—adding little pieces to itself —ideas about who it might become. It is borrowing items that interest it, examining them, and trying to fit what it's learned from characters in the play to its own existence. Is it a king this week, or a witch? A murderess, or a knight fighting for their lord? But the Scottish Play is closed now, and we have a new production on the boards: the School for Gossips."

"*The School for Scandal*," I corrected her.

"I know the title. It's a play of clever words and mean people who say nasty things about each other. It is a terrible influence on a young spirit just forming its character. It will bring out the trickster side of its nature." She sighed. "But there's nothing to be done about it now except wait out the run."

"You think the theater spirit has become a gossip?" I almost laughed, but I could see Maggie was dead serious.

"Foul whisperings are abroad in the company, and fouler deeds. The drama among us is going to be wagging off the stage and into the hallways and dressing rooms, causing all sorts of vile chatter until this show closes and the spirit has something new to focus on." She pressed her lips together, thin and tight like a string stretched, pinched between two hands. "Be careful, Kit. Don't fall prey to false friends and gossip."

I thought about the rumors Gil claimed were going around about Bernie. The play had been in rehearsal for a few weeks and was about to open.

Mister Lester had announced that our next show would be *Hamlet*.

"Oh God," I muttered.

Act One, Scene Thirteen: Drake House, Washington Square, April 1863.

As *Hamlet* went into rehearsal, the bump and push of rumors within the company subsided. Concerned about the play's effect on a young spirit, I held on to the fact that the production would have a short rehearsal period and a short run.

Pushing away my worries that Maggie's hypothesis about the theater spirit was a fantasy that would lead me away from the halls of reason, I excused my belief by telling myself that the seamstress and I were merely indulging in a bit of fancy connected to old theater traditions, something I would wink and smile about when I was older.

Drake House was not where my heart lived, but it was a far better option than boarding school, and, aside from Kit Becket's suspicions, I enjoyed my life there. Still, feeding suspicion with one hand and hiding it with the other was becoming exhausting.

But if the Drakes were stubborn, the Becket's were stone.

There were things going on in Drake House, beyond the unexplained residence of a little blue man, things its occupants did not talk about in my presence. When I entered a room, sentences crumbled and fell apart, abandoned words dangling from the cliffs of the staff's tongues as they scattered nervously.

The insecurities sparked by this behavior woke me in the wee hours when the clunk of the cast-iron walls of the fireplace contracted as the night-fire's embers cooled. The limbs of the trees outside my window seemed to tap out Morse Code messages, every draft in the old house an exhaled secret, each carpet-strangled creak a confession of the house's conspiracy.

Was I on edge because I was being watched, or was I watchful because the household was on edge? Did the house whisper only to me, or had the other residents stopped their ears?

I was on my way to breakfast when I passed Aunt Bernie's door. It was partially open, so I could easily see into the room. She was sitting in front of a landscape painting of a Victorian folly fashioned after a Roman temple. Two ravens guarded the staircase. My aunt was so still that for a moment I entertained the thought that she might be ill. But then her hands began to flow in graceful gestures mimicking pinching invisible threads, drawing them from one side of an invisible loom to the other, before tying them off to something that, again, I could not see. When she finished this exercise, she sat back, studying her invisible work.

Suddenly, the little blue man peered out from behind the puddle of Bernie's silk skirts, his expression cold and malevolent, startling me.

"You do not belong here," his voice stabbed my brain. *"Forget."*

Bernie's door slammed, the sound disturbing the house's morning peace, and Ida appeared.

"What is she doing in there?" I asked.

"Nothing." She placed herself between me and the door, as if protecting my aunt from me.

"She was doing something," I persisted.

"No. She was doing nothing. It is a Hindu practice. You sit and do nothing. It's supposed to relax you. Don't ask me to explain it. You people do all kinds of senseless things. Dweeti has breakfast up." She walked on, taking the stairs down to the main floor. A moment later, I heard the front door open and close behind her.

I expected, since Ida had left, and Bernie was in her room doing "nothing," that I would be breakfasting alone, but an elderly stranger was at the table spooning down porridge, much of it on his chin whiskers or the napkin he wore like a bib tucked into his starched shirt collar. He had the most alarming pinfeather-fine white hair, which stood up in every direction, making him look like an avian barnyard saint. He introduced himself as Albaugh Drake.

"I am pleased to meet you, Uncle," I spoke louder than was my custom as Bernie had indicated that her brother was hard of hearing.

"No need to shout," he coached me. "My hearing is perfectly adequate. I tell Bernie I don't hear her because she prattles on so. Too many words. If each person were allowed a quota each day, Bernie would use hers up in the first fifteen minutes and be forced to remain silent all the rest of it. I imagine that is why she became an actress. They pay her to talk."

There was nothing I could say to this that would not doom me to trouble with one or the other of the siblings, so I changed the subject.

"Did you enjoy the conference you were attending?" I meant it as a polite inquiry, the expectation being that he would offer a brief, polite reply, but there was nothing brief about Albaugh Drake. His intellect was a maze of twisting pathways with points of interest along the way. Long, detailed descriptions of the Scientific Society's Annual Meeting and the new inventions and discoveries that had caught his interest followed, most of it incomprehensible to the average person, to whom his lengthy explanations would have resulted in boring non-comprehension. I, however, having interests aligned with his, was thrilled, though I realized that his earlier remark about his half-sister using up her quota of words was less about his desire for quiet than about his desire to dominate the conversation.

"Ah, so you two have met. Good," Bernie observed as she entered the dining room.

Did she look calmer after her mysterious Hindu practice? I did not think so. If anything, she looked more distracted. I checked the space below everyone's knees to see if the blue man had come to breakfast. I deduced that he had when a muffin and two strips of bacon levitated from the sideboard, disappeared, then reappeared at the other end of the table, not far from Uncle Albaugh.

"No doubt you will find endless minutia to share and will get along like a pair of turtledoves," Bernie offered as her blue companion bit into Dweeti's baked goods.

"Do not stare, Half-man. It is rude," the blue man scolded me, aware that I was observing him. I looked away, trying to ignore his presence. Everyone else seemed able to, but I proved to be incapable of it. The creature's fingers, especially his nails, were very long. He stabbed his food, then ate it off his nails, like a soldier eating from his knife.

"You have been making the poor boy go with you to the theater?" Albaugh was accusing his sister. "He has a serious mind, Bernadette. Far too serious to get caught up in all that foolishness."

"I did not force him, Albaugh. He has been pleased enough to go along, and you were not here to take him under your wing and lock him within the walls of logic. I filled in as best I could."

"But the *theater*?" Albaugh shuddered.

"I quite like it, Uncle," I defended my aunt, hoping it would help her forgive my trespasses the night of the Livingston party. "Not the acting part--I hated that. Being on the stage was terrifying, but watching the play was quite wonderful." The blue man's face reflected his own opinions on the subjects.

"Infernal machines," he croaked between muffin bites. *"Terrible things. There's nothing wrong with a good candle."*

I tried to hide a smile that I would have been challenged to explain if anyone inquired.

"What play?" Albaugh asked my aunt.

"*MacBeth* with Forrest in the title role. It was a good run, but it has closed now," Bernie replied between sips of tea.

"One of your better roles. But I cannot believe you have already corrupted the child by putting him on display on the stage. Whatever were you thinking, Bernie? Did you not consider the damage to the boy's reputation? You will ruin any chance he has at being accepted into a good university if these shenanigans become known."

"He has no reputation to ruin." My aunt buttered her toast. "Which is why he has adopted the use of our surname. We are introducing him as Christopher Drake."

"Jolly! But won't the boy's father be offended?' Albaugh demanded.

"His father is dead."

"Oh, jolly good. Problem fixed." Albaugh fumbled with a poached egg in the shell, trying to scoop out the gooey insides. "What about his mother, Manon?"

"Manon is his *grandmother*, Albaugh," Bernie informed her brother patiently. "And she passed away last winter. Christopher's mother is Leonie."

"Leonie!" The old man's face brightened. "A lovely girl. I haven't seen her for weeks. Where is she? Touring?" My aunt pinned me with her eyes as if to gain my complicity, saying, *"See what I have to deal with?"*

"She is out of town at the moment, brother. Which is why Kit has come to stay with us." The stern look she gave me warned me not to cross her by trying to clarify what she had left out regarding my mother's absence, but I was more concerned with her choice of the impermanent word "stay" in her description of my position in the household, rather than the more permanent choice she might have made: "live". I remained a probationary member of the household.

"I only took a role temporarily, Uncle. Just a few nights until they found a replacement," I defended myself feebly, unsure which sibling I needed to please to secure more permanence. "I like it very much at Wallack's, but it has not changed my interest in science," I volleyed between them.

Albaugh harrumphed. "I should hope not. The theatre is no place for a keen mind: puppetry with live dolls. An actor is not allowed to do anything they are not *told* to do."

Bernie rolled her eyes. "That is not true, and you know it, Albaugh."

"It is the machines and effects for the gas and limelights that I find fascinating," I told my uncle. "And the sets, and the rigging. There is this place called the flying bridge high up in the theater," I warmed to my subject, my passion being honest. "Did you know that rigging for raising and lowering backdrops is based on the rigging of the tall sailing ships? Most of the stagehands were sailors. But the new effects we can create using this lighting changes everything. It is positively magical."

Albaugh's head whiplashed toward where the little blue man was sitting.

"We'll have no talk of magic in this house." He scowled. For a moment, I thought his and the blue creature's eyes met. The blue man looked amused, and my uncle looked away, clearing his throat before speaking again. "This family has had no good magic for the last three hundred years," he proclaimed. The blue man threw a bit of muffin at Albaugh, which landed in the old man's beard and remained there, ignored. "The lad has been here a month and already you have undermined his good sense with talk of magic," Albaugh growled. "What uneducated people call magic is only a naturally occurring phenomenon viewed through the lens of ignorance."

"I understand," I replied, trying to contain my laughter at the morning sideshow between my great uncle and the blue man he had declared did not exist. It was a strange world when crumbs in a beard became empirical evidence, but Albaugh had no muffin on his plate, and the crumbs had come from somewhere. The little blue man was indeed a natural phenomenon being observed through the lens of ignorance.

"I only meant that it *looks* magical, Uncle," I tried to repair my faux pas with my reason-clutching relative. "I realize it is not actually magic. The lighting and design pieces are, in fact, quite scientific, using modern geometry to create the illusion of depth and distance on the sets, and mechanical devices that control chemical reactions to create light. Wixx is teaching me about the lights. He is the theater's gasman."

"I know who Wixx is," Albaugh responded drolly. "I have been a member of the Coterrie..."

"We shall talk more about this later." Bernie stopped her brother, casting the elderly man a warning look.

At Albaugh's mention of a Coterrie, the little blue man's head came up, and his grotesquely large eyes bugged out like a fish. He put one long, sticklike finger to his lips and shushed me as if I was in on the secret. I was not and had no idea what any of them were talking about.

"Right. Of course." Albaugh turned from what he was going to say as if the subject had a "no trespassing" sign on it.

My hope that my uncle might prove to be a confidant in Drake House vanished. Whatever hugger-muggery was going on, Albaugh was complicit.

It was possible the entire Drake family was eccentric.

Act Two, Scene One: April 1863, New York City

"Ah, nephew," Aunt Bernie hailed me as I was leaving Wardrobe. "I was going to look for you, but you have saved me the trouble."

A wave of anxiety rushed through me. Had she finally decided on the sentence for my transgressions at the Livingston party? I had hoped Albaugh's return might change things, and as he and I got along well, he might advocate for my continuance in the household. But my great uncle was very much involved in his thoughts and studies, and though he occasionally invited me to assist with an experiment and talked to me incessantly at breakfast about any new idea that caught his fancy, he mostly kept to his rooms and his books, his involvement in the household minimal.

I understood that if my aunt decided that my presence so close to her secret world was inconvenient, arranging a school would take time. I also realized that when that happened, I, undoubtedly, would not be informed of those arrangements until everything was settled and I was about to be bundled into a carriage. But as time passed with no mention of such a move, I stopped worrying, comfortable where I was… until this moment. I held my breath, fixed by my anxiety.

"Wixx told me of your interest in knowing more about theater," my aunt said casually. "So, I have arranged for you to tour some of the other theaters in the city." I exhaled the breath I had been holding, my fears dissipating. "You will have a chance to view their facilities and hear how the different companies do things. As far as performances go, you will mostly see only rehearsals, but let me know if there are plays you would like to see in their entirety, and I will arrange it.

"But what about…I glanced toward Wixx's station.

"Wixx has made arrangements to replace you tonight. You have Weaver and the carriage for the evening, but you will want to visit as many theaters as you can before curtain, so you should go. They are waiting for you out back," Bernie directed.

"They?"

"Oh, I am sorry, I forgot. Charlie Stratton will be your guide."

Relieved that my fears had been for nothing, I fetched my coat from a prop chair and exited through the stage door.

Weaver sat on the carriage's box, his muscled arms bulging against the cotton duck of his coat, his long whip in one hand, the team's reins in the other. He never wore the black top hat and tailcoat most carriage drivers wore; instead, sporting a pork pie hat and practical clothing in practical brown. I often wondered if Weaver had been the driver of the carriage that whisked my mystery person away that first night—I say person because I was now uncertain if it was a man, or if it was Charlotte Cushman dressed like a man.

Weaver was no more "just" a carriage driver than Bernie was "just" an actress, or Burke was "just" a butler. In fact, no one in the Drake household was who outsiders presumed them to be, except Frostine, the young Irish housemaid who had only been hired a month before I arrived, and of course, Dweetie. There was not a dash of mystery about the motherly queen of kitchen spices.

Charles Stratton, dressed like a bon vivant, stood on the porch deck outside the stage door, conversing with Weaver. I wondered what they could possibly have in common to talk about, but, knowing Stratton, it was probably women.

"Thank you, Weaver," I greeted him. He touched the brim of his hat and readied his reins. "So, Mister Stratton, we meet again." I greeted my new friend as we descended the stage door's stairs together. I climbed into the carriage, taking one bench while he clambered onto the bench opposite me. "Are you all right with this venture? It seems an odd favor for my aunt to ask of you. I fear she has presumed on your friendship."

"Come now, Master Christopher, it will be fun," he declared.

"Please, call me Kit," I said. "It's what my family calls me."

Stratton bowed politely. "And you may call me Charlie, which is what no one calls me, except my closest friends. Most people only know me by the stage moniker that Phineas gave me." He rapped on the carriage's ceiling, and Weaver clucked the horses into action.

"Mister Barnum didn't like your real name?"

"Charles Stratton is a perfectly good New England name, but it does not zing from a marquee. P.T. felt a clever name was required.

One that set my persona apart as much as my stature did. Tom Thumb defined me as small. General, defined me as a person of authority and intelligence; two opposites in people's minds that encouraged curiosity, so they would pay a nickel to come and ogle me. But to his credit, Phineas made me a curiosity without making me a clown. The strategy benefited me in ways I would never have foreseen when we started all those years ago."

"How old were you?"

"Five. But Phineas lied and said I was nine, so I would seem smaller, and maybe so women wouldn't be upset with him for taking such a young child from its mother."

"It must have been hard for you to leave your family."

"Not as hard as it should have been. They were quite ashamed of me, you see. What were they to do with me? They could not send me to school with other children. Was I even capable of learning? Since there was something gone amiss with the way my body was growing, it seemed likely there was something equally wrong with my mind. Mostly, they expected I was going to get sick and die, and they hoped I would do it before our neighbors realized that the little boy next door was not getting any bigger. My parents did not mean any cruelty. They did not treat me poorly. They just did not know what to do with me. And they were so terribly embarrassed."

"Did it bother you, having to become someone else?" I asked, thinking of my situation and the guilt over feeling the freedom becoming Kit Drake had given me.

"No. At least I was someone. Does it bother you?" Charles turned the question back around. "We do what we must, we freaks. We are masters at getting by in a world that has no place for us. If Phineas had not marketed me as he did—if I had not been able to charm audiences with my talent and wit, my life would have been very different, and for that I am grateful to him. Because of Barnum, I have respect, a reputation, and every expectation of living out a pleasant life.

"So, here we are, two men out on the town together. 'Take my nephew out and make a man of him,' Bernie said. Well, those were not her exact words. Oh, stop frowning, Kit. I am not taking you to a brothel to give up your virginity—that is assuming it hasn't been given already." I felt my cheeks burning. "Forgive me, I forgot how terribly shy you are. I was just getting into the spirit of things," he assured me.

I gulped. "Aunt Bernadette said this was to be an educational evening. That I was to see some of the other theaters and the style of their shows." Nothing had been said about brothels or manhood.

"She said the same to me. We'll start at Niblo's Garden and work our way south. The New York theater season runs from September through June," Stratton began his narrative. "Then, while the gentry travel to Europe or remove to their beach cottage mansions, theater companies tour. Well, not lately. Since the war started, travel in the South has become too dangerous, which leaves only New England, and the Puritans have never been fans of the theater. It is nearly impossible for a company to keep afloat without touring in the summer, which is why so many have folded or relocated to cities willing to subsidize a resident company so they could brag of having that elusive commodity, culture.

"Of course, touring has its challenges, even before the war. A play heralded in Boston could cause a riot below the Mason-Dixon Line. In San Francisco, audiences may cheer the stabbing parts of a Shakespeare play but will fling mud and rotten vegetables during the speeches."

We pulled up in front of Niblo's Garden.

"I think you'll find the buildings similar in layout: a proscenium arch frames the stage, with larger or smaller aprons below the curtain line. Niblo's rooftop garden is what is most unique here. It is used to extend the season into summer because it's cooler on the roof, and now that we are trying to woo the middle class and those who cannot afford to leave for the summer, Niblo's figures that they will need something to do: hence the rooftop theater. But productions destined for an outside venue must be carefully chosen, because there is no proscenium, no fly system, limited ability to change backdrops, and lights are an issue. Staging designs must be simpler."

Stratton was right, the theater buildings were quite alike at the core. Most had made the changeover to gas and limelights, or were in the process of doing so. The more common use of this new technology was changing every part of production from design to acting styles, and most theater managers understood that if they did not change with the times, audiences would simply stop buying tickets to their shows. All the theatres we toured had ample lobbies and huge houses, their décor designed to give audiences the sense of luxury that they were paying to be part of. Tiny, cramped, backstage areas for actors and crew were also universal. No one spent money on the comfort of the actors or the crew.

Stratton introduced me to E.A. Sothern at the Chatham. I already knew Mister Forrest from his term at Wallack's as *MacBeth*. I just missed seeing Charlotte Cushman, who was closing a run as *Queen Catherine* at The National before she prepared to leave for Italy. When we arrived at The National, pieces of the set for the rehearsal of the soon-to-open *A Midsummer's Night's Dream* were just being struck.

"Not in costume runs yet, Mark?" Charles asked, searching for any sign of scantily clad fairies.

"No, not yet, Charles, but come back when we open. There will be plenty to see then." He winked at his friend.

"I wouldn't miss it." The set, though unfinished, looked intriguing enough that I, too, wished to see the full production and said so. "We can attend together. I will tell Bernie." Stratton grinned like a child with cookie crumbs clinging to their cheeks. "How did you get the old biddies on your board to agree to such daring designs, Mark?" he prodded Smith.

"They did not give themselves the time nor have the patience to look at all the costume sketches," he admitted. "And it's not like we are going Burly. Our fairies wear body stockings under strategically placed bits of moss, vines, and leaves. The suggestion that the fairies will be costumed in only what the forest provides is generating good free press, though. Suggestion is far more interesting than nakedness."

"I don't know. I am rather fond of nakedness," Stratton demurred.

"Just use your imagination, Charles. The lighting of those woodland scenes will be exquisitely shadowy."

"I can use my imagination at home and not pay for your bloody ticket," Stratton grumbled. "What about Puck? Is he to be reduced to wearing vines and playing in the shadows?"

Smith laughed. "Our boy fairies wear even less than the girls, though in our play, it may be hard to tell the difference."

"I can tell the difference between boys and girls, Mark," Stratton retorted.

"I fear our Puck will not be up to your level, Charles." Smith gave Stratton a respectful bow.

"That is very kind, Mark, but if Puck is not to be fully dressed, do not call me in to substitute when your actor comes down ill. No one wants to see a half-dressed dwarf."

"That's not what I hear." Mark ribbed his friend. "The papers claimed that ladies in Europe were lining up to get a private peek during your last tour."

"Europe has a broader definition of male virility."

"And more sexually adventurous women?"

"Unquestionably." Stratton grinned.

We spent the afternoon viewing the facilities and talking to managers, stagehands, and actors at the different theaters, but as eight o'clock and curtain time drew near, more important tasks required the theatrician's attention.

"Are we going back to Wallacks now?" I asked Charles. It had become so much a part of my life that as the hour for the curtain's rise approached, it felt wrong not to be there.

"No. Now we going to the New Bowery Theater." I remembered what Old Gideon said about Bowery audiences, sex, and gore. "Mister Lester performed with the Bowery Company when he was younger," Stratton began his tutorial. "Edwin Forrest took a turn or two. Charlotte Cushman worked with the company for a time, but it has had a troubled history, and the days of performances on those levels are behind them. The building burned down several times and had to be rebuilt. The current theater has four thousand seats."

"Four thousand?" I repeated incredulously.

"Exactly, and with the money moving uptown, it is impossible to fill. Plays like what Wallacks or The Chatham put on won't sell down here anymore. The neighborhood's changed too much, and the audience with it."

"So, what do they do?" I asked.

"Burlesque, specialty acts like you see at a circus, minstrel shows, a singer or two whose material is on the bawdy side, or a variety show satirizing popular plays or operas, and, of course, hootchie-kootchie dancers. Good burlesque acts can be very entertaining, and being flirted with by females dressed as if they are in their boudoir does raise the spirits and get the blood going. After the burlesque and vaudeville acts, there will be a main play, which tonight is *Uncle Tom's Happy Cabin.*

"The one Old Giddy is in?" I asked.

Stratton shrugged. "Might be."

The first acts were, as Charles had said, stand-alone pieces with no story; their purpose was to sell alcohol and whip up the crowd. Chorus girls from the opening number worked the room afterward, selling drinks and encourage drinking.

The costumes for the burlesque were not that different on the top from what you might see at a high society ball or dinner party, but the bottom parts were missing, revealing hips, legs, and the outlines of that exciting conjunction Stratton had gone so poetic about. Men whistled and shouted at the performers who performed to the oompah of a brass band blasting over heavy drumbeats and crashing cymbals until I wanted nothing more than to curl up in a ball and cover my ears. The audience cheered, punched the air, and each other. I was miserable.

We waited for the main play.

Uncle Tom's Happy Cabin was everything Harriet Beecher-Stowe's book, *Uncle Tom's Cabin,* was not; dishonest in its portrayal of slavery, rank with prejudices that catered to the worst impulses of an audience already decided on the issue of race, certain that their whiteness made them better, smarter, and more skilled, regardless of any character flaws or the lack of experience or education. White men in black-face makeup mugged and postured in disgusting parodies of Southern stereotypes about the African race, portraying slaves as childlike half-human half-apes who adored their leisurely Southern plantation lives and the kind and genteel masters who cared for them. I found the performances degrading to every race. This was the dark side of how theater magic could be used. Even more ribald and goonish in his blatant mugging to the audience than he had been at Wallack's, Old Giddy's talents fit well here.

The performances brought their audience to the edge of rioting, then brought them back toward civility just enough to buy another beer, anger building alongside the drunkenness until I could feel it as a presence in the house. When the doors opened and this spirit spilled out into the world, the result would be neither enlightening nor benevolent.

My hands ached from being clenched, my jaw tight, the sense of impending danger so like when the robbers had boarded the train to Cincinnati and killed Lieutenant Lewis that I kept seeing the hapless young man with his dead eyes on different faces in the crowd. The guilt I was feeling that my skin color alone would keep me safe in this crowd was unbearable.

When the performers came out for their bows, I stood and announced, "We're leaving." I began to push through the crowd without waiting to see if Stratton followed. "Why would you bring me to such a place? What could possibly have been your purpose? To frighten me? To humiliate me? I thought you were my friend," I declared as he and I got into the carriage, and Weaver called the horses to a trot.

"You seemed capable enough of saving yourself," Charles replied. I realized that he, too, might have felt endangered, a little person, accustomed to bullying and the scorn of society, amid a crowd overflowing with prejudice and at the edge of violent action. As he pointed out before, my differentness was something that could be hidden. His could not. His answer had been to earn enough money that he could keep himself apart from the common world, protected behind the structures of privilege, but he had come from behind those protections tonight to accompany me.

"I am sorry," I acknowledged my shame. "I should not have left you behind. It was thoughtless and ungenerous of me. But I could not stay one minute longer. All I could think of was getting out."

"High theater is not the world, Kit," Stratton pointed out. "That was what your aunt and Wixx felt you needed to understand--not just in your mind, but in your gut. A theater company is an insulated world. It helps us deny the existence of the nastiness outside. People who would spit at us on the street will applaud us in the theater, but when we leave the sanctuary of those walls and its illusions, the world's ugliness is still there, ready to bash us down."

"That was no sanctuary." I pointed back toward The Bowery.

"No. But there are ideas being churned out there, the same as at Wallack's or Niblo's. Just not the same kind of ideas. Theater is wonderful and magical, but don't mistake it for reality. Poverty and hopelessness are not merely tragic plot devices. Most of the poor in this city are not one line from being rescued by a rich relative. There is nothing genteel or polite about desperation. Words cannot adequately explain what you just experienced: the lethal combination of heated anger, the sweat and desire for release at the end of a hard day, when you stop working only to find the realities of the life you hoped would be better laughing at you. What does a poor father do when the faces of his starving children accuse him? He goes to the burly where sex, anger, laughter, resentment, bitterness, and violence all collide with drunken camaraderie, and every man faces the same failures. The producers who perfected this money maker know exactly what they are doing. They have considered the possibility that these performances play into the city's violence. They just don't care."

As Weaver circled the carriage around to head North, a young black man darted out in front of the horses and ducked into an alley. Seconds later, the carriage skidded to a halt before three roughs who only hesitated because it was blocking their way.

"Go! Go, you fool." They waved us on.

"Come on, boyos," One shouted to his fellows. "Don't let the coon get away!" They ran behind the carriage and fanned out across the alley's opening. "It's a dead end. He can't have gone far." The men called out rude words, making nasty noises and cracking their clubs against the alley's brick walls as they scuffed forward in a menacing line.

"What are they going to do?" I asked, my voice tight and high. It was a stupid question, a weak question. In my gut, I already knew. "Will they beat him?"

"If they catch him," Charles replied stiff-jawed.

"Will they kill him?" Charles did not answer. For all his talk, he was no more prepared to accept the world's cruelty than I was. "What are we going to do, Charles?"

"*We* are not going to do anything," Stratton insisted. "Neither of us would last a minute against those men." I tried to open the carriage door. Charles pulled it shut, pushing me back into my seat. "I am not going back to Bernie's apologizing that you can no longer spell your own name."

Weaver jumped down from his seat, landing on the left side of the carriage.

"This is no business of yours, Mister," one of the roughs warned the driver. "The nigger ain't going to get anything he don't deserve."

Weaver stood like a circus muscleman in day clothes. The roughs had florid faces, jumped-up adrenaline, and wooden clubs.

"Fuck." Charles winced. "Stay here," he pointed at me. Throwing the carriage door open, he stood in its frame, which made him almost as tall as everyone else standing on the ground.

"You hush puppies seem to have taken a wrong turn," he addressed them, affecting a slight Georgian accent. "This is not Alabama or Kentucky. This is New York City. We're in the North here, meaning that young man," He pointed to the black man cowering at the end of the alley. "Has as much right to walk these streets as any of you."

Weaver growled, a bear in brown trousers and a pork pie hat.

"Another traitor to his race." One of the roughs spat.

"There are no traitors here, my friends," Charles spoke like he was trying to tame a rabid dog. "Just men, out for a bit of fun, making our way at the end of the day. Isn't that right?" he glanced at Weaver. It was a caution—a request to stand down but stand by. The driver took a wide stance, his thick, muscled legs like the dock posts pounded into the river's edge to hold fast the big ships. One of the roughs snarled, spun, and sprinted toward the back of the alley. Before I had registered that an attack had begun, one of the man's friends pulled a pistol and shot the poor fellow they had been chasing. Weaver blurred into action, taking the closest two men down with one punch each. The third man saw what the driver had done and began running up Bowery Lane.

Charles climbed down from the carriage and hurried to where the young man lay panting, streaks of blood on his face, slicking his skin and shirt collar. The wound beneath his coat, where it covered his shoulder, was growing a red bloom.

"We need to get you somewhere safe where your injuries can be seen to," Charles offered. "Can you stand? Can you walk?"

"I'm fine. I can…" The young man tried to rise, wobbled like a cornstalk in a high wind, and Weaver scooped him up, depositing him in the carriage.

"We'll get you cleaned up and sorted out," Charles told the young man.

"Don't trouble yourself. I am fine, Sir. Truly." He tried to rise and climb back out of the carriage. Weaver pushed him back in and held him there.

"You are not fine. You have been shot," he said gruffly. "You think you are fine because the excitement is masking the pain, but it won't last."

"We're not kidnapping you," Charles insisted. "But that wound needs attention—maybe even a doctor. We've got people who can take care of it. After that, you are free to go on your way as it pleases you, but right now, there are a thousand men just like the three who attacked you, about to come out of that theater." He chucked his chin at the New Bowery. "We can't stay here." Our erstwhile guest nodded reluctantly, and I crawled past him into the carriage as Weaver climbed up onto the box. Charles joined us, and a minute later, we were bouncing over the cobblestones as Weaver shouted to the team to step out smart.

"I am Charles Stratton, and my friend here is Christopher Drake," Stratton made introductions. "The brute who just saved our lives is Weaver."

"Ira Aldridge," the young man introduced himself, trying not to breathe too deeply. "Drake, did you say? Are you by chance related to Lady Bernadette Drake?"

I nodded. "She is my aunt. We're going to her house now."

Ira Aldridge shook his head, chuckling. "My father, Ira Aldridge Senior, always says the theater is a small community. He and Lady Drake worked together onstage in London for many years."

"I knew him well," Stratton shared. "Then it is doubly lucky that we happened by. Lady Drake would have been very displeased if you had visited New York and not come to call on her."

It was such a small social lie; I hoped Stratton would be forgiven.

Act Two, Scene Two: Drake House, the Next Morning

Having cleaned and bandaged our guest's injuries and loaned him nightclothes so Begam Dweetie could wash and mend his torn clothing, Burke and I settled the young man in, hoping the draught for pain that Dweetie made would help him sleep. Charles insisted on going with Weaver to pick up Aunt Bernie from the theater so he could explain everything. I did not know if my aunt had planned a free night or begged off from any other engagement, but she and Charles both returned shortly before midnight.

"How is he?" Bernie asked as Burke took her cape and hat.

"The bullet only grazed his arm.

"Does he need a doctor?"

"I was able to take care of it, Madam. Other than the bullet wound, he is a little beat up. He's had a fright, but he will mend," Burke finished his report.

"Good. It is better not to complicate matters by calling a physician to the house." Charles clasped Burke's hand in greeting.

"How could this happen?" my aunt demanded. No one attempted an explanation. Prejudice was rife in the city, fanned by the mistrust and enmity between immigrants, Nativists, the resentment of successful free black families and their businesses, and the surge of freed slaves. There were Abolitionists, Wide-Awakes, Union loyalists, Republicans, Copperheads, and Peace Democrats, and the other sort of Democrats, every one of them set against someone or something else. "Did he say why he is in New York? Is his father here with him?" Bernie was exceedingly rattled.

"Ira Junior is 'traveling to broaden his experience,'" Burke informed her. "Ira Senior is still in London."

Bernie's face registered disappointment. "I doubt this attack was what Ira envisioned when he agreed to the adventure."

"Aldridge knows the temperament of his native country better than most," Charles reminded her.

Burke nodded. "But some understandings a young man must experience for himself."

"A gruesome lesson. I hope you are never so foolish, Kit." Bernie's eyes moved to Idabelle. "Have you heard of other such attacks, Ida?"

"Every day, Madam," the young woman replied coolly.

Bernie blanched. "I do not want you going about the city alone anymore. I forbid it. Do you hear? I know the orphanage wants you to do things for them, and I admire your commitment, but you are not to expose yourself to the violence of these ruffians, Ida. Weaver can take you anywhere you need to go."

The young woman lifted her chin in defiance. "With all due respect, Lady Drake, you are a generous employer, and it is your right to make demands of me during the hours I work for you, but I am a free woman, and you cannot tell me what I can or cannot do on my own time. I will not live in fear. That is how these bullies win."

"There are plenty of other ways they can win, child," Bernie countered without restraint. "It is my job to protect you. When they agreed to let you come work for me, I promised the Reverend Washington and his wife that I would keep you safe."

"And it was a naive promise to make." She seemed to have surprised even herself with her boldness, but she did not back down. "Forgive me my forwardness, Lady, but to keep that promise you would have to make me white and even then, I'd still be a woman." Ida swirled her skirts and stomped up the stairs to her room.

"I can never do the right thing—never *say* the right words." Bernie appeared on the verge of tears.

"That young woman is...?" Charles dangled the question unfinished.

Bernie glanced at me before glaring at Stratton, which shut him up. "She's my Lady's Maid: Idabelle Washington, an adopted daughter of the Reverend and Missus Washington," Bernie's emphasis on certain words of this brief explanation might have been enlightening to Charles, but it was confusing to me. "I should take her home to London," Bernie despaired.

"Nowhere is free of prejudice," Charles reminded her.

"She should not have to live with the threat of assault. We could go to Italy. She is light-skinned. She could pass there."

"Pass for what?" Charles demanded. "A white woman?"

"Miss Idabelle is a young woman of strong character and high moral values," Burke declared. "If you believe she would agree to pretend she is someone she is not, you are mistaken, Madam."

Bernie's glare was an arrow unleashed. I did not understand the silent subtext going on between Bernie, Burke, and Charles, but it was so strong it was like a fifth presence in the room—sixth if you counted the cocky spirit sitting on the arm of the sofa, grinning as if the conflict between the humans was a sideshow treat. No one else acknowledged his presence, leaving me to assume they did not see him and that privilege was mine alone. He looked at me, perhaps sensing my thoughts were focused on him, his expression becoming a cruel taunt. He knew I dared not say anything about him, as doing so risked my being declared mad.

"She is too young to understand. She does not know *who* she is," Bernie rounded on Burke. I wondered if Bernie did.

"And you are too white," Burke retorted. "Forgive me, madam, but you cannot understand what you have not experienced." It was not the sort of challenge a butler threw at their employer and remained employed, but then Burke and Bernie's relationship regularly trespassed such social norms.

Bernie crumbled onto the sofa, her face forlorn, her spirit friend hovering, his strange blue face looking up at her with genuine concern.

He cares for her, I realized. It was a surprise.

Burke poured Bernie a brandy. Charles said goodnight, and I went up to bed.

When I came down in the morning, a thick, leatherbound book lay on the table where Bernie had been sitting. I took it up and began to thumb through the pages. There were news clippings, sketches, and programs from different plays, the years progressing with the pages, all of it chronicling Bernie's career. Eventually, the ink sketches became daguerreotypes, like those used to advertise the performances of actors, actresses, and singers of some fame. During Bernie's years in London, some of them included a striking black man beside her. The captions identified him as Ira Aldridge. Sketches of Bernie as a fetching Desdemona to Aldridge senior's commanding Othello. Rosalind and Orlando, Cleopatra and Caesar; they played opposite each other many times during their careers. Some sketches caught them in productions where they were present, but not the leads. I noted the dates of the pictures. Bernie and Ira Senior had worked together for well over a decade.

I turned a page and found an article announcing a European tour featuring the two of them playing several of their most popular roles in a limited series.

The following page was an announcement of Ira's return to London and his impending marriage.

The page after that explained that the newly appointed "Dame" Drake was taking a restorative health break in Italy for the season. A flattering portrait-style daguerreotype of Aldridge graced the facing page. The resemblance to his son was unmistakable. But there was another, less easily explained familiarity. Idabelle looked very like him.

'Turn the page." The little blue man appeared at my shoulder, looking at the pages as I did.

The next several pages were dedicated to my mother's stage career, featuring daguerreotypes of her costumed in the typical ingenue roles, Ophelia, Juliet, and Rosalind.

"Leonara." This single utterance was filled with longing. A memory of my mother singing in Bernie's West End townhouse flooded my mind. I was only an infant. The blue man's face was peering at me over the edge of my crib.

"He smells." The blue creature frowned in distaste.

"His nappies probably need changing." My mother lifted me into her arms and took a long, deep sniff, drawing in my infant essence. "What are you talking about, Spin? He smells like a miracle." She nuzzled her nose into my neck. "What is bothering you, my friend? You have been quite out of sorts lately."

"He smells like that man," the creature complained.

"You mean my husband?" The blue man scowled. "We have spoken of this, Spin. Johnathan Becket and I are ..."

"Don't say it..." Spin disappeared.

"It is a truth you must accept," my mother spoke to the empty air.

Another memory replaced the first.

Act Two, Scene Two

We were still at Aunt Bernie's, and the blue creature, Spin, was watching me suspiciously from across the room as I played on the floor. I smiled at him, but he would not smile back. In a quick series of memories, I saw myself crawling after him tirelessly whenever I found him, keeping at it until he was forced to disappear to avoid me.

"I don't like you, half-man," I remembered him hissing at me.

In a third memory, I saw his sad, angry face, Bernie's, and my mother's as our baggage was carried out of Bernie's townhouse the day we moved to Becket's flat. Everyone had been so dreadfully unhappy—everyone but Johnathan Becket, and as a toddler, I could not understand why we had to leave this place where we were happy to go to some other place when it was making us so miserable to leave.

I had not seen the little blue man for years, but it was clear there was some connection between my family and the fey creature. A puzzle Kit Becket longed to dissect.

Look at him—how he looks at her picture.

The creature was enthralled.... *By my mother.*

There were many tales warning humans about becoming enthralled by the fey folk, but I could not think of one that warned about the dangers a fey could face if they became enthralled by a human. None of my memories held a hint of romantic interest on my mother's part. Leonara had married Johnathan Becket, born his child, and moved away with him, leaving the blue man behind. If he had been so attached to her, why had he stayed with Bernie, not coming away with us? Why did he stay with Bernie?

Burke startled me from my reverie. "The elder Aldridge is a handsome man," he commented. "There is a strong family resemblance." He gently took the book from my hands. The blue man frowned, crossing his arms in a pout.

"There is," I agreed. Burke walked to a closed cupboard built into the wall and slid the door open.

"Some memories are such a pleasant nostalgia. Others, however, are best left to the pages of books not often visited." He placed the scrapbook inside and closed the cupboard door. "I am sure you understand." I did. He was asking for my silence, and I gave it.

More secrets. The house shivered with the chill of them all. Ira Junior's arrival saved me from second-guessing my decision.

"You look better…rested," I addressed him. "Did you sleep well?"

"Well enough, considering. Thank you," Ira replied.

"No new pains?" Burke inquired. "Excitement often disguises injuries so we do not feel them until later."

"My ribs are sore." He touched them tentatively. He was wearing his clothes, washed and mended. "And now I can see all the bruises where stick knocks landed." Ira stretched his shoulders and torso cautiously. "I am not accustomed to brawling. It was fortunate you and your friend came along when you did. And your man, of course."

"Weaver," I said, taking exception to the description of Weaver as "our man," which reeked of the British class system. "The name of the person to whom you owe your thanks, Mister Aldridge, is Mister Weaver. Without him, the whole affair would have been a tragic disaster. Mister Weaver drives for our household."

"My apologies," Ira replied. "I did not mean to offend. I fear I am not entirely myself."

I feared he was. Britain had declared an end to the buying and selling of human beings, but its policies of colonialization encouraged undisguised prejudices against people unlike themselves. Still, people of African descent were more accepted there than in the United States, where the institution of slavery remained, and, as Charles had said, the theater community was an insulated world.

Bernie arrived downstairs, already fetchingly dressed for the day, hours before it was her custom.

"Good morning, young Mister Aldridge," she gushed as she flooded the room with her perfume and her presence. "As the son of my dear friend, I am taking the prerogative of greeting you like an old family friend." She folded him to her breast before releasing him and holding him at arm's length to take a good study. "Oh my, how like your father you are. I see much of him in you. How I do miss him." For a second time in less than twelve hours, her eyes teared up, a phenomenon I had never imagined I would see from the stern, stoic Dame. I looked around for the blue spirit, Spin, as she continued, "Your father is well? And your mother and sisters?" she added in an awkward rush. "Tell me everything." She sank to the sofa in a rustle of skirts.

Ira did as he was directed, Bernie responding to the brief parts of his narrative involving his father with great attention, but wandering when Ira started in on the accomplishments of his mother and sisters.

Then Idabelle appeared, and as she did so, Spin reappeared on the top of a tall cabinet. It would provide an excellent view of the drama to come. He seemed to have a penchant for emotionally charged scenes. Perhaps that is why he shadowed actresses. I wondered if Wallack's theater spirit and the blue man knew each other. Did they occupy the same 'other' world, or two different worlds that just brushed against each other? Maybe their fey natures were too self-interested to share a space or engage with another, and they simply ignored the other's existence, like disapproving in-laws.

Stopping abruptly at the doorway, Idabelle gaped at Ira Junior. He rose, acknowledging her arrival, as any gentleman of breeding was taught to do, and the two young people stood, staring at each other: mirrored parts; twins born of different mothers. Which was exactly what I guessed they were.

I had noticed before how some of Idabelle's expressions uncannily mimicked Bernie's, but dismissed it as a younger woman imitating an older mentor. The evidence of my mistake was before me.

Idabelle was a Drake and an Aldridge, kneaded together.

Bernie lived her life like she was made of bedrock, but Idabelle was evidence that for the past twenty-odd years, she carried a secret heartbreak, paying in a currency of deceit that twisted her and Ida's relationship. I thought my aunt was brave. But knowing the pain a child feels when the adult they trust most chooses something else over them changed that. My aunt's sacrifice of her child was not motherly bravery. It was cowardice.

The blue man was circling Ira Junior, sniffing his pant legs, ducking under his coat in the back, and inhaling more intimate parts, like a canine checking another dog. If I had liked Ira Junior more, I might have been disgusted, but his arrogance made me dislike him just enough to find this secret humiliation amusing.

"Breakfast is ready if you would like to adjourn to the dining room," Burke said, pivoting attention away from the awkward silence between Ira and Idy. Everyone began to breathe again. Spin, I noticed, had already gone.

"I am headed to the orphanage," Ida offered a weak protest, her attention still a prisoner of this look-alike guest.

"I am so sorry, Idabelle, but I sent Weaver out on an errand this morning," Bernie lied. "When he returns, he can take you." She took Idabelle's hand in her own, a gesture so out of character that Ida looked at her mistress as if Bernie had lost her mind. "It will only be a few minutes—just have a little something. Please, Ida." My eyes met Ida's, and I shrugged, now doubly amused. I thought perhaps I understood the subtext of the scene better than she did, but only because I had been privy to a history she had not.

"Mister Aldridge, this lovely young woman is my companion, Idabelle Washington." Bernie brought Ira Junior and Ida together, looking from one to the other, misty-eyed. "I was never as much a part of her life as I would like to have been, but I knew Ida's parents, and I have kept an eye on her since she was a little girl."

"Then perhaps my father knew your parents as well?" Ira suggested to Ida.

Bernie blanched. "I doubt he would remember," she stuttered. "Ida was born soon after your parents were married. Aldridge's life would have been rather full and hectic at the time."

"Of course."

"Perhaps Weaver could drop Ira wherever he wishes to go when you go out, Ida?" I suggested, feeling mischievous.

Idabelle looked flustered. "Of course."

"But I thought he would stay here, with us," Bernie protested, crestfallen. "Surely, you will stay here, won't you, Mister Aldridge?"

"It is very kind of you, Lady Drake, but I have lodgings, and my hosts will be very worried that I did not return last night."

"Then we must send a message."

"Unfortunate that Weaver is already out on an errand," I reminded Bernie of her lie. "And when he returns, he will be taking Ira and Ida to their destinations, so there would be no point in a message." Bernie scowled at me, but a smirk flitted across Burke's usually oh-so-serious face.

Young Ira was gracious, polished, and good-looking, possessing the same large, brown, sincere eyes, beautifully shaped mouth, and strong chin as his father. I thought it fortunate that he lived in London and Ida lived in New York, because Bernie had not thought through the awkward possibilities of introducing these two attractive young people and the potential result of their developing an unsuitable regard.

Talk at breakfast ranged from the lives of Ira's sisters to the work Idabelle was doing at the Colored Children's Asylum, eventually working around to last night's events outside the Bowery. Bored, Spin was eating as if there were ten of him.

"My father warned me what it would be like here," Ira admitted. "But I thought with the Union freeing the slaves, it would be different now, and this is the North."

"New York City is the most Southern city in the North," Idabelle informed him sourly.

"I see that now."

"Your father was not wrong to leave," Bernie interjected. "The prejudices he faced here were not imagined. He had a great deal of talent and promise, and audiences and producers in the United States treated him very unfairly."

"And you think it is any different today?" Idabelle challenged. "How many black actors are there at Wallack's?" For the first time since breakfast began, Spin became interested.

Definitely drawn to human drama, I decided.

"There is a war on," Bernie tried to defend Mister Lester's lack of diverse hiring. "Theater owners need to fill seats, or they will be forced to close their doors. Many already have. You know this, Ida."

Ira frowned. "Social change is the business of politics, Lady Drake, not art. Art is not political. Nor should it be."

"I must politely disagree, Mister Aldridge," Idabelle responded. "The root of the word theater is 'theatron': Greek for 'a place of seeing'. The church produced passion plays because common people could not read. Early plays were staged propaganda performed in the streets featuring bible stories that delivered whatever message the clergy felt aligned with their goals, manipulating public opinion and moral codes to their liking. Theater has been political since it began, because truth is a political pawn, and art is an effective, if manipulative, method of communication."

"I stand corrected." Ira blinked at being so verbally accosted, but nevertheless, he inclined his head to Ida in a polite gesture of concession. "I should not have voiced an opinion on a subject I was clearly so ill-versed on. Last night's performance at the Bowery was unequivocally a political expression. I have never seen such raw hatred…and afterward." He shook his head. "How can this country possibly hope to come back from such a crevasse of hate and prejudice?"

"You are too hard on Americans, Mister Aldridge, and too idealistic about your homeland," Bernie replied. "We cut off the heads of several of our kings and quite a few queens. We effectively enslave other countries and rape their resources, and yet every British citizen will tell you they are civilized. Humanity finds its way back from many horrors."

"Then turns around and commits new ones." Idabelle was always outspoken outside my aunt's presence, but she always appeared much more restrained around Bernie. Was she showing off for Ira Junior, or had something else changed to make her so bold? "If the Confederacy wins this conflict, slavery will have a hold in this country for generations. There is nothing that might be asked of us that would be enough, and nothing that would be too much."

She is a Drake through and through, I told myself. I had never been prouder to share the same blood.

Act Two, Scene Three: Ada Clare's Salon 46th St., NYC, May 1863

Bernie sailed into Ada Clare's Sunday Salon like a stately ship.

"Greetings, everyone. This is my nephew, Kit. He is only seventeen, so please refrain from corrupting him."

"Bernie! Come settle this. We are discussing…." I lost the details as my aunt was enfolded into a group at the far end of the parlor.

"You are such a cynic," I caught a sliver of an ongoing discussion. Gerald, the silver-haired gentleman from Pfaff's, was scolding an excessively thin, dark-haired gentleman with a stiff, full beard. "How can you live without hope, Clapp?"

"I drink…a lot." Clapp downed his whiskey and went to refill his glass.

"Beggar Kings and Royal Puppets!" I was surprised to see Cyril Fitz-Royale, but he appeared quite comfortable, one arm draped around the shoulders of a middle-aged man with a boxer's build and a nose shaped like a lazy S that declared him a pugilist.

Ada Clare's Sunday Salon was where The Bees and New York's intellectuals came to discuss the state of the world as they saw it. The house was several blocks North of the fashionable addresses of Union Square, where new houses were bursting from Manhattan Island's farmland, a few blocks off Broadway. I looked around the room and recognized Henry Clay, the Editor of Harper's Weekly, and the venerable actors Charlotte Cushman and Edwin Booth, also our hostess, Ada Clare, but there were many more, some of whom had their backs to me, so I could not see and recognize their faces.

Buzzing with a half dozen different conversations, the room lacked Victorian ostentation, furnished instead like an open invitation:

"Come, sit here. Pull up a chair. Here's a drink. Let me tell you a story," it promised.

"You don't imagine Lincoln closed those papers just because they said bad things about him, do you, Clay?" I heard Bernie's voice rising from the back of the room. "They were passing information to the Confederates using coded messages in editorials and speech quotes. That is not free speech. It is treason."

I knew Bernie's stand on this and turned my attention to another group.

"*MacBeth* is about revenge and ambition, but audiences love it. And in *Hamlet,* everybody dies," a lovely, frail brunette woman with skin like ivory was speaking. Her dress was loose but form-revealing, gauzy and clingy enough to show she had no need for the tortured undergarments women corseted and pinioned their bodies into, trying to pretend they possessed what she had naturally. It was very unconventional, as was her short, curly hair.

"Yes, but that's Shakespeare, Mencken." Edwin Booth was currently performing in the title role of *Hamlet* at Wallack's, having beaten out his younger brother, John Wilkes, who my aunt had refused to play opposite, as the younger Booth had a reputation for being moody and hard to work with. "Time, and poetry have granted The Bard's material absolution. Audiences tolerate the message of *The Octoroon* because it is a love story. They went to *"Uncle Tom's Cabin"* because they had to--everyone was talking about it, and they go to see *Rip Van Winkle* because Joe is a national treasure." Booth raised his glass. "Audiences may or may not understand the message in a play, but we cannot bludgeon them over the head with it to make sure they do."

"Are you saying that theater should not be used to educate, Edwin?" the lovely brunette, Mencken, challenged him.

"I am, Adah."

"Then where?"

"Reverend Beecher draws a considerable audience in New Jersey on a Sunday," Booth replied sardonically.

"If plays have messages, then how the devil will audiences tell the difference between the stage and the pulpit?" Cyril Fitz-Royale demanded.

"The theatre has better costumes and lighting," Adah Mencken joked.

Passing other conversational notes, ditties and symphonies, some the quiet, the gentle whispers of flutes, others the bombastic claxons of cymbal and drum, or the gallop of quick string ensembles; so many ideas, so many fluid, creative minds discussing the problems and promise of culture and humanity. I breathed it all in. I adored the theater. I loved helping Uncle Albaugh with his experiments, but this dazzling company, so uniquely Manhattan, was utterly divine.

I moved deeper into the apartment, turning into a side room where a strident voice attracted my attention.

"The West was never ours to buy or France's to sell." It was the actor whom Booth had just toasted: Joe Jefferson, his face, a pair of dreamer's eyes, and a broad mouth, was familiar to audiences across the country. Dressed as Rip Van Winkle in all of his daguerreotypes, his name was synonymous with the role he had made a career of playing, the work itself an allegory for the American Revolution, satirizing Old-World British and European values and celebrating its hero's uniquely American, easygoing, childlike charm. In person, Jefferson's posture, like his clothes, was casually disheveled. Rather than sitting on the furniture, he seemed to drape himself over it. If he owned a comb, he had forgotten to use it. The persona of Rip Van Winkle suited him.

"A European country across the ocean cannot sell people's homelands," Jefferson insisted.

"I think the Louisiana Purchase says otherwise," Henry Clapp disagreed, entering the room, his drink refilled.

"This is what happens to a conquered people, Joe," Fitz-Royale offered the British Empire's fatalistic justification.

"But that is my point, Cyril. These Native people have not been conquered," Jefferson argued. "They are our *allies* and we owe them everything, to the very notion of democracy. Their homelands are not open for settlement, and Horace Greeley needs to stop saying they are."

Jefferson's argument made me think of what Weaver had shared about how North America, never having been one nation, never would be, as it was too large and made up of too many different cultures.

"It would be awkward to trample states' rights, then insist we honor our agreements with the Indian Nations, Joe," Clapp suggested. "It would be as if we were saying the Indians have the right to self-determination, but white people in Georgia do not."

"I don't understand why people are willing to stand up for the plight of the black man but not for the rights of our country's original inhabitants?"

"A good question, my friend, but one I cannot answer," Clapp retreated. "Perhaps you should ask Bernie." He indicated my aunt, who had just joined the group.

"Change does not come with a pair of twenty-league boots, Joe," she cautioned Jefferson. "You are only eighty years from being subjects of a king."

"Lincoln's insistence on treating everyone as if they are just as ethical as he is makes me want to shake him until he wakes up and realizes the world he *thinks* he lives in and the world he actually lives in are as far apart as the banks of the Mississippi," Jefferson grumbled. "And when I tell him what is happening, Bernie, he just smiles and says, 'I will have a talk with the rascals,' and nothing changes."

"It has taken decades to get public opinion to this point," Bernie repeated her advice for restraint. "And that holds by a thin thread. We would all like to see a better world tomorrow, but our tall friend must move with caution."

This was what Bernie really did at parties, expanding awareness of these ideas to a broader audience. Versions of what I had heard tonight would be repeated at other social events. Newspapers would write articles. Orators would give lectures. Edwin Booth said that society could not be brought to awareness through theater, but it was not because the art was not capable; it was because the audiences were not yet ready. Bernie and her friends were trying to get them ready.

Joe Jefferson turned to Henry Clay, the Editor of Harper's Weekly. "Why doesn't your paper write stories about this injustice,

Henry? Why is it always heathens murdering God fearing white people?"

"Because heathens terrorizing Christians sells newspapers, and publishing a paper is a business, Joe," Clapp answered with sardonic honesty.

"People won't buy what they don't like, or understand," Henry Clapp said, speaking around the cigar in his mouth.

"No one understood *Leaves of Grass* when it first came out, and now Walt is hailed as America's poet," Jefferson declared.

"Because *he* understood it." Clapp bobbed his head toward an older gentleman with an eagle-beak nose and bushy sideburns seated in a chair by the fire.

Our hostess, Ada Clare, was perched on a footstool at the man's feet. Bernie had made her way to one end of the sofa closest to him. Charlotte Cushman had pulled up a chair, and a half dozen men stood behind the women, silver-haired Gerald and his lover James, and Lord Fitz-Royale among them. Unlike other discussions where you could pick up the conversation by focusing on a predominant voice, this group was engaged in a close, quiet sharing, and oddly, the older man at the center was not speaking. He was listening. Those surrounding him followed his lead, listening closely to when someone spoke, and I wondered who this man was to capture such admiration in this group of luminaries.

Then, Charlotte Cushman addressed him as "Waldo." Joe Jefferson's discussion about Native people's rights and the Lincoln Administration's failures faded from my mind.

Ralph Waldo Emerson. America's philosopher and conscience was here at Ada Clare's Sunday Salon. Well, of course he was. He did not come to New York often, preferring the quiet New England countryside of his home, but he was one of them. Emerson was a Bee.

If Joe Jefferson's Rip Van Winkle characterized Americans as they wished to see themselves, Ralph Waldo Emerson was responsible for molding the young nation's ideals about who they should aspire to become and how their values should be expressed through conscience, self-reliance, and individual action. His words were freeing America from its feelings of cultural inferiority to Europe, claiming that because of the Democratic ideas Native born Americans grew up with, ideas learned by living close to Native people, they were inherently different from the recent European immigrants. Native-born Americans had never lived under the thumb of the old feudal system. They did not think or act like serfs. It was in their nature to be more independent, more inventive, and self-reliant. The elder essayist offered these ideas to the young country, and they took them up, holding them as their new truth.

Emerson's grizzled head turned toward me. Bernie followed his gaze.

"Ah, Kit, join us, won't you?" she called me to her side, reaching out her hand to draw me close. "Mister Emerson, this is my nephew, Christopher Drake," she introduced me. "We call him Kit."

"Like 'Kit' Marlow, the Elizabethan playwright," Emerson noted, looking me over. "Leonara's offspring, yes?"

"Yes. Manon's grandson."

"I know your family well." Emerson offered me his hand. I wondered why he knew anything about my family, outside the Drake women's stage work. "You have been listening to Joe's thoughts on the injustices perpetrated on our Native neighbors."

"Yes, Sir."

"We might live in a very different world if Europeans had not refused to accept that Enlightenment philosophers based their new models of government on Native American cultures."

"Yes. I have read your work." I said, shyly. "It is an honor to meet you, Sir." I wanted to ask him about the truth of everything, but I could not find the words to ask him anything.

"Charlotte, I do not think you've met my nephew yet," Bernie interrupted my introspections.

"Not properly, Bernie, no, but I believe I saw him at Pfaff's some time back." Miss Cushman's words were casual; her study of me was not. "Your aunt has told me that you have a newfound passion for the theater."

"Lighting and design," I informed her.

"Albaugh must be disappointed."

"He has not given up entirely, seeing theater as frivolous, but I do not see it as mere entertainment. I believe theater has the potential to change how people think. Books are wonderful, but it takes time to read them. With a play, you just go to a theater and in only a few hours you are exposed to many new ideas." I blushed, realizing the naive exuberance of my outburst was its own kind of impropriety. "I apologize for getting so carried away."

"You need not apologize for having passion. At least not to me." Emerson looked over at Bernie and chuckled. "Quite a young man, our Fox's Kit."

"He is," Bernie agreed, surprising me. She had never complimented me before. "Have you said hello to Mister Stratton yet, nephew?' She indicated a window enclosure. "He has been very generous with his time in mentoring you. It would be rude not to say hello."

"Of course, Aunt. I did not realize he was here. Excuse me."

Stratton was seated on the tufted pad on the window bench's sill.

"When did you get here, Charles?" I asked."

"A bit before you and Bernie. Heady company, eh? Did she bring you tonight so you could meet our American Merlin, the Sage of Concord?"

"All she said was that since I had experienced the fractious wealth of New York Society, it was only fair I should have met the other side, its artists."

"They are an impressive bunch," Stratton commented. "I don't steam in from the islands every week, but it's always worth it when I do. Talking to other creatives helps me feel less isolated in my thoughts and concerns."

"The theater is the only place I don't feel invisible," I shared.

"Everyone feels invisible sometimes, Kit," Stratton commiserated. "It's a symptom of not having your voice heard. They tell us we're too young, too old, too odd, too female, or not female enough, too short, too tall, too poor—they have a hundred justifications to set us aside. They just wish we would do the right thing and go away, so they would not have to deal with us and our strangeness anymore."

"I don't feel that way at Wallack's," I mused. "I feel like I belong there. You have experience, Charlie. Why don't you join the company?"

"And have to deal with actors?" Stratton winced. "The Gods preserve me, no. I prefer the freaks. They are less entitled." We sat together in companionable silence before he spoke again. "Some of New York's most celebrated beauties are sitting right over there." He pointed to the gathering of brunettes near Emerson. "You should go sit by one of them."

"I'm not interested."

"Yes, but if anyone asks, and they will, having something to say is a camouflage for a hidden freak. And don't tell me you can just make something up. You are the worst liar." He leaned in conspiratorially. "'The Mencken' is currently the most highly paid actress in America," He indicated the frail brunette I had noticed earlier. "She plays the title role in *Mezuzah*, a breeches role. At the end of the play, her character is forced to ride naked through the streets. The audience always stays for the final scene. Your aunt would not call her an actress, but she does look amazing on that horse." Stratton sighed.

"Why aren't there any beautiful young men here?" I demanded grumpily.

"Because Walt is in Washington." I blinked in shock at what he was inferring. "Publicly, artists play the roles required of us, Kit, but privately, we do what we want and love who we will. Artists don't care who you fuck as long as you are interesting."

"Charles Stratton, you are a disgusting little man."

"And you are a naïve little twat. Now, go sit by someone whose life story you do not already know," Stratton shooed me off.

Needle Maggie Walsh had stories, not only because she had been in the theater forever, but because she teased memories out of actors as she "uh-huhed" around a row of pins held between her lips. She would not have those stories if she remained hidden in a corner, which was what I preferred to do.

I wove my way through the Bohemians and sat on the floor next to Charlotte Cushman.

"Ah, Kit, and how is it living at Drake House?" she asked politely.

"Odd," I replied before thinking.

Cushman raised one eyebrow. "Well, perhaps you won't stay long."

"I should not have said that," I attempted a quick retreat.

"But you did."

"Please, forget it. I did not mean it," I pleaded.

"Ah, but the power and danger of words is that once spoken, they cannot be taken back. Don't worry, I won't say anything. Neither you nor Bernie needs more small troubles. If either of you catch some, they will not come from my lips."

I was still churning over my unfortunate lapse when Mark Smith entered like a tornado.

"Bernie? Where is Bernie?" he demanded, naked of niceties. "Is Lester here? Bernie, it's Mark. I need you. We're in trouble—the show is in trouble!"

My aunt made her way toward her friend, the room's attention following suit.

"What is it, Mark? What has happened?"

"The show." His shaking hands scraped his face. "They've canceled the show!"

"But we're about to open," Ada Clare processed out loud.

"In five days," Smith moaned. "That Missus Van Buren dropped in on a dress rehearsal, saw the fairy costumes, and went running to Missus Astor. Now the whole board is in an uproar. They fired me and canceled the show."

"Cowards. I am so sorry, Mark. What are you going to do?"

"I was hoping you could talk to Lester and get him to buy the show." Mark looked like a child who had just asked for a pony for the tenth time, hope and the expectation of being told no wobbling back and forth. "As it stands, the board will have to write off all production expenses. If Wallack's offered them something—anything, they'd take it. I know they would. Then Wallack's could open the show."

"Your cast…"

"They'll come over. They're contract players. If the show is canceled at the National, they're out of work. The production is ready, though—everything is done, and Bernie, it's good. I mean, really good. I don't care about my fee. I'll waive it. I just—we need to save this show."

Bernie looked thoughtful. "I'll talk to Lester," she promised. "Why don't you come in and sit a bit, settle your nerves. You can tell me about the show." She guided him to a settee, and someone handed him a drink. "If he is interested, he will have questions, but to get you a meeting, I need to present compelling reasons for Wallack's to take the show on. We close *Hamlet* at the end of next week…"

"That's why it's perfect," Smith insisted. "We can come right in behind it."

"That might work. I can't promise anything. It's Lester's decision."

"Of course. I know. I know." He took Bernie's hand. "But you will try hard, won't you, Bern? I mean, really try? It's such a good show. Really. You'll see."

"I'm sure it is," Bernie encouraged him.

Smith knocked back his drink and stood. "I need to go somewhere--do…something. I just can't remember what. But I will, once I can settle my thoughts down."

"Of course." Bernie followed him to the door. He was out and gone in seconds.

"Thank you again, Bernie. And bless you." Like when a parent has a sick child, disaster brings out the desire for divine intervention, and to Mark Smith, saving his show-child was like saving his flesh and blood, and Bernie's intervention seemed divine.

My aunt summoned me, indicating we were leaving. As I approached, I saw Mister Emerson slip my aunt an envelope of what appeared to be documents.

"I will give them to Burke." She tucked the packet beneath her cape.

"Stay safe, Little Fox," Emerson bade me quietly as I passed him. "And remember you have friends in the forest."

I wondered what he meant. I was still wondering when I climbed into bed.

Act Two, Scene Four: Wallack's, The next day.

"What you are proposing is risky, Bernie," Mister Lester replied. "We could alienate the entire Knickerbocker society. That is a lot of tickets."

"The production is a work of art," Bernie argued. "The sets, the costumes."

"The costumes," Lester groaned. "The damned costumes. They are what started this whole thing."

"Have you seen them? They are beautiful," Bernie declared.

"Wallack's is a business, Bernie. We need to pay the bills."

"Wallack's is a theater. A place of social modeling where ideas intersect with humanity."

"There's a war on. We can't intersect with anybody if we can't keep the doors open!"

"The costumes are inspired, Lester." She flipped her hand in the air, dismissive of this 'problem.' "So, add a few more leaves and vines, but don't let these old biddies kill something really amazing. The board of the National will sell you the sets and costumes for pennies on the dollar. The actors are contract players; the investment in rehearsal time has already been made. Wallack's can pick up the show for almost nothing. Think of all the free publicity created by this hubbub around the costumes. Ticket demand will soar. Everyone will *have* to see it, even if they don't admit to seeing it at first, because everyone will be talking about it."

"The biddies will pressure the other Knickerbockers to stay away."

"Let them try. These women would put sheets over Botticelli's 'The Birth of Venus' for God's sake. The costumes are more covering than the Greek statues at the British Museum or in some of their own homes. When the show opens and it's a hit, which it will be, their hypocrisy and medieval notions will be revealed for the ignorant, prudish idiocy it is. Ada Mencken wears a body suit on the back of that horse--no vines or leaves, and she's packing houses. Mezuzah is about to start a European tour."

"Europe is more open-minded about these things than New York," Lester replied.

"It's Shakespeare, Lester, not Burlesque. Just put up a rehearsal and see it for yourself. Lighting controls how much the audience sees, leaving much to the imagination. I assume we are not yet trying to control that. Mister Clare studied the backdrop and curtain mechanisms of Giancomo Torelli in Europe, and he's been talking to Wixx about how to use some of those ideas here."

"You said the production work was finished," Lester growled, thinking he had caught Bernie in a lie.

"It is," Bernie insisted innocently. "It was just a discussion between colleagues sharing what was possible, and this was weeks ago. The show would be yours, Lester. You would be in control of how much is seen or not seen, either in small costume design changes or lighting. We'll plaster the town with posters. I'll promote it at society events, and we'll get my journalist friends to write about it."

"And say what?"

"That it is beautiful, and groundbreaking. That it is art and cannot be compared to burlesque. Curiosity will fill the first week's houses, the romantic beauty and humor of the show will keep them buying tickets. Non-artists believe the human story can be defined by the wins and wars of politics, the births and deaths of great leaders, but when archeologists explore ancient history, it is the craftsmanship of the relics that defines a culture. Art tells the world who we are."

"No one will be digging up a performance of Midsummer Night's Dream, Bernie," Lester scolded her for a bad example.

"Theater is storytelling made visual," she ignored his argument. "It reaches across history to draw us into humanity's soul. That is the power of it, and that is why we sacrifice, putting so much of ourselves into doing what we do."

There was a lengthy pause on the other side of the door I was listening at.

"I will need to see an actors-only rehearsal before I decide to see where Mark has taken the direction. We're building a reputation with audiences, and we can't have any melodramatic posing. It would confuse our ticket buyers about what to expect from us."

"Of course. We can arrange a run-through for this afternoon," Bernie assured him.

"I'm making no promises, you understand?"

"I do."

There was some indiscernible grumbling, then I was required to jump quickly back from Mister Lester's office door to avoid getting hit by it as it swung open.

"He's in," Bernie announced in low tones as she marched past like a general who has just won a major battle. She might or might not be able to influence history and win the war between the states, but by God, she could get a show up.

Wixx, who had been in the meeting with Mister Lester, hurried to catch up with my aunt's long, natural stride. She was a woman of passionate energy who usually kept that energy contained, walking genteelly, like a proper British Lady, but this woman, like her ancestor, Sir Frances Drake, could conquer the seven seas from the bow of a pirate ship. Here was the Drake heritage in all of its grandeur, despotic charisma strengthened by an unrelenting certainty.

"That's not what he said," Wixx disagreed. It was a brave and foolish thing to do when my aunt was fully unfurled.

"He was going through the motions so he could justify his decision to Wallack Senior, but in his heart, he knows what is right. Lester is theater through and through. He was raised in it. He can no more let this show die than he could walk past a baby abandoned in the street and not pick it up. He won't let this show go when he has a chance of saving it. Excuse me, Wixx. I need to talk to Mark."

And she was gone.

"Should we begin the lighting plan?" I asked Wixx, as dazed as any fresh survivor emerging after a natural disaster.

"Quietly," Wixx cautioned. "I have a script. We can find a quiet place and begin to imagine what we'd like to see, but don't say anything to anyone. We have to wait until Lester announces to the company, Kit. We don't want him harboring bad feelings because he feels sidestepped. We'll need his full support."

Even though some roles had to be read in by Wallack's company members for the quickly thrown together rehearsal, by the next day, Mister Lester announced A Midsummer Night's Dream would be added to the end of Wallack's Theater season after Hamlet closed, opening one week later than it's originally scheduled opening at The National, with a few cast changes to utilize key Wallack's company members. Bernie would play the queen of the fairies, Titania, and to leverage his rising status as a leading man, Gil Colmeyer would step into the role of Lysander.

Hamlet's run had brought out the haunting aspects of our theater spirit. Whining and moaning had been heard, and a few ghoulish appearances, re-enacting scenes from the show, had given some of the cast and crew a fright, but the advent of taking on A Midsummer Night's Dream had energized more than just the company.

Watching rehearsal from the fly bridge, I could see that the young actor playing Puck was struggling; new building, new director, new leads. His skill was not able to capture what Mister Lester was asking him for. His Puck was mawkish and forced. The other actors had taken a break while this actor remained onstage, repeating his lines with varying inflections.

Someone moved quietly along the wooden walkway and sat down beside me, softly whispering the lines with the poor fellow.

I turned, and I blinked at the unfamiliar young person. I had not seen them before, and yet I felt as if I knew them, which naturally made me curious as to who they were and what they were doing here on "my" flybridge. Their legs hanging over the edge of the bridgeway were longer than my own, their arms equally long and willowy. Their hair was deeply black with distinctive and implausible white roots…like Kindle's fur. The reflection gave me pause. I considered being afraid. My heart was beating wildly, but they turned and smiled, revealing tiny, sharp teeth, and they had shockingly feline gold eyes.

"I'm sorry," I stammered, uncertain of everything about them, their gender, their clothing--a mixture of materials, vines, leaves, and patched together material remnants that screamed "fairy" costume, but more like a child's dress-up version than any of the designed creations we would be putting on stage. "I don't think we've met," I said after a shamefully long pause, just staring.

"But we have. Of course we have. Many times. Now hush," they silenced me, focusing intently on the actor below. "I must study."

The other actors returned, and the rehearsal resumed, my strange companion continuing to frown in concentration as they monitored and mimicked the action below.

"Are you the understudy?" I whispered.

"I am. I have decided," the newcomer announced.

"It isn't done that way," I warned them against disappointment. "The actor is not the one who makes that decision."

Again, they turned their attention to me. "I care not about playing a role. I care only that the show goes on as it should with all its players. That is my responsibility. I have learned three roles: Hermia, Helena, Peasblossom, and Puck."

"That's four," I pointed out.

"I did not count Peasblossom. I understand that there are no small parts, only small actors, and if the company requires a Peasblossom, I will be ready. But it is such a small role, I did not think it fair to count it."

"Kit!" Wixx was calling me.

"Well, break a leg." I exited, hurrying back to the end of the bridge that connected to the stairs, answering Wixx's call.

I enjoyed the tradition of a theater cat, and Kindle was a great theater cat. I had accepted the charming idea of a theater spirit; now I had to wonder, were the two one? Was the theater spirit inhabiting Kindle's body? Maggie had almost said as much when I was talking about the theater's spirit, and she pointed to the cat's dish and claimed she was feeding the theater's spirit. But could our theater spirit occupy, not just a cat but a human? The person I had met did not seem entirely human with its tiny, sharp kitty teeth and exotic, gold, cat eyes. Even their hair had been like Kindle's, white at the roots and dark at the tips.

All afternoon, as I held gadgets that created effects for Wixx, I thought about this strange meeting. The odd person's presence had felt so familiar, yet their appearance had been completely baffling with their feline grace, catlike eyes, and unexplainable hair coloring.

I was exploring different lighting effects, holding up objects to see what kind of shadow they would make, pulling the object closer or further away to view the changes, when Kindle came down the theater's aisle, sauntering through the house, the cat's black coat with white roots rippling with the movement of its muscles. It leaped effortlessly onto a seat and settled down to watch rehearsal.

It watched the entire rehearsal.

"This is not a cat," Wixx had said. *"It's a spirit in the body of a cat."*

Maggie was the only person I could confide my suspicions to and not end up on Blackwell's Island in the asylum.

I pulled up a chair opposite the seamstress and began badly stitching up a hole in the toe of a fairy's stocking. The seams did not have to be neat, she had informed me when I protested over trying to sew something other than a straight line, because a fairy would not be any better at wielding a needle and thread than I was. I worked on the task for a time before asking my question, as it hardly seemed fair to take up the seamstress's time so close to opening a new show without giving something in return.

"So, Wallack's theater spirit is able to inhabit the theater cat, Kindle, right?"

"They are one and the same," Maggie agreed.

"Can it make itself look like something other than a cat?" I asked, trying to seem like I was just making idle conversation. Maggie Walsh set her sewing down.

"That's not what you came to ask me. You've seen something. So, go on, out with it. What did you see?"

"I'm not sure I saw anything," I lied.

She harrumphed. "You either saw something or you didn't. If you don't have the bollocks to admit what you've seen, don't come bothering me." Maggie had little tolerance for my cowardly side-stepping about the existence of a magical world that existed alongside what most people thought of as the real world. I kept sewing, trying to sort and put order to the words I wanted to use and make them come out of my mouth, but before I had managed it, Maggie spoke again, "Go ahead then, tell me what you *almost* saw."

"I met someone up on the flybridge…"

That is not uncommon. What you mean is that you met someone you do not think is human up on the bridge." I nodded. "And you spoke to them?" I nodded again. "More than just repeating lines, this was a conversation?" I nodded. "And this time it was not Kindle?"

"Yes. Well, maybe."

"Our little spirit is growing up," she declared, gleefully.

"They were wearing a sort of wrap-around toga with bits of the vines and leaves like on the fairy costumes for Midsummer all patched together, and they looked almost human, only they had a cat's gold eyes and hair like Kindle's fur...." I could not finish. "They were watching rehearsal, saying the lines along with the actors."

"How else would they understand the show and enfold it into themselves?"

"They looked so much like Kindle, though, Maggie, but they were a person. How can a theater spirit become a person?"

"Are you asking me what the rules are? I don't know. A spirit is a wild thing, Kit. It isn't going to follow human rules. But a theater spirit is going to follow the theater's rules, and that means it will learn about transformation and changing so it looks like something else. This is a good thing, Kit. Kindle has gotten past the murder and guilt of the Scottish play, the mean-spiritedness of the School for Mean People, and the self-destruction of *Hamlet*. *A Midsummer Night's Dream* celebrates a spirit's nature. It is a good play for a young spirit to build their character around."

"So, you think this person I saw could really be Kindle?"

"Don't ask me. Ask it."

"It did say we knew each other." How did you ask a person if they were a cat?

"Spirits appreciate honesty, Kit. That is one of the reasons most people get confused and make poor bargains and bad relationships with the fey. The Fey admire honesty. They may dance around something, but they won't lie. You should stop worrying about what other people think. You are not other people. You are Christopher Drake, and the Drakes keep secrets as old as stone. Your family has an unusual history with the fey that goes back to the days of Good Queen Bess. Trust yourself, Kit. You will find more peace when you accept the world as it is in your experience, not as you have been told how it should be according to them."

Ticket sales were booming, and under Wixx's expert guidance, the lighting looked exquisite. As Bernie had predicted, the show's move to a new theater and the story of how it was saved were everywhere. Bernie and I did our part by making the rounds of society parties. A chance meeting of Mamie Anthon and her beau, Stuyvesant

Fish, now officially engaged, gave me the opportunity to tell them about the play, pointing out that it was exactly the sort of thing Mamie wished to encourage and fit right into her plans to shatter stuffy Knickerbocker notions.

"It is a very fun and understandable play, Mamie," I explained.

Mamie frowned. "I would like to go, Christopher, I really would, but I don't think Papa would allow it with all the talk of scandalous costumes."

"Then have Styvie take you." I was not giving up so easily. I looked to her young man, a rather plain fellow of good Dutch stock, with common features that kept him from standing out, which served Mamie just fine because she was animated enough for both of them and enjoyed being the center of attention. "Mister Fish, are you up for the adventure, Sir?" I prompted him.

He smiled first at Mamie, as if to make sure he had her support before replying that he was and that I should call him Styvie as Mamie did, for we were all three friends and accomplices now as well.

"Thank you. The cast will be truly grateful for your support. I can have tickets set aside for you," I offered.

"I wouldn't think of it, Mister Drake. I am perfectly able to pay for a box for our friends, if there is one available."

"I will make sure of it. Opening night?"

"Of course," Styvesant Fish agreed. "I consider our attendance a small, but important way to show my support for the endeavor. It cannot have been easy for young Wallack to make such a leap of faith in the face of a potential boycott by the Old Guard. I commend his bravery. We will be proud to do our part, however small."

"You promise there won't be any long-faced lectures, Christopher?" Mamie demanded. "I cannot abide being lectured."

"I promise, Miss Mamie. Just watch the show and allow yourself to be caught up in the story.""I will try," she agreed.

I thanked them again and moved on to work my pitch into another group's conversation. It was easier than I had imagined.

"Please thank your aunt for the kind invitation to dinner last Sunday," Charles Stratton found me. "It was a pleasure to meet your Gil."

"He's not *my* Gil," I said in a tone that was meant to keep the conversation only between us.

"He is handsome and charming in a you-are-much-too-innocent-to-survive in this world way. I can see why you are so smitten."

"I am not smitten, and neither is he," I protested. "At least not with each other."

Stratton shrugged. "Whatever you say, Kit. I like him as Lysander, though, and of course Bernie's Titania is always a treat, though this new touch of evil she's added is interesting. Trust Bernie to find some refreshing nuance to add to a role."

"And what do you think of Puck?" I asked.

Stratton winced. "I'm glad I do not have to wear the costume."

"No one would want that." I poked him in the belly.

"I think I liked you better when you were a shy, callow youth who barely spoke," Stratton teased me back.

"You are avoiding my question. What did you think of Puck, Charles?"

Stratton took a deep breath and blew it out, buying himself time before he had to answer. "I know this sounds like sour grapes because he is playing a role I have played, but you asked. I think Lester should watch him. I do not know how he measured up before this Wallack's version, but in this cast, he is in way over his head, he knows it, and he's scared shitless to get on the stage with Bernie and Gil and the rest of them. He is out of his league."

I understood what he was saying. Watching rehearsals, often with some of the best actors of our time and listening to the direction given to the actors, then seeing how it was applied to their performances, or not, depending on the actor's skill, had been an education. I was no actor, but I recognized a good performance from a mediocre one, and a great actor from a good one. Anyone could recognize a bad actor.

"Compared to the depth that Bernie was bringing to Titania, or even the expanding skills of Gil Collmeyer, the young actor playing Puck is just painful to watch. He's like a drowning puppy who inspires only pity."

Charles was right. What should have been the magical thread that held the performance together kept twisting, knotting, and breaking. Mister Lester kept working with him, calling extra rehearsals, but that only weakened the actor's confidence. He simply could not grasp the fey nature of the character and that fey did not mean clownish.

Aside from Puck's less-than-outstanding talents, the production was running smoothly until the night before we opened, when the actor playing Puck did not show up for costume or makeup call.

Needle Maggie had once told me a story about how, in his declining years, the once great Junius Booth Senior had fallen into drinking so heavily that a stagehand had been assigned to tend to him, searching all the local pubs to locate him and bring him to the stage to make his entrance cues.

I shared the story with Young Giddy.

"I used to do that for my old Grand Da' when he was here, at Wallack's," Giddy had confessed at the time. "It wasn't official, like, but all the stagehands knew when it happened. Grandad would exit the stage and wander out the stage door and into one of the local pubs, then, as his next cue was coming up, I'd go fetch him, bring him back, and push him onstage. I'll look for the bloke," Giddy assured us. "I know all the pubs."

An hour before curtain, Giddy had not found our Puck.

"Get a message to Charlie Stratton," Mister Lester commanded his assistant.

"He won't do it," Mark Smith groaned. "The costume is too…"

"I don't care if he wears his steamship commodore suit," Lester shouted. "I need a Puck, now!"

I licked my lips. "I know someone who could do it," I admitted cautiously. "They know the lines and the blocking. They've been watching rehearsals…"

"They've been watching rehearsals?" Mister Lester did not like that at all.

"I think they're one of the minor fairies that came over from The National," I prevaricated. "I will try to find them and ask if they'll come see you."

Bernie joined us. "If you are able to get word to Charlie Stratton and he agrees, and he is even in town, Lester, it will be at least an hour before he gets here," she added her pull to my suggestion. "The house is filled with journalists and investors. They're already primed by their preconceived ideas to either love this show or despise it. We can't hold the curtain. It will signal there's a problem, and with all the controversy this show has already seen, we will lose them. They are going to think the worst and leave. Just let Kit's little replacement muddle through the lines before Charles gets here." Bernie looked at me, silently informing me that she had just stuck her neck out for me, and my mystery replacement better come through.

"All right." Lester nodded. "See if you can coax your friend to walk the role until Stratton shows up. But I want to see them in my office first, hear them give a few lines of one of Puck's speeches. I am not going to be embarrassed over this."

And that is how the theater spirit, Kindle, became Puck in A Midsummer Night's Dream.

Perched on the stage right tower, I noticed when the door at the back of the house opened and Charles Stratton slipped in, standing at the door so he could see down the aisle. Remaining very still, he watched Kindle play Robin Goodfellow, the iconic Puck. Maybe it was the theater spirit's thin and sprite-like physicality, maybe it was the strange feline grace combined with kittenish leaps and rolls that made the performance so charming. Their piquant face and cat-like eyes required no makeup to become otherworldly. Kindle's delivery was effervescent; all sparkles and bubbles before plunging into unexpected darkness, their long fingers and the small-toothed smile were threatening menaces our bodies recognized as dangerous, and our instinct reacted to as such. And still our eyes could not look away. Kindle knew the lines and delivered them with mastery. And they knew how to work their audience. How could they not? They were Theater.

I could not see Charlie Stratton's expression from my tower perch, but I could see that he neither left to come backstage to take over the role nor left to go home.

At the end of the show, I climbed down from my tower and hurried through the house. Mister Lester's office door was open, excited conversation spilling out, accompanied by the musical ring of crystal decanters and self-congratulatory celebration. Stratton was headed for the lobby doors to the street when I caught up with him.

"So, what did you think?" I stopped him.

He turned, the biggest, silliest grin stretching the lower portion of his face. "Was this your discovery?"

"I can't take credit."

"Then where did they come from? They can't have just magically appeared out of nowhere."

"Something like that." I smiled, keeping my friend's secret as if it were my own. "Some of us are just born with theater in our blood."

"He…she…they were exquisite, Kit." Stratton tipped his hat. "Absolutely wonderful. Please tell them that I said so and give them my congratulations."

"You'll be here tomorrow night for opening?" I asked.

"I wouldn't miss it. I'll bring P.T. After the show, you can introduce us."

I gulped. I had not thought about what would happen after the show. Everyone would want to meet this new actor. The newspapers would want to know their name, where they grew up, a hundred details that Kindle did not have; a hundred questions they could not answer.

They had been too good. They might have hidden onstage as Peasblossom, but they could not hide as Puck.

Kindle's shy, kittenish nature had found all the attention after the curtain came down overwhelming, and they had disappeared like Cinderella running from the ball, leaving the cast and Mister Lester with questions. As soon as I returned from the lobby and reappeared on the stage, I was engulfed.

"They are very shy," I explained again and again. "Quite young. No, not experienced. This is their first time on the stage as an actor. Yes, that makes it their theatrical debut." I was making up Kindle's story as I went. "Yes, it was a big night for them—quite unexpected. It is a lot to take in. They live with an uncle who would not approve if he knew what 'Kay' was doing." The improvisation of the name Kay, using the cat's initial, had not been planned, but I had to call them something. "They will use a stage name," I explained.

Finally, people began to drift off to their dressing rooms or make their way home. While the actors soaked up the audience's praise, and the audience basked in performance-afterglow, the stagehands quietly tucked the theater in for the night and set up the ghost light.

Helping Wixx shut down, I invented an excuse to go up to the flybridge, knowing that was where I would find Kindle.

"There you are," I said, speaking with soft affection I always used with Kindle. "Everyone was asking about you."

"Was it all right?" the theater spirit asked shyly.

"It was better than alright. I didn't think about what would happen afterward, though, so I had to make up a few things about you. I couldn't exactly call you by your cat name." There, I had said it. "You are Kindle, aren't you?"

They frowned. "I did not think about what would happen after, either."

"We'll have to go over what I said, so that our stories match, or you can just say I didn't know what I was talking about. You really were amazing, Kay."

They smiled. "Kay?"

I shrugged. "Like I said, I had to think of something fast. If I had used Kindle, the whole company would be in on your secret."

"Our secret," she corrected me. "I like that we have a secret together. It was exciting to be seen, but also frightening. Then after, when everyone crowded around me, I didn't know what to do. There were so many people, they were so close, and they wanted so much. I did not know the lines I should say. What did they want from me, Kit? I gave all the cues—I did all the lines. What else did they want?"

"More," I said sadly.

"They wanted to hold me and pet me, so I purred for them?"

Of course, Kindle thought of physical interaction like a cat, which was all they had known, until now. This was going to be complicated. Kay could not be left alone to navigate this new world. They could too easily be taken advantage of. They needed a protector.

"They don't really know what they want, Kay, but I have seen this before, with my aunt, Bernadette. After a good performance, people's emotions are raw and all churned up—like there is too much emotion and it's overflowing. They don't know what to do with it, but they connect those feelings to the actors, so they want to touch them and be close to them." I had seen audience members crowded around the stage door waiting with such longing, such confused hope that seeing the actor would somehow return them to themselves.

"I cannot give them anything more," Kay said.

"When the lights are up and you are onstage, that is as true a knowing as anyone ever has," I explained. I was not sure if it was *the* truth, but it felt like *our* truth, Kindle's and mine.

"The way they looked at me—*at* me, not through me. It felt so different."

I understood that.

"The audience sees the actors, but they don't see what you do, Kit."

"Stagehands work the magic, but they are supposed to be invisible."

"Like me."

"Like you, sometimes, but whether they see us or not, we are all part of the performance."

"The secret part."

"Yes."

"Like me."

"Yes. We have some decisions to make about your future and how we keep people from discovering who you really are."

"They cannot know me. I am in disguise."

"Yes. You are enchanted, like Bottom."

"Bottom is funny, but stupid. I am not stupid," Kay disagreed.

"No, you are not, but you are a spirit--a magical being, and most people would be afraid if they knew that."

"Not you?"

"No. Not me," I agreed.

Kay looked perplexed. "But isn't that why they come to the theater, to see the magic?"

"Yes, they need to believe what they are seeing is an illusion. They would be frightened if they knew it was real, because then they wouldn't understand it."

"They come to a play wanting the performances to seem real, but they would be afraid if they knew it was? That really is stupid. It doesn't make any sense."

"People don't usually make sense, Kay. It's just the way they are."

"And they need to be loved, anyway."

"We all need to be loved," I agreed.

"I think I'd like to be a cat again now." The illusion of Kay's image came apart, becoming transparent, then reforming into the little black cat, Kindle. I could not say I was not pleased. Kay was a fascinating creature, but Kindle had been with me at Wallack's from the beginning, and I loved the little cat.

It crawled daintily into my lap and curled into a ball. It had been a long day.

Act Two, Scene Five: Drake House, NYC, May

I always knew we were an uncommon family. I did not realize how uncommon. Maggie claimed the Drakes had a long history of connection to the fey. Kit Becket wanted to know why. Somewhere, there was an answer, and it called me.

As quiet as dust, I spied on Drake House's occupants, my hauntings now a nightly ritual as I stalked secrets. Lurking at windows, I marked shuttered lanterns tossing spears of light into the darkness as shadows stole from the alley to the carriage house. They always came at night. None were blue, or wore crowns, or quoted Shakespeare. These were the shadows of men, their comings and goings unremarked pieces of the house's secrets.

It was not a slamming door or a scratching branch that brought me from my uneasy slumber. It was fear. Rising through the house like river vapors from the Hudson, it seeped through the crevices between the floorboards.

There is nothing to fear, I told myself, drawing the stillness of the room to me, waiting, feeling the familiar creaks and moans of the wooden building. Embraced by layers of cotton quilts and down comforters, I shivered, reaching for invisibility: my only true covering.

The sheets whispered fears I did not know, cotton rubbing cotton. I climbed from my bed, padding on bare feet to the window that looked out over the street.

Everything was quiet. The other houses around the square, night-dark, the park empty.

Had Bernie come home yet? I had not heard the carriage, but sometimes when the yard was not wet, she rode around to the back and came in from the carriage house.

It had not rained for several days, but the wind was up now, and fat raindrops began splattering against the windowpanes.

I pulled on a robe, eschewing my hard leather-soled slippers, and cautiously turned the knob of my bedroom door. Having learned which treads squeaked and which stoically bore human weight without complaint, I stretched my steps to remain in contact with the stoic. Not a drawn breath revealed my progress along the gallery to the stairs.

It was not an audible sound that led me to the back of the house and the stairway to the cellar; it was a lament that vibrated the air, my flesh, my bones; a ripple shed by humanity, groaning beneath the weight of desperation.

Replaying my slow, stealthy knob-turning, I breathed the must and mold of the cellar. The unplastered lath in this part of the house swelled and shrank seasonally. Spring rains had swollen the wooden strips, thinning the cracks between the boards. A wink of candlelight revealed movement on the other side.

If I were an innocent bystander, unaware of Drake House's secretive nature, I might have called out to demand that whoever was there identify themselves, but those who hid here had been assisted with the intention that they remain hidden.

I held, motionless, watching the candle's flame flicker with the tempered breath of the Hidden Guest. A brown eye circled by a fringe of dark lashes and ebony skin pressed at the space between the lath slats.

"Is someone there? Who are you?" The shadow's tremulous breath formed words.

"I am no one," I replied in my head. "I am no one," I repeated, wishing to comfort the lost soul. "You have nothing to fear from me. You are safe."

"I am so hungry. How much longer?" The tight, half-spoken syllables felt cut from the hunted slave's throat.

"It is almost day. It will not be long now." My assurance was met by a whimper of gratitude and some moist snuffling.

I tiptoed up the stairs, using the stealth I had gained during weeks of nocturnal wanderings, closing the door with the same silent care I employed in opening it.

Drake House is a station on the Underground Railroad.

All that suspicion, and in the end, it was so simple—far simpler than my imaginings, but it explained the secretiveness and why Bernie had been so quick to help Mister Livington's escapees.

The Livingston estates were on Staten Island. If his family operated a Station House there as well, and refugees had arrived unexpectedly while he was not at home, it would have presented a problem. But, as my aunt insisted, we never spoke of the events of that night.

When I returned to my room, I found the little blue man, Spin, perched on the end of my bed.

"What are you doing, half-man?" he growled, his voice as gritty as sandpaper.

"When I cannot sleep, I walk." There was no point in trying to lie to him. Charles said it, I was a terrible liar, and I suspected this creature was quite a good one, if he was real.

"I am real," he informed me, though I had not spoken my question out loud.

"Which is exactly what a figment of my imagination would say," I countered.

He leaped across the space between us and slapped his long, bony fingers and claw-like nails across my cheek. The sting of their slice was real. When I reached up to touch it, spittle-like beads of blood stained my fingertips.

"Tomorrow, you will have marks there on your cheek. And there will be no more questions about me being real."

"How will I explain that?"

The blue man shrugged. "However you wish." He smirked.

"What if I tell Bernie that you did it?"

He cocked his head from side to side. "Humans are…unpredictable, and she has not been very honest with you so far."

"Neither have you. You made me forget," I accused him.

"You should still be forgetting," he complained.

"What's changed?"

"You."

"I remember it all now, you know." One long eyebrow quirked up as if to say he doubted the veracity of my statement. "Even as a baby, you did not like me. People always like babies."

He looked bored. "I am not 'people'."

"I figured that part out. What are you then?"

"I am me. Your Mother called me Spin."

"You used to run away from me. You aren't running now."

"You used to smell of Becket. You don't so much anymore. Though your right hand and left ear still do. I would be happy to cut them off for you." He dropped to the floor, threatening to move closer to me.

"Please no," I said quickly. "I would rather you did not. Perhaps if I scrub them extra hard next time I wash…

"It would have to be with vetiver, with some sage and frankincense in the soap," he informed me.

"I will ask Burke to pick some up. You should know that I bore no love for Johnathan Becket. I am happy he is gone from our lives."

"You think I should know that? Because you imagine it will make some difference between us?"

"It might. It is another thing we have in common, besides my mother." My honesty seemed to calm him.

"You are less him now. Less Becket," he said quietly. Because…you are all her." His face sank as if his soul was falling and might fall forever, bits of it shaved away to nonexistence by the strong emotions overtaking him, aunts, uncles, cousins: all the relatives of Sadness.

"Mother," I clarified.

"Yes. Leonie." He had endured his separation from her for years, as had I. I knew that feeling…the emptiness of her absence, the grief.

"Do you know where she is?" I asked him.

His entire being slumped, limp, like a leaf in drought. *"Far away. Too far away,"* he despaired, disappearing from my room.

The next morning, I was reaching for an egg in the backyard coop when a shadow engulfed me from behind. Whirling around, I found Weaver hovering, his bulk too large for comfort. I took a step backward.

"I saw you last night." His expression was foreboding.

"I couldn't sleep." I forced myself to face him, though every part of me wanted to cower down on the hay at my feet.

"We are none of us idiots here."

A pitchfork lying on the straw behind Weaver began to rise without the aid of a human hand, rotating until the tines pointed toward the driver's broad back. Spin appeared, holding it, prepared to thrust it into Weaver. "I told them bringing a child into this house would be trouble. They should have sent you to school before you unpacked your bags."

"I'm sorry. I meant no harm."

"There's no need to go sneaking around," the driver muttered, backing down from his threatening stance. "If you need something, ask." He stalked back to the horse stalls.

He would tell Bernie, and that would be it. She would know that I knew, and she had not told me. She would decide what was to be done next. I thought about Wallacks and all my friends there: Kindle, Maggie, Wixx, and Gil. I thought about Charles Stratton and Dweetie. I was building a life here. I could not lose that now.

My choices were to back down and plead to stay or press forward to understand my aunt's secrets. Running a Station House was one thing; having a fey creature living in it was quite another.

"You were up late last night," I greeted Albaugh as soon as I finished breakfast. He did not break his focus on the book before him.

"I am a gentleman-scientist of leisure. I work when I can, and sleep when I cannot."

"And Bernie was not yet home." I waited to see if he would respond to my bait. He did not, continuing to read. I went a bit further. "It seems no one in the household sleeps until she returns from her parties and dinners." Albaugh looked up over the edge of his wire-rimmed spectacles. Was he looking at the long, red scratch on my cheek? He did not mention it.

"If you have a point, Kit, please make it so I can return to my book uninterrupted."

"I just wonder why everyone worries so much when Aunt goes to these society functions. Parties and soirees are not generally considered to be that dangerous." Albaugh continued looking at me, waiting for me to finish, though I thought I had.

"I understand that you escorted Bernie to one. What do you think?"

I thought through the night, the political conversations, the attempt by Wood to get me drunk and make me an ally so I would reveal information about Bernie, the social intrigues I observed, the way the night ended in a secret spiriting away of refugees.

"Social danger is not physical danger. One can be ignored, and probably should be; the other is immediate and possibly life-threatening and should not be."

Albaugh shook his head. "Wrong. Because the first may quickly become the second. Danger is a master of disguise, and this city is a viper's nest of political intrigue, spies infiltrating every echelon of society from the highest social circles to the mobs of Five Points. Informers lurking in the shadows, hoping to glean a secret they might leverage or sell. Street vermin will slit your throat for the coins in your pocket. The rich are afraid for their futures. The poor drown daily in desperation."

"The household stays up because they worry that Aunt Bernie may stumble into trouble due to the war?"

"When you've lost someone, you'll understand." A shadow passed over Albaugh's face. "I'm sorry, Kit. Of course, you understand, though you are too young to know such sorrows."

I appreciated his kindness, but questions still itched beneath my skin.

"If it is so dangerous, Uncle, why does she go?"

"That is a question only your aunt can answer, but I do not recommend asking." Albaugh returned to his book. "She will not answer. Not honestly anyway."

Act Two, Scene Six: Drake House, NYC, May

"What did you do before you drove for my aunt?" I asked Weaver. Weaver, whose activities were many, and for whom the explanations were few, though now that I knew about Drake House's status as a Station House, some of his activities made more sense.

It was early, before breakfast for the late sleepers, but I had been up for some time and hoped by helping him with the horses, I might soothe any ill feelings he still might harbor toward me after catching me spying.

He continued trimming Tad, one of the team's, hooves while I smoothed a clean cloth over the large animal's shiny black coat.

"Were you a soldier in the war?" I asked him.

"A soldier in *a* war," he replied. "Different decade, different continent, but it's all the same. Somebody wants something, so they give you a gun and tell you to go kill people who don't look like you, or talk like you, or call God by the same name, so they can have it and when it's all over you are left with the guilt and a gun, and if you are lucky, all your arms and legs. I fought in the Anglo-Sikh War in the Punjab with Burke."

That explained the trust between Weaver and Burke.

"Were you ever out West?"

"How far West do you mean?" Weaver asked. It seemed like a yes or no question to me, but apparently, he did not see it that way.

"California?"

"Never been to California."

He did not seem very interested in answering my questions, but I plodded on, keeping them casual and unrushed. "Where…?"

"Texas," he answered, to stop me from talking. "I've been to Texas." He paused. "But it wasn't Texas then."

"You were there when it was still Mexico." He nodded. "Did you like it? Do you think you'll go back someday?"

Weaver stopped trimming and straightened up. The scratch on my cheek was obvious, quite red, and a bit angry, but Weaver made no comment. Men like him did not discuss their injuries.

"Life changes," he said. "I never would have figured I'd live in New York City either. But the West… is complicated."

"You don't think people should be settling there?"

His brown eyes grew distant, as if he saw and felt a pain unknown to the rest of us.

"The West doesn't need settling. People already live there," his speech was laconic but steady. "Been living there since time began. Now these refugees from European countries are coming, tossing all these different people together on this land they have no shared history with and no understanding of, everyone with their ideas about how life should be lived, and what they're owed. But life doesn't owe us. The land doesn't owe us. We owe it. If people listened, they'd know that." His dry, callused hand smoothed the big horse's rump, and he shuffled away. He was done talking.

I thought about Weaver's rough, weathered face, his dark, silver-streaked hair. I assumed his coloring was a result of the hours he spent outdoors, but maybe I was wrong.

"And what will we do today?" Bernie mused as she came to the breakfast table. "Get ready for the show, do the show, recover from the show, and tomorrow we will get up and do the same again. It will be a relief when the season is over. I am ready for a break. Bernie dished up spicy eggs from a side table. "Oh, Kit, the Lowdons sent a trunk of your grandmother's things. I've asked Weaver to take it up to your room. Who knows, perhaps they've sent Leonie's rapier."

"Thank you, Aunt."

"And I wish to speak to you about your future," she surprised me with a new subject. "Albaugh has pointed out that I may have imposed my ideas of career choices on you in ways that might be uncomfortable for you. I assure you that was not my intention, and if you would prefer to go to…"

"I don't want to cause trouble," I stopped her finishing, sure I knew what she was going to say.

"And, as far as I know, you have not." She sat and unfolded the latest edition of Harper's Weekly. "Is there something you feel you need to confess?"

"I won't interfere or go off on my own anymore," I promised. "I won't watch from the windows. I am careful. I would never say anything about what goes on here at the house. Please, don't send me away."

Bernie lowered the newspaper. "Who said anything about sending you away? Is this some invention of Albaughs? Where did you get such a notion?"

I almost said, "Charlotte Cushman," but that would have been unfair. The situation was not Charlotte's doing, but my guilt.

"I know Uncle Albaugh believes I should be at a school and that many people consider that sending their young men away to boarding school makes their future, but I am not like them, Aunt. I am like you. I won't fit in."

Bernie looked nonplussed. "And I wouldn't want you to. Dreadful places, boarding schools. You are perfectly well educated, Kit. I cannot think what more an American school would teach you, except their own constrained values. It is true your education was rather unorthodox, but Manon did not send you to me so I could ship you off to some academic manufacturing plant that turns out snobbish young men unable to think for themselves. Don't worry about Albaugh. He is his own universe. I thought you liked going to the theater, working with Wixx and his gadgets, and learning about set design."

"I do."

"Then what is all this nonsense about school? Has something happened to upset you?"

"No," I lied. We looked at each other for some time before she spoke again.

"Keep your secrets then. When you are ready to trust me, I am here."

"But I do trust you, Aunt," I protested. "Of course I trust you."

Idabelle walked by the doorway and waved as she headed out to the orphanage. Bernie's mood changed.

"You shouldn't," she stopped me from saying more. "Just because a person has power over you, does not mean you should trust them. Adults are always putting their needs before those of children, and people like me can be quite blind to others' needs. Manon and your mother made choices I was unwilling to make. I am no one's idea of a young person's guardian, but they are gone, and we are here."

"My mother is not gone," I reminded her.

We intently did not look at the other.

"May I be excused?" I said finally.

"Of course."

I went upstairs, closing the door of my room before kneeling beside the trunk the Lowdon's had sent. My hands shook and my vision blurred as I unbuckled the straps and turned back the lid. The scents of leather, lavender, and parchment memories rose from the contents. I had no confidence the Lowdons would send me anything I cared about. They would not have recognized an item of sentimental value. To them, emotion was a foreigner not to be trusted. But buried in the detritus of my grandmother's life, I might find a small relic sacred only to me.

Or perhaps deadly snakes.

Below a layer of crumpled newspapers were the daguerreotypes that had decorated my grandmother's piano, an image of my parents and baby-me at my christening. There were others of my mother and me in exotic locations, India, the Sandwich Islands, and Massachusetts. Mixed among them were pictures of my mother dressed in the costumes of characters from stage plays she had done in London before she married Johnathan Becket, many of them duplicates of those I had seen in my aunt's scrapbook. The next layer down was more pictures. These, I knew well, as they had been displayed in Manon's home. Beneath them were ink drawings of my grandmother as a young woman costumed in roles she had portrayed in London: Helena, in *A Midsummer Night's Dream*, and Beatrice, in *Much Ado About Nothing*. These were also new to me, theatrical images being thought unacceptable for display by the conservative Lowdon's, part of their campaign to scour my grandmother's past as a Drake.

Below the framed sketches and daguerreotypes was a christening gown, tiny, white embroidered slippers, and an equally elaborate cap. I set them aside and peeled back the next layer, sorting through books and journals with satin ribbons marking the writer's progress. Within one, I read a page describing Abott Lowdon's brief courtship of my grandmother. Her decision to remarry had not been precipitated by romantic love but by common respect and friendship for her husband's former partner and the life he offered her and her young child, Leonara. Security and compatibility were a common trade-off for a woman in Manon's position, widowed with a young child. After her first husband, Avery, died, Bernie's anger at her sister for leaving their life together to marry had made it awkward for Manon to return to live under her sister's dominance. Marrying Abott Lowdon seemed the easier path.

I was reminded of Gil's statement that men could not understand the limited choices women faced. I had little confidence that my maleness would grant me the crown of superiority other men accepted as their due, trapped in an in-between world neither confined, nor protected, as a female might be, nor admired and respected as was the expectation of a family man. Gil could take these things for granted. I could not.

I opened another marked journal. The page held only this brief entry:

Leonie has had a letter from our Dear Friend. The Fox departs for California this week. May God be with her and protect her and her kit, because Johnathan Becket certainly will not.

It was unsigned, but the journal and handwriting were my grandmother's. Manon had never spoken ill of my father in my presence, but her words on the page were evidence that she had harbored misgivings. I wondered who "our dear friend' might be.

Thinking other entries might provide a clue, I chose another journal, a fabric-bound collection of art and personal writings, with loose folded letters inserted between the pages. I drew one out and opened it.

Dear Friend,
It has been some time since we last corresponded. I recognize much has changed in our respective lives, but presuming on our former relationship, I am compelled to put down my thoughts and fancies on paper.

E.F. Winters

I am living on the West Coast, far from friends and family. My husband is often away, leaving me much leisure time. I have come to treasure my freedom, roaming the fringing forests and sandy beaches of San Diego Bay, riding out to the coastal cliffs on horseback, or rowing out in a small rowboat. A local has offered to teach me to sail, and I think I will accept, as it seems that learning to navigate and using sails to capture the wind would be a useful skill.

The small inlets around the bay here teem with the wildlife following their pursuits, and the coastal view from the cliffs, called Punta del Loma by the Spanish, and Amat Kunylily by the local Kumeyaay, allows one to see for miles to the North, the South, and far out to sea. There is much to observe if you are patient and do not frighten the wildlife during their activities.

Most days, the coastal weather is very fine, and I take advantage of it, walking or riding in the morning and again as the day wanes. I find the habit suits my constitution and improves my health.

The ships that sail along the coastline fly flags of many colors. A child from our village who often accompanies me on my wanderings informs me fancifully that the vessels we spy on are pirate ships seeking gold and silver treasure. If I had a telescope allowing him to see the flag's details, I could prove his error, but as I do not own such an apparatus and there are no shops here where such an item might be obtained, I am unable to prove my case. Perhaps the child is right, and it is only adult certainty in a world we pretend to know that keeps me from seeing the world as he does. If you visit, and I hope you do, you might bring your device so the question may be settled. If you are unable to visit, perhaps one of our mutual friends in the forest could be persuaded?

Having no one else to whom I may pour out my thoughts, I am grateful for your patience in reading my ramblings, though you may find them of little value and may wish to simply burn them.

Yours in friendship,
L B

I could not guess to whom the letter had been written. "Dear Friend" was so nondescript that it granted the recipient complete anonymity, but the text lacked the intimacy between a daughter and a mother. Whoever the original recipient of the letter was, they must have passed it on to Manon. Was this the same person my grandmother referred to in her journal? I opened the second letter.

Dear Friend,

I write again, imposing on your patience with my habit of putting pen to paper to sort my thoughts. Despite its challenges and the lack of comforts here, there are things I love about life in Southern California. The people in the village have an honest nature and a refreshing openness, and the country around us is both wild and gentle with long, golden days and stunning sunsets reflected in the bay waters.

Today, my young companion and I spent the afternoon on the shores of the bay observing mink playing with fish they captured. There were at least a dozen silver-scaled varieties, and half as many with golden scales. Hidden among the trees and remaining quite still, we were able to observe them for some time without being seen.

The mink stored their catch in a hole under a large rock near the confluence of two seasonal creeks that empty into the bay, North of the village. I do not know the creek's names, or even if they have names, but I am confident I could find them again and intend to return to observe further episodes of the mink's drama. Walking the two miles home in the late afternoon sun, I had to wonder what the effects on the local wildlife's activities will be when the military engineers arrive to build the new fort the administration is considering. If these plans come to pass, I think our animal friends will find their freedom to pursue and capture their silver and gold prizes much confined.

I have not heard from you regarding the possibility of a visit from you or one of our friends. The challenges of travel here are not exaggerated, but sailing vessels do put in with some frequency at the Port of Los Angeles, and there is a coach service that runs irregularly from that town to San Diego. I recommend making inquiries at Banning and Alexander, as the schedule changes weekly.

Yours in Friendship,
L B

Uncertain what to make of this, I opened the third letter.

Dear Friend,

I send you the following story, hoping you might pass it along, confident you will know the proper contact. I understand it is unlikely anything will come of my scribblings, and if you find them unworthy, I beg you to spare us both embarrassment and burn them at once.

Despite my lack of confidence in their contents, I am sincere in my need to share my story and ask advice about the best direction for the character of the vixen regarding the safety of her kit.

"In a burrow-house beneath an oak tree where the woods gave way to the pastoral haunts of men, lived a vixen and her kit. Theirs was an isolated existence, but sometimes the farmer's hound, a creature of a changeable nature, came around to brag about his grand life in the big house South of the woods. His visits were always unexpected and a bit unnerving as the vixen did not trust the hound's friendship or his sharp, flashy teeth. Whenever she caught the hound's scent, she always hid her kit so the hound would not see her offspring.

They were fox-kind, not wolves, and not rabbits. So, the vixen taught the young kit the skills a fox needed to survive: strategy and stealth; how to blend into the brush and tall grasses, how to run and change directions, and hide. However patient she was, she recognized that her kit was very young, and this worried her. Their burrow was cozy and dry inside, but outside the world felt more dangerous every day, and if something were to happen to her, her kit would be all alone."

That is as far as I have written. I hope that with your greater experience, you may offer advice to the vixen, and me as her voice, on whether she should send her kit away, or should rely on a mother's instinct that a kit is always safest in its mother's care. There is also the danger, not revealed in the body of the story, that the kit's father might return, increasing the mother and her offspring's danger. Please share your thoughts.

I look forward to your reply. Yours as ever,
LB

I lowered the last letter, looking at the wall without seeing the floral design of the wallpaper.

This last letter was written while my mother and I were both still in San Diego. She never mentioned having any literary ambitions. Her advice to the reader to burn the letter if they found its contents unworthy favored it having been burned. Yet here it was. Was there a different purpose for the odd style of this story-letter?

The possibilities wrestled to populate my mind, but I could not decide which should be allowed to settle into first position. If the characters were myself and my mother, why hide the vaguely concealed dilemma about a mother fox and her kit? And why call me a "village child' instead of owning our relationship?

My friend, Mateo, the son of the woman who helped us with housekeeping and cooking at the saltbox house, was the only "village child" in our lives, but Mateo had never accompanied my mother and me on our wanderings. He and I explored alone together. So, why the pretense?

I answered myself: *Your mother feared if her letters were intercepted, it would put you in danger.*

But our lives were not a dime ʹnovel. No one would have any interest in reading my mother's correspondence.

I recalled how Grandma Manon scoured newspapers and journals for references to events on the West Coast. What was she looking for? A lone female in the background of some artist's sketch of a skirmish between Union and Confederate forces along the California Coast?

Leonie Becket was not a soldier or a pirate. She was a mother. *And a spy.*

Imagination dangled the impossible possibility before me, and once the thought was formed, it had to be accepted or entirely dismissed.

I favored dismissal, but Aunt Bernadette's transformation into Lady MacBeth stopped me. Onstage, night after night, my aunt skillfully flogged her fellow actors with raw emotion before tossing them to smash on the rocks. What would it be like if she imported her onstage skills to her offstage life? And my mother was my aunt's student.

The mysteries of Drake House squeezed me until I could not catch my breath. I needed more information—information I did not have.

But there were others who did. I got up from the floor and started for the door.

"You do not know what you are doing," the little blue man appeared, blocking my exit.

"No, I do not," I admitted. "Are you going to tell me?" He just looked at me, not moving. "That's what I thought."

"There will be consequences," he warned.

"I welcome them."

"Only because you underestimate their outcomes," there was a pleading to his gravelly voice. "Your mother would not want you to do this."

"What do you know of it?" I hurled my words at him. "She is *my* mother. What is she to you? Nothing."

"I know everything," the little man argued. "All the dirty little secrets of the Drake line for hundreds of years, all the lies and deceptions and infidelities that made you who you are today—I know them all."

My hands wrapped around his turkey gobbler's throat. He gasped and began to vanish, then phased back in, unable to complete the action.

"Take those words back!" I shouted at him.

"To do that, I would have to put my fingers down your throat, for you have already swallowed them." He wiggled a hand before my face, long, bony, claw-like fingers with talon nails moving inches from my face. I released his neck, starting to gag. "By all that's true, I wish you were truly a Becket." He stepped out of my reach. "Because then I could kill you and be done with your idiocy." He disappeared.

I fell against my bedroom door, slamming it open, and stumbled down the stairs, letters in hand.

"What are these?" I held them out toward Bernie, fear and anger still a swarm of wild bees inside me. My aunt's eyes subtly widened, but she maintained her poise.

"Letters? Sent to your grandmother, I presume." She reached her hand out to take them, but I pulled them back, holding them to my chest.

"They are in my mother's handwriting," I said, unapologetic.

"Your mother wrote to your grandmother," my aunt replied with exaggerated innocence. "Of course, she did." Disguises: Bernie donned them whenever she stepped out of her private rooms.

"Grandmother never said anything about mother writing to her."

"And we cannot ask her why. Perhaps if you read them carefully, the letters themselves offer an answer." Behind her calculated calm, she watched me with the attention of a rival predator.

"They're nothing--small talk and fanciful descriptions of animals she observed in the wild around San Diego." A connection leaped into my mind. "What did Mister Emerson mean when he said that I had friends in the woods?"

"You will have to ask Waldo that. I cannot speak for him," she tried to put me off, but I knew all the actresses' tricks, the rise and fall of her breasts mounding above her bodice, the quickening of her breath, the way her mouth worked, and her lips pursed. "And what he says is often quite inscrutable to a common actress like myself."

I knew better than to believe that. She was smart, an accomplished strategist. I was the unknown in this confrontation. I had become someone neither of us recognized.

"May I see the letters?" She again held out her hand to take them. This time, I gave them over, though reluctantly. "These are dated before you left New San Diego--a renewal of an old correspondence, then perhaps? Odd, though that they were in Manon's possession, but perhaps this 'friend' sent them to Manon out of kindness after Leonie went missing."

"They are lies," I responded. "What she writes about the mink and the fish? It never happened. I was there. What we saw were Confederate soldiers unloading trunks of silver and gold from a ship anchored in the bay. They buried them near those two creeks." The fierce hunger of my fiery emotions was fading. "*I* am the village child. *I* was with her. Why did she lie?"

"I cannot say, Christopher." Bernie's heightened emotions were fading as well, leaving her shaken, a flutter in her voice. "This third letter…"

"It's just a request for this Dear Friend to have some publisher look at a silly story." Bernie scanned it as I spoke.

"The vixen is worried her kit is not safe where they are, and questions if he would be safer elsewhere," she summed up the letter's contents. "You see no familiarity in that?"

"Just because my nickname is Kit doesn't make the story about me."

"No, it's about the mother trying to decide what to do when all her options are bad," there was a bite to my aunt's reply. She handed the letters back to me.

"These are not all of them," I said. "There must be others. Who has the others?"

"I cannot say."

"Can't, or won't?" I accused her. Her stubbornness flared again.

"There are secrets that are not mine to share, Kit."

"Oh yes, Drake House has lots of secrets," I said scornfully. "It lives and breathes them. They are everywhere--in everything, like salt. Well, go ahead and keep your secrets, Aunt. I won't tell anyone, but someone knows where my mother is, and I am going to find them, then I am going to find her." I turned to stomp upstairs. Bernie stopped me.

"Kit, Leonie may not be ready to be found. If she isn't here now, there must be a reason."

"Why would you say that? You know something, don't you, Aunt? What do you know that you are not saying?" I waited, but she gave no indication she would reply. "The Pinkertons could find her. Hire them. You have the money." It was a petulant demand, clutched like a hand around the ache inside me.

"I am sorry, Christopher. It would not be safe."

"Not safe?" My eyes welled up, so I could not see. "Why? Because she is doing something dangerous? Please, Aunt, she is my mother! She is all I have."

"Don't whine, Christopher; it is unbecoming. Here." Bernie handed me her handkerchief. "Wipe the damp spots. You are about to spill over." Once I had recovered, she spoke again. "I am going to share something about the Drake family that you do not know. Something we do not tell people outside our family circle. Will you listen?" I nodded. "You can never speak of this to others. Never. It would do great damage, and it could cost people their lives. Do you understand?" Again, I nodded.

"We were children, at least I was. Manon would be of marriageable age in a few years, but that is when we discovered her special ability. At first, it was just fun to create little adventures, scheming together—we called them 'workings'. Being older, when we were caught doing our 'workings', she got most of the blame, but I learned my part; we became more skilled, and we stopped getting caught. As we grew older, we found more mature, important uses for our skills, and eventually our work expanded to fields where the outcome was broader and the stakes higher. We began to work for governments, Britain at first, then as our reputation grew, we expanded to other European nations, eventually including the United States after I relocated to New York.

"Large projects required increased support, so we began to gather colleagues who worked well together, each with their area of expertise. This helped reduce the danger and stress involved in our work, as we were also required to live public lives, and it meant we had a high rate of success. With her marriage to Avery Marchand and her pregnancy, Manon took on a more administrative role. Then Avery died. A year later, Manon remarried his partner, Abbott Lowdon, and he moved her and Leonie to Cincinnati. I stopped doing workings. I could not continue the work alone.

"Couldn't someone else have taken on her duties?" I asked.

"No. It is an uncommon talent, and my abilities lie elsewhere. Sixteen years after my sister left New York, your mother came to live with me in London, intending to pursue a career on the stage. We discovered Manon had passed her talent on to Leonie. I helped Leonie hone her skills, and we began doing workings again; a nudge here, a tickle there. But we made a difference.

"I was away on tour when your mother met Jack Becket. In her letters, she described him as charming, well-traveled, and an excellent conversationalist. She insisted he was open-minded, supportive of her independence and commitment, and would not get in the way of our work, but the man I met was not the one she described. He was arrogant, surly, and self-involved. Leonie insisted that this was not really him, that some temporary stress was making him act differently. She is a very loyal person, your mother. Against my advice, she married Becket. He cut her off from the theater, then anyone in our social circle of artists, and anything to do with workings, though he did not know about them specifically. He resented anything that took your mother's attention from him. She might have rebelled against his control, but by then, she was pregnant with you, and such rebellion is particularly difficult when there is a child involved. A mother has no rights. The husband owns the child, and if the mother leaves him, he can punish her by not allowing her to see the child."

At this point in the narrative, Burke entered. I was not surprised. I had always known he was involved in the Drake House mysteries.

"But our group decided, though we could not accept the same type of assignments, we would continue to work. There were wars, threats of wars, and intrigues, and we created a way to influence events that did not require Leonie's abilities, but simply spy-craft, disguises, and strategies involving the planting of ideas in the minds of those who influenced policies.

"You were all committed to bettering the situation. I understand. I have seen the people coming and going from the carriage house. I know that Drake House is a Station House on the Underground Railroad."

"We've been going to tell you for some time," Burke acknowledged. "The right moment had not presented itself, and after Weaver discovered you found out…"

"We were going to tell you, Kit," Bernie assured me. "We did not mean to make you feel we mistrusted you, or to make you mistrust us, but we have to be very careful. People's lives are at stake. You have seen more of the world's dark side than most boys of your age and class, and for that I am sorry, but this world does not favor the innocent."

"I understand."

"No, you don't, yet," Bernie disagreed. "But you deserve to." Burke frowned, trying to catch her eye, but she ignored him. "I have spoken of the ability my sister and your mother had…"

"*Has*," I corrected her.

"*Has*," Bernie acknowledged my correction. "But I have not yet explained what that has to do with you. You see, I believe you have inherited your mother and grandmother's talent; the talent of invisibility." The statement was dropped as casually as if it were a loop fallen in a circle, but I recognized it was a coiled snake.

"I-I don't have that," the syllables tripped and stumbled over my tongue. "I don't know anything about that." The lump that bounced up to clog my airway made it hard to breathe.

My aunt cocked one eyebrow. "Come now, you never listened in on the Lowdon's when they did not know you were there, or explored a room you were told was off-limits, knowing you would not be caught because you are never caught? The night you stood in for Gil Collmeyer, no one could see you onstage, but you insist you were there. And I believe you were, but you were invisible. That night at Pfaff's, you said that the Bees did not notice you. They would not have simply failed to notice a strange young man listening in on their conversation."

"But they did," I insisted. My throat felt dry and scratchy.

"Because they could not see you, because, again, you were invisible. I spoke to Charlotte. She claims that night at Pfaff's, she saw you, then suddenly didn't. You are probably not aware when it happens, but there is a trigger, something in your life that made being invisible a useful skill."

My Father, I thought.

"And you certainly cannot control it, but this skill could be important. It could make a difference." I stayed silent. I was admitting nothing. "Manon is gone now, your mother is missing, but you are here."

I did not know what to say. I believed my invisibility was a construct—a response to my father's outbursts of temper I had, then incorporated into my character until I lived with the expectation of being overlooked and dismissed by people as a matter of course. Invisibility was my weakness. But here was Bernie, naming it something unique. Something more.

"Imagine an agent who can walk into a room and listen to high-level discussions without being seen," she dangled adventures. "Imagine having someone who can search a room or a military tent for documents, entirely undetected. There are things you can do that would be impossible for someone without your ability. No one else knows this has been part of why we were so successful. Outside our immediate circle, no one knows how we do the work we do. Only a very few."

"The animals in the woods."

"Yes." Bernie nodded. "Your mother's code name is The Fox."

And Emerson knew because he was part of the 'family'. I turned to Burke. "You're not a butler, are you, Burke?"

"I am, but I am also a soldier, a scholar, a husband, a friend…. We are none of us one thing, Master Kit. My position is unique, but my service here in the house is appreciated, and someone must care for home and hearth and prepare things."

"Prepare them for what?" I asked.

"Whatever happens."

"What could happen?"

"Nothing we cannot handle, I assure you." He said it with such confidence, I believed him.

"Who are *we*?" I asked.

Bernie and Burke exchanged a silent question and answer before she spoke.

"The Coterie. It is an organization with foundations going back to the Age of Reason."

"We provide a service," Burke explained. "Sometimes, if our goals are aligned, we work with a country's government, sharing strategic information, but we always retain our autonomy."

Bernie sniffed. "The leadership among governments changes, and we often know more about what is going on than they do. But we cannot control whether they take our advice or not, and that can create problems. Social events offer an opportunity to influence thought. Even though our target may not be present at a particular event, ideas may be passed on. Without these efforts, some of the world's most progressive ideas would languish in books or essays read only by elite literati."

"Understand, Kit, that what your aunt has just shared is a secret," Burke cautioned me. "Not a simple secret, like a gift, but a secret that affects multiple lives and the future of countries. We are engaged in a battle for the very soul of this nation, and too often the Coterie believes we achieved a goal only to find victory dashed from our hands. The Declaration of Independence was such a blow. 'All men created equal' was not meant to be inspiring words applied only to white men of property. It was a pivotal moment in history."

"We thought we had won." Bernie's face was earnest, her eyes honest. "The Great Compromise of the Thirteen Colonies embedded slavery into the new dream of American Democracy. This is the work we are asking you to join, Kit."

"I am not a spy," I replied.

"We have been watching you—your quiet, open manner…your humble intelligence. People trust you."

Not you, I thought.

"Who do you think saw Manon or Leonie and thought they were spies? No one."

Someone thought Leonara Becket was a spy. I remembered the footprints around our house in New San Diego. They were why the Fox worried over her kit's safety.

"The best spies are those who seem most unlikely."

"And what about him?" I pointed to Spin perched nonchalantly on the balustrade at the foot of the stairs. He scowled at me. "Your little blue friend, who follows you around like a loyal puppy."

"I am not a puppy," Spin grumbled.

I looked from Bernie to Spin and back. "You don't see him, do you?"

Bernie hesitated, but for once, truth won over lies. "No," she admitted. "But you are Leonie's son. It should not surprise me that you do. It makes sense that if you inherited one talent, you might have inherited others. But no, that is not my talent."

"But it was mother's."

Bernie nodded. "Leonie saw him and befriended the sprite. I can only communicate with him under specific circumstances."

"In front of that picture with the temple and the ravens," I surmised.

Bernie huffed and rolled her eyes. "Are there no secrets in this house?"

"There are," I declared. "Too many of them. So, what *is* your 'talent', Aunt?"

"I am a Weaver. I see patterns in The Weave, and sometimes I move the Threads to alter them." I recalled the pinching and moving I saw her doing with the invisible lines in the air.

"You change the future."

"Sometimes. Just a little," Bernie nodded. "But the threads have their own will. A Weaver should never try to bend The Weave to her will. Encourage the threads to accept a slightly different pattern, yes, but the Weave does not take well to too much interference. And of course, I am not the only Weaver; there are others. Some are aware of what they are and how to use it; others do not recognize their gift or what they are doing when they influence situations."

"So, you were not just being kind when you didn't argue with me about Mother not being dead? You know."

"Yes."

"And do you know where she is?"

"No. But we have more of her letters." Burke reached into his inside jacket pocket and pulled out a small stack of papers. Some were on fine stationery. Others were written on butcher paper or envelopes.

"You are not mother's 'Dear Friend?'" I asked Burke.

"I am *a* dear friend, but not the person she wrote the letters to, no, Kit. These were passed on to me."

I remembered Emerson giving Bernie a package at Ada Clare's as we were leaving. *"I will give them to Burke,"* she said. And it suddenly came to me, Ralph Waldo Emerson was the person my mother was writing to. He was the "Dear Friend". He was the head of The Coterie in America.

Sitting on my bed upstairs, I sorted the letters by postal dates before opening the first.

Dear Friend,
Though I have returned to the scene where I observed the mink, I have witnessed no repetition of their activity with silver and gold fish. I believe I was right, and the increase in workers arriving to build the new fort has forced local wildlife to move their activities. This will complicate my efforts to observe them, but as I have few distractions here, I believe I will eventually stumble onto their new hunting grounds.

Ever your friend,
LB

I held the letter, frowning. Once again, Mother referred to the activity of the mink and the fish, reporting to her 'friend' that she was unable to find the animals but would continue trying. The letters gave every appearance of being nothing more than a chatty correspondence, but I knew now that, in light of her work for the Coterie, the letters were more.

Burke spoke of how the Coterie felt the Thirteen Colonies' agreement to become one country, including the practice of slavery, was a failure for them. The war between the states was an attempt to rectify that mistake. After eighty-seven years, slavery was being removed from North America. I looked at the pile of 'letters'. They were not letters. They were field reports from an agent to their leader.

I kept reading.

Dear Friend,

Though it is my habit to write about my ramblings and observations of local wildlife, I have recently been most surprised to find tracks circling my front door and the windows of my house in the village of New San Diego. What do my animal friends spy through the glass? Who do they think we are after observing our simple lives? I think it best that our activities remain a mystery to them, to have wildlife too close among us might present a peril, and so we will follow the tracks and hunt each other seeking them out in their habitats, hoping to learn more of their activities. I have been cautioned that Black bears, cougar, coyotes, and wolves may be found hiding in the forests and woodlands here. Therefore, I now carry a sidearm at all times. Even something as large as a bear may be stopped by a well-directed bullet, and as you may remember, I am a competent marksman.

Your Friend,
LB

This letter's date showed it was written shortly before the "children's story" letter.

I remembered telling my mother about the tracks I found outside our house--not animal tracks, but human ones. After that, she began carrying a firearm in town, and a rifle when we went riding, which we did more often, even when our destination was so close we might have walked. We also began to race on the beach and up to the top of the cliffs.

"A good horseman can not only trot down a city street or a woodland path, but can keep their seat riding at a gallop in the dark, in a storm, or if someone is chasing them. You need to know how to control and calm your mount if it is skittish or afraid, Kit. If you are thrown and injured, or left alone, it could be dangerous. You must not only ride, but ride well."

My mother was training me so I could handle myself in the event something happened to her.

I pulled out the story letter from the batch and double-checked the date. She had written the story letter shortly after the tracks appeared. That matched the timeframe of when she began coaching me to ride at a more advanced level. Perhaps she intended to teach me to shoot as well, but then the soldiers and smallpox arrived and moved up my departure.

I wondered if I had ever really known this woman?

I read the next letters with a fresh eye.

Dear Friend,

It is not for lack of dedication that you have not heard from me in some weeks. Events here turned so suddenly that I've had no time for wandering or writing. Therefore, this letter will be brief.

The soldiers who came to man the fort brought smallpox with them, and it is taking a terrible toll on the Kumeyaay and those of mixed Mexican and Native heritage.

Fearing for his safety, my young adventuring companion is being sent away to family in the Midwest. It is my hope you may look in on him there, or you may encourage another of our friends to do so. I expect to follow soon, but cannot leave while so many are so ill. The need is great, and much is at stake.

The business of managing the details surrounding my late husband's death still lies before me as well. No one seems able to verify the circumstances or where his remains were buried, and irregularities in the official report abound. I will leave as soon as the epidemic has subsided. Send future correspondence to our mutual friends. They will know where to find me.

Your friend,

LB

But they did not know. The letter was direct, falling just short of naming Manon and Bernie. Were these the letters Emerson handed Bernie, or did Burke have these letters before? The letter writing was a weak subterfuge based on Leonara Becket's persona as an innocent wife and mother. By the time The Fox had written this report, though, she had no time for such intrigue; she had dropped the flowery tone. If her true role was revealed, anything she wrote might be read by Confederate spies. However, if she stopped her activities and mired herself in helping with the sick, ending her wanderings, all the Confederates would have were suspicions.

Shadows of unconscious memories washed through my mind like over-wet watercolor pigments dripping down the paper, images of my mother as someone, not herself. Images of someone who was, and was not, Aunt Bernadette—fragments of the Drake women's other life. I opened and read another letter, feeling I was leaving childhood behind and closing in on my present.

Dear Friend,

I have had the good luck to observe a most determined dolphin searching for the gold and silver fish that make the Pacific Ocean so rich. I am, however, not the only one watching the creatures. The newly arrived sea hunters have taken to scouring the coastline looking for these clever thieves who plunder California's great natural resources as they travel from the North.

Yesterday, the sea hunter's efforts were successful. After relieving the dolphin's belly of its catch, they plugged its blowhole and sank it. Watch for an influx of gold and silver fish in the markets of Washington. If you do not see it, you should draw our friends' attention to it and encourage them to reconsider the sea hunter's credibility.

Your Friend,
LB

Sea hunters, dolphins, silver and golden scaled fish…. According to the date on the letter, the epidemic had been over for some time. I had been in Cincinnati for nine months, but my mother had not yet left California.

I did not know what to feel, emotions tumbling all in a jumble. I needed…someone…a friend. A confidant. I gathered the letters up, stuffing them into the pocket of my overcoat and snuck out the back door to the alley. In minutes, I was running North along Broadway toward Wallack's.

Act Two, Scene Seven: Wallack's later that night

From the street, Wallack's looked empty, dark, and locked tight. *A Midsummer Night's Dream* opened strong, filled houses, and was now being held over, extending Wallack's season. If the cooler summer weather held, we would run right up through the first weeks of June. But this was Monday, so the theater was dark.

I went around the back into the alley that led to the stage door and found the small basement window in Wardrobe was propped open, letting in the afternoon breeze.

"Maggie," I called out quietly. "It's Kit. Can you let me in?" Maggie's face appeared at the window, and she gestured that I should meet her at the stage door.

"Thank you." My eyes welled with gratitude when she opened it for me.

"Did your aunt forget something? Are you meeting Wixx?"

I shook my head. "No. I just need to be here for a bit." I could not explain. It was too personal, my insides too raw. My eyes pleaded with Maggie not to press me.

"Do you need anything else?" she asked kindly. "Tea? A biscuit?"

"No. Thank you."

Maggie nodded. "A theater is rather like a church, waiting for us to need it. If you need something, I'll be here for another hour or so."

I tried to calm myself, breathing in the odd mixtures of scents of the place, the leftover fumes of gas and limelight, makeup, and sawdust, before beginning the climb to the fly bridge, each step heavier, my sight blurring with unshed tears.

"Kindle? Kay?" The cat appeared at my call, adorable with sleepiness. I scooped it up, hugging it close as I sobbed out the story of my discoveries and pain, how I missed my mother, my feelings of abandonment, my father's abuse, the loss of my last reliable relative, Grandma Manon—all of it twisted up inside me.

Kindle wriggled from my arms and became Kay, and we sat together on the bridge, my head in their lap while they petted my arm.

Once I was cried out, I felt better. I pulled my mother's last letters out and read them to Kay.

"I like fish." Kay licked their lips.

"These aren't real fish," I explained. "It's a code for gold and silver metal."

"A king's ransom." Kay's understanding of the world was based on theatrical stories. Human life and its commonalities were charmingly unfamiliar.

"The 'dolphins' are Confederate privateers--pirates essentially, and the 'sea hunters' tasked with stopping them are the Union Navy." My mother's story was beginning to come into focus. I picked up the last unread letters.

Dear Friend,

Under a new moon, a dolphin swam into the sea hunter's net. Moving heavy and strangely ponderous in the water, it reeked of deceit. And our suspicions proved true. Black Gold filled her belly. If it had gone undiscovered, a hundred ebony babies would have been brought ashore on some deserted beach and sold on the black market.

We helped them into this new world as gently as we could, but now, the leader among the sea hunters is claiming he cannot spare the resources to care for their stolen lives. The dolphin's children are unable to fend for themselves. They were stolen and have nothing. It is unconscionable to abandon them. My colleagues and I have refused to do that. Please discuss this with your friends and advise what action is to be taken. I await your reply.

LB

"She wrote this just as my grandmother became sick. She was still in California," I mused.

The last letter was scrawled on ragged paper scraps. I smoothed the crumpled brown paper, imagining its journey from my mother's hand to mine, squinting at the faded script, and read:

Dear Friend,

The dolphin's sons and daughters are learning to ride the waves. If you would direct their course to a safe port, the time for that is now. Neglected fish spoil. Neglected people die.

LB

The letter was brief to the point of being curt, a challenge, a rebuke. The treatment of the dolphin's children left my mother bitter and disillusioned.

"I don't think the sea hunter's captain was a very good director, not like Mister Lester," Kay commented. "He did not help his cast like he should have. He did not give them the tools to play their parts well." With Kay, everything was examined through the lens of plays and theater. We fell into a companionable silence. "It's nice you are here," Kay said after a long stretch. "Sometimes I get lonely when everyone goes away. Then I feel sad, like Ophelia, so I go sit by the ghost light and wait."

"Wait for what?" I asked.

"Morning. Maggie comes first. She brings cream, and sometimes an egg, a leftover dumpling, or some fish." They licked their lips again. "She is always kind to me. I like this show," Kay's mercurial mind leaped to a new subject. "The fairies, and the sweethearts. I feel bad for Helena, though. It is not her fault that Demetrius falls out of love with her. It's just a bad magic trick. I do not like Titania and Oberon's kind of love, though. It is cruel and selfish. It must be nice to be loved, though, if it is a kind love, and not a bad trick."

"I think so too." I looked up at Kay from their lap.

The theater I loved had a curious spirit. They would never have a human life, and that was all I would have. They were a spirit and would live forever—or as long as this building stood. I would not.

Love was cruel, to give us so much forever in the shadow of loss.

It was just before dawn when I woke, uncurling myself from where Kay and I had lain cuddled up together on the bridge. Maggie was long gone, the building dark and empty, except for us.

The ghost light on the stage below cast its flickering light up at us.

"Thank you, Kay, for helping me feel better. I will be back this afternoon," I promised softly, not wanting to disturb the shadowed silence of our sanctuary.

"I'll be here." Kindle disappeared from the flybridge, reappearing on the floor in the circle cast by the ghost light.

Act Two, Scene Eight: Drake House, early the next morning

Tip-toing quietly up to my room at Bernie's, I found an envelope slipped under my door. Inside it was a torn and mangled bit of paper with my mother's hasty handwriting. The note was unsigned. I sat on my bed and read it.

Dear Friend

We have taught the dolphins' sons and daughters to sail and returned them to the sea. I dream of riding away on the waves with them, but we both know I will remain, and why.

So, the dolphins were finally gone. Where would my mother go now?

Back to her family. *Back to me.*

I walked to the front windows and looked out over the park green and the streets surrounding it as dawn slowly brightened the world. But if Leonie was so close, she would not be out there. She would be here with me, and she was not.

I lay on my bed staring at the ceiling until I heard the household stirring below, then splashed cold water on my face, changed my clothes, and went downstairs.

Bernie was standing at the front window in the dining room, tea in hand. Spin was nearby. As soon as I entered, Burke joined us.

"Thank you." I handed the letters back to Burke.

He looked surprised. "I thought you might…" I cut him off.

"They are not mine. They were not sent to me." The little blue man turned away. "Perhaps you could read them out loud to Spin. He has been without word of my mother far longer than I have." I was not the only one Leonie left behind. I turned to Bernie. "I will assist you in your workings, but I have conditions." She cocked an eyebrow. "The first is: no more secrets."

"Agreed." Bernie nodded.

Burke did not.

"No more secrets," I repeated, waiting for his agreement. A conversation transpired in silent looks between Bernie and Burke before he finally nodded. "I recognize you are a man of your word, Burke, but you must say the words to make the bond."

"No more secrets," he agreed. I returned my attention to Bernie.

"Whatever you know, Aunt, whatever you are willing to teach me, I will learn, but I will not kill for you, or for this Coterie. I will decide what jobs I accept. That, too, must be part of the bargain."

"We are not monsters, Kit. We would never ask you to act against your own conscience."

"That is good, but you should understand that though I am agreeing to help you, my goals are still my own. I mean to find Mother."

She was part of something bigger than her own small life, and now I was, too.

Act Three, Scene One: Armory Square Veteran's Hospital, 6th and S.W. "B" Street, Washington D.C. June 1863.

Wartime Washington City was an ant's nest of fretful activity, pedestrians and carts dodging saddle horses, traffic of every kind churning the muddy streets into a stinking mix that wheels and hooves splattered onto people without respect to their status or task. As we traveled along Fourth Street from the Baltimore-Ohio Train Station, it seemed like men in uniform were everywhere, and men in suits or workmen's clothes were everywhere else.

Only forty-eight miles from the Confederate capital in Richmond, Virginia, Washington City was a town of mosquitoes and snakes; many of them human, and the scent of power encouraged swarming. As a child, I imagined adult leaders as chivalrous knights fighting for the less fortunate, but Washington was not Camelot, and politicians were not fair-minded knights.

A smelly haze rose from the swampy, tidewater lowlands, tainting the air with a stink so dense with bugs you could chew the air. The unfinished Washington Canal's waters rose and emptied with the tide, but the garbage and excrement tossed in were a constant, adding to the disgusting smell of our nation's capital.

Aunt Bernie had donned veil and gloves, keeping her chest and throat hidden beneath a high-necked blouse. Dweeti had made us an ointment of lemon balm herb and bees wax, which we slathered on to any exposed skin, so we moved in a cloud of our own herbal apothecary. The scent was preferable to swamp and sewer.

"This is the capital city?" I wrinkled my nose, disgusted. "The streets are not even paved."

"They built it on swampland." Bernie made a face. "It really is a very young country, Kit. The White House was only rebuilt forty-five years ago. We British burned the first one during the War of Eighteen Twelve." She shrugged. "I won't apologize. Madison attacked us first, but the city's problems have not been helped by this wartime explosion of population."

"Can't they do something about all these bugs?" I groused, swatting at one that was trying to bite me through my coat.

My aunt smirked. "At the moment, I think the administration is more concerned with keeping their country a country."

Our train passed through towns scarred by war, the eyes of their inhabitants sprouting the resentment that would be this spring's only crop.

And yet there was purpose here, men and women challenging the overwhelming needs of a wartime country. Nurses, volunteers, and dedicated clerks, weary from the weight of their work, shoveling mounds of paper, trying to sort out disguised avarice from true need.

Outside the carriage window, I saw a tawny, ginger-haired woman threading her way through the crowd, her build and movement as familiar as my own heartbeat. I threw the carriage door open.

"Mother!" I leaped into the street's moving miasma, deaf to my aunt's pleas to stop and return to the carriage.

"What are you doing?" Spin demanded, trotting after me.

"It's her! Mother!" I declared, breathlessly. "I saw her." Pressing through the crowd, I craned my neck, pausing to jump up and see over the people's heads. I had lost her. I walked along the street, peering down every side street and alley, hoping for a glimpse of the russet bonnet with the black feather on it that the woman was wearing. The broader street I was traveling intersected with another popular thoroughfare without me finding her. "Do you see her, Spin?"

"Not in the physical world."

A group of toughs began moving toward me, and I turned away from them. A cocky lad who could have been with the toughs or might be working alone was approaching from the other direction. His eyes flickered to my jacket pocket. Before he was within reach of it, a strong brown hand clutched my shoulder. I spun around, trying to remember what Weaver taught me about throwing a punch, then recognized the hand's owner. It was attached to Burke.

"It was Mother, Burke," I tried to justify my escape. "She is here in Washington."

"Then we will try and find her," he spoke calmly, eyeing my potential attackers with a warning not to come closer. They melted into the crowd. "But you cannot run off into a strange city filled with soldiers, spies, pickpockets, and con men, Master Kit. You will probably not find your mother, but you most certainly will find some misadventure."

"I don't care about that. I need to find her."

"Listen to the man, boy. He is trying to talk sense into you before you land yourself in real trouble," Spin shoved his opinion into my head. I did not like that he could pop into my mind whenever he wanted. It made me feel naked, but I did not know what I could do to stop him.

"What you need is to return to the carriage so we can keep our appointment," Burke reasoned. "You cannot defend yourself, and you have only the barest rudiments of anything resembling spy-craft. Your aunt would be devastated if something happened to you." That seemed Aunt Bernadette might have finally unlocked the family skeleton closet, and that I was now useful. She was still her prickly self..

"But we need to find Mother before she leaves Washington, Burke."

"Inquiries will be made," he assured me. "But right now, we have an appointment with Mister Whitman, and it would be rude to be late." He gestured for me to return to the carriage.

Walt Whitman met Aunt Bernadette and me outside the Armory Square Veterans' Hospital. It was on the East side of the public park grounds that connected the White House to the Smithsonian Castle, the Capitol Building, and the site of the Washington Monument. The still unfinished Washington City Canal marked the park's Southern edge.

As we stepped from the hired carriage, I could see the red sandstone Castle of the Smithsonian Museum, directly to the West, just beyond the hospital barracks. The Capitol Building was on my left, situated by symbolic design at the highest point in the landscape. The White House occupied the next highest rise, the architect making a very permanent symbolic statement that the people's role in this new democracy would always be above the President's.

Walt Whitman clasped my aunt's hand. "Thank you for coming, Bernie."

"How could I not when it was you who asked?"

"I am ashamed my country requires such a favor, but the need is so great, and the resources so terribly few. Come. You will see yourself."

"May I introduce my companion?" Bernie asked politely, indicating me. "Walt Whitman, this is my nephew, Master Christopher Drake. Christopher, this is America's Poet, Mister Walt Whitman."

The poet chuckled. "So formal, Bernie." His clear blue eyes touched my own with an interest that was not dismissive, causing me to blush. "Hello, young fellow." His lack of formality was a kindness." He turned to Bernie. "Perhaps young Christopher would prefer to wait outside? The effects of war on men's bodies can be rather alarming."

"It is thoughtful for you to consider Kit's youth, Walt, but it is too late to shield him from the harshness of life. He is what spiritualists refer to as an 'old soul'."

The poet studied me, his perpetually upturned lips softening fears on my part regarding his scrutiny.

"And do you hold the dream of so many young men to go marching off to war, Master Drake?"

"My talents lie elsewhere."

"An artist then?" He looked to Bernie.

"Kit has an interest in design and theatrical lighting," Bernie explained.

"Ah." Whitman's eyes lit up. "Myself, I did not discover a passion for poetry until I was inspired by seeing my first opera. It was as if my soul was set on fire, and before that, I had been walking through life half-awake. The experience transformed me utterly."

"I felt that when I saw my first play," I shared. *MacBeth.*

Whitman grimaced, then laughed. "The Scottish Play? How dreadful! The bard did write less dismal works."

"Rather like an opera," my aunt scoffed.

"It is not the plot of an opera that is so edifying, my dear Bernie; it is the music," Whitman declared.

"I think it is the connection between the performers and the audience, reaching across the footlights," I shared. "The truth of tragedy, the bitter sweetness of romance, the excited-pumping gallop of looming death; that is what transforms the audience's experience."

"And the words," Whitman added, excited by the subject matter. "The words are the foundation of every brilliant performance."

"But it requires an actor of skill to make those words come to life," Bernie spoke up for the actors.

Whitman shook his grizzled, gray head. "Even a skilled actor cannot breathe life into a poorly written work."

I agreed with him. Though audiences laughed a good deal during *The School for Scandal*, I had found its brittle, shallow parody of social manners unequal in emotional intensity to the works of Shakespeare I had seen Wallack's produce.

"But *MacBeth* is what you propose to perform here in Washington for the benefit?" Whitman asked Bernie.

"It is popular with audiences, I have a reputation in the role, and since it recently completed a run in New York, all the production pieces remain available, making it financially attractive. The Wallack family has promised to donate the use of all the costumes and sets and pay the actor's salaries as their contribution to the benefit. There is also a young actor, Gil Collmeyer, whom people will have heard of but, unless they've come to New York recently, will not have seen yet. He is quite the Greek Adonis, and that also increases interest." Whitman raised his eyebrows. "Sorry, Walt. He's not your sort at all." She smiled slyly.

"Your aunt is a formidable woman," the poet stated.

"She is," I agreed. "But she is also a woman of passion." Bernie glared at me as if she thought I was going to reveal something embarrassing. "She owns a copy of *Leaves of Grass*," I confided. "I have seen it in her library."

Whitman looked delighted. "And have you read it yourself?"

"I have, Sir," I replied. "But please do not embarrass me by asking me what I thought. I am no critic of literature."

"I did not write it for the critics," Whitman insisted. "I wrote it for common people who feel the joy in a sunrise, or a loved one's smile, and have the capacity to acknowledge that the sunset-death of a day, or the poignancy of a loved one's long goodbye, exist simultaneously in our lives and gives those lives depth and richness."

I dropped my eyes to hide the emotions his words had churned up, then raised them, solemnly revealing my pain and loss.

"An 'old soul' indeed," he said quietly. "Leaders use the youthful desire to do heroic deeds to get young men to don a uniform and parade off to war, but Death is not an easy companion to walk alongside. This, however, is a quiet day, and we do not expect new arrivals from the battlefield."

The barrack-style wards were laid out linearly behind white picket fences on the property surrounding the original armory building. The sun was shining, and infirm soldiers whose health had improved and who would soon be released, loitered outside, leaning on crutches or against the white clapboard buildings. Their eyes followed Bernie and me like we were exotic visitors from afar, a place where people lived whole lives and parts of them had not been cut away and left behind. But Walt Whitman, they knew. He had a kind word and encouraging touch for any whose expression said they would accept his approach, nodding with compassionate understanding to those who cringed from social contact and looked away.

We entered a ward where the floors were unfinished wood planks. The walls, ceiling planks, and visible rafters were all painted white, giving it spaciousness on this sunny day with the door and windows open. I imagined the cold of winter in such a place, though, and it made me shudder.

Spin was already walking slowly down the center aisle between the beds, his hands clasped behind his back like a miniature Napoleon.

Just inside the door to the right, a large wooden bin held discarded arms and legs tossed together like cordwood, most pieces wrapped in bloodied cotton stained in shades of fresh pink to rusty brown, revealing how long ago they were separated from their owner. Bernie held a perfumed handkerchief to her nose.

"I am sorry. Perhaps my concerns over the suitability of this exploration were wrongly placed?" our guide suggested.

"I have no expectation of comfort in this," Bernie replied.

"The staff does what they can, but they are overwhelmed by the number of sick and injured. Common military field practices are well behind the modern understanding of how disease and infection may be prevented. As much harm is done in the camps as on the battlefield. We are continually fighting misinformation about health practices."

We gazed down the long rows of white, blanketed cots placed with their heads against the walls, their feet jutting out into the open space down the center. Most occupants were lying down, eyes closed, or staring at the ceiling. A few were sitting up. All of them looked gaunt and dispirited, their troubled eyes too large for their thin-cheeked faces.

I walked ahead of Walt and Bernie, creating an opportunity to address Spin without notice.

"Are you following me?" I asked, my voice barely a whisper.

"I am your aunt's protector." It was an implausible statement considering the creature's size, but as he was a magical being, I gave him the benefit of the doubt.

Whitman led Bernie and me through the ward, introducing some of the patients and asking them to share their stories if they felt inclined. Witnessing the men, many of them too young in years to deserve the description but who had earned it on the battlefield, was both expectedly sad and unexpectedly life-affirming. Some of them clung to life with committed desperation. Others were accepting Death's companionship with calm clarity. Both were profound to witness. Neither being open to the judgment of un-blooded civilians like ourselves.

"These boys have seen so much horror, violence, and loss," Walt spoke softly. "And they are so far from home and the care of their families. Meeting their physical needs is, of course, paramount, but we may feed their bodies and still fail them if they are starved for a moment or two of reassuring human connection." Whitman pulled himself from his reverie. "But that is not the assistance the Sanitary Commission is asking for from you, Bernie. It is for supplies, bandages, crutches, and the care for widows and orphans."

Bernie took Whitman's hand and squeezed it as we bade him farewell. "Thank you."

"No, thank you, my friend. It has made my heart lighter to see friends from home. Say hello to The Bees for me, won't you?" Whitman said. "Lodgings have been arranged for you with Secretary of State William Seward. It's quite near: Lafayette Park, just North of the White House. They are expecting you."

"Will you be joining us later?" Bernie asked.

Whitman shook his head. "No. I have no interest in social gatherings outside our small circle. I cannot speak to these political folk. My place is here." He indicated the ward behind us.

"I liked him," I commented as the carriage retraced its journey along Main Avenue back to Fifth.

"I expected you would. You will find his advice much more useful than a man like Fernando Wood."

"I wouldn't trust Fernando Wood with my old shoes," I growled. "And I most certainly would not take his advice. He has not earned my trust."

Bernie smiled. "Good. Though it might be useful if you could find yourself included on the fringes of his circle and learn what his people are planning after the Confederates win at Chancellorsville. It needs to appear to be his idea, though. If he suspects you of duplicity, you could be in danger, particularly if Undergrove is with him," she cautioned me. "He, too, has 'abilities'."

I was not surprised.

Act 3, Scene 2: Seward's house, "the President's Neighborhood", Lafayette Park, Washington, DC

We turned North onto C Street and merged into the heavy wagon traffic approaching the Center Market, which I only recognized because the words were painted on the long side of the white building. Vendors who could not afford the market's rent sold their produce and wares, and offered their tradesmen's services from wagons or carts as Washington City's residents sought to survive the hardships of war.

Beyond the market, the road continued along the Washington Canal, passing the half-completed Washington Monument standing alone and looking ashamed of its naked neglect. It was not the war that stopped the monument's progress. The Know Nothing's, a virulently anti-Catholic organization, had taken over its board, and the private funding that was supporting the raising had dried up, leaving the structure unfinished at one hundred fifty-six feet tall.

We came at the invitation of the Sewards, William Henry Seward being Secretary of State to the Lincoln Administration. Seward, an Abolitionist, worked for years to create the Republican party and had every expectation of being its candidate for president in the election of 1860 when Abraham Lincoln, a back-woods lawyer from Illinois, appeared and clinched the nomination.

C street dead-ended at the Executive Park grounds attached to the White House, and our carriage turned North. Passing the White House on the left, we turned briefly onto Pennsylvania Avenue, jogging onto a spur of Fifteenth Street that separated the elite green known as Lafayette Park from the houses that surrounded it on three sides, the fourth side being open to the White House. Locals referred to the park and its houses as "the President's Neighborhood," and it was here that the Sewards, being a New York family, rented a house.

Taller than wide, it was a multiple-story red brick building, small dormer windows built into the Mansard-style fourth-story roof. White trim and decorative green shutters dressed the rows of windows on each story. An add-on behind served as the servant's quarters and workspace. While double chimneys on the North and South ends of the house would keep the brick house comfortable in the winter, the many mature trees in the adjacent park shaded it so completely that as we drove up, we could not see any other house, making it feel like we were in the country and had left the city behind.

A butler of senior years, his white hair contrasting deeply with his dark skin, approached our carriage, indicating to a boy, younger than myself, that he should assist Burke with our luggage while he led Bernie and me to the house.

The institution of slavery had been illegal for over a year in the District of Columbia, but many of those who were freed stayed in the area where employment was readily at hand and their reputation for good and honest work was known.

"Secretary Seward apologizes that he is unable to greet you personally, Lady Drake, but both Missus and Miss Seward are here from Auburn and invite you to take tea with them if you feel so inclined, after you have refreshed yourselves, of course. If you and the young gentleman would prefer tea in your rooms, no offense will be taken. Missus Seward understands the challenges of travel from New York. She rarely makes the trip here from Auburn herself for that reason."

"Please tell Missus Seward that I would be pleased to accept her kind invitation once I have washed off the dust from the road and changed." Aunt Bernie glanced at me. "I believe my nephew would prefer to stretch his legs after our journey."

"Dinner is at eight," the man advised us. "It will just be yourselves and the family tonight. No other guests are expected." He showed us to comfortable rooms on the third story, facing out over the central green.

I splashed water over my face and hands to remove the soot and dust of the train and carriage, then made my way back downstairs. The boy was gathering my aunt's luggage at the foot of the stairs.

"Let me help." I reached for one of Bernie's bags. I had taken my own up with me.

"It is alright, Master, I can do it." He kept his head down, not meeting my eyes.

"My name is Kit Drake, and I am no one's 'master'," I told him. "Please call me Kit."

"It is true, we don't have 'masters' anymore, but you younger misters are supposed to be called 'master' to be polite."

"It seems a wicked trick when the word must have so many bad memories attached to it. At least let me help you with the large trunk…" I waited for him to fill in his name.

"Joshua," he introduced himself. I put out my hand.

"Pleased to meet you, Joshua." He looked at my outstretched hand, hesitating. "It's a new world, Joshua. In a few decades, people like you and me will be the adults running things. I would like you to remember me as a friend." He smiled and clasped my hand firmly. I reached down and lifted the leather strap on one end of Bernie's largest trunk. Joshua hefted the other side.

"You're a young fella, but you talk like those old ones who come here to talk to Mister Seward, Mister Hay, and President Lincoln."

"President Lincoln comes here?"

"Rides right over from the White House on a military horse called 'Abe', named for its extra-long legs. It takes a long-legged horse to carry the president."

"You have met him?"

"Many times, and I've shaken his hand."

"You've shaken a president's hand but hesitated to shake mine? I am no one, Joshua, a stagehand at a theater."

"You are nephew to a lady," he pointed out.

"It is not that special," I confided. We finished dragging the trunk up the stairs and deposited it outside Bernie's door. "Do you know where the National Theater is, Joshua?" I asked him. I am in need of a walk."

Act Three, Scene Three: Streets near Grover's Theater, Washington, DC

I was walking south on Fifteenth Street, once again tracing the east edge of the Executive Park grounds, when a carriage traveling the other way slowed. I recognized its passenger, New York Congressman Fernando Wood. The carriage continued, though it slowly passed me, then turned and came back, traveling South as I was.

"Young Master Drake," Wood greeted me, touching his fingers to the brim of his hat. "What a pleasant surprise. You remember my colleague, Hieronymous Undergrove?" I nodded at the sullen second man in the carriage. He did not react, looking out the window, bored by this interruption. "What brings you to the Capitol, Drake?"

"I accompany my aunt." He was hoping for more, but I did not give it to him, determined not to share more than necessary with a man I knew to be looking for ways to twist anything he learned to his benefit at my aunt's expense.

"I did not realize she was to perform in The District. What a treat for the local population, a performer of her caliber."

"She is not performing this trip," I corrected his assumption. There seemed to be no danger in revealing this, as it would soon be public knowledge.

"A visit then?"

Admitting Bernie was on a social visit to someone high up in the Lincoln Administration would raise Wood's and his friend's suspicions. Of course, performing in the benefit would be a sort of declaration of loyalty as well, but as a charitable event whose goal was to support the acquisition of bandages and health care supplies, it could be argued that her involvement was beyond politics. The Sanitary Society's efforts benefited Confederate wounded in Union hospitals as well. Whatever Wood wished to take from Bernie's involvement, she agreed to the performance, and there would be no hiding it.

"Only a meeting to discuss the possibility of an engagement," I replied, choosing to focus on the universally accepted path of making money.

"Very good. The wheels of commerce keep spinning, despite the war." His disingenuous smile made me nauseous.

"Or because of it," I tugged the weasel's tail. He did not hear my insolent reply, however, or perhaps he pretended he did not.

"May I offer you a lift?" he asked.

Bernie's suggestion that I allow myself to be drawn into Wood's circle to spy on him and his colleague's activities was fresh in my mind, but what Wood was proposing was not a sit-in-the-background-and-listen sort of engagement. This would be a close-up interrogation by Wood, with him questioning me and dissecting my replies while I attempted to remain within the realm of social acceptability and reveal nothing, all the while under the scrutiny of Undergrove's gaze, which felt like a snake crawling over my skin.

"Thank you, but no," I replied, keeping my hands firmly in my pockets so Wood would not see them shaking. "I am only going to the National Theater. It is not far, and I feel in need of a walk after the journey from New York." Wood's mouth tightened.

"But..."

"He is a child, not a fish on your hook, Wood. He knows nothing. Let him go." Undergrove did not alter his blasé focus on whatever was outside his window.

Wood wanted to continue to question me, certain I knew things he wished to know, but he dared not relinquish his superior position as a government official and my elder.

Undergrove turned toward me, his attention caught by something over my shoulder. His jaw set and his eyes slitted like a reptile's.

"We need to go. Now," he snapped.

"Another time perhaps." Wood touched his hat again. I glanced behind me. Spin was leaning on the fence around the White House grounds; his eyes locked on Undergrove's. "Please, let me know if there is anything I can do to be of assistance during your stay," Wood continued, unaware of the staring match between his companion and the little blue man. "I lodge at Mrs. Pittman's Boarding House on Third between Pennsylvania and C. There is a private dining room set aside for government officials who board there, so if you come, we may speak privately." He waited for me to share my own lodgings, but I pretended not to understand his expectation, continuing cheerfully on my walk to the National.

"Do not think about Bernie and her Weavings in that creature's presence," Spin warned me vituperatively. *"He is fey and dangerous."*

"You are fey," I pointed out.

"Yes, and dangerous."

The National Theater had been closed for nearly a decade after a fire gutted it, and the previous owner had not rebuilt. Leonard Grover purchased it, rebuilding it with the intention of competing with the Washington Theater and the recently renovated Ford's Theater. Now that the quiet little government town had burgeoned into a vital hub, it was proving to be a wise investment.

The rebuilt building's exterior was a compromise between commercial needs and Grover's desire to present a theater admired for its architectural appeal, resulting in an altogether disappointing outcome. A tailor's shop and a saloon bookended the entrance. A gentleman could buy a new suit, see a show, and have dinner or a drink within the same hundred feet. A balcony with a balustrade perched like a lady's hat over the entrance. Here, luminary performers might greet their adoring fans, or speeches might be made. It was, after all, D.C.

The requirement of every structure in the city celebrating patriotism was evidenced by an eagle sculptured mid-flap, its wings frozen in frustration, perched at the center of the building's façade and flanked by copies of classical statues depicting human females, strangely sized to be no taller than the bird. Without the size or power to make any artistic impact on those standing on the street below, these statues, rendered in the Roman style, functioned as mere exclamation points to the eagle. One had no head but boasted naked breasts, the other had a head and modest cloth sculpted to cling but cover its carved female anatomy, as if, even at forty feet in the air, the only way a woman's figure was acceptable was if it was either blanketed or headless.

Mister Grover was not at the theater, but once I introduced myself and my purpose, the manager allowed me to explore backstage, the fly system, the theater's rigging, and the available lighting. When he remodeled, Grover installed a gas lighting system, including modern ventilation to keep the gases from asphyxiating the audience, but word among theater folk was that the rebuild put appearance before comfort. In the winter, the building was freezing. In the summer, everyone was on the verge of fainting. Accordingly, actors refused engagements at certain times of the year. Our performances were scheduled for September.

I exited the theater and paused. It would be an easy walk back to Lafayette Square. The Executive Park grounds and the White House's classical structure and painted sandstone walls were stunning in the fading day's light, but I only had to walk in the opposite direction to return to the downtown area where I had seen my mother earlier. Searching an unfamiliar town for a person who may or may not be present with night coming on reeks of futility, but returning to the Sewards and simply waiting for dinner sounded boring.

I could not keep waiting for someone else to do what I thought needed to be done, then feel frustrated with them when they did not do it. It was a new city and available for me to explore. I turned left toward the Center Market.

As my aunt said, Washington City was a relatively new capital, but the original plan by French architect, Messieurs L'Enfant, had already been revised. What was built according to his design was visually impactful, with the Capitol Building set on the highest hill at the center and roads laid out in a grid-array surrounding the Capitol with several roads crossing the grid at angles, which created irregularly shaped spaces that were difficult to build on and therefore became parks. From any direction, it was a conscious plan, an idealist's vision that celebrated beauty and aspired to inspire. It was meant as a lesson in the positive effects of inspirational beauty's use as a focal point designed to affect those who lived and worked in the space.

But this was Washington City, not the Palace of Versailles, and the Parisian Architect's plan ran afoul of a government in need of workspaces and housing for multiple departments and many people, not the Sun King and his court. The design needed to be more than pretty. It needed to work.

When the war came, the quiet city, still finding its footing, was suddenly launched to the very American status of a boom town. The juxtaposition between L'Enfant's designed elegance and people's immediate need to put something somewhere, often themselves, found them at odds. The juxtaposition of swiftly thrown-up wood shacks cowering in the mud at the feet of grand, marble-colonnaded buildings declared artistry lost.

As the sun went down, the hordes of flies that had swooped and landed on us all day were coming to rest on every unmoving surface, like spilled black seeds sprouting not at one point but four, with tiny legs and wings complicating the outline of their bodies.

The mosquitoes, barely held in check in the warmth of the day, now rose in bloodlust-driven swarms, their little proboscis hunting for any crack or crevice to stab flesh and suck up the sticky, sweet blood of a warm body. Horses swished their tails and shook their heads to clear the nuisances. Dogs yelped and tucked their tails, racing to get away from the actively hunting swarm clouds. Cats, being cats, bit and swiped at the air, rippling their tails, their ears laid back flat against their heads, silently damning the determined insects.

When the bats appeared, swooping through the air and scooping up mouthfuls of the tiny disease carriers, I wanted to whoop and cheer the black avenging angels.

But the mosquitoes were not the only creatures that preferred the dark. As I approached the market block, the last vendors were tying tarps over the beds of their wagons and heading back to their farms or workshops. Spin appeared, striding beside me.

"Bernie is not here, but you are," I pointed out his lie that he had been following my aunt. The little blue man shrugged, unconcerned. "Why are you here?" I asked.

"I am touring the city."

Down the street, a man, bent and bloated into the likeness of a summer squash, watched me with slitted snake eyes. His long, unwashed hair was twisted like vines, his torn pants striped like the rind of a watermelon. The new cloak he wore over this haphazard ensemble screamed it had been kidnapped and was being held for ransom. He had no wagon or cart. No companions or assistants. In fact, he looked to have no trade at all outside of troubling others, and he had set his sights on troubling me.

"Can you help me if he attacks me?" I asked the blue man.

"No." He vanished.

"What about the pitchfork? You were willing enough to help then." My would-be attacker was moving closer. My breath quickened, the march of my chest moving at the long loping pace of a tall man's strides. My body wanted to run, but to where? The market building was to one side of me, the Washington Canal to the other. The tide being out, the canal was empty except for garbage and sewage. The honest working people were all leaving. I needed to disappear.

I spotted a single wagon nearby. Its owner, fiddling with the harness at his horse's head. I ducked around to the far side, out of view of Squash Man, and dove beneath the cart. I had been practicing summoning my skill to become invisible at will, as well as holding it off when disappearing might be inconvenient, but since Bernie and I identified being afraid as my most dependable state for success, I had high hopes for now. I squatted under the cart's cover, breathing deeply, willing myself to disappear.

I am nothing. I am no one. No one can see me. I am nothing. I am no one. No one can see me," I chanted.

The wagon rolled away, leaving me squatting in the roadway, exposed…or, if I was successful in my efforts, not.

I looked to see if Squash Man saw me. He turned his neckless body left, then right, then made a slow circle, like a coiling snake. His squinty eyes disappeared behind facial features reminiscent of scabby growths on a diseased vegetable, but he did not see me. I was invisible. No longer seeing this as a weakness of character, I smiled.

Act Three, Scene Four: The Armory Hospital, Washington, D.C., the Same Evening.

Being invisible did not fool the mosquitoes. I was briefly amused by imagining the horrified reaction of someone seeing my invisible form covered by the insects, but once I was invisible, I quickly left the market area, headed for the Armory Hospital using the Smithsonian Castle as my guide.

Passing along the backside of the Smithsonian, I cut through its orchard. Crossing the canal via a railroad bridge, I arrived at the Armory Hospital grounds from the opposite direction our carriage had taken earlier.

This was a side of the barracks compound not included in Whitman's tour, shacks snuggled like pebbles around the northernmost barracks, bare-bone domiciles tacked together to shelter the soiled doves and camp women that accompanied an army. Those who were not engaged in their duties stood in doorways or lounged half-reclined on makeshift benches made of stumps and boards, clad in corsets or chemise, pantaloons or skirts that outlined their hips, long dressing robes or short bed jackets hanging over their shoulders as a nod to decency. Unaware of my presence among them, they talked together without affectation, sipping from flasks and smoking tobacco rolled inside thin leaves of unbleached paper.

The sun had gone down below the heights that protected the city, and lamps were lit, their glow turning the camp into a place more romantic in appearance than it deserved. Making my way around to the front door of the nearest barracks, I spied Spin sliding into one of the soiled doves' hovels.

You are safe. No one is hunting you. There is no one here to hurt you. Taking deep breaths, I willed myself to relax and become visible. Holding my hand out, I tested the result, but it was no barometer. Whether I was invisible to others or not, I always saw myself.

I walked up the center aisle of the barracks between the beds, moving as if I belonged, a physicality somewhere between Cyril Fitz-

Royale's "no one questions my place" and Walt Whitman's humble "I am useful and polite, and therefore my presence is acceptable". I nodded at a nurse, watching her reaction. If she acknowledged me, I would know she saw me. I was gratified when her eyes focused on me, even more so when she refrained from asking me the dreaded, "Can I help you?" question. My plan was based on the truth: I was looking for someone, not a male someone, and not a soldier.

As I approached the back of the ward, I began the speech I had rehearsed in my head: "Gentleman, excuse me, but I am hoping you may be able to help me. I am looking for a woman."

I had not considered the reaction to the unfortunate wording of my request, the snickers and mixed chorus of, "Aren't we all?" and "The ladies are out back, son."

"Excuse me, no. I am looking for my mother," I corrected my misleading wording. Immediately, the soldier's expressions changed. A mother was not just a woman; they were warriors of the womb, who defied death to bring us into the world. "She is petite with ginger hair, pale skin, and freckled. Her name is Leonara Becket, but she could be going by Leonie Becket. The last we heard from her, she was in California."

"California's a long way from D.C.," one of the soldiers commented.

"We have information that leads us to believe she may have made her way here."

"Are you a Pinkerton man?" Another asked. I shook my head. I could not imagine that I bore any resemblance to such a person.

"Does she know you're looking for her?" the first man asked.

"She does not know I am in Washington City," I replied.

"Maybe she doesn't want to be found," the man suggested. "Sometimes that happens when a man is…unkind."

Johnathan Becket had been "unkind", but he was dead. Whatever kept my mother away, that was not it.

"Did you check at the camp out back?" One man tossed his head toward the dove's camp.

"She wouldn't be there," I replied.

"You'd be surprised. There aren't many ways for a woman alone to make a good wage, especially if she's hiding from her family."

I was loath to say too much, but this assumption was not going to help me. "I am her son. We are close. She is not hiding from me," I said firmly. "It is possible that she is working for the Union," I added. "Not for Pinkerton but…" I left the sentence dangling, allowing them to draw their own conclusions.

"That's a big leap, young fellow." An older man, his neck rope-burned, the skin chafed red, stepped forward. His voice sounded scraped like shattered shells on the beach.

"We've had a few letters," I shied to the left of the truth. "It sounded as if she might be in trouble. I am worried she needs help. If any of you have seen her, or know of someone who might have, please let me know."

"And how are we to do that?" the man asked.

"You can tell me," Walt Whitman's gentle voice spoke from behind me. "I am a friend of the family. I will know how to get word to him."

"You're a friend of Walt's?" another of the soldiers spoke. "Why didn't you say so? Of course, we'll keep an eye and ear out."

Whitman walked forward, closing the space between us so that we were speaking more intimately.

"It is very kind of you, Mister Whitman. I did not mean to trouble you."

"What are we here for if not to make the paths of our fellow travelers easier, Master Drake?"

"Please, call me Kit, Sir."

"Then you must call me 'Walt' and we can do away with the sirs and masters. After all, I have been a friend of your family for many years. There are eleven more barracks. Is it your intention to visit them all?"

"It is."

"Then we should move on." I nodded my gratitude to the men as we exited. "Why did you not mention this search for your mother when you were here earlier?" Whitman asked as we walked to the next building.

"I thought I spied her on the street while we were on our way to see you, but I could not be sure, and I did not think it appropriate to insert my business into my aunt's, that being the reason for our visit.

Burke said he would make inquiries but…" I was not sure how to explain my impulsive decision to begin the search on my own.

"Some things a person must do themself," Whitman finished the sentence for me.

"She is my mother." I fought the tears blurring my eyes. "There is nothing I would not do for her."

"Except leave her alone." The bluntness of his words startled me, but when I looked up, I saw he meant no rebuke. He was a poet, and breaking the conventions of how words were stitched into phrases, forcing our ears to hear them anew, was his gift. "The bond between a parent and child is a love that cannot be broken, even by death."

"My mother is not dead," I said.

"I hope that is true, but whether the situation with that is, you live, and you are the summation and testimony of who she is, and what she believes. It is a special sort of guise they gift us, which we then carry throughout our lives."

Whitman and I walked together in a silence that was not empty.

At the second barracks, I repeated my plea, better worded so as not to replay the misunderstandings, and ending with Whitman's offer to be the go-between for any information that was discovered after I left. Once we left and were moving on, our conversation resumed.

"This draft seems a hard thing…sending men to war when they have not chosen it. And there is so much hatred. I believed we would be a country of promise for all."

"It is a difficult time to be starting in life. My young friends tell me they feel like the world is broken and they fear there will be no future left for them."

I felt the same concern for our country's future as Whitman's other young friends.

"And so, you write poetry because your words give people hope."

"Poetry will not fix what is wrong with this world. Longfellow said it best when he said the written word is fragile, the pages easily torn, burned…scattered. Time destroys paper. What remains of worth will be what was written on the hearts of men." He smiled disparagingly. "Not an exact quote, but the idea is there, and still, I must write because it is like breathing to me. Thoughts sweep in, and they won't stop badgering me until I write them down."

"I have felt that," I confessed. "Sometimes when I get an idea to improve some gadget, I have to scribble it down, or I feel like I will go mad. It is as if this thing I am drawing already exists somewhere, and it is going to pound on my door until I open it and introduce myself."

Whitman chuckled. "Creativity is gloriously messy. Not everyone understands that."

My mother does, I thought wistfully. And yet she was not here. We walked along in further silence.

"I met your father once. You are nothing like him."

"The difference is intentional," I confessed. "But thank you." It was not my shame that led me to seek the comforting shroud of invisibility. It was Becket's, and I was not required to bear it. I needed to set it aside.

Sometimes our talks in the barracks were brief; sometimes there were questions, but as the evening progressed, we kept moving and talking. The early summer night was warm, frog song drifted up from the nearby swamps and riparian pond edges. The common folk were settled in for the night, while Washington City's social set prepared for an evening out or relaxed with a smoke and a drink.

We had five barracks left when Whitman announced it was nearing 'lights out' and we would have to stop.

"You can come back and finish tomorrow," he suggested.

"It is unlikely I will be allowed to go anywhere tomorrow," I confessed.

"You did not tell Bernie what you planned, and she does not know where you are," Walt surmised.

"I did not plan. I previewed Grover's Theater, and when I came out, I simply chose to turn one way instead of the other. No one knows where I am."

"You know, your aunt will be worried to death." I did not think that was true. "I will send a runner to the house and have them meet us, but not here. We have one more stop to make." Whitman called over a young chap who looked neither injured nor ill. The poet-nurse wrote a quick note on a page from the notebook he carried in his pocket, tore it out, and handed it to the boy along with a coin. A minute later, I heard the clop clopping of a horse setting off on the road that ran in front of the Smithsonian Castle. Whitman and I continued South.

As we neared our destination, the poet paused. Moonlight shimmered on the dark, high tidewater now filling the Washington Canal. Back at the barracks, a lonely harmonica began to whine, an Irish tenor joining, the tune weighted by loneliness.

"A complicated people, the Irish. But they write a tune to make your heart bleed," Whitman mused. "Even with all the savagery and ugliness of this war, there is still beauty, Kit. Don't forget that. If there wasn't, what would we fight for?"

We walked toward a collection of buildings in the far Southeast corner of the open area that stretched from the White House to the canal, and Whitman guided me to a four-story brick house. A carriage was just pulling away, having dropped off an older, heavyset man dressed like a gentleman but without the flair of New York. He approached the door and was let in by a comely woman dressed and made up to look like a wood nymph, her yellow tresses entwined with leaves, her arms bare, decolletage pushed high.

"This is Miss Mary Anne Hall's house," Whitman explained as we entered the walkway. "It is a place where men in government come to enjoy what is referred to as 'horizontal relaxation'.

"I understand what kind of a house it is, Walt," I assured him.

"Miss Mary and her sister, Lizzie, have many important connections and hear a great many things about what is happening in Washington and around the country. The lady of the house also knows things in an uncanny sort of way."

"She is a spiritualist?"

"I would say more of an artist who sees patterns and weaves." My stomach clenched. Was Mary Hall a Weaver, like Aunt Bernie? "She is also very active in women's charities, helping females who find themselves in need of assistance," Walt continued his biography of the woman we were about to meet. "If your mother found herself in need, she might have come here. Whoever Bernie is sending to fetch you will be here soon, so 'best to be direct. Ask what you need to know and try not to gawk at the ladies."

"I would never gawk at ladies," I promised in mock sincerity. Whitman looked at me, eyebrows raised, and we both burst into laughter. "There are a few fine-looking young men as well," he warned me as he lifted the fine brass knocker.

Act Three, Scene Five: Miss Mary Hall's Bawdy House, Washington, D.C., the same night

Inside Miss Mary's, wealth was the word, the scent, the flavor. It smelled like expensive tobacco, spiced alcohol, and French perfume. A piano forte played in a nearby room. The furnishings were upholstered in burgundy velvet, the drapes the same color, with gold fringe. Every stick of wood, the carved legs, knob tops, and side tables were walnut or cherry. No expense was spared to make Miss Mary's guests feel comfortable in luxury.

The round table next to the door presented a silver tray with fluted champagne glasses, their bubbles effervescing in the golden light of the crystalline gaslight chandeliers.

"Lizzie." Whitman kissed the owner's sister on both rouged cheeks. Her long sausage curls brushed his graying whiskers, glossy tubes of curled hair, the color of wheat straw.

"Walt." She eyed me with a playful smile. "A new toy? For us or for you?"

"A new friend," Whitman corrected her kindly.

"How sad. Such youth and innocence makes my…mouth water." She smiled at me seductively, pursing her lips. I blinked at her in astonishment, uncomfortable with this sort of attention.

Whitman stepped closer to me. "He is not a street urchin you can lure from my side, Elizabeth. He is Lady Bernadette Drake's nephew." Lizzie dropped her act. "Kit, may I introduce Miss Elizabeth Hall. Miss Elizabeth, Master Kit Drake."

"Ooo. Will you be a lord when your auntie dies, foxy little Kit?"

"No. My aunt's is an honorary title, Miss Hall. It is not inheritable," I replied, still on edge.

"We are here to see your sister, Lizzie. Can she make the time? It will only take a few minutes."

"I'll ask." Miss Lizzie swished out of the room, tossing me a last look over her shoulder.

"Well, what a surprise," a familiar voice rose above the piano music, "Come to get your wick wet, eh, Young Drake?" Fernando Wood slapped me on the back. I pressed my lips together and tolerated the overfamiliar gesture and assumption. Looking as weaselly as seemed humanly possible, Wood's mutton chops and the cut of his hair added to the unflattering characterization. The congressman took in Whitman's work clothes, his end of a long day hair, and the smell of the hospital clinging to his skin. "And who is this…gentleman?" I glanced at Whitman, uncertain if, under the circumstances, he would wish to be introduced, but Walt saved me from my confusion.

"Walt Whitman." The nonverbal 'You may have heard of me' was a triumph I would have stood in ovation for. In a beat, Whitman the humble had become Whitman the intellectual giant. A lesser man would have treated Wood like a bug crawling across his shoe—not an interesting bug you wanted to study, the kind you flick away or squash. Whitman might have avoided society's games, but he knew how to play. The subject of my reason for being at the house vanished from Wood's mind, and he took a step back, blinking as if that could reset his faux pas.

"My apologies, Mister Whitman," the Congressman recovered himself. "I did not…"

"Recognize me? It happens to people not in literary circles. Writers do not seek fame. It simply comes to us." I turned away to hide my amusement. "Excuse us, I believe Miss Hall is waiting for us." Lizzie returned and was waiting at the edge of the room.

Miss Mary was the antithesis of her sister; all the rich colors of a chestnut, polished and smooth, artifice applied so subtly, its presence remained uncertain. Intelligent eyes and a gentle mouth balanced a handsome face, which made no effort to be coy, girlish, or seductive. She was a woman firmly grounded in her own intelligence. I liked her immediately and had to remind myself what Bernie said about waiting until people earned trust.

"Mary," Whitman greeted her fondly. "Thank you for making the time to see us."

"I always have time for you, Walt. You know that." The close echo to what Bernie said in her meeting with the poet did not escape me. Whitman's friendship was treasured. Even more remarkably, his female friends trusted him implicitly. I understood. I was proud to walk at his side and would be proud to follow him wherever he led, as I was sure many before me had been, and many more would be in the future. Walt Whitman was a navigator of souls.

After introducing me, adding the Becket name and my mother's, Walt explained my task.

"You have gained an impressive knight-advocate, Master…Drake is it, or Becket? Which do you prefer?"

"If you called me Kit, it would please me very much," I replied. "When I use a surname, I take to my great aunt's: Drake. But last I knew, my mother was using her married name, Becket, or she may have reverted to her maiden name by now, that of Marchand."

"I have had the honor of seeing your great aunt perform," Miss Mary sidestepped my unasked question about my mother. "She is truly the actress of our age."

"She is brilliant," I agreed. "As a stagehand, I have the fortune to watch her nightly from the light towers. Her performance is always impeccable. We are here to arrange a benefit for the National Sanitary Commission in the fall. You must come. I can have tickets set aside for you if you like?"

"You are very kind. I would enjoy that. But I am sure that inviting me to the theater is not your purpose here. You are seeking your mother. Does she not write?"

"Not to me."

Miss Mary looked to Whitman, and he gave her the subtlest nod of encouragement. "If your mother is in Washington City, Kit, it is likely there is a reason she has not written."

"I hear that a lot," I replied, but I did not back down.

"This is not a small rural town, young man. It is a city at the center of a war. You do not seem aware that making such inquiries could put your mother and yourself in danger."

"I believe she is already in danger," I stated.

"The danger you perceived as a child because of her absence," Mary countered. "But you are not a child anymore. You are a young man able to understand the nuances of compromise that life demands of us, particularly in a time of war."

"You are saying, politely, that I have indulged selfish and childish notions."

Mary nodded. "I am. And I think you have already realized this, but the child in you fears that letting go of your search would be an abandonment of your mother."

"How could you possibly know that?" I demanded.

Whitman chuckled. "He is not going to let this go, Mary."

"And his aunt has failed to keep him in check," Mary countered. She turned back to me. "This is what I am able to tell you, young Kit. Since before the war, our government had a system for gathering information that was not a system, where each field officer reported to a different military man, each of those officers tasked with deciding whether to listen, act, pass on the information, or ignore it. Too often, they did just that, and it cost the Union's military efforts dearly. The rates for information being acted on or passed up the chain of command were disastrous, and mistakes were made that should never have been made. Pinkerton did what he could, but he was a civilian contractor not allowed to be present at military strategy meetings and therefore often lacked information that might have helped his agents in the field. Likewise, he often had information that might have helped the generals, but which was not shared with them because they refused to allow him to attend their meetings and did not read his reports. The rivalries between some of these generals are an embarrassment.

"The good news is that McLellan's leadership in D.C. is finally finished, and Burnside is out as the head of the Army of the Potomac. Joe Hooker is now in charge, and Joe is a thinking man, not interested in a political future, so he has no agenda outside of his commander-in-chief's. With the administration's support, he has organized a new department, The Bureau of Military Intelligence, under Colonel Sharpe. This is not a secret in D.C., but folk outside the capital only pay attention to news of the battles.

"Now, it is possible that Sharpe, or someone who works for him, knows something about your mother's whereabouts, but whether they are at liberty to tell you anything is another matter. If you go to see them, which I recommend you do if that eases your mind and sends you home to New York safely, you should be prepared to learn nothing, or learn something that is not what you hoped for. Please, remember that until this war is over--and it will be over someday, many men and women are making great and terrible sacrifices for the ideal of freedom. If your mother is among them, and she is not communicating with you, it is a decision, not an accident. If I were in danger, I would avoid drawing attention to my loved ones to protect them, even if it was painful.

"I am asking you to consider respecting your mother's decision, Kit. But recognizing your determination, I have told you what I am able. Good luck." She turned to Whitman, her expression indicating she had said all she was going to. I was sure she knew more.

"I will be there in a moment." Whitman nudged me toward the door, indicating he had further business with Miss Mary.

I returned to the main room and took a second glass of champagne. People always claimed that alcohol steadied the nerves, but I have never had champagne before. It did not seem to do anything for my nerves. It went right to my head.

"You are back." Fernando Wood was seated out of sight to one side of an archway that separated the main entry room and the adjacent parlor where the piano was being played.

"I am." I was not in the mood to partake in a conversational sparring match. "So, is this when we continue the game where you try to coerce information out of me about my aunt, and I prove my loyalty and manners by not revealing whatever it is you imagine she is hiding?" I spoke with rash honesty.

Wood frowned. "How many of those have you had?" he indicated the fluted champagne glass.

"My aunt is famous, Congressman Wood, and therefore a public figure, but she is also British, and the British find it ill-mannered to share their private lives. I understand for Americans this can appear like deviousness, but I assure you Lady Drake's desire for privacy has nothing to do with a need to hide underhanded activities," I lied, feeling quite clever. When I drank champagne, I was quite a good liar. I took another sip. It went down much easier than Wood's scotch or Charles Stratton's bourbon.

"I do not need a lesson on the differences of etiquette between ourselves and our cousins across the pond," Wood replied brusquely.

"I am simply trying to be helpful, Sir," I protested innocently.

"Somehow I doubt that."

"I think we both understand why I would wish to please my aunt. I live with her," I babbled on. "I work with her, and she is my guardian. But what I do not understand is why you imagine I would wish to please you? You are practically a stranger. Powerful, yes, and with some influential friends, though I imagine they are not as friendly as they once were—nor as powerful."

Beneath his gray whiskered cheeks, Wood's face was coloring red. "As I suspected, your mind has been tainted by proximity to your aunt's Bohemian friends, but the world is not built from cloud-fantasies. The Union may win a few battles, but they will lose this war, because no matter how you dress them up or school them, no white person in any state is going to accept people of color as their equals."

I thought of Idabelle, and Burke, and Dweeti, and my fists balled at my sides. I wanted nothing so badly as to punch Wood, even if I did it badly. Even if it would cause trouble for Bernie. Fortunately, at that moment Bernie and Burke burst in.

"Kit! Thank God, you are safe." My aunt rushed toward me as if to crush me to her, stopping when she saw Wood. Her composure reset, her spine straightened, her manner resuming its imperious habit.

Miss Mary joined us. "Lady Drake, your nephew is a prodigiously stubborn young man to be unleashed in Washington City. So purposeful. I believe it is a family trait." Her sarcasm was subtle. The smile she gave Bernie was rife with a complex history I was not party to, but if Miss Mary was a Weaver, it made more sense. "I assure you, no harm has come to him, not even the frolicking type we offer our clients. He arrived in the company of our friend, Mister Whitman, and he will leave in your custody. But I would caution you not to lose him again, Lady Drake. The city is overflowing with rascals and rogues."

"Thank you," Bernie acknowledged the madam with cool politeness. "And thank you, Walt." She turned back to Miss Mary. "Do we owe you anything?" She indicated the champagne.

"There is never a fee for champagne at my establishment," Mary assured her. "I am relieved that things turned out so well. I gave your nephew the information he was seeking. Which is nothing really, except to inquire at the Bureau of Military Intelligence. Ask for Colonel Sharpe. And please be careful on your return journey to New York. Travel is quite dangerous these days." Her eyes went to Wood, telegraphing her mistrust as she raised a graceful arm, gesturing toward the door. "You might want to avoid it for your own safety."

Taking me firmly by the arm, Bernie marched me out. Behind us, I heard Miss Mary telling Wood that his lady friend was ready for him in an upstairs room.

Walt doffed his hat, holding the carriage door open as Bernie settled herself inside.

"People of difference are everywhere, Kit," he spoke to me quietly. "Most of us remain half hidden, but we are there, and now and then, here and there, we find each other. Thank you. It was a surprising and most delightful evening."

"I know you only meant to be of assistance to the boy, Walt, but I am not sure how helpful it is spreading my niece's name all over Washington," my aunt chided the Great Gray Poet.

"He is an artist, Bernie. He needs someone he can speak his heart and mind to. It is dangerous to have a youth of such tender years stewing in his own thoughts and imaginings."

"God forbid, they might write poetry," Bernie retorted. Walt took her hand and held it in silence, just looking into her eyes. After a long moment, she dropped her head. "I am not unaware of my nephew's private pain and his need for a confidant, my friend. It is being handled." She knocked on the carriage ceiling to signal the driver to go.

As the carriage pulled out and made its way along the street, it came up alongside a woman wrapped in a wool shawl, her head and face covered even in the warm evening. Age and infirmities made her movements slow, dripping honey. As we passed her, just for a moment, she glanced up at my window and our eyes met. Hers were wells of hollow sadness; a sadness that mirrored my own.

We moved beyond her before my mind asked why I felt such kinship between us. Had her gray hair had streaks of tawny red? Had there been a recognition between us connected to the sadness we shared? I leaned out the window looking back, but she was gone, dissolved into the grounds of the Smithsonian Castle.

"You have put us in a spot, Kit." Bernie's head was turned toward the window on the other side of the carriage. "My private life needs to remain private. My *name* is known, not myself. In the past, you understood my job was acting, but you know better now. My true job is subterfuge. When we get back to the city, I will put about my version of tonight's adventures. You will be cast as the inexperienced youth who foolishly puts himself in danger, and Wood will join the small group responsible for rescuing you, for which I will express my gratitude. There is a chance that flattery will appease his ego enough to keep him from spreading wicked stories and trying to cut us off socially."

"The man is a traitor and an ass."

"Please do not mimic Charles Stratton's worst attributes, Kit. Damn it, Walt insists you are in need of male companionship, but all the men available seem determined to lead you into more trouble. Ah, well, things without remedy should be without regard. What's done is done. The affair is over, and no one was physically injured. That is something." The carriage pulled into Lafayette Park. We were back at the Seward's.

Act Three, Scene Six: Seward's house, Lafayette Park, Washington, D.C., later that night.

Missus Seward met us at the door, a smile of relief sweetening her wan face.

"Oh, thank the Lord, you found him and he's safe. Let's get you inside and fetch you something to steady your nerves." Which was code for serving a person an alcoholic drink. I understood now why champagne did not have this nerve-reviving reputation. I imbibed nearly three glasses of it, and the floor was rippling beneath my feet.

"Tea would be fine. Thank you, Missus Seward. I really am rather done in." Bernie laughed in deprecating embarrassment. "I think I will go up to my room, if that is not inconvenient?"

"Of course. Of course." Missus Seward patted my aunt's hand. "I will have Fanny bring a nice cup of chamomile up."

"That would be lovely." Bernie dragged herself up the stairs as if her dainty feet supported the body of a large beast. Emotion streaming from her.

Had I done that? Was I the cause, or maybe we did it together, she by making the choices she did, and me by pointing them out? I did not mean to hurt her. Or maybe I did. But I did not mean to crack her open like an egg and expose the soft yolk of her. I would not have thought there was such softness there.

I looked at Burke, wondering which of us should go up and put Bernie's pieces back together. Without exchanging a word, it was decided that it would be me, as it was my transgression that caused the problem.

I climbed the stairs and knocked on Bernie's door.

"It's Kit, Aunt. May I come in?" After a few moments, she opened the door, her eyelashes wet, but her cheeks freshly dried. "I am sorry. I should not have wandered without notifying you. I did not think about how worried you might be."

"I do not wish to coddle you, Kit, but your impetuosity leads me to believe you do not yet understand the intrigues and dangers of this new world you have stepped into with the Coterie. I have no children…"

I stopped her. "You do not need to hide the truth from me, Aunt. I looked at your scrapbook, and I saw Ida and Ira Junior staring into the mirror of each other's faces. I know she is your daughter. I won't say anything. It is your secret to keep or reveal, and I do not judge you for grasping at happiness, however complicated the outcome. You have not allowed yourself enough joy, Aunt."

"You analyze me like a character you are going to play. Are you sure you're not an actor?" she jibed.

"I am not interested in the attention and notoriety."

"Not a drop of Becket in you." I smiled at the compliment. "In the morning, we will go to the Bureau of Military Intelligence and talk to this Colonel Sharpe. I am sure Secretary Seward can get us a meeting."

There was a tentative knock on the door. Seward's daughter, Fanny, had arrived with Bernie's tea. The child was stick-thin, with hound-dog eyes, the curls alongside her face like floppy ears, and apologetic in manner.

"Thank you, Fanny." Bernie took the cup, and the girl tiptoed away. "Now, I have had a long, challenging day, nephew, and I just want to sit here and drink my tea, then go to sleep, so go away."

I closed Bernie's door behind me.

Fanny Seward was sitting on the stairs halfway down, peering into the room below. She turned and held her finger to her lips to let me know to be quiet. Intrigued, I stepped down and joined her. Squatting so my head was nearer her level, I could see into the parlor room to the right of the foyer.

It was dark, lit only by the fire's flames and a gas lamp on a side table. Lean and craggy like the twisted root of a grandfather tree, Abraham Lincoln sat before the fire, his long legs stretched out, his booted feet resting on the grate. The silhouette caught and carved by the fire's light was a man of layered complications. Sadness, fatigue, and regret were wrought on the peaks and pinnacles of his face, his troubles limned in the set of his shoulders, and the resigned curve of his spine.

"Common folk don't think too much on change, Mister President," a voice like unplowed earth spoke. It was a woman's voice, too unapologetic and strong to be a Southern woman's, despite the drawl in the accent. "We're too busy trying to do for our sick children, putting food on the table, and trying to avoid the lash. We know change will come. There's no holding it back, but whatever it's going to do, it has to take care of itself 'cause we're just trying to survive."

"It will be better now with Emancipation," Seward assured the petite woman.

"That's Harriet," Fanny Seward whispered. "Harriet Tubman. She is a special friend of my mother's. Her house is near ours in Auburn. She's a guide for folk escaping the South."

On the Underground Railroad.

"Black people have always been free," Missus Tubman spoke plainly. "We were born free. Since we came to this country, we've just been held prisoner," Harriet Tubman's voice was all smoke and loam, crackling like breaking twigs.

"Black people will not accept chains forever," Seward declared. "Things will change, Harriet. Look at Haiti. I know waiting seems like a poor strategy, but change takes time."

"Beg pardon, Mister Seward, but these men aren't going to change. Why should they? Where's the profit for them in changing when they sit on top of everything, taking the best for themselves? They believe that because they're white, they're God's chosen, picked to wield the bullwhip, and they're going to hold onto that belief. They're gonna pass down those beliefs about being better to each new generation like a family heirloom. It's part of the culture that's worked its way deep under their skin, like a worm, and that worm will kill its host before it leaves. The South is playing a long game."

"The laws of the land are being changed, Harriet. People will have to change with them."

"I know you mean well, Mister Seward, and I'm grateful for all you and Frances have done to help my people, but when your back has never felt the lash, I don't see that it's your place to say 'wait a few decades.' What if it were Fanny being taken from you, her little body used in cruel ways by heartless men? Would you still be saying 'wait: slavery will end itself'?"

"Daddy is here in Washington too much," Fanny confided quietly to me. "He isn't in Auburn with us. He doesn't see what Mama, and I, and Miss Harriet see when the people come to stay in our Old Kitchen."

I understood. The Seward's house in Auburn was a Station House. Before the Emancipation Declaration, the Sewards risked everything for their belief that all people being created equal meant all people, of all colors, and they had broken the laws of their country to stand by that belief.

"Laws don't change what people believe," Missus Tubman's exhortation continued. "Folks will just find a way to go around the law or wait until no one's looking and do what they damn well please. I know. I spent my whole life among them."

"But other countries have done away with slavery, Harriet," Missus Seward pointed out. "The Netherlands, Britain. Most European countries have already changed their laws. If they did it, we can."

Missus Tubman shook her head. "A person can have a description of a river crossing, Frances. They can read about where the deep spots were last season, or a month ago, where the footing could be dangerous, how the currents have run in the past, but rivers change constantly, and for folk to be safe, they need an experienced guide who knows that river and can look at it and read its currents." She turned to the president. "You be trying to lead us across this American river called Freedom with no guide, Mister President."

Lincoln smiled ruefully. "'I challenge you to look into the seeds of time and say which grains will grow and which will not', Missus Tubman." It was a line in *Macbeth*, Banquo challenging the sister-witches over their foretelling of MacBeth and his companions' futures.

The feisty little woman grunted. "We don't need a gris-gris woman to read this country's future. Look at what folks been doing, and it will tell you what they're gonna keep on doing."

Lincoln looked around the room. Fanny shifted her position, the silk of her dress swishing, and he turned enough to see us crouched on the stairs. The sharp angles of his face softened. I expected the lanky thinness and the angularity of Lincoln's face, having seen it lampooned many times in newspaper sketches. What I did not foresee was how quiet the man was on the inside.

"A lack of knowledge is its own kind of enslavement. We must help our brothers and sisters in the South see the value of giving others the freedom and respect they claim for themselves. That is the vision of America."

Fanny leaned over to whisper to me again. "This has been a particularly trying day for the President. Papa told me President Lincoln spent the whole day judging treason trials of captured Confederate soldiers and trying to find reasons to pardon them." Her kind nature brought a shine of tears to her eyes at the revelation of this powerful man's compassionate character. It was not something Lincoln donned to impress others. It was the core of him.

"You are right, Missus Tubman, laws aren't what change people's minds," Lincoln agreed. "Our stories are what guide humanity, even now as we enter the Industrial Age and thrust old ways aside as if they have no worth to modern lives. I believe that change makes heroes every day, Missus Tubman, and everyday heroes make history."

I thought these things myself, though I never voiced them so eloquently. Walt Whitman could have. Ralph Waldo Emerson probably had, but here was Lincoln, a politician, saying stories mattered; the stories people told were important because, through them, humanity was reminded of the best qualities in ourselves and the character we should aspire to embody. People needed stories that inspired them--stories that held ideas that felt so big inside that they had to be shared with friends, family, and our children—especially our children. Humanity needed leaders with the vision and courage to bring us into a better future, not just look back at what was and pretend it could be again.

Stories without worth or meaning? They served no purpose. They were a distraction…noise.

"But I cannot subscribe to your vision, Missus Tubman," the President went on. "If the world were made from your words, our country would eternally struggle, with little hope. Giving up on the belief that we can make positive change is a declaration that human beings are lost and will never embrace their better nature, and I cannot accept that and live. I have made mistakes as the leader of this country. There are things I would do differently now--compromises I would not make, but I cannot accept that our country will not become whole again and our differences will be healed. I beg you to leave me that solace of hope, Missus Tubman, for it is all that keeps me going."

This oak of a man, with his tree-bark exterior, was done in…exhausted. In the past two years, he had lost friends, a favored son, and countless young men who were not his blood but for whom he mourned. He was the writer and director of a future, only he had the vision to execute. A grand production to inspire the world, every piece, from teacups to ties, placed on the stage by his own hand. And he was having to fight for his vision every step.

"I should not have been old till I became wise," Lincoln quoted a line from *King Lear*, adapting it for his own situation rather than keeping it sacrosanct like a cue to the next actor. The President sighed, wiping his eyes. "I am tired, Henry. I am so tired, and my family has already given so much—I know many families have given more, but that does not stop the ache inside me. I am not sure I have the heart left to run again. We need a fresh hand at the tiller. You should run next term, Henry."

Abraham Lincoln was a man who had seen the hole in the boat and accepted that it would sink, and he would drown.

I wished with every part of me I could fill that hole and promise him the boat would not sink, but Truth lay like a lake around us, and I could not dishonor it with a lie dressed up like a promise that would be broken before it was said.

"No, Mister President," Seward turned away from the suggestion. "My time has passed. You must be your own successor. You are the only one who can lead us to the end of this work."

Lincoln shook his head. "No, my friend, for if there is one thing I have learned these two years, it is that I would rather be right than be president." He unfolded his long legs and stood to go, stretching to the ceiling like a pine tree. A gangly arm placed his tall hat back on his head. A lesser room would have felt crowded by his presence.

Before I thought about it, I found myself down the stairs and standing before him.

"I would give you my hope," I stepped from invisibility into the history of Lincoln's notice. "But you cannot give up, Mister President. You cannot. What will the world be like for young people like Fanny and me, and my friend, Matias, in California, and Joshua, and your son, Tad, if the progress we've made in taking this stand for freedom for all is abandoned, half-done? Fanny told me you spent today listening to treason cases and trying to find reasons to give pardons and save lives. How many other men could have resisted the pull of revenge when they lost so much? How will this country heal without a man of true character leading us?" Standing as tall as I could, I looked into Lincoln's face, an invisible boy speaking as if he had the right to be seen and heard.

"There are roles that are defined by one actor, Mister President," I told him. "And this is yours. Do not give it up to a man of lesser ability. Run for a second term. Please." Looking into each other's eyes, we both knew there would be a cost, but there was no one else. "Excuse me, Sir, I should have introduced myself. I am Lady Drake's nephew."

He studied me, amusement playing across his face. "Here with your aunt to make arrangements for the benefit in the fall?"

"Yes, Sir. I run lights—That is, I am a crewmember on one of the towers that make the lighting effects."

"So, you are 'learning the ropes', as they say."

"Yes, Sir."

"The play is to be *MacBeth,* I am told."

"It is, Sir. And it is glorious."

"As it should be. Then I will see you in September, Lady Drake's nephew." He doffed his hat to the room, then to Fanny, now standing on the stairs, and went out into the night.

What did I say? I had the sense I might have poured out my soul like a libation at his feet.

Outside, I could see Joseph holding the reins of a very long-legged horse while the President raised himself into the saddle.

Secretary Seward returned to his place near the fire, and Missus Seward closed the door.

"I didn't like him in the beginning, you know," Seward confessed in the low tone of a private musing. "I was angry that he was the nominee and not I, after so many years of working to get a Republican nominee. When he asked me to be Secretary of State, I was going to refuse him, but then he arrived in Washington--no entourage, no staff, just his family. The South already hated him. He had only gotten through Baltimore and avoided an assassination plot because Pinkerton's people disguised him as a widow-woman. I know of two such plots to violently remove him from office since then. But let me tell you a story about Abraham Lincoln," Seward addressed Missus Tubman and we children.

"Soon after his little boy, Willie, died, the White House barn caught fire. All of the children's ponies, including Willie's, were inside. The president ran to the barn to save the animals, but it was too late. The fire had already engulfed the barn. The guards on duty had to fight to keep the president from going in after those ponies, but there was nothing that could be done to save them, and the soldiers knew it. The President, though, could not accept that, and he struggled and struggled to get to those ponies.

"Later, after Lincoln finally went back inside the house, one of the guards looked up and saw him at an upstairs window watching the barn burn. He just stood there at the window, sobbing."

It was a horrible story, but it spoke to the soul of the man, and the personal cost of what the man, Lincoln, was trying to do for our country.

In that moment, when I stepped forward and stood before him, asking him to run again, I felt so proud. Now, haunted by remorse, I questioned that pride.

What had I done? A second term? It would kill him.

Act Three, Scene Seven: the office of the Bureau of Military Intelligence, the next morning

My Dear Friend,

I write not to tell you anything of my life because I have given up on that. I have no life; it has been given over to others' needs for so many years that there is nothing left I may call my own, except this tiny hope of life within me. If I expect to continue, I will need to borrow someone else's life for a term.

I will miss the wildlands and the wildlife in California, but I must leave this place and those wild parts of myself along with it.
LM

Knowing we had a full day ahead of us before our late afternoon train, Missus Seward had the cook provide an early breakfast of the sort that would not suffer from getting cold. I grabbed a few things and was about to go out when Joshua came in from the front of the house.

"A messenger just delivered this for you, Master…uh, Kit," he corrected himself with a grin.

"Thank you, Joshua." He handed me a velum envelope, which I opened, reading silently:

My Dearest Son,

Forgive my absence and my silence. There is no excuse good enough, but here is mine: There is a world I wish you to live in, and it is not the world I saw being created. I could not–I cannot, stand by while your future is stolen before your life has started. Someday, I hope you will understand that one must do what one can for their children. Present circumstances prevent me from doing that in New York, and it would be too dangerous for you all if I were to live under the same roof.

Please, thank the family for doing for you what I cannot. I am forever grateful. I will return to walk in the woods with you as soon as the path is clear. Look for me."

LB

I folded the paper carefully and tucked it into my breast pocket. It was good paper, her penmanship firm and flowing. She had written it at a desk in a civilized room with a steady hand. It smelled of Mary Anne Hall's bawdy house. Though it sounded as if her life still included elements of danger, she was not living in a shack on the edge of the world. Her mind was clear, her purpose and her sanity no longer holding on by a pulled thread.

"She sounds better," I said, hoping Spin was about and would hear me. If anyone else overheard me, it did not matter. "I am going to finish packing. Joshua," I caught the young man as he was passing by, going the other way. "Will you make sure my bags all get onto the carriage to the train station if I am not back in time?"

"Of course, Kit."

"And let my aunt know not to wait for me to join them at this morning's meetings. Tell her I am going to the Armory Hospital to bid goodbye to Mister Whitman. If I run late, I will meet them at the train station."

"Are you going to get yourself in trouble again, Kit?"

"I hope not." I smiled, hoping to relieve his worries so he would not hurry to inform anyone of my leaving. "I am just making a quick call on a friend." My plan was to do more than that, but it was a plan still being formulated.

I walked swiftly over the now familiar terrain between Lafayette Park and the Armory Hospital, no longer distracted by Washington's historic sites, hoping Whitman would be at the hospital on a Sunday, as he would not be required at his job as a clerk for the government. The oddity that America's premiere poet needed to work a clerk's desk job to feed and house himself so he could stay in DC and volunteer to help succor our injured soldiers did not escape me. Some artists made a living from their art. Many did not.

I asked an on-duty nurse if Whitman was about, and she pointed me to Barracks Twelve, where Confederate soldiers were cared for.

There was visible security, but it was not difficult to gain access. All I had to do was mention Walt's name, and one of the guards fetched him for me.

"Kit. I did not expect to see you again this trip." The old poet looked genuinely pleased to see me. I thought you and Bernie were leaving today?"

"We are. I just wanted to say goodbye, and to thank you again."

"In person. That is very kind. Come. We can talk inside." He led me into the barracks. Aside from the guards at the doorways and the bars on the windows, it was much the same as the other barracks. Whitman took a large pitcher of water and began to make rounds, filling cups for the men and holding them for the men who needed assistance. "I sense there is something more to your visit," he said. "Something you are reluctant to reveal."

"Bernie and Burke are meeting with Military Intelligence, but I do not expect them to be of much assistance." Whitman did not look surprised and continued ministering to the soldiers.

"It was always only the merest of chances. It is not in the nature of the government or a spy agency to share," Whitman commiserated.

"I had a letter from mother this morning," I confessed. "I think Miss Hall knows more than she told us last night. Maybe this morning she will reconsider."

"It is rather an insulting supposition, my friend," Walt cautioned me. "Rather like calling the lady a liar. It would be more socially correct to believe Miss Mary told us all she knows."

No one wanted me to talk to Miss Mary. There must be a reason why.

"And how are you doing today, Cleatis?" Walt asked another patient. The young man was emaciated, his cheeks and eyes sunken, his skin yellowish.

"I think it will not be long now, Mister Walt. I see more of other worlds than I do of this one," he answered hoarsely.

Whitman pulled up a chair and sat beside the young Confederate soldier. "I am sorry, son. Can you not find the strength to keep fighting to live?"

"The war was never supposed to last this long," Cleatis spoke as if he had not heard Whitman's question. "We all thought we'd be home in time for harvest. But then fall turned to winter, and spring came. Before we knew it, it was summer again, and on, and on it went, everything turned upside down and inside out. Two years," he mused. "I thought I'd be a married man by the time I turned twenty. I don't know if my sweetheart has waited for me or not. We hadn't settled anything, but I thought she was the one. Back when I still thought I'd have a life."

"You could still have a life, Cleatis. The war will end," Walt assured the young man. "You could still marry that girl—still have a family. No matter who wins, some things won't change that much, unless you were enslaved."

"My family don't have slaves," Cleatis said. "Most people around us don't. Maybe a few merchants in town and the like, but mostly not. We're not plantation folk. But everyone was so sure those Wide Awakes was about to invade, and we couldn't let that happen."

"There have been a great many misunderstandings," Walt replied. "As there are in any family, brothers fight, then make up. Hold onto the image of that young woman and try to get better, Son."

The young man's gaze grew misty. "I wish I could see my mama again—just one more time. She did everything for us. It didn't matter how tired she was or how long she'd been working; if we needed something, she'd find a way to do it. When I was little, I remember thinking how pretty she was. You can still see that pretty woman in her eyes, but mostly I remember before I left, thinking she looked used up. I wonder if she knows how important she is to me," Cleatis said wistfully." I felt my eyes tearing up. "I'd like her to know that before I die."

"We could write her a letter." Walt pulled out a pencil and opened his notebook to an empty page.

"She don't read," the soldier said sadly.

"Let's write it anyway. She can find someone to read it to her," Walt suggested. The young man nodded, beginning to speak the words that sat heavy on his heart. Embarrassed to be listening to such a personal conversation, I turned away and tried to focus on the barracks.

Without their uniforms, the Confederate soldiers were like the men in the other barracks, sick at heart and lonely.

"Dearest Mother…. I feel your love wrapped around my heart, holding the broken pieces together… I am forever grateful…I miss you more than words can say." Walt wrote down the words, his eyes misting so a tear or two stained the paper. What a thing he had taken on in ministering to these poor soldiers.

"We are fighting for the very soul of this country," Bernie had said, but watching this young man write a dying message to his mother made me wonder if that was as much hyperbole as the grandiose statements the Confederates made. Who made Cleatis think the Wide Awakes were about to invade? Who encouraged him to believe their intentions were violent, even though they always marched peacefully? Had there been no voice of reason on either side that might have stopped this conflict before it started? Was there no one whom people from both sides would listen to?

I remembered one of the Bees talking about how, before 1835, people were willing to listen to those they disagreed with and made the effort to find common ground, but after the rise of newspapers, people stopped listening to each other and became more divided.

When this war was over, how would our country bridge that divide and heal?

We needed Abraham Lincoln, the father who tried to save his son's ponies and sobbed over his failure to do so, the compassionate man desperate to find a reason not to give a death sentence. He was not a perfect man, but he was a good one. Ambition, power, and wealth were not what motivated him, and there were few others in the political realm of whom that could be said.

When I looked back, Cleatis's eyes were closed. Walt folded the paper, clutching it in his hand.

"It's important what you do, Walt," I said.

"It is a small thing, and never enough."

"This cannot be the democracy we dreamed would change the world," I confessed my disillusionment.

"That you can still be surprised by greed and avarice, Kit, is a good sign. It means your soul has not been lost to pessimism."

"And yet time and again naive optimism makes fools of us," I complained.

"You must count me and Waldo among those fools," Whitman contended. "Waldo will tell you that stubborn optimism is the core of our young country's energy and charm. Hold to those idealized notions, Kit. Do not let the jaded pessimists convince you that belief in something beautiful is a weakness. It is the only true bravery."

"I am not brave," I grumbled.

"You know that you stand alone, and yet you still stand. That is brave, my young friend. The common experiences of joy and tragedy bring people together, reminding us how we are more similar than different." The scabs of his emotions were bleeding. "I need some air." He exited the barracks, drawing in gulps of air heavy with humidity, but clear of the sadness permeating the barracks behind us. Cleatis's letter in his hands shook like a distant thunderstorm.

"I'll see to this." I gently took it from him.

"His family is in Richmond," Walt whispered. "The Pingletons, on River Street."

"It doesn't matter to you which side these young men fought for, does it?" I asked. Walt shook his graying head.

"There are those who have been twisted by lies and hate, and I see them, but mostly I see young men who went to fight alongside their brothers and friends because Honor demanded it. Politics wants us to see the other side as evil, but that's about what's in a person's heart, not where they come from. There are people in the North I would not break bread with—people who abused the nation's trust to enrich themselves, people who are churning up hate on both sides because the war benefits them. Rousseau said man's basic nature is good, and civilization helps smooth our rough edges, but those who are exposed to brutishness and forced to struggle and kill to survive become brutish. I want to agree with him, but some days I think I am just another naive fool."

I reached out to take the poet's hand. "From one naïve fool to another, I hope I will see you when you return to New York."

"Stay safe," Walt clasped my hand.

Walking out of the short picket fence on the south side, I left the hospital grounds, but I did not turn North toward Lafayette Park. Crossing the canal, I retraced the path Whitman had taken me on last night, walking the short distance to Mary Hall's.

As all things did when robbed of the romantic glow of candlelight or gas flame, Miss Hall's brick house looked very different in the harsh light of day. The canal looked like oily sludge, bugs hovering over its surface like a quivering blanket, the smells rising from it strong and fetid. The house was not unkempt, but the neighborhood was less than desirable--outside of a desire for its clients not to be seen. The neighboring buildings to the rear were manufacturing plants. One had a tall smokestack that towered above every other building nearby.

At this hour, no carriages were arriving, and I was uncertain if my plea for a second interview with the madam would be granted—or if anyone would answer the door. The house was kept very late after business hours.

I rapped smartly and waited. A girl of indeterminate heritage peeked through the curtains, disappearing for some minutes while I waited before Miss Mary appeared at the door.

"Master Drake." She scrutinized the emptiness behind me. "Have you run away again?"

"I did not run away the first time. I was visiting a friend, and he brought me here to introduce me to you in the belief that we had similar interests, Miss Hall."

"Come around the side, and I will let you in the garden gate," she suggested.

I followed her directions around the house, and she opened a wrought iron gate, letting me into a lush, flower garden with a vegetable garden behind it.

"It is better if you are not seen here," she explained.

"I understand."

"Do you?"

"I think so. Walt said you were a woman who knew a lot of things. I am guessing that includes something about my aunt and her 'forest friends'."

"I read the papers," she dissembled.

"I think you read more than newspapers, but I am not here to pry."

"I do not know where your mother is," Miss Hall repeated her earlier dissemblage.

"But you know where she has been?" I could feel the answer longing to pry open her mouth and dive off her tongue, but she resisted. "Fine. I will stumble around on my own then, but whether you help me or not, as Walt said, I will not give up, and I should let you know that I received a letter from my mother this morning."

Miss Hall sighed. "Come inside. I was serious when I recommended your aunt should be cautious in her travels," she explained as we walked. "The train line between New York and Washington dips into Confederate territory, and the trains are attacked or sabotaged regularly. If her activities have come under scrutiny, it is ill-advised for her to travel."

"We have no plans to return to Washington City until the fall for the benefit," I assured Miss Mary.

"Good. Just across the Potomac in Alexandria, I have a small farm that I use as a retreat." She went to a bureau, removed a cedar box, and took out a letter. "On occasion, a woman in difficulty who requires a place to disappear for a period of time, approaches me and I let her stay there. There is no such woman there now, but a few months ago, this was found under a mattress." She handed me the letter.

The paper was a torn and much-folded scrap, scrawled onto the back of a list for market items. I unfolded it.

Dear Friend,

I will not tell you where I am. Do not ask. It would not serve either of us. Long before you receive this, I will be somewhere else. Whatever I was when you knew me, I am no longer. Whatever I have been, I am now a ghost, drifting silently, my passing unheeded, myself unseen. If we passed on the street, you would not see me. And that is as it needs to be, for this is the role I must play in this moment of history. I have been sniffing out the secrets of the scent trails you have left me like fairy tithes left outside a cottage door for years now, and I am done with it.

I will not write again. Pen and paper fall through my hands. Being invisible has taken a toll, and I have remained too long in it.

LB

The words had the tone of a wounded animal who wished to crawl away and burrow beneath a bush to lick their wounds until they healed or they died, alone, and without witnesses.

"It is a rather pretty house, white, with blue shutters. It is just off the main road after you exit the ferry. Two lilac trees shade the entry to the lane."

"But no one is staying there now?"

"That is what I was told." She did not look at me, focusing away across the fence to the south. "A short ride, though, and you could see for yourself. I would not get my hopes up. It is only a modest house. I would hate for you to be disappointed. Use the back way, please."

"Thank you for your time, Miss Mary." I left through the back gate.

E.F. Winters

Act Three, Scene Eight: The Farm

I was in sight of Mary Hall's farmhouse, a neat, white clapboard with cornflower blue shutters and a bank of red poppies in front. The flowers on the two lilac trees beside the lane were brown but were distinctive enough in shape to confirm Miss Mary's description.

A woman came out from the back of the house carrying a wicker laundry basket in her arms. A scarf was tied over her hair, but when she turned, the braid down her back revealed it to be a unique, muted ginger color. The line of her…the way she moved: it was my mother.

Spin appeared beside me.

"You said you wanted to find her because she was in danger. As you can see, she is safe."

My mother approached the clothesline and began pulling laundry from the line, dropping it into a basket. A baby's cry crossed the lawn between us, and she stopped to adjust the sling-bundle nestled against her chest.

Settling herself in the grass, my mother pulled the infant from its makeshift pouch, opened her shirt, and began to nurse it.

"You wanted the truth. This is it," the blue man said, not unkindly. "Truth is an onion, Kit. It comes in layers. This one particularly."

"She did not join me because she had another child." I wanted to feel sorry for myself, but a different feeling was bubbling up: the relief of understanding, pride in my mother's bravery, love.

I have a brother.

"The father is one of the Dolphins' children that Leonie and her friends rescued, a proud African, captured and shipped across the ocean to be sold. When the Union Navy, Leonie, and her companions intervened, it changed the Dolphin Children's fate. Eventually, Leonie saw to it that they were able to sail back to Africa, but she would not leave you. When she discovered she was with child, she realized she could not return to New York. Uncertain of Bernie's reaction, she knew what society's reaction would be. She could no longer work as she had been, and she would not abandon the child."

But she could abandon me.

"The infant needs her, Kit. You no longer do."

"Did you know she was here?"

"Only recently."

"But you did not tell me."

"She wrote to you, did she not?" I now suspected that Spin had something to do with my mother's letter. "If she wanted you to know she was here, she would have told you."

"Why are you here, Spin? What do you have to do with all this?"

"Some stories are not easily heard."

"I am her son," I retorted. "Who are you? A hobgoblin obsessed with a human woman he can never have."

"How did Leonie beget such a son? You are undeserving of her," the little fey man's temper rose to meet my own. "I declared myself Leonara Marchand's friend decades before you were born. No human could ever protect her as I have." The sharp, lipless edges of his mouth pursed in disgust.

"And yet she left you behind," I sneered. It was not Spin I was angry with, but I needed to be angry with someone.

"The mouth is a threshold between thought and speech, a magical space where what is ethereal becomes physical, like the edge of a stage, which is another such threshold between worlds. Be careful what you say, Kit, "the blue man cautioned. "When you stop acting like a brat and are ready to listen, I might agree to tell you the story of our families," Spin offered haughtily.

He was right, and my recognition of that deflated my anger.

I sat by the road, letting the sunshine and the breeze swishing through the tall grass calm the flurry inside me before I spoke again.

"Forgive me, Spin. You are right. She is safe, and that is what is important. My mother did not raise me to be so rude or arrogant. I am ready to listen now." He studied me before he began.

"Our families have been connected back to the time of your ancestor, Captain Francis Drake. He was not a 'sir' then. He was not wealthy, but he was a man of great ambition—a man who wished to raise himself to be the equal of the titled members of Queen Elizabeth's court who snubbed him, despite the dangers he risked for

E.F. Winters

Queen, country, and the national treasury. To get what he desired required boldness, which Francis had in abundance, and wealth, of which he had none. What he did have, though, was a plan to steal silver from the Spanish.

"To avoid the treacherous route around the Horn, shipments of Spanish silver were being unloaded on the Pacific Ocean side of South America, portaged across the narrowest part of the isthmus of Panama, and reloaded on the Caribbean side, where they continued their journey to Spain. Captain Drake's plan was to steal the silver along the isthmus trail before the Spanish porters reached the Caribbean Sea. But Francis knew little of South America and its challenges. By the time my people found his entourage, they were in dire straits. We could easily have killed them, but Francis had a panache that amused my lord, Toranado. You can see a remnant of this charisma in your aunt, Bernadette," Spin explained. "Your mother had her own version. After some negotiations, a price was agreed upon between Captain Drake and Lord Toranado, and aid was given.

"But the agreement was not just about silver. Toranado needed leverage against Michele Ghislieri, a man who was the Grand Inquisitor of Spain and was raised to become Pope Pius the Fifth. Ghislieri was a fanatic whose twisted pursuit of anything smelling of magic had proven dangerous to our fey family. His portion of Captain Darke's stolen silver would buy Toranado revenge, and Drake could function as his physical representative.

"What was this Lord Toranado seeking revenge for?" I asked.

"While Ghislieri was an inquisitor, he captured an important member of our family, a Weaver of unsurpassed ability, La Dulce'. My Lord Toranado was devastated. He and La Dulce' were more than lovers. She was his consort. Ghislieri tortured her to death.

"But months before she was captured, La Dulce' showed Toranado a future that included our family entering into a strong human alliance. So, when he found Drake and his crew, my lord felt he knew what he must do, and he helped them.

Toranado had a son. Drake had a daughter. The bargain they made was sealed in a shared bloodline."

"Our bloodline." I thought about this. "My bloodline."

"It was a long time ago," Spin pointed out. "Many generations have passed since then."

Act Three, Scene Eight

We watched the bucolic scene, the mother nursing her baby amongst the green grass and rolling hills of West Virginia on a spring day.

"You would have me leave her here," I said finally after a good deal of thinking.

"It would be a kindness," the little blue man agreed. "If you leave now, you can still make the train back to New York."

I stood and we began to walk back to the ferry that would return us across the Potomac.

Act Three, Scene Nine: Washington City, D.C. June 1863

"Where have you been?" Bernie demanded as I approached her and Burke on the platform at the train station.

"Stretching my legs before the long trip. Saying goodbye to Mister Whitman," I played her game, offering partial truths. Perhaps sensing my dissemblance, she scowled.

"We nearly missed the train."

"You could have gone on without me. I would have been along," I made a point of acting grown up enough to be unconcerned. Bernie's brows knit together. "Don't do that, Aunt. I hear it gives a person wrinkles." I passed her and boarded the train.

"You should be kind to the old girl," Spin scolded me as we slipped onto a bench seat in our compartment.

"It is a strange world when a blue fey creature lectures a human boy on being kind."

"Not so strange," Spin disagreed. "It is far more common than you realize."

Burke entered the compartment, seating himself stiffly beside me.

"Your aunt was not pleased with the outcome of our meeting with the new Bureau of Military Intelligence," Burke advised me.

"No one by the name of Leoara reports to him." Aunt Bernie grumbled as she, too, sat, settling her skirts so there would be minimal ironing needed to restore them after the long trip. Burke, Spin, and I were on one bench. Bernie and her skirts filled the opposite one. "The man we met, a John Babcock, was a detective who left the Pinkerton Agency to start a more organized spy ring for the Union," Bernie caught me up. "But with the limited resources granted by Congress, or more correctly *not* granted by them, and without access to Pinkerton's files regarding what was done before, who worked for them, and such, the project was doomed. Now, however, the Office of Intelligence has become a recognized department with all the resources and power to force cooperation from field generals and their kind. Colonel Sharpe is the man heading it, but Babcock stayed on, hoping things would get better, but he did not tell us anything."

"He would not be very effective in his position if he could not resist sharing information on the identities and locations of his agents, Madam. If Leonie is working for this new bureau—or worked for the previous one under Babcock--he cannot tell us. It could jeopardize their plans, and it could endanger her."

"Bah! We are professionals—partners even, and he treated us like common civilians."

"That is what we presented ourselves as, Madam: common civilians."

"Well, uncommon ones anyway." She fluffed her dress. "I am sorry, Kit. We did try."

It did not matter. With some assistance, I had done what was needed on my own.

Burke reached into his front pocket.

"A letter was delivered to us at Seward's before we left." He offered it to me. "It is from your mother." *Another one.* But this one was not meant for me. I opened it, every second, a sharp pain.

Dear Friend,

I was surprised to learn there were woodland animals in Washington. Please encourage the Badger Queen to sheath her claws. It will not help our cause.

Correspondence is nearly impossible. Please, respect my silence.

LM

The train began to move.

I looked up at Bernie. "You are the Badger Queen?" She did not reply, but that, in itself, confirmed my suspicion. "Did you and my mother quarrel? Is that what happened?"

"More than once. I argued with Manon as well." Bernie shrugged this off. "Mostly about their life choices, because I was sure they were making the wrong ones and dropping family commitments needing to be upheld."

"Your certainty was based on what you observed in the Weavings?"

"I understand Charlie Stratton's hubris, because it is my own," she admitted. "And I have sacrificed the affection of those closest to me because of it."

"Mother does not feel welcome because of something you did," I suggested.

"Everything wrong is because of something I did," Bernie confessed with more sadness than rancor.

That was not true, and I knew something of carrying a burden of guilt that was not my own. I leaned forward and took my aunt's gloved hand.

"You are a tough, mean old badger, Aunt, but we Drakes are a stubborn lot, and not keen on doing what others tell us to. Our forefather, Captain Drake, stood up to a queen." I grinned as I released her hand.

"Who have you been talking to?" I did not think I needed to answer. We both knew who knew all the family secrets. Bernie's eyes became hard, black obsidian marbles, buried beneath an avalanche of grimace. "Spin, you little ink spot. What have you been telling my nephew?"

Spin sat back, unconcerned. "Don't worry, she can neither see nor hear me without the painting and her little ritual. Tell her I said I merely explained your family history."

I did as I was bidden.

"You speak to him so easily?" Bernie looked disgruntled. It must be hard for her to always need an interpreter.

"We talk." I shrugged. "He has more secrets than you do, Aunt. Some of them are very interesting."

"You cannot believe his kind, Kit. They lie."

I cringed. "That's prejudicial talk from a woman whose family has benefited for generations from fey blood." Bernie stumbled through gasps, a couple of harrumphs, and a growl, ending with looking at Burke as if she expected him to do something, but the genie was out of the bottle, and it was not going to go back in.

"That was a very long time ago," Bernie declared. "And anything fey about the Drake's has long since been so diluted it has no pertinence."

"Whatever you say, Aunt." I smiled. "Now, we have a lot of time stuck here on this train together, so we can either tell ghost stories or make plans for what comes next. What spy activities do we have coming up?"

Bernie made a face. "No one calls them that."

"Because *they* are boring," I complained.

"Because they are professionals, not children," Bernie countered.

"Ah. I see. Humor is not encouraged."

"Well, cheekiness is certainly not," Bernie argued. "You have been spending too much time in bad company, nephew."

"Do you mean the blue fey, Spin, or the Little General, Charles Stratton?" I teased.

She rolled her eyes. "Your mother is going to blame me for ruining you."

I doubted it. "So, what workings are we planning?

"I am sorry, but I think we have reached a dead end with the search for your mother, Kit. If Sharp and Babcock do not know Leonie's location…

"I know where Mother is." Bernie's jaw dropped. "She is fine, and no, I am not going to tell you her location. As a new member of the Coterie, you need to have confidence that I, too, can keep secrets and promises." The look on Bernie's face was worth every lie and uncertainty I had endured.

Act Four, Scene One: Drake House

"Aunt Bernie," I spoke quietly, knowing that when her study door was closed, she was doing something *important.* When there was no reply, I called out again, knocking softly. Still getting no reply, I considered entering unbidden, but fearing I would distract her analysis of some vexing Weave, I went down to the kitchen, then out to the garden to see what help I might offer Dweetie. Spending time in our cook's cheerful, earthy presence always eased my anxiety and soothed my fretfulness.

Wallack's was facing a summer hiatus, which meant the daily routine that was the foundation of my life, of going to the theater, seeing my friends, and doing shows, was coming to an end until fall.

Now that I understood the nature and goals of Bernie and Drake House and knew Mother was, if not safe exactly, at least not in imminent danger, and I was reassured of my position in the household, the concerns that formerly consumed me had all found organized spots to be set aside and were fading.

However, by joining the Coterie, I was signed into the ritual of worrying over Bernie's safety as she went about town meddling and muddling in the nation's affairs.

The instructors Bernie selected for my gentleman-spy education continued their parts, my schedule now filled with hand-to-hand combat, the use of sword and dagger, reading and breaking codes, the proper use and care of guns, disguises, dissembling, and its opposite: truth reading. I seemed to have a knack for the more esoteric skills, but, aside from marksmanship, I had no aptitude for the physical arts, and therefore no confidence I would be of any use to Bernie in the event she was attacked. Despite my ancestor, Sir Francis's, rumored skill with blades, I was by nature a cabin boy, not a pirate.

Still, Bernie continued to have me accompany her, grooming me for the greater role she expected I would grow into, along with the skills she believed I would master with practice now that I had stepped forward to take my place in the Drake family tradition of espionage.

My early-season weeding and harvesting with Dweeti was interrupted by Idabelle's strident shout from an upper-story window.

"Help! Kit, come up here now! Begam Dweetie, get Burke. Lady Bernie is in distress!"

I was running up the back steps to the kitchen door before Ida stepped away from the window.

"What is it? What's wrong?" I burst into Bernie's study. My aunt lay draped in a chair, her body limp and likely unconscious. Without the armor of her indomitable spirit, she looked frail, her age striking me as it never did when she was animated.

"She fainted or something," Ida said trembling. "I knocked earlier, and when she did not answer, I did not intrude, but after several more attempts without a reply, I let myself in and found her like this."

"Aunt Bernie." I patted my aunt's hand repeatedly, then moved to trying to stimulate a wakeful state by tapping her cheek with my fingers. "Aunt, wake up. Wake up."

"It's not working." Ida wrung her hands. "Shall we call the doctor?"

"No," Burke said as he rushed in. "A doctor would only complicate things."

"Are you sure? How do you know?" Ida demanded half pleading and half accusing.

"She has been Weaving night and day for a week now," Burke explained. "She has worn her energies too thin. I urged her to stop and rest, but you know how well she takes direction. She obviously did not heed my warning." Dweeti hurried into the room with a bit of herb crushed into honey in a small bowl. She handed it, along with a spoon, to Burke, and he held it to Bernie's lips. "Bernie, take this," he commanded her. No one expected her to comply, but it was polite to ask first. "Ida, open her lips."

Idabelle stepped back. "No."

"Ida, she needs this. It will help revive her."

"What is it?"

"Herbs I grow in the garden," Dweeti tried to reassure the young woman.

"How do I know that?"

Dweeti looked hurt. "Miss Idabelle, you know I would never do anything to harm Lady Bernie."

Ida did not move.

"I'll do it." I stepped forward and pinched my aunt's cheeks between my thumb and forefinger, forcing her jaw to open slightly and her lips to pucker. Burke slipped the mixture in with the spoon.

"Now stroke her throat," Burke directed me. I did. Burke took Bernie's hand, pressing on points on her palm, and we waited. Bernie's chest shuddered, her eyelids fluttered, then her eyes opened.

Abruptly, she sat up. "The Weave…the threads. I have to… She did not seem to notice us gathered around her, her entire being consumed by whatever she was seeing and doing before she fell unconscious. Burke pressed her back into the chair.

"Give it a moment, Bernie," he commanded. "You lost consciousness. You've worked too hard—used up all of your resources. You must give your body time to rebalance itself."

She looked at him, her eyes misting over with despair. "I can't, Burke. There is no time. The Weave… " She could not bear to say what she had seen.

"Ida, Kit, please leave us," Burke commanded.

"No more secrets," I countered. It was all that was needed.

"If Kit is staying, I am—" Idabelle followed my lead and stood her ground, refusing to exit.

"Of course you may stay, Idabelle." Bernie reached out and clasped the young woman's hand. "I am sorry to worry you all. Burke is right, I have been working too hard. I just need a little rest."

"What were you trying to say about the Weave, Aunt?" I asked.

At my mention of the Weave, a wave of remorse and despair tumbled over her.

"Bernie? Are you alright?" Ida knelt by my aunt's side.

Bernie did not answer, taking a few moments to breathe deeply and gather herself. "Things are happening," she finally spoke. "The Weave has been very active—the threads thickening unnaturally. They are being woven too tightly, so it's hard—nearly impossible to change them. It is not a natural Weave."

"Someone is manipulating the Weave," Burke said. Bernie nodded.

"They are trying—no more than that, they are determined to force events to their will," she explained.

"Can they do that?" I asked. "I thought you said that did not work."

"I said it did not work out well," my aunt corrected me. "If the Weave is firmly decided on a particular outcome, it self-corrects to reinstate something as close to that pattern as possible, but whoever is interfering is not giving up. They keep moving the threads back, re-knotting to get the pattern they want."

"Can you tell what they are trying to do?" Burke asked.

Bernie bit her lip, hesitant to answer. "I recognize some of the threads, yes," she admitted solemnly. "It is about Lincoln. They are targeting Lincoln through the Weave." I gasped. "I have been trying to correct what they're doing, but every time I change it, they find a way to work it back."

"How much of what you are trying to correct is the Weave itself?" Burke asked. "Does the Weave require this future?"

"No." Bernie snapped. "It is not the Weave. It is this person, manipulating things."

"Then we must stop them," I declared.

"That is what I have been trying to do," Bernie wept. "But..."

"She cannot keep this up," Burke cautioned me. "Her strength affects the threads she interacts with, making them and their pattern weaker. She has to rest."

"No," Bernie spoke forcefully. "The Weave will move on in the pattern this person has forced it into, and we will no longer be able to change it."

"Because that would mean sacrificing the president," I surmised.

"There is only so much change The Weave will accept," Burke explained. "It tries to reassert its natural pattern, but eventually it will adjust its patterning to accommodate another."

"If that pattern's threads are repeated often and persistently enough," Bernie added. "At that point, anything that works against the new pattern that has been accepted will be against the Weave."

"We can't let that happen," I protested.

"It may already have." Burke looked to Bernie.

She shook her head. "I don't know. I passed out." Despair stained her cheeks.

"Well, there is nothing you can do about it right now," Burke declared. "You are too weak, Bernie. You do not have the strength to battle this other Weaver's determination."

"Then use me. Let me do it," I spoke up. "What do I have to do?" I looked around the room. "Spin? Are you here?"

"Kit…." Burke stopped me, tossing a glance at Idabelle.

"Oh, for God's sakes, Idabelle has lived here for years," I responded. "You don't think she knows all about your little secrets by now?"

"I assume you are referring to the 'invisible' creature that follows Bernie around?" Idabelle said. "Yes, I am aware of his presence. You see it too, Kit?"

"The Drake family has some unusual talents," I informed her, making no attempt to hide being a Drake herself; she might have at least one of these. I turned my attention back to Bernie, sensing she was the one I had to convince to accept my help. Burke might be standing in the way of her continuing to fight this invasive Weave, but only because it was taxing Bernie. "Is there a way to do this that is safe for you, Aunt?" I asked.

Spin appeared. *"Kit, I appreciate your desire to help, but there has only been one male Weaver in my lifetime,"* he informed me.

"Which has been how long?"

Spin smiled slyly. *"Let's just say I was a dashing young spirit during Henry the Eighth's reign."*

"But you were still short, and blue, and had that long pointy nose?" Spin frowned. *"Then not that dashing."*

I turned to the others. "Spin says that it is rare for males to see the threads, but it has happened. I vote that we try it."

"You see and *hear* him?" Idabelle's eyes were dark, round stones on wind-smoothed sandstone.

"Unfortunately." I rolled my eyes, grinning. "He is rather a pain in the ass." Spin thumbed his nose at me. "And he has picked up some very rude human habits. Now, let's see what other gifts Drake blood has granted us, shall we?"

"First, you will need to get very calm and quiet inside," Bernie coached me. "I usually sit. Here in front of the picture." I sat on the floor. "And I close my eyes."

"I need to see what you're doing," I objected.

"Not with your physical eyes."

"Is that true of all Weavers, or is that just you?"

"I don't know about other Weavers. I am informally educated," Bernie admitted. We got me settled, and she opened a "window' as she called it, which really consisted of opening a portal between the archways of the Victorian "folly" temple in the painting. Bernie began to reel.

"Spin, can you keep that window open without Bernie, so it doesn't draw on her strength?"

"Toranado will not be pleased. He does not…"

"Just do it!" I commanded.

Spin stepped in.

Bernie's whole body was trembling, tears of frustration sliding out from beneath her closed eyes.

"What do you see?" I asked her.

"The Weave…" she muttered. "Moving too fast—too adamantly. She is going to break it," Bernie moaned. She tried to lift her arms into the air, but could not hold them up. They fell back to her sides, shaking with the failed effort.

But I saw something…thin threads glinting within the dark swirls that represented shadow within the painting of the temple's interior.

"What am I looking at?" I asked Spin.

"You see the Weave?"

"I do."

"The gifts of your heritage," Spin commented. It was just possible that I was growing on him. Perhaps a little on my own account, and not only because of my connection to Leonie, though her presence always loomed large between us. *"This is The Weave as it appears in this moment."*

"What do I need to be looking for to change it?"

"What is your purpose in this?"

"To save Lincoln."

"Not good enough. Think larger, Kit," Spin redirected me. *"What is your true purpose in interacting with The Weave? What would you wish of it?"*

"To restore its natural pattern."

"You are prepared to accept whatever that pattern might weave for you, your world, and those you love?" the blue man asked.

"I am."

"Then tell it that."

"How?"

"Speak to it from the heart, in truth and sincerity. Let go of any sense of self-importance and let compassion and kindness wash away personal will and prejudice, sieving out Threads that are heavy or cumbersome. Those Threads are easily recognized by their denseness and muddy color, marked this way by ego and a desire for control.

"The threads you will have left should be pure of color, light in form, flexible, and feel alive in your hand."

"The right Threads will feel like a tingling to your touch," Bernie whispered, as if hearing Spin and watching what my hands were doing.

The threads I wished for came to me in open graciousness. Gently cupping them in my hand, I separated them, draping them over my fingers.

"What do I do now, Bernie? Can you guide my hands?"

"You do not need Bernie," Spin admonished. *"You are a Weaver."*

"But I don't know what to do."

"Do nothing," Spin directed me. *"Simply offer the threads, drenched in your pure intention, back to the Weave."* I hesitated. *"You are strong, Kit. These Threads are now strong and once again unencumbered."*

"The Weave as it is meant to be—as you see it," I whispered to the universe.

"You are doing it, Kit. It is working," Ida whispered. "The muddy threads are breaking and falling away. The ones you added are overworking their pattern."

"Can the other Weaver's threads still be hiding behind the new Weave?" I asked Bernie.

Drained and pale, my aunt answered, "They could. It is possible. The Weave has great depth, and a single session, like this, reveals only the surface of a single working area. But your Threads are strong, and you did not try to include anything foreign to the Weave. This will make it more resilient to modification."

"Enough?" I asked.

Bernie shook her head. "There is no certainty for a human working with the Weave."

"We need to close the window," Burke said.

"I will do it," Idabelle stepped forward. "I have seen Bernie do it hundreds of times." With her fingers set in a particular configuration, she made a motion in the air, and the portal began to iris shut, the Weave, shimmering behind it, continuing its slow, meandering creation.

Bernie opened her eyes and looked at me. "So, we have another Weaver in the family."

"Two," I corrected her, but her eyes were already closed. I looked at Idabelle. "I am sorry."

She smiled at me. "It doesn't matter." And I believed she meant it.

Act Four, Scene Two: Castleton Hill Gardner-Tyler house, West New Brighton, Stanton Island, New York, July One, 1863

The discovery of my ability meant I was able to stand by and assist her as best I could, which helped, but I was still inexperienced, and the talent required training as well as natural ability. Idabelle quietly removed herself during these sessions, making no declarations of her abilities or offers to assist, and I respected her right to do so. Bernie gave no indication she recognized Ida's part or that she heard me proclaim Ida as a Weaver that night, and Ida seemed satisfied to keep it that way.

Threads of pure color curled in the rippling air, shimmering in and out of sight.

"A Weaver can only understand what they see in patterns through years of training and experience, noting how particular patterns align with specific kinds of events," my aunt instructed me. "We learn to analyze and interpret what we see long before we learn to subtly guide the Pattern, always careful to be sensitive to working with the Weave and what it will accept as natural, or try to insert our will, as that creates a resistance by the Weave.

"A subtle, light touch is best," she coached, watching me work the Threads. "Threads in the active part of the weave are always moving and changing, but eventually they settle, and the active section moves on. Areas of The Weave that are in the past and out of the active area are difficult to change, and if an attempt is made, it is hard to make the change hold once it is beyond the active area that represents the immediate future or present. The Weave is too well set, the threads locked, and their inflexible bend resists being altered," my aunt explained. "Newer threads are looser and may be plucked free of a position. But this is always a gamble. The Weaver cannot predict how the Pattern might shift after such a move." She studied the Weave before speaking again. "When a thread remains in a particular position, it represents a possible future, but it is always subject to change."

"There is never an absolute future?" I asked.

"Not in my experience, no. Possibilities, probabilities, shifts, changes; those are the constants of the Weave, not certainty. Never certainty."

"But individual threads represent individual people? Like how you recognized Lincoln?" Her uncertain pause told me she was reluctant to answer, but after some consideration, she did.

"At this point in history, Lincoln's is a very strong thread. It is more recognizable than most. What you really wish to know, though, is if I have identified which thread is Leonie's?"

"Yes."

"I have seen it," she admitted. "I knew she was alive, but I have not interfered with Leonie's position in the Weave. We avoid searching for or following the Thread of someone we know. Such knowledge gives a Weaver an unnatural power over that person's future—not sole power, because no one can control the Weave, it is too chaotic and random. But having the ability to influence someone's life is both dangerous and unethical. What we are doing is more than moving pretty threads around in the air, and the outcome of intentional interference is rarely what was intended because..."

"No one can control The Weave," I repeated her words back to her.

"To manipulate the Weave to our will requires the Weaver to remain in the 'in-between' we place our minds to interact with it. Forcing the Weave into a Pattern in opposition to The Weave's natural tendencies is wrong, and to accomplish it, the Weaver must keep moving it back over and over again. This is why it becomes dense and muddy."

"Human interference."

"Yes," Bernie agreed.

"But isn't this kind of interference what the Coterie is asking you to do, Aunt?"

"No." Bernie made a face. "The Coterie does not know how we Drake's do what we do, and guiding and encouraging the Weave is not the same as trying to force it into an unnatural pattern. Those who fall into thinking they can force the Weave become quite lost. Did you see that?" Bernie gasped. "That thread there." She pointed to a brown-rose thread more solid and less translucent than its neighbors, woven in behind other threads. "I helped shift that area, but it just moved back—not languidly like the threads move naturally, but decisively, with purpose. Too much purpose."

"Someone moved it."

"The other Weaver," Bernie agreed. "I did not expect them to give up."

"Will what we've done hold?"

Bernie looked back through the Weave as far as she was able. "So far, but the Weave is not static. It is ever-changing."

"So, we still do not know what will happen?" I did not like the uncertainty.

"We never know the future until it is the past."

As we approached Castleton Hill, the Greek Revival mansion of the Gardiner-Tylers, I noticed newly fine, etched wrinkles around Bernie's eyes and a hollowness in her cheeks, evidence of her recent endeavors to restore the Weave.

Arrows of light burst from the windows of the Gardiner-Tyler mansion, spearing the driveway and night lawn.

"Let us see what damage we can do tonight, shall we?" Bernie spoke lightly. She was less the socially starched and buttoned-up lady she had been in my presence before, and more the wry, passionate rebel she must have been in her youth, and still with The Bees, and I liked her better for it.

I, too, was changing, far less shy and compliant, and I was gaining confidence and strength that surprised me.

Slowed by the trip across the Hudson to Staten Island and the carriage ride to the island's Northern end, we avoided the crush of guest arrivals. Many of them came earlier in the day or the day before. Some would stay at Castleton Hill, as it was quite a large estate, while others would stay with friends on the island or at the popular Confederacy crowds, the Planters Hotel. A very few, like ourselves, would make the trek back to Manhattan in the wee hours of tomorrow after the party ended. Bernie avoided investing more than a day by claiming theatrical commitments, though the theater was now closed for the season.

As we disembarked our hired carriage at the foot of the portico steps, a rider enveloped in a storm of summer dust could be seen galloping up the road. "That young man is in a terrible hurry," Bernie noted.

"A late arrival?" He did not turn down the drive leading to the front of the house, but instead headed to the back, where the stables drew up in a line pointing to the rear door, encompassing one side of the work yard used by the household's staff.

"Not a guest," my aunt concluded.

Since our return from Washington, messages had been passed daily between Coterie members and Drake House. New York newspapers churned out editions focused on our Federal troops in Pennsylvania moving to protect D.C. as Lee's men made a run for the Capitol. Stories updating the nearly month-long siege of Vicksburg, where civilians were living in caves carved out of the hard yellow clay of the surrounding hillsides, while the rebel troops protecting them chewed shoe leather, had been moved to page two. No one in the Union expected the rebels to hold out much longer, but both sides continued to spend a good deal of paper and ink, gossip and rumor, creating anticipation of a war-turning victory on one front or the other, and the nation waited.

Bernie believed the pattern in the Weave indicated Union forces would be the victors, but we all knew victories often balanced on a nail's head.

With the company on hiatus, Bernie and I were busy attending listening-luncheons, parties, and, in my case, some strategic loitering. It required little acting skill to take on the persona of a New York newsboy, mostly costuming and a Lower Manhattan patois, and savvy newsboys heard things people who spent their days insulated within townhouses and carriages did not.

The occasion for the event at Castleton Hill was a reception given by Missus Ex-President Tyler for the visiting Governor of New Jersey, Joel Parker, a Democrat who ran as a War Democrat, then voted like a Peace Democrat. New Yorkers groused that you could not tell whose side he was on. I guessed he was a politician who wanted to remain in office and voted accordingly.

"I'd like to know what he's about," Bernie muttered, watching the messenger racing to the back door even though the lady of the house was clearly entertaining and otherwise engaged.

"I could find out for you," I offered.

"You could, but then I would have to explain your absence and sudden reappearance when you returned."

"Frivolous young men are so easily distracted by their friends."

"You are not a frivolous young man."

"Perhaps I am," I suggested coyly. "I certainly showed poor judgment in Washington, running off at night in a strange town and showing up at a bawdy house."

Bernie chuckled. "You did. I was so terribly disappointed in you."

"I will be along directly." I spun away, crossing the lawn toward a stand of trees where I slowed my pace to make certain I was fully invisible before I came out on the other side. As soon as I did, I ran toward the back of the house, as the horse and rider were much faster than I, and I did not want to lose the man if he entered before I got there.

I did not need to worry, as the rider neared the work yard, he slowed to a fast trot, then slid off his horse.

Spin was at the back door before me, leaning nonchalantly against the cladding. I glared my question of why he was here at all, and he replied by ignoring me.

The kitchen help and the house staff drafted to assist with the party flowed in and out the back door, hauling water, wiping and dipping dishes and cloths, plucking birds, and carrying armfuls of wood to the kitchen for the cook stoves.

"I have a message for Missus Ex-President Tyler," the messenger barked the long title that Castleton Hill's owner required, panting to catch his breath.

The back-house servants refused to take the document from him, backing away as if it were a rattlesnake, but a boy was sent to fetch someone who had more authority, giving me time to join the messenger, check the condition of his horse, and any indications that might tell me where they had traveled from.

The animal had been ridden fast, but not for more than a few hours. The livery stamp on the saddle connected it to New York.

The young man did not know where to stand amid all the activity, seeming to always be in someone's way as the staff buzzed about, but he neither slouched nor sat, waiting with commendable, if foolish, formality, to deliver the message in his charge.

A Servant of Greater Responsibility arrived and took the document, assuring the messenger that it would be delivered to its intended recipient. The messenger lingered, having difficulty accepting that his mission was complete, but the Servant of Greater Responsibility was firm and, after pointedly asking the messenger if he required anything else for himself or his horse, water, or food, before he departed, the rider admitted he did not and mounted his horse.

I saw him no more after that, as my goal was to follow the document, and it was now entering the house in the possession of the Servant of Greater Responsibility, and I needed to be close enough to that person to enter behind him without the necessity of opening the door a second time to let my invisible self in.

The Servant of Greater Responsibility's power of demeanor caused his colleagues to part before him like Moses at the biblical Red Sea. I used his body as a shield to keep from bumping into them like a billiard ball.

At first, my ears were full of the cacophony of the kitchen, but as we moved deeper into the house, I caught the chorus of crystal and conversation flirting with the early evening twilight of Missus Ex-President Tyler's event, the aroma of dinner replaced by the scents of whiskey and rose water.

I shadowed the document up the Turkish carpeted stairs to the mistress's office.

The servant was cautious and did not open the door overly wide, but neither did he close it behind him as he crossed to deposit the ivory envelope on his mistress's massive, mahogany desk.

I was easily in the room when he promptly retreated, efficiently closing, then locking the door behind him. I heard the lock click, but still tried the knob myself before I could accept the ridiculousness of my situation.

"How are you at locks, Spin?" I asked, keeping my voice low. There was no reply. "Spin? Spin, are you here? Where the blazes are you?" Swearing at the creature's lack of loyalty and poor timing in taking off on his own, I set to my first purpose before tackling this new problem.

Of course, the envelope was sealed, and there was no way for me to steam it open or conceal it having been tampered with, so I tore it open and stuffed the envelope in my pants pocket before reading the letter.

Dear Mother,

Orders from Lee to evacuate Vicksburg have been rescinded. President Davis has ordered us to hold the city at all costs, which I fear will be severe. There is not a man among us who is not ill, the water here having been fouled, and the siege, being nearly a month now, leaving us without supplies. There is no food worth describing to be found in Vicksburg. I tell myself it is important for us to stay to protect our fellow Southerners, but the civilians have been less than kind, hiding food they will not share, leaving us to starve. I want to believe that General Lee's insistence that we not retreat is because of the Mississippi's importance and has nothing to do with his desperate need for a military victory, but I fear that Jeff Davis is not the man my father was, and has neither Papa's quiet confidence nor his wisdom. Still, you have instilled in me that orders are orders, so we will stay until the end, whatever that may be. Tell our friends not to send anything more via the river. It is lost. The Yankees control it.

Your loving son,
David

This was good news. Not unexpectedly, Vicksburg's fall was imminent. But this was not a formal dispatch. It was a letter from a son to a mother. There was nothing in it not already known to the Coterie or the Union, or anyone who avidly read the news. It was interesting that young Tyler was able to get a letter out to his mother from a city under siege, but I presumed that being the son of an ex-president came with privileges, and perhaps General Pemberton wished to show the young man a kindness. Pemberton himself was a Northerner by birth, which was presumed by many to have played into his decision to remain in Vicksburg after Lee ordered him to leave—

a command retracted by Jeff Davis, but one that if Pemberton had acted on immediately, Davis would have been unable to change.

I folded the letter, found an envelope in Julia Tyler's desk, placed the letter inside and sealed it, crumpled it, and dribbled some water on it from a flower vase so it looked well-traveled, before turning to search for something to use to pick the door's lock.

As I was twisting and turning Missus Tyler's letter opener in the lock, I heard footsteps approaching, which stopped me just in time for the metal-on-metal announcement that someone with a key that fit the door was on the other side, and it was about to open. Stepping back quickly, I tossed the letter opener onto the floor beneath the desk. The door opened, and Julia Tyler rushed in, accompanied by a gust of jasmine water and the papery rustle of layers of black silk. The Missus Ex-president was still in mourning.

"Where is it, Youseff?"

"I placed it on your desk, Ma'am."

I held my breath, waiting for the Servant of Greater Responsibility to notice that the envelope his mistress was lifting was not the one that was delivered, but to my relief, she dismissed him.

"Close the door and wait for me outside," she commanded. "I require a moment." She searched her desk drawer for her letter opener, but not finding it, she ripped the envelope open, her eyes scanning the letter silently. "Oh, my poor dear." She sank into the chair behind her desk. Her sadness gave her no more than a moment's pause before she dashed tears from her eyes and returned to the door. "The messenger?" she asked the servant, Youseff.

"Gone as soon as the message was delivered," the servant replied, though this would not have been true if he had in any way encouraged the rider to remain. In fact, in retrospect, I suspected the rider expected to wait for a reply, but Youseff hurried him off. He was hardly going to mention that to his mistress, however. The Tylers retained more than sixty slaves at Sherwood Forest, their Virginia plantation, and though the servants working at Castleton Hill would technically all be free men and women, it was not uncommon for newly freed persons to continue laboring under rules of indenture to the family that held them enslaved, a gray area that survived full ownership.

Missus Tyler closed the door again, crossed the room to a handsome cherrywood cabinet, and opened the doors. I shifted my position to see what was inside.

A landscape painting of a dark forest, thick with ivy and bracken fern, moss hanging from the trees, hung behind a stone sculpture of a gamboling faun dancing to impress a waifish young woman sitting modestly at his feet.

Missus Tyler began to hum, alternating between the hum and a whisper, while dusting the tips of her delicate fingers over the sculpture's curves. As I watched, the faun's eyes opened, a light appearing in them. The stone figure of the young woman animated, rising as if in a daze, and walked into the painted forest.

Missus Tyler began to move her hands gracefully through the air, tracing, pinching, and slicing invisible threads with a tiny silver knife.

I must have audibly gasped because she stopped, her hands frozen mid gesture, listening. Slowly, she turned enough to look behind her and scan the room.

I held my breath, looking down at the carpet so she would not sense my gaze, and after a minute she returned to her work, completing the gesture she had begun.

Focusing on the picture, Missus Tyler waited for the stone woman to return to the faun's pedestal before carefully closing the cabinet doors, leaving the tiny silver knife inside. The faun's eyes, too, closed. She was done, but she remained suspicious, moving slowly about the room, tracing its walls, then its interior sections, while I cautiously moved from her path, practicing the lessons Burke taught me to calm myself, controlling my breath, stilling my heartbeats until they were less than a cat's footfall.

Missus Tyler stood in the middle of the room studying the air. What was she looking for, ripples? She moved to a lamp and turned it on, rechecking the room.

I backed up to the wall, hugging the dark edges of the cabinet, impeccably still, as one by one, she turned each light in the room on, then off, studying the shadows they cast.

Perhaps she imagined she was playing a game of cat and mouse, but this was a game of cat and fox, and in that game, the fox wins.

Finally deciding there was no one else in the room, she patted her elaborate coiffure with her elegant hands and went to the door.

"I must return to my guests," she muttered as she opened it.

"Would you like me to make your apologies to Governor Parker, Ma'am?" Youssef asked.

"No. I do not want to draw…" She stopped herself. "No. I will see the event through." She straightened her back, threw up her chin, sniffed in the physical expressions of her emotions, and exited like a professional.

Youssef locked the door.

I threw myself to the floor, crawling under the desk to retrieve my makeshift lockpick.

Missus Tyler was halfway down the grand stairs, and I was just exiting her office when a commotion at the front door drew her guests' attention.

Another rider had arrived. This one came straight to the front door.

"I have a message for Governor Parker," he announced. I paused on the balcony above.

"I am Governor Parker." Joel Parker stepped forward. The messenger handed Parker the letter he carried, which the governor opened while those in the room waited in tense silence.

"Grant's forces have met General Lee's in Pennsylvania, a place called Gettysburg." Everyone in the room began to chatter.

"Did they stop Lee's march?" someone asked.

"Will they still make Washington?" Questions flew across the room, swift as twilight swallows.

"How far from D.C. is Gettysburg?"

"What about Vicksburg? We expected news from Vicksburg, Parker?"

"Vicksburg has fallen," Julia Tyler announced from the stairs. "The Union now controls the Mississippi."

P.T. Barnum's voice rose over the din. "I hear Lee's troops were in Gettysburg because his troops are barefoot; he got word there was a warehouse full of shoes there."

Some of the attendees tittered, others looked shocked.

Congressman Wood turned on Barnum, and Charles Stratton, my aunt had the misfortune to be standing beside him.

"You smile at a soldier's misfortune?" he attacked them as if they were all complicit in Barnum's joke.

"Irony, not humor," Stratton demurred. "You and your friends spend money like water on parties and balls while the young soldiers you claim to support march without shoes. You should be ashamed of yourself, Wood."

Fernando Wood's hands bunched into fists at his side. "The way was clear for this march. Washington should be ours," he hissed. He turned to my aunt, his face flooding red with anger. "What have you been doing, Lady Drake? Cutting and twisting your little threads as if you alone should decide history's outcome?"

I was shocked at what Wood was openly accusing Bernie of, but then realized that Hieronymous Undergrove was standing beside Wood, so, of course, he knew about Bernie and the Coterie, but our little scene was not the main show, and my attention was drawn back to what most of the guests were paying attention to.

"I am sorry, Missus Ex-president Tyler," Governor Parker apologized, but I..." he indicated he needed to leave.

"Of course, Governor. In truth, I think no one is in the mood for a party anymore, though if anyone wishes to stay, they are welcome, and naturally dinner will still be served as planned..." Their hostess tried to keep a brave front, but she was losing the battle. Her guests began to move, muttering quick apologies as they found the other members of their party and made for the door. In moments, Wood erased the space between him and Bernie, and he was now standing face to face with her, close enough that he could touch her without effort or notice. Though it was unlikely Wood would attempt to abduct my aunt in a room full of socialites, my heart was banging on the walls of my chest, shouting danger was imminent.

Bernie melted to the floor.

"Lady Drake!" Wood said too loudly. "Oh dear, the lady has fainted!" He knelt beside her. His delivery of what was obviously a line was abominable, his words a poor attempt to cover his actions. "I have my carriage. We will take the lady..." Wood started to claim the first position to aid the distressed Dame, indicating to Undergrove that he should pick Bernie up.

No, no, no! My mind shouted.

Suddenly, Spin was there, a curved dagger glinting in his hand.

"Touch her again, Wood, and I will eat your balls for dinner." Wood toppled back from his knees to his bum, shock blowing a hole in his face where his mouth had been. He scrabbled like a crab across the floor until he hit Hieronymous Undergrove's oak tree legs.

"Heironymous…? What…?" was all he managed to wheeze.

Charlie Stratton stepped forward, unable to see Spin. He did not understand what he was seeing, but the Little General was as game as they come.

"Lady Drake and her nephew arrived with me," he lied. In a contest of hierarchy, a vaudeville performer would always lose to a congressman except when there was a male relative at hand. Old-world misogyny still had its uses.

I walked behind a column and came out the other side, visible, shooting down the stairs.

"Aunt Bernadette! What has happened? What have you done to her, Wood?" I turned on him. "Did you give her laudanum? Opiates?"

"No! Of course not." Wood looked around at the crowd. "I was merely trying to…"

"Step away, Sir," I improvised. "I understand your admiration for Lady Drake; you are far from the first to become fixated on her, but she is *my* aunt and under my care." I pushed him away.

Stratton's voice was near a whisper. "We need to go, Kit, before they marshal any assistance they may be able to call on." He turned to his friend. "P.T., Meet us outside."

I wriggled my hands under my aunt's shoulders and midsection and tried to lift her to a sitting position.

"Bernie? Aunt Bernie?" I whispered. "You can get up now." I waited. "Bernie, please, get up." I tried to move her on my own, but I was not strong enough. "Damn. Where are Weaver and Burke when you need them? Spin," I whispered under my breath. "I could really use your help."

Undergrove's muscled arms slid under Bernie, lifting her easily. "No! Stop…"

"Let him be, Kit," Spin interrupted. *"Heironymous will do your aunt no harm."* A wavering figure appeared on the stairs, tall, slender, and with dark hair with streaks of white fanning back from each temple. His posture was imperial, his manner lordly. *"He is under obligation to Toranado."* As I heard the name in my head, the princely being on the stairs gave me a subtle nod. I knew him. Oh, I knew him.

In the depths of my own soul, I knew him, and it made me sick to my stomach to realize it.

Confused, I stood, walking right by Bernie's side, holding her hand as Undergrove carried her outside. If anyone tried to whisk her away, I was going too.

"Do you want to tell me what all that was back there?" Barnum, Charlie, Spin, Bernie, and I were safely onboard Stratton's yacht, steaming toward Manhattan. Bernie tucked away inside, wrapped in a light wool blanket to keep off the river air's chill.

I shook my head, no. "What you already know, or guess, will have to do."

"Bernie did not faint," Charlie declared.

"No."

"Wood tried to take her. Because of who she is and the things she does." Charles' statement was vague but truthful. Not being sure how deep he was in Bernie's confidence, I dared not say more.

"Thank you for your help, Charles."

"Of course. I thought I was going to piss myself when Undergrove came lumbering toward you and Bernie, but then he just picked her up like he was your pet retriever and took her to my carriage." He shook his head in disbelief. "I always thought Undergrove was Wood's man."

"Wood is a pissant. Purchased loyalty spoils quickly, but Bernie and Undergrove were acquainted before in London. I suppose this was a repayment for some past favor."

Stratton snorted. "You are not the boy you were when you arrived in New York, Kit."

I'm beginning to wonder if I am a boy at all, I thought.

Staten Island was falling behind us. The water in the Hudson rippled blue and silver in the fading moonlight as dawn began to brush the high sky. We were closing in on New York City, the bright points of street lanterns and early morning candles winking through the fringe of trees and down the canyon streets. We had survived another night of misadventures.

Act Four, Scene Three: The Streets of New York City, July 13, 1863

Gil Colmeyer was a good person—a good man. Not that one's goodness should be defined by whether you went to war for your country or not, but for most men, it was. Fundamental issues of character were wrapped into such life-or-death decisions; was a man willing to put himself on the line for the freedoms and rights he enjoyed? For his beliefs?

For three hundred dollars, a man could buy his way out of the draft lottery and have his name removed. This was the first such draft in the history of our country, unless you counted the Southern states that were in rebellion. They began conscripting soldiers over a year ago. But three hundred dollars was more than the average working man, who earned sixty dollars a month if he was unskilled, could afford to pay.

The wealthy had that kind of money, giving them a truer choice over whether their sons became soldiers or not. The wealthy could pay for someone else to take their place, or, if their family were slave-holders in a non-rebel state like Kentucky or Delaware whose slaves were not affected by Lincoln's Emancipation Proclamation, a slave could be sent in the place of a son, though few persons of color were being placed in the lists of fighting soldiers, as a good portion of society was against arming black men. I was told repeatedly at society parties that this was simply the way things were done, which was obviously not true since there had never before been a military draft in the United States.

Because of all this, and perhaps because Ginevra Wellbelove refused to take Gil seriously and consider him a suitor despite his fervent devotion, Gil Colmeyer declined Lester Wallack's offer to pay the $300 for his name to be removed from the draft lottery.

Lester argued that it was a business decision because Gil had gained a solid following, and the company relied on him for young male roles. Most of us, however, suspected the theater manager worried what war would do to the kind, young man.

"Even if your name is not drawn, Gil, the laws around the draft say you cannot travel more than twenty-five miles from your place of residence. You will not be allowed to tour with us," Mister Lester tried to coerce Gil into accepting his offer.

"I am sorry, Mister Lester, but my mind is made up."

Everyone hoped Gil would change his mind, or the war would be over before September, when we were set to perform the Sanitary Benefit in Washington.

And so it was that on Monday, July thirteenth, I accompanied my friend to the second round of drawings in New York City, held at the Ninth District's Provost Marshal's offices on Third and 47th. We stood among the other white families, black men being exempt due to their legal status as only being three-fifths of a human being, and waited for the names to be called. Most of the people waiting with us had friends and neighbors who were signed up to fight as soon as they stepped off the ships from Ireland. Offered two thousand dollars and immediate citizenship, many agreed. Many also died.

The lottery drawing a few days before was peaceful, though, it being a Sunday, pubs were full of men complaining about the state of things and how they might as well have stayed in Ireland if they were going to be so taken advantage of. This led to a good deal of fist pumping and the hearty singing of anthems.

A murmur rippled through the gathering as the volunteer firemen company, the "Black Jokes," arrived at the marshal's office, their numbers and reputation opening a path for them to the front of the crowd, where they stood, sticks, cudgels, and rocks gripped in their work-calloused hands.

With the reading of the first name, stones began to fly.

"I think we should go." I tugged Gil with me as I backed up. "We do not want to be part of this."

"I think you are right," Gil agreed, turning. "But where?"

The erstwhile firemen and their friends quickly escalated to attacking the government men who were tasked with organizing the lottery, beating them with the cudgels and whatever else they found at hand. Prying paving stones from the streets and tossing them at buildings, the crowd began breaking windows and anything else in the trajectory range. From somewhere, lit torches appeared, and before we could extricate ourselves, the Provost Marshall's building was on fire, the neighboring government buildings quickly following.

Government officials were being run down and overwhelmed by the attacking crowd, which quickly took on a mob mentality. Anyone who looked, in any way, official or wealthy, was being targeted.

Gil and I were working our way out of the chaotic center-crush toward Lexington Avenue, which he informed me, seeing over the crowd's heads, was clear, most of the action being confined to the portico and stairs of the government building on Third.

We made our way to the fringes of the crowd when a small group of rioters broke off from the main group and began chasing men in suits who were issuing from the back of government buildings and were trying to escape via a passing streetcar. Boarding the trolley, however, brought them no safety. The rioters boarded behind them, tossing them off and into other rioters' hands, before proceeding to yank bystanders already on the trolley from their seats and throwing them into the street as well, or beating them where they sat.

Four of the rioters grabbed the streetcar's horses' heads and began beating the animals' legs with cudgels to hobble the streetcar's progress. Their intention was clear: the trolley would not be used to escape or get help.

"My God..." Gil's body flinched with each blow assailed the poor animals. "Who are these people?"

I had no answer. The violence was born of a surge of desperation and loss of hope by people who had everything taken from them. Reason would not be heard over the angry blasts of their drumming hearts and throbbing blood. Compassion had no place here.

As we were trying to pull our horrified eyes from the tragic scene of the horse's destruction, Police Superintendent Kennedy arrived. Leaping out of his carriage, he mounted the steps to the Provost Marshall's building, prepared to address the crowd, thinking his position and his Irish heritage might sway the group, and that he would certainly be seen as one of them. This was not the case.

The mob swarmed him, falling on him with clubs and knives.

Gil tried to run forward, but I grabbed him and pulled him back.

"You can't do anything to help him, Gil. You are one man. They will turn on you and kill you, too. And for what?"

"But we cannot stand here and let them murder him, Kit," Gil threw me off. "That is the coward's way."

Better a living coward than a dead hero, I thought, but I did not say it. I could not bear the thought of watching my friend die in valiant futility. I remembered Charlie Stratton's words the night of the Livingston party; *Sadly, those who are given great gifts often meet a tragic end. We used to blame jealous Gods. Now, we can only blame ourselves.*

"That's enough, lads. It's enough!" An Irishman shoved his way through the rioters, assaulting Superintendent Kennedy. "Stop!" he knelt by Kennedy's beaten and bloodied body. He was bruised, his skin mottled and broken, many bones crushed, blood streaming from dozens of stab wounds where he had been knifed. "You've done the job, the Irishman announced. "He's dead. Now get away from here before someone sees you." He motioned the mob away as if his first concern was for them. As soon as they moved far enough away that their attention was elsewhere, he looked around. Seeing us, he motioned us over, whistling for a wagon that had just turned onto the street and stopped in surprise and shock at the state of things. The wagon's horses were dancing with fright at the smell of fresh blood, the noise, and the fire taking hold of the government buildings. "Help me get him into the wagon," the Irishman commanded us.

Streams of blood were crossing Kennedy's chest like an alluvial plain.

"He's dead," Gil said, his eyes wide with horror.

"Not yet," the man assured us. "And I'm hoping he can still be saved. Help me, quick." Kennedy groaned as the three of us lifted the poor bloody sod into the wagon. The Irishman turned to us. "Thank you. It may not be much, but if the angels have mercy, we saved this man's life today." He climbed into the wagon beside its frightened driver, and it drove off quickly, headed uptown.

Looking up Lexington Avenue, we could see people and goods being loaded into carriages and wagons all along the street. Those with the sense and means were leaving the city.

"Ginny…. I must find Ginny," Gil muttered.

"Don't be daft. Ginny's apartment is all the way downtown," I argued against this folly. "It's too far, Gil. The rioters are stopping the trolleys--attacking anyone they think isn't with them, and you no longer look like one of them, Gil." His clothing, though not ostentatious, was of too fine a cut and fabric to blend in with these low-end laborers, as was my own.

"Ginny and her mother moved uptown a few weeks ago," Gil informed me. "She has a flat up on Forty-Second near Broadway."

Near Ida Clare's. I thought about the beautiful Ida. Would she be alone? Did she need help? I was considering how long it would take me to get there and what I could do if I did, when the crowd burst into a roar.

"The black brat's orphanage is over there! Follow me."

The Colored Children's Asylum: they were going to attack it next.

And Ida was there.

I gripped Gil's shoulder. "Go, and good luck."

"Be safe, my friend." Gil began to run west ahead of the mob, which was now fixed on Sixth Avenue.

Act Four, Scene Four: The Colored Children's Asylum, NYC, Day One of the Draft Riots

It was only four blocks to the Colored Children's Asylum, which stretched between Forty-second and Forty-fifth Streets off Fifth Avenue. Adrenaline made the run feel shorter, fear made the time feel longer. I turned in the gate, ran through the trees and green lawn that set the asylum apart from the encroaching city, and threw the front door open, shouting, "Ida! Idabelle Drake." I could not remember her adopted family's name and did not know what other to use, but the not-so-secret secret of Ida's birth felt terribly unimportant under the circumstances.

The first staffer to appear was a black man in a white coat. He hurried forward, shushing me.

"There is an angry mob right behind me," I shouted, ignoring his censure for silence. "And they are bent on destroying this facility and everyone in it."

"We have done nothing…" the man began to protest.

"It wouldn't matter if you were the sainted mother herself; they are not going to listen to reason. They just attacked Supervisor Kennedy and beat him almost to death. How much do you want to gamble on their mercy for black children?" The man was no longer shushing me. "Get everyone in here, now. We need to get all the children out of the building and off the grounds." I could see the white's of the man's eyes; he was sufficiently afraid, maybe too afraid, because he did not move. Several of his colleagues appeared from hallways and rooms on different levels. An older white man wearing a long white doctor's coat approached me, speaking in a practiced voice of measured reason.

"Please, calm yourself, Sir."

"I am Kit Drake, Idabelle's relative." I introduced myself perfunctorily. "Do you smell that smoke? Rioters set fire to the Provost Marshall's offices. The other government buildings near it are now burning. Rioters are attacking people on the street and pulling them from carriages. They smashed a trolley horse team's legs." I stopped, realizing I was babbling as if words could release the trauma I had seen. It couldn't. "Where is Idabelle?"

"There is no Idabelle Drake here," the doctor informed me.

"There is." Ida appeared. "I am Idabelle Drake." Our eyes met. I suspected she knew. Now it was in the open between us. Good. I smiled at my cousin.

"Ida, please make them listen. The children--all of you--are in danger. The rioters are on their way here. They won't see innocent children. They're too angry. All their hate is the color of these children's skin. We have to get everyone out now."

Ida looked to the white doctor. "Doctor Smith, my cousin is a good person. He would not lie about such a thing." The man nodded.

"Staff, gather all the children and bring them here as fast as you can. Make sure we don't leave anyone behind."

"Shall we pack their nightclothes and such, Doctor?" one of the orderlies asked. Doctor Smith looked at me. I shook my head, no.

"There's no time. Everything but the children's lives is replaceable." We could hear the roar of the mob approaching across the lawn, shouting ugly epithets and making brutal threats. Ida ran up the stairs with me right behind her. "What can I do, Ida? Tell me."

"Stay with me," she commanded. "We're going to get the littles. Some of them will need to be carried."

I followed her into the stark, barracks-style room. The walls and ceiling were white, the floor unpainted wood. There were rows of beds, some narrow, others able to sleep multiple children. All the beds were occupied by sleepy-eyed young children. We had interrupted their nap time.

"Put on your shoes, children, quickly. Older children help the little ones. This is my friend, Kit. He has come to take us on an adventure."

"What kind of an adventure, Miss Ida?" one of the children asked. "One with pirates and rogues?"

"Yes," I jumped in. "Pirates, and ships, and…"

"Will there be Indians?" one asked.

"Possibly."

"And fairies?"

"Anything is possible on an adventure," Ida played along. "That is why it is an adventure. We don't know what will happen. But to have an adventure, we must all be very brave and do what our captain tells us. All crews know the first rule of an adventure is that they must follow orders, or the adventure may go amiss, and the pirates could capture them. We do not want the pirates to capture us."

"Where is the captain?" one of the older children asked suspiciously.

"Miss Ida is the captain," I informed him. He made a face.

"Girls cannot be captains," the boy stated. "Only boys."

I was prepared to argue that point, but Ida stepped in. "That is why Kit is here. He is a Drake, like the famous sea captain Sir Francis Drake, who sailed the seas for Queen Elizabeth of England." She gave me a look that said I had better support her in this, or I was going to be in big trouble. "Captain Kit, what are your orders?" The children were all lined up now at the end of their little beds.

The noise from the approaching mob was a train racing into a station without brakes.

"We need to move fast. Who will have trouble keeping up, Ida?"

"Oscar and Tootie." She pointed, and I hurried to pick up the two small children. I placed Oscar on my back, keeping the smallest, Tootie, a toddler with kinky sand colored hair and blue eyes, in my arms. We led our little troop of child-adventurers downstairs.

The last groups of children were pulled from classrooms and work chores. Those old enough to realize there was a problem were restive, their expressions melting down their faces like hot wax.

The front door exploded open, rocks and paving stones bursting through the ground-floor windows. Broken glass tumbled across the carpet like circus acrobats, coming to rest in the puzzled formations of a spring ice flow breaking up.

The children shrieked in fear, the younger ones beginning to cry, their dark eyes flooded with a chiaroscuro of emotions no child should be so familiar with. It broke my heart, but who knew what terrors these innocents had witnessed? Fear shredded a child's confidence in the world, destroying what should have been burgeoning trust. A child always blamed themself, as I had, because the adult knowledge-holders who built their world could not possibly have made such a mistake.

And just like that, a child's doubt in their worth was planted, roots stabbing deep. I could see it on their faces, the melted hopes of a new start, a better childhood puddled at their pudgy feet, leaving bare fear, doubt, and hopelessness writ large like yellow journalism newspaper headlines.

I would not let them die, murdered by anger and prejudice.

The rioters began to push into the large foyer, the children and their adult attendants instinctively pressing toward the back wall.

Doctor Smith, in his long white coat, came forward, separating himself from the group. He was white, but that was not going to save him today. He was a friend of the enemy. He could die with them.

"We have nothing of value here," Smith told the rioters. "Please, go on your way and pass this place by."

"Nothing of value," the man at the head of the rioters harrumphed. "You're right about that."

"You will find no enemies here, my friends. Only children."

"Black children who will grow up and take the jobs of our children."

"There is room for all of us to thrive here in this country," Doctor Smith tried to reason. "Preserving the lives of these children costs you nothing."

But it would. The man looked behind him. If he backed down, everyone would see him and think him weak. He could not let the orphans live and save face.

The people outside were not patient. They could not hear the conversation taking place inside, but they were well past talking, hot blood fueled by more blood, the release of bitterness, rage, and the manic spirit of battle lust.

Oil-soaked rags attached to sticks sailed in through the broken-toothed maws of the windows, landing on the asylum foyer's carpet, the flames quickly spreading to the drapes. The screaming children cowered, clinging to their friends and favorite caretakers.

"What are you doing?" Someone outside shouted at the mob. "Mary and Joseph, they are only babies."

"Black babies!" Someone shouted.

"Don't do this, I beg you, my friends. How will you face your own children with the blood of these innocents on your hands?"

Someone threw another torch through a window. "Stop!" the man outside shouted. "You should be ashamed of yourselves!"

But a mob has no conscience. No one is responsible for what happens. Someone else is always to blame.

I could not accept that. The people outside could not be allowed to hide their inhumanity within the anonymity of a mob. Every one of them needed to understand they were responsible for any blow they dealt.

One of the leader's companions pushed through to our defender's side.

"What are you doing, Seamus?" our defender stopped him. "What are you thinking, man? We are not the kind of people who murder children? No amount of Hail Marys could cleanse this from your heart. God will not forgive this. If you do, you will regret it for the rest of your life." The defender turned and shouted at the crowd. "If you do this, you will carry it carved on your souls to the end of your days."

"Then let it be so!" the man, Seamus, spun on his friend. "Our folk are dying in this God Forsaken land so the likes of them can be free. What about us? When do we get to be free? I am tired of being beaten down into the mud, Con. I'm worn thin as a shroud with seeing my little ones starving in rags, no matter how hard I work. My children will not live like slaves in this world. Do you hear? I am done with it."

"I hear you, Seamus," our defender, Con, said. "We'll see to it our children get a good life here and don't have to live with the shame of signs saying 'No dogs. No Irish,' but this is not the way. How will we make things better if we become the animals they claim we are?" Con pulled his friend's head toward his, forehead to forehead, eye to eye, making a pact between them. "We'll do it right, Seamus, showing them we're upright men, who know a Godly path, even when we've been wronged."

I stepped forward. "Let them pass." I let the older toddler, Oscar, off my back, but I still carried little Tootie in my arms. Seamus looked at the mob, shouting, shattering, and breaking whatever they could get their hands on. The torched interior of the Asylum was burning well now, the flames lapping at the upper story, catching the well-oiled walls, and spreading. The children's eyes reflected the flames, the sweat from the heat, and fear beading on their smooth, young skin.

This was not about black orphans. It wasn't about a military lottery. It was the anger and bitterness of generations of abuse rising to the surface.

Inside, the foyer had gone quiet, except for the rumble of the flames. Seamus looked at the tear-streaked faces of the children, their youthful determination making a fragile stand in what they believed were the final moments of their lives.

Doctor Smith picked one of the children up. "Please, let us pass."

"Think of your own Michael and Rosie and let them go, Seamus," Con echoed.

The truths Seamus wailed had cut out his heart, and it lay there on the floor for all to see. He did not have the energy to pick it up. Slowly, he nodded.

Con went to the door and shouted, "They're coming out. The building is ours." There was a jubilant cheer. "Step to the side and leave a path down the middle. Seamus promised them safe passage." There were mutterings and grumbles, but the crowd separated into two lines, leaving a corridor down the middle.

Doctor Smith came out first, leading the way between the hecklers as the orphanage's attendants sorted themselves among the children, encouraging them to clutch each other's hands and walk forward into the noise, the violence, the white-hot anger spitting at them. It was an anger based on wrongs done long before they were born, in a land far away, brought to the docks of New York, hidden among the poor possessions of poverty the immigrants brought with them from across an ocean. Hope had sustained them. Reality had burned it from them. I wondered how they would find it again, and how Abraham Lincoln would ever heal this country, or if he could.

I looked back at Ida. "I am so sorry." All of my feelings of injustice and abandonment were nothing in the face of hers. I was loved, cared for, and encouraged to find my best path to a future of my choosing. Ida's mother never dared to tell her she loved her. Ida had never known the protection of being part of the Drake family, and still, she was brave and good.

"It was not your mistake that defined my life, Kit. You are just a boy."

Her inference that she thought I was not a boy any longer made my heart swell.

"But all the support I've had reminds me of what you should have been given and were not. Walk ahead of me, cousin. I will be right here, protecting your back." I would not let her die while I was still alive.

Idabelle took the few steps that separated us, leaned in, and kissed my cheek.

"See you on the other side."

As the orphans walked forward, some of the rioters spat at us. Others tried to strike us or threw stones, shouting words I hoped would give them sleepless nights until their deaths and beyond. I hoped their God would read those words blistered on their hearts.

"Don't look at them," I whispered to the children clustered around me, holding Tootie close to my chest. "Don't think about them. Just look forward to that green lawn up ahead. That's where we're going."

"Is this the adventure?" the little suspicious child asked me.

"It is the beginning of one, and beginnings are often the hardest part. Just keep being brave. We will get through this. Miss Ida and I will be with you the whole way."

"Ay yay, Captain Kit," the little boy said, pretending to be brave.

The slightest twitch, any contact between the heckler's eyes and ours, a stumble, a word, a look of defiance—anything could trigger the lines into breaking and collapsing in on us. The children walked the gauntlet like it was a death march, their faces set, bodies and spirits surrendered to the end they expected would come at any moment.

I thought of my mother, valiantly working to create a better world for her children…both of us, for mine was not the only life she was the caretaker of now. I felt her presence in the love I carried inside me. It was strong, and it was real, and it made me strong as well. I visualized it surrounding me, enveloping me, but not only me, but Ida, and the children, too.

Then I thought about the lines of angry people hemming us in, but instead of seeing them as rabid beasts, I forced my mind to shift. These people were bitter and frightened, but they were fathers and mothers, brothers and sisters—fellow human beings struggling through the same pain of prejudice we knew.

I expanded the love that protected me to include them.

Their hands dropped to their sides, the crush of cruel words dying on their lips.

"Remember a time when someone did you a kindness," I whispered, making myself a hollow vessel without importance or ego, like I was learning to do when Weaving. *"Repay that kindness now and let us pass."* I visualized the lines of rioters, not as threatening us, but guarding us by standing between us and the violence in the city.

And they were.

We walked on, flames and smoke rising behind us.

Ida slowed her steps so that we could walk together.

"Where to, Captain?" I could feel how her smile, though hard-won, released some of the tension hovering around us like the black smoke of burning buildings.

"That would be Doctor Smith's decision."

"James Smith is a quiet, studious man, Kit," Ida replied. "An admirable man, whose life's work has been taking children's temperatures and putting bandages on their skinned knees, but he has barely been holding himself together since the rioters broke down the door. He has no idea what to do."

Doctor Smith joined us. "What next, Mister Drake?" he asked. Ida gave me a knowing look.

"We need to go South to avoid the government buildings and that area where the rioting has been," I suggested.

"The police will arrive soon, I expect," Doctor Smith suggested. "We just need somewhere to go until they restore order." I was less confident about the police's ability to stand against the mob I had seen. "The children have had a fright," Smith went on. "We cannot expect them to walk far, especially at this pace. It is nearly impossible to keep them together. One or the other is always falling behind or getting sidetracked by some alley cat or insect."

"They are curious children, Doctor," Ida defended the little ones. "Right now, they need to feel normal, and looking for bugs or petting a cat helps them do that."

"They are going to need to rest and gather their strength," Smith insisted. "Perhaps a board member's house who lives nearby?"

"Those people have already left town," I informed Smith. "And if they have not, hiding among the wealthy, who are being targeted, seems like a bad idea. We have just escaped by the grace of a miracle, but we cannot expect two."

"A church?" Smith suggested.

I shook my head. "Protestant churches, abolition support, Irish Catholic rioters… That's too risky."

"They'll be after anyone they suspect of being abolitionists," Ida agreed.

"Do you have another destination in mind, Mister Drake?" Doctor Smith asked.

"Think, Kit. Where is safe?" Idabelle whispered.

There was one place where I felt safe.

"The theater."

Act Four, Scene Five: Wallack's Day One of the Draft Riots

We brought all two hundred-thirty-three children and their caregivers into the alley that led to the stage door. I set Oscar and Tootie down, my arms and back grateful for the break, and climbed the steps to the platform porch.

"Please, someone be here. Please," I whispered under my breath. The knob turned, and the door opened. Distant sounds of violence in the city were expanding and getting closer. "Inside quickly," I encouraged everyone. "It's dark, so be careful—dark but not scary dark," I edited my statement, seeing the worry on the children's faces. "It's a good dark--a safe dark." Kindle appeared, their bright gold eyes startled by the flood of strangers. I scooped the cat up, snuggling it to my chest. "See, here is our theater cat, come to say hello."

"Can we pet him?" someone asked.

Kindle wriggled from my arms, nipping my hand as they leaped away, retreating to the darkness.

"Maybe later." I laughed, hiding the bite marks. "Kindle is very shy," I apologized as children sifted past me into the dark halls.

"Is it a girl cat or a boy cat?" our suspicious, inquisitive child demanded.

"No one knows, Isaac. It is a mystery," Ida answered for me.

That was true. Kindle, being a spirit, did not ascribe to a human-specific gender, and none of the company seemed interested enough to face claws and teeth to investigate. The question of my spirit-cat friend's gender was never an issue for me. I simply fell into referring to Kay as Kay, leaving the rest nebulous. As Kay, the spirit understudied both male and female parts. Once it became acceptable for women to perform on the stage, Puck was played by both men and women, and Kay's portrayal was so fey, it defied categorization. Audiences and the company accepted this as part of the actor's enigmatic genius.

"I will find out," the precocious Isaac proclaimed. His gender was obvious, with his stout little legs and low, raspy voice.

"Do you think they will forgive me for disturbing the sanctity of their abode?" I asked Ida as she passed.

"Kindle? Probably not. Mister Lester? It's a toss-up, but we will try to keep the children from getting into things they should not."

The hallway was nearly pitch black, illuminated by only one lantern down near Wardrobe, and packed wall to wall with curious, frightened, and exhausted children, some of whom needed their nappies changed.

"Everyone just sit down and rest," I ordered.

"You're not leaving us, are you, Captain?" I was assaulted by a chorus of "Don't leave us, Captain" and versions of "I'm scared."

"Wait, Wait. We are on an adventure," I reminded them. "And sometimes on an adventure we will get tired, thirsty, hungry, or get poopy pants. Those needs are easier to take care of at the orphanage, but on an adventure, we don't necessarily have all the comforts of our usual lives. That is why I expect my crew members to be not only brave, which you are doing very well, but also to be tough. As a crew, we feast together when there's food, we rest when we can, and we always follow orders because that is what will keep us safe. Right now, my orders are for my crew to sit here quietly, because we have more adventuring ahead and we need to rest while we can. Now, who is the captain here?"

"You are, Captain Kit," Ida declared.

"And when I am not here, Doctor Smith and First Sergeant Belle are in charge."

"Her name is Idabelle," Isaac corrected me.

I stared him down. "Her name is Belle Drake, and she is an officer in training on the high seas. You think of her as Miss Idabelle because that is the name she used while in disguise, but she is really a notorious privateer, like her ancestor, Captain Sir Frances Drake."

"She is a Drake, like you?" Oscar asked.

"Yes. Sergeant Belle is my cousin and a fine officer."

"I thought she said you were friends," suspicious Isaac caught me out.

"Cousins can be friends," I declared, as if it were the most obvious thing in the world. There was no more arguing about who was who. "I will be right back," I promised.

Maggie Walsh came out of Wardrobe into the hallway, and her eyes went wide. "By all that is holy, what is this?" I hurried down the hall and into the light where she could see me. "Kit Drake, explain yourself."

I looked back at the crowd of children. "If we could just step into your office for a moment, Mistress Walsh, I will do that."

It did not take long for me to catch Maggie up, but before I finished, several more company members joined us in Wardrobe.

"The rioters are spreading out all across the city," Wixx explained.

"And the police?" Maggie asked. "Where are they?"

The gasman shook his head. "I don't know, the mobs are now breaking into houses and looting them before they set them on fire. Most of the people in big houses have abandoned them. The neighborhoods being hit hardest are those where people of color live. The rioters have no mercy for persons or property." We all knew what would happen if such mobs discovered the children in our care.

"What about The National Guard?" Maggie asked. "When are they arriving?"

"The National Guard is in Gettysburg," Wixx informed us. "As are most of New York's troops."

The truth sank in.

"So, there's no one here in the city to stop the riots."

"There is a small contingent still stationed here, and we have the local police force," Wixx ran the situation down. "But it is not nearly enough. We need to plan as if we are on our own."

"Has Mayor Opdyke recalled The Guard?" I asked.

"No one has heard anything," Wixx admitted. "Governor Seymour gave his speech against the draft the other day, then promptly left on vacation, so he is not in town. No one has heard from Congressman Wood or Mayor Opdyke."

I thought about what happened to Superintendent Kennedy when he tried to reason with the mob, and he was Irish. Most of the Metropolitan Police Force were Irish as well, whatever that might mean. Would they fight against their own? George Opdyke was certainly not going to do anything that put him in danger. He would do what he usually did: nothing, waiting for the situation to work itself out. Which meant waiting until someone else did what he didn't, but should have. And Wood would be smugly waiting for local government to fail, hoping it would mean they would favor his plan for the city to secede from the Union.

Wixx turned to me. "Kit, you have met Mayor Opdyke and Wood at these society functions Bernie takes you to. Can you find out what is being done?"

"I see them at parties, Wixx. We are not friends."

"But you know where to find them?"

"Like you said, people who have the means have left town."

"But not the city leadership, certainly?" Doctor Smith exclaimed. His expectations were, again, higher than my own.

"Surely, there is something you can do, Cousin?" Idabelle asked me.

Maggie raised an eyebrow. Wixx did not react at all, which told me he already knew. I was not surprised. He might not be a Bee, but he was almost certainly a member of Bernie's support team.

"I can go to a few places and ask around," I agreed.

"And find some way to get the children out of the city," Doctor Smith suggested. "Somewhere safe."

"They are safe here."

"For now," Wixx agreed. "But for how long? If the theater is attacked…" He did not finish the sentence. The theatre was not a fortress, and a handful of stagehands were not troops. "It might be safer for the children if we could get them off Manhattan Island."

"For that, we would need a ship."

"I know a man with a crew who might be willing to help," Wixx suggested. "Check all the doors and windows and make sure they're closed and locked, Kit, then head out. The rest of you, keep the children contained and quiet. We don't want to draw attention to the fact that anyone is in here."

"We can't just leave the children sitting in the hallway," Ida pointed out.

I had already been considering this. "Divide them up into small groups and set them up in the private boxes."

"What about food? They're going to be hungry."

"And nappies." I made a face. "We're going to have to do something about nappies or the rioters will just follow the smell."

"There are stores of cotton here in Wardrobe." Maggie went to find it.

"Is someone going to tell Mister Lester what's going on?"

"I'll go by his house when I go to the docks," Wixx offered.

"Assuming he has not left town," Doctor Smith said.

"Lester won't leave his theater." Wixx turned away to signal we were done talking and the time had come for action. We each knew our job.

Ida approached me. "Bernie will be worried."

"There's nothing we can do about that right now, Ida."

"You don't think you could…?"

"At the moment, there are more important things than Bernie worrying. I'll get to Drake House when I can and update Bernie. Meanwhile, take care of the children and stay safe. Keep an extra eye out for that little scamp, Isaac. If he starts hunting Kindle, he could get into all kinds of trouble in a theater. I'll be back." I hurried down the dark hallway before the mass of children came this way as they were led to the theater boxes.

I almost left behind the faintest light from the hallway outside Wardrobe when I passed the stairs leading up to the wings, stage right, and the ghost light caught me.

Kindle was alone on the empty stage. I crooked my finger at the cat and sat off to the side where we would not be seen as the children began to fill the boxes. Kindle joined me with a deliberate saunter, an act I was meant to read as punishment for bringing strangers to invade the theater.

"What are you doing?" The cat hissed, changing into Kay. "I don't like all these little people running around, screeching, and grabbing and chasing. Why are they here?"

"Things are bad outside," I explained. "There's a riot. I'm sure you've heard." Kay began licking their shoulders, arms, and hands, bathing themselves like a cat. Only they were not currently in the form of a cat. It was…disquieting. "We needed somewhere safe to hide the children." I pointed at the boxes now filling with children."

"Humans are always fighting," Kay shrugged this off as unimportant. Of course, Kay thought people always fought. Shakespeare's plays were full of fights and battles. That was part of the entertainment.

"This is not a play, though, Kay. It is real, and there are people set on hurting people who they see as different than them. People like these children. It was the only place I could think of that was safe."

"But this is *our* place," the spirit wailed, like a toddler.

"Why are you being like this, Kay? There have always been other people here; the company, the audience."

"The audience comes and then goes away. And the company is our family. You brought strangers here, and now you want to go away again and leave them here with me, without you. You said you would be here with me, always."

"I did not mean I was going to set up house here. I can't be here every minute."

"You can." Kay produced a sword and pointed it at my chest. It was not a wooden prop. It was one of the finer steel points Gil and I trained with. "If you are a ghost, we can be together always, and I won't have to share you."

And there it was. Kay and I had a bond, and the spirit saw my concern for the children as a threat to that bond.

"It doesn't work like that, Kay. Dying won't make me like you. If you kill me, I will just be gone. They'll bury my body in some churchyard, and you will be here with the company but without me. I don't want you to ever doubt that I love you, Kay. Killing me so you don't have to share me is not love. You said you did not want a love like Oberon and Titania's because it was cruel. This," I indicated the sword still pointed at my chest, "is cruel, and it's not what you really want."

Kindle dropped the sword. "I love you, Kit Drake. Without you, I would die."

"No, you wouldn't." I pulled them into my arms. "You would feel sad and alone for a while, but then the season would start up and the company would return, and there would be a new show, and after some time, I would become a memory, like any show you love while it's running, but you begin to forget once it closes.

"And I don't want to be alone," Kay wailed, in tragedian distress. "When I am alone, I feel confused, and I don't know who I am. I hate summer hiatus. I need people. I need an audience. I need a show, Kit!"

"Then, maybe you should put one on for the children? Just a little one. It will help them feel more normal, and it will help you not feel so lonely. Go to Idabelle as Kay and offer to help distract the children by doing a show. Now, I have to go take care of something, but I will be back. I promise."

"You should not make promises you can't keep," Kay reminded me, pouting. "You are not a witch with future-telling gifts. You are only a human. You cannot know the future."

"You are right. I will try to come back," I corrected myself. "I will try very hard."

Act Four, Scene Six: The Metropolitan and The Nicholas Hotel, July 13, Day One of the Draft Riots

The first thing I noticed was: no trolleys were running. The city was shut down, the only traffic headed West, away from the forties blocks near Fourth and Fifth Avenues, where the first fires were set. The carriages passing me raced as if a burning stick was tied to their back axles. The violence was escalating. If you looked like you had money, if your skin called your race into question, if the mob suspected you were an Abolitionist, a Protestant, a Quaker, or a member of any group that supported freedom for people of African descent, you would be targeted. Realizing order was not going to be restored by nightfall, even the middle class was fleeing.

A young man of African descent ran furtively from one side alley to another, crossing the street in front of me, believing the street was deserted. Disappearing down the second alley, I heard low voices followed by a door thudding shut and a bolt being slid back into place with two clicks. He was safe. For now.

Apparently, the rioters were expanding the violence and arson South toward the entertainment district, and I questioned leaving Wallack's. I did not think there were enough adults at the theater to fend off a determined mob, but we needed a plan, and it was hard to plan without information. We needed to know the city's status and when we could expect help.

I knew where to look for New York's gentleman-leaders. I had seen them often enough, lunching or drinking at the Metropolitan, Astor House, The Nicholas, Del Monico's. I considered borrowing a few costume pieces so I would blend in better with the working folk who made up most of the rioters, but to gain access to the lairs of New York's decision makers, I needed to look the part of a gentleman. I would cloak myself in invisibility until I reached my destination.

Stopping on Prince Street, around the corner from the Metropolitan, I made sure no one was nearby before returning myself to visibility.

Once inside the hotel, I paused, taking stock.

Anxious families of means occupied every available chair and settee, late-comers standing against a wall or sitting on the floor. Their hands were clasped together in their laps, their faces blank or troubled. Children dressed in broadcloth, laces, and satins, like smaller versions of their parents, played on the Turkish carpets or clung to their nannies.

My attention was grabbed by a familiar voice.

Cyril Fitz-Royale sat on a chair, telling a story to a bouquet of children settled around his feet. He looked up, and our eyes met. The acceptance of difficult truths made his face look vulnerable and years older than the last time I saw him. I had judged him unfairly, believing the character he played for Bernie was his own. He played it well, humbly accepting society's disrespect of the doddering old British dandy they thought him to be. I hoped we would both live long enough for me to meet the real Cyril and apologize for my mistake.

"Are you seeking Wood?" he interrupted his story. I nodded. "They're at The Nicholas." He resumed.

It was not far. A block South and one East.

"Third floor. Sixth door on the left at the end of the hall," the clerk informed me when I asked at the desk.

I followed his directions, moving as if I knew where I was going and acting like I belonged. I could smell the smoke as soon as I arrived on the third floor. No one stopped me, though once I entered the room, several assistant types turned to scrutinize me, trying to decide if they needed to intervene between me and their person of importance, or if I was one of the group.

I looked for Wood--not because he was the most important person, but because we were acquainted, and however murky his morals, he expressed an interest in me I hoped to leverage. He was, however, not present. One of the assistants strutted up to me, his beady eyes looking down a very long nose.

"Can I help you?"

"I don't know, can you?" I acted as much like Cyril Fitz-Royale as I could. "I am here to see…" I glanced at the gathering of cigar-smoking poker players. "Mayor Opdyke." Hearing his name mentioned, New York's mayor looked up from his cards.

"Ah, young Drake, isn't it?" he greeted me, a cigar clenched between his teeth. "You are looking for Wood?"

"I expected to meet him here," I prevaricated to make it seem such a plan was in existence.

"As did I. Apparently, we have both been bamboozled. As you can see, the scoundrel has gone missing."

"You were meeting to discuss what actions can be taken regarding the riot?" I asked.

Opdyke guffawed. "You show people, always so melodramatic. There is no riot. Just a bunch of malcontents whipped up by that fool Seymour."

"The Governor doesn't want his name or career attached to this mess any more than the rest of us do," the man beside the mayor grumped.

"How long ago was the National Guard called up?" I asked.

"Ten days," Opdyke growled around his cigar. "They were 'called up' to Gettysburg."

"But you've requested their return?"

"Not my job." Opdyke shrugged, continuing to play his hand and smoke his cigar. "It was a Federal Draft. That makes it a Federal Problem--Wood's problem."

"Arc you playing or talking, Opdyke?" one of the mayor's colleagues demanded.

"But surely, Sir, someone needs to do something. Tell Washington what is happening. People are being attacked…"

"The police are handling it," Opdyke interrupted me. "That's their job."

But they weren't. Wherever the police presence within the city was, whatever they were doing, it was not enough.

"Perhaps if you were to send a telegram, Mayor…"

"My hands are tied," the man said, putting me off. "Go talk to Wood. He is your congressman."

I barely held my tongue and temper as I exited.

Hurrying down the stairs, I made the lobby when I encountered the stern Mister Undergrove.

"May I offer my assistance, Master Drake?"

"It is kind of you, but no, thank you," I tried to dodge around him. He moved subtly to thwart my effort.

"You are seeking Congressman Wood, are you not? I know his location. Let me take you to him. I have a conveyance just outside, and I can guarantee we will not be bothered by the mobile. You do not want to be traveling on foot in the city right now, Drake. The situation is…volatile."

"Drake?" Cyril Fitz-Royale was crossing the room. He had ended his entertainment of the children at the Metropolitan and seemed in some hurry to speak with me. "Excuse me, I must interrupt for a moment. I require a word with the young man," he addressed Undergrove with his usual air of refined dismissal.

Undergrove's expression remained controlled, but his eyes were red embers in his dark face. He was an uncommonly frightful figure. Fitz-Royale pulled me away.

"You are not thinking of going with him, are you, Drake? Your aunt would not approve."

"My aunt knows him and has for many years…"

"They are not friends. They are, in fact, decidedly unfriendly."

"I need to see the Congressman, Lord Fitz-Royale. The city…"

"Where is the little man?" Fitz-Royale interrupted.

"Charles Stratton?"

"No, the blue creature that trails after your aunt."

I was so shocked I nearly stumbled. Cyril Fitz-Royale could see Spin? My mind had seconds to decide if I should pretend that I did not understand his reference or let Fitz-Royale's statement stand and see where that led. Under the circumstances, lying seemed a waste of time.

"I would suppose he is with Bernie, as you say," I replied, giving away as little as possible.

"Summon him, or conjure him up, or whatever you do," Fitz-Royal demanded.

"I don't do any of those things. The creature is his own master."

"Oh, my Lord, he is not!" Fitz-Royale objected. "He is that tall man's creature—the tall fellow with the lovely hair and marvelous tailor."

I knew of whom he spoke, the fey lord, Toranado. "Spin appears when he wants to," I repeated. "It has nothing to do with me—us."

"I am aware Bernie cannot control him," Cyril continued. "But I hope you have greater talents and might be able to."

"We should go, Drake," Undergrove hailed me.

"Lord Fitz-Royale, I really should…"

"You should not go anywhere with that creature," Fitz-Royale argued. "He is not who or what he pretends to be."

I cocked my head to one side. "Few in my aunt's circle are," I let him know I knew the role he played.

"Damned stubborn family," Fitz-Royale swore. He took a breath. "Just be careful. Keep your eyes open and take nothing for granted. See things as they are, not as you assume them to be," he cautioned.

"I will. Watch yourself as well." I took his forearm and shook his hand with my other hand.

"Master Drake, my carriage awaits." Undergrove gestured to the door. I walked ahead of the man, feeling the skin on my back pressing toward my spine, as if to get as far away from him as possible. It was possible Fitz-Royale was right, and I should not have accepted Undergrove's offer, but by the time I realized it, I was already in his coach.

Act Four, Scene Seven: Federal Hall, 26 Wall Street, NYC, Day One of the Draft Riots

Moving through the city, we passed roving groups of rioters, but few turned their heads to look at the carriage. It was as if it were invisible--not one person, but an entire vehicle. I was in the presence of magic far beyond my experience or understanding. The smell of smoke permeated the carriage's black, leather, tufted benches, its fabric-covered walls, its dark brocade curtains. I noted the deep purple embroidered curlicues and fleur-de-lis on the curtains before seeing the lines they were made of were thorned branches and poison ivy vines with tiny skulls and clawed hands painted over stylized skeletonized bodies. My first impression was to view them as more common designs, but as I examined them, they either changed, or my view of them had, and I saw them as they were.

"See what is truly around you," Cyril had cautioned me. *"Do not assume."* Sound advice from a doddering old fool.

Working to retain this unguised view of the world, I looked at Mister Undergrove himself and wished I had not. It was not that he was ugly. There was a gravitas to the ill-favored creature, his build and features not unlike the human sleeve he used to conceal his true self, but without a glamor, he appeared more demonic than gave comfort. I was not religious, but in the Western World, it was very difficult to avoid being impregnated with ideology involving heaven and hell, and one could not avoid using language that referred to angels or devils.

"I see you truly, Mister Undergrove," I informed him. I was not sure what possessed me to make the declaration, as it revealed me not to be as naive as people supposed. The inclusion of the word "possessed" in the thought was unfortunate, but once my mind made the connection, the damage was done.

"And I see you, Mister Drake." Undergrove inclined his head toward me in a sign of respect. "Even when you are invisible to human eyes."

I peered out of the window, looking ahead to parse where we might be going, and caught a clear-sighted view of the creatures that drew the carriage. Night-black and hellish, they were akin to the horses of our world but with less flesh and more bone. Their black manes were strands of black fire, blue lightning crackling and flashing within.

"Fine steeds," I complimented him, as gentlemen were wont to do. "I am unfamiliar with the breed. Did you get them at auction?" I playfully poked his otherness.

"No, a former acquaintance who passed on owed me a substantial debt." He grinned, enjoying the sortee.

"My condolences to his family."

"Oh, he did not die. That would have been an undeserved comfort."

"A business rival then?" I tried to keep him talking. Anything I could learn about his world, his desires, or his goals could be helpful, now, or in the eons to come, for such a fay creature must have, like Spin, a very elongated life span, and I very much wanted to understand his interest in the small events of humanity.

"There are no small events, Mister Drake." Undergrove mined my unspoken thoughts as easily as I might have eavesdropped outside an open door. I should have realized he could do this, since Spin did it all the time, but now I knew to watch for it. "The future is spun of the sticky threads of humanity's every conscious and unconscious question, and every thoughtless action," Undergrove explained his thinking. "You must see how your kind's negligent, self-centered choices are breaking this world."

"It is not your world. Why would you care?" I asked.

"We are neighbors, and I do so enjoy visiting and playing games here. My kind would count it a great loss if this world and its inhabitants ceased to be available for our entertainment." He had no reason to be truthful with me. He could tell me anything, and probably would, assuming I was naïve enough to believe whatever he said. That was the role I must play today, the callow youth, nephew of a long-time Coterie member and Weaver. Someone who lived near greatness but was not great themselves.

"You should ask Spin for a history lesson. You really are frightfully ignorant," Undergrove informed me. "It puts you at an unnecessary disadvantage."

"I am," I admitted. "Frightfully." I smiled. "But what has any of this to do with the rioting here in the city, or the war between the states?"

"What indeed," he replied enigmatically. "Humans' lives, like our fey lives, have a purpose. One of the most frustrating and amusing differences between us is that we are born knowing our purpose, while you humans struggle to locate yours, like a missing sock, always getting distracted and severing the patterns of the Weave. The notions of this new *democracy*," he said the word with a sneer, "that you are in charge of your destiny—that you make your own decisions, are the most laughable hubris, but this belief has made you inconveniently difficult to manipulate. Humans were much more malleable when you were unwashed peasants. You might grumble behind the master's back, but you knew to cower when he drew his sword because he was just as likely to cut out your heart as he was to shit in the morning. In medieval times, humanity understood its lives were worthless. Now, every damn one of you in America thinks you are important. It is so tiresome."

"I am not going to apologize for the evolution of my kind."

Undergrove snorted. "You flatter your fellows. Slugs are beyond any ability to evolve. To do that, they would have to accept that growth is desirable, and the cosmic inevitability is change, which they do not. In their struggle to remain in the familiar mud and goo of non-understanding, humans continually rupture the natural growth defined in the concept of a future, to the misfortune of themselves and every other being."

"You make mismatched generalizations that seem in direct opposition to each other, Mister Undergrove," I argued. "I know of men and women whose nature is so completely opposite to your description that their very characters defy it."

"I know some as well," Undergove agreed. "I have sought them out. And, like yourself, I wished to believe their vision of humanity might prevail. It would make our games much more interesting. And there was a time, some centuries ago, when I, too, believed as you do, but I had less experience of humanity then and a more romanticized notion of their nature and capabilities. Now, I know them. My eyes have been opened. Whatever promise humanity once had, they have failed.

"Look at this conflict: creating death-fields in the name of a belated insistence on freedom and equality for a race your countrymen do not like. Even an idealistic dreamer like you must see it is a political farce."

"What about men like Emerson and Whitman?"

"A few bright spots in the dark heavens do not make the night sky blue, Mister Drake. You only need to look to your life for confirmation."

I let that comment go. I did not count myself as the subject, but spoke of men and women of greater abilities than I.

"So, you have given up on us?" I demanded. "You are working toward our downfall now?"

"We watch the Weave, Little Fox. We watch it closely. We know when new threads appear and study how they bind or undermine the strength of the cosmic fabric."

"The Weave, as you wish it to be," I accused. "A Weave that favors the fey."

"At some level, all Weaves are one."

"Human beings are flawed," I admitted. "But we are unfinished- -still evolving. We are worth saving."

"That has not been my experience," Undergrove retorted. "Nor, if you are truthful with yourself, has it been yours." He paused. "I am not your enemy, Little Fox."

"Perhaps, but I do not think you are my friend either, or the friend of my kind."

"Your *kind*?"

"Humankind."

"Is that how you see yourself?" He cocked an eyebrow, reminding me I had Drake blood, however diluted it might be. The carriage pulled up to the marble colonnaded Federal Hall building. "We are here."

As I stepped from the magical conveyance, I took in a breath and blew it out, trying to shed the foreboding I felt. Was it industry or intrigue making heavy the steam venting from the buildings nearby?

The original building at this location on the Federal Courtyard was once the center of the United States Government. George Washington was inaugurated here. The new building was much grander, with all the changes of architects and architecture, but when Federal offices were moved to Philadelphia, then to Washington, the country's needs outgrew the current structure's space and purpose. It now served as a financial arm of the National Treasury connected with the Port of New York and all the vast sums that passed between merchants, banks, maritime organizations, federal and state governments. But we were not entering by the grand staircase as the public did. Undergrove led me around to a side entrance and down a set of steps to the basement.

The door shrieked open, and we entered, going up another set of stairs that clung like ivy to the wall, to enter the ground floor beneath the rotunda. Stacks of gold bars, both in and out of heavy metal chests, ringed this floor level, stations with heavy ledgers and scales set in another circle defining the space. My guide ignored this casually displayed wealth, leading me to a narrow wood stairway concealed behind a wall at the far back of the ground level, far away from the elegant street entrance.

We climbed these stairs, up, and up, until I could look down at the marble floor far below as if from a bird's eye view. And still we climbed.

The stairwell ended at an upper-level mezzanine that maintained the ring-shape of the base below, continuing up a narrower, steeper stairway that took us above the rotunda's open space to an attic tucked high beneath the rotunda's crown. We walked out from behind a support post to find Fernando Wood.

"Look who I found," Undergrove announced as if I were a lost puppy.

Wood looked as untrustworthy and ferrety as ever, and I noted how odd it was that, as unabashedly strange as Mister Undergrove was, it was Wood who set my teeth on edge.

"He was asking about you at The Nicholas."

"Asking the piss pots about me? Was his aunt with him? Did you bring her?" Wood craned his neck to see behind us.

"Your friends were wondering where you were," I ignored Wood's questions about Bernie. "They seemed to be expecting you.

No doubt you were delayed in notifying the government of the situation here in the city."

"That is not my responsibility," Wood countered.

"Strange. That is exactly what Mayor Opdyke said."

"Opdyke is a jellyfish without a spine," Wood spat. "But you, have you finally seen reason and have come to accept the opportunity I offered you?"

"You mean the opportunity to betray my family?"

Wood snorted. "Your family? You do not know who your family is."

"And now you are going to show your superior knowledge by enlightening me." I sighed to indicate I was resigned to being bored.

Wood's eyes grew narrower, his face more pinched. "No. I am going to let you wonder and stew over it. That is far more entertaining. Don't you agree, Undergrove?" Undergrove did not answer. As had been demonstrated at Julia Tyler's, the fey was not Wood's creature, though Wood certainly believed he was. Wood did not control Undergrove. Theirs was an alliance of convenience for the fey, one he endured at the moment because it suited him. For the fey, Wood's rude treatment of him was as unimportant as an insect buzzing in his ear.

"Where is the Blue Duke?" Wood demanded. I frowned, not understanding. "Spin? Where is the creature you call Spin?"

I shrugged. "I do not know what you are talking about." Undergrove guffawed. "I came here to ask if you have sent a request to return troops to New York, Wood. You have indicated you have not. Now, I must ask: will you?"

Wood looked disgusted. "That is the mayor's job, and I am no longer the mayor. Let them reap the benefits of their decision to put Opdyke in my place."

"The city is burning, Congressman Wood. The police are overrun; the rule of law is gone. Someone needs to declare Martial Law, and get the government to send our troops back," I tried to refocus him by appealing to his civic duty.

"Why should I help Lincoln look like a hero, his Union soldiers valiantly returning to save the city?

"New York needs to understand it stands and falls alone. The rest of the country does not give a damn what happens here. They are jealous and resentful of our wealth, our power, our opportunities, and the ability of our businessmen to seize those opportunities and make something of themselves. New England does not consider us a part of its little club. They cannot forgive us for being Britain's last foothold in the War of the Revolution."

"People are dying, Congressman."

"Not *my* people," Wood countered callously. "Join us. Just tell me where Bernie is and how to get to her, and I will have my people do the rest."

Disgusted, I began to leave, hoping I would not be stopped.

"You know you are nothing more than a pawn tossed into the game to be sacrificed? Don't you? But if you worked for me, you could be more."

"I am a Drake," I disagreed. "And we Drakes have been playing chess with queens and kings, lords and ladies since the seventeenth century. You, however, are an elected official who will lose all power and friends with the next election." I looked at Undergrove and grinned. "Isn't that right, Mister Undergrove?"

"My connection with Mister Wood is…transactional," the fey admitted without embarrassment.

I looked at Wood and smiled. I had made my point.

"Your father is not dead, you know," Wood fired a parting shot across my bow as I reached the stairs.

"He absolutely is," I countered, not slowing.

"He is not." Wood shouted after me. "Ask the little blue man. He will tell you. He does not have to tell you if you don't know to ask, but if you ask him directly, he cannot lie. It is only right that you have given up the name Becket because Becket did not beget you."

It would have been natural to ask who did, but I was angry at the man's blatant attempt to manipulate me and could not get the words out.

That, and I was afraid of the answer.

Act Four, Scene Eight: To the East River, July 13th, Day One of the Draft Riots

"Becket did not beget you," Wood's statement echoed in tunnels and shafts in my mind as I made my way back up Broadway to Wallack's.

The sky darkened, threatening rain, while I was occupied with Wood and Undergrove. Even so, the contrast upon entering the theater required a pause so my eyes could adjust. Also, I still practiced my ritual of pausing at the threshold between my two worlds.

The voices and laughter of the children brought a fresh life to the hallowed, often hollow, space. I hoped Kindle found it in themselves to enjoy our guests.

I helped Idabelle line the little ones up in pairs, preparing to walk them out of their theater-box holding areas, through the theater, and down to the alley. Using his connections from his sailing days, Wixx arranged multiple drays to move the children and their attendants to an East River dock where a barge would take them across to Blackwell's Island.

I stopped to refocus myself more than once. *"Pay attention to what you are doing. The issue of your parentage is not the mission here."*

More company members and their families joined the stagehands and production people now staying at the theater, and found purpose and distraction in helping feed and care for the orphaned children. A scavenging of Wardrobe provided pieces of old costumes and lengths of material to keep the river's chill from the children as they crossed. A dozen company members would accompany us to the docks to help herd the children and solve any problems that might arise.

Unable to turn around in the narrow alley outside the stage door, the first drays to be loaded were lined up at the mouth of the alley on Fourth Avenue. The need to avoid notice by roaming rioters played against the tedium of getting the little ones down the stairs, through the alley, and loaded into the cargo areas of the vehicles.

Kindle was nowhere to be seen.

Wixx stood beside the box seat at the front of the wagon, overseeing the load.

"That's enough in this wagon," he informed the driver. The first load was ready. I waved to Ida, and two stagehands pulled the canvas cover closed, tying the flaps. The same action was repeated for the other two wagons. "Move on." Wixx motioned the next three drays forward.

The plan was that we would stay in small groups, taking slightly varied routes to the docks, again, hoping to avoid drawing attention, which a train of drays carrying over two hundred children traveling together would certainly have done.

Stagehands dropped the back gates of the second set of wagons, throwing back the tarpaulins stretched over the hoops that covered the payload area.

"Load them in," the gasman ordered.

The next group of children streamed forward, an army of dark-headed ants with white bodies. The stagehands closed the back gates, pulled down the tarpaulins, and secured them before signaling that the load was ready. The process would be repeated until all the children and their helpers were loaded.

I hurried back to the theater, still hoping to find Kindle. The cat was pacing on the porch, their skinny black tail twitching with anxiety.

I squatted beside them. "Go to Wardrobe. Stay with Maggie. She will look after you." I walked up the steps and held the door open. Padding inside, the cat turned and looked back at me, their golden eyes sad. "I will come back," I whispered as I shut the door between us and hurried to catch the last loaded dray.

Twelfth Street, take a jog onto Avenue C to avoid Tompkins Square, then travel Columbia or Cannon to Grand. That was the plan.

Gil sat on one side near the back of the wagon, Giddy on the other. My body was tense, my ears focused on every sound on the streets outside, but my mind was back at the theater with Kindle-Kay. If something happened to Wallack's, it happened to Kay. With the danger in the city, the risk to them was no longer an abstract. And then there was Kindle.

New York cats lived fragile lives. There were so many ways a cat could be injured or killed in the city. Though a theater cat's life was different than most, they were not immune to these dangers. Since Kindle and Kay were essentially one, if Kindle's cat body was injured, would the theater's spirit be as well? Could the spirit merely move to a different cat's body if it had to? What if that new cat did not like me? What if it did not take to theater life and ran away? Imagining all the possible dangers was making me a wreck, but eventually the rhythmic sway of the wagon lulled my overwrought senses, and I nodded off.

I was awakened by a shout outside--someone yelling at the dray driver, calling for him to stop. Gil, Giddy, and I exchanged looks, shushing the children. The wagon's pace picked up, the big cart horse's hoofs booming against the paving stones.

"I said, stop. Are you deaf?" a man with a heavy Irish accent shouted. The cart wobbled, jolted, then stopped. "What are you about, driving on a day such as this?" the Irishman demanded.

"A man's got to make a living, whatever kind of day it be," our driver replied. "There's mouths need feeding at home."

"What are you carting?"

"I don't ask," the driver said gruffly. "I just drive. That's all they pay me to do." I cautiously lifted the bottom edge of the canvas cover and peeked out. The man held the horse on the left side head gear. The cart behind us was in a similar situation, but whether the third cart in our caravan had gotten away before it made the turn or not, I could not see. I tried to explain to my friends our situation in gestures.

"So, it could be anything; guns, whiskey, gold," the Irishman prompted the driver.

"They're not that kind of customer. More likely coal or iron from the weight and how it makes old Tom and Tim work to pull. None of us can take this hard work like we used to."

"Isn't that the truth," the man holding the horse's head agreed.

"Take a peek if you want to," the driver spoke loudly, warning us we were about to be discovered. Giddy had a big stick he'd found somewhere, and he stood, holding it up high, ready to whack a head if it poked inside the canvas flap. Gil sat frozen, looking worried. I heard a jingle as the man released the horse's head. Then the driver's whip cracked. More jingling. He was shaking the reins, jiggling the traces. The horses, Tom and Tim, leaped forward, whinnying.

Giddy and I were rocked off our feet and went rolling onto the floor of the wagon bed. One child let out a tiny squeal, but this wagon held older children, not the littles, and they knew how important the command to remain silent was.

I stumbled to my feet, balancing precariously against the galloping pace. Giddy was staying down.

"Right turn!" the driver warned us, taking the corner at a furious pace that tossed us like water sloshing in a pail. We had only just sorted ourselves out again when he shouted again, "Left turn," and we fell to the floor again, rolling to the opposite side of the wagon bed. While we were scrambling to right ourselves, a third directive was shouted, "Right again," followed immediately by, "Hold on!" Unable to make the sharp turn, the bulky dray rose on two wheels and spilled over onto its side, skidding over the pavement as the horses shrieked, trying to sort out their legs, desperate to avoid the tangling traces and keep their footing, and just as desperate to get away from the alarming sound of the wagon boards and wheels cracking apart.

"Is everyone all right?" I asked, trying to keep my voice calmer than I felt. There were a few minor injuries that would require attention, and one boy who would need assistance walking. Gil was swiftly improvising a sling for a girl who had probably broken her arm.

Young Giddy yanked the canvas tie free and tossed the flap open.

"We need to go," I said. "Everyone out! Move!"

The horses from the dray following us were right on top of us. Giddy jumped out and ran toward them, urging the driver to pull his animals back enough so we could get out without being crushed under the draft horse's feet. Running to the back of the second dray, Giddy ripped open the back flap, repeating the command," Out! Everyone out!"

The drivers of both vehicles were cutting their horses loose. The second wagon driver leaped onto the back of one of his horses, preparing to lead the other.

"You're on Columbia and Houston," the second dray driver shouted at me. "Go five blocks south." He pointed down Columbia. "Then turn left. That'll be Grand. It's six blocks from there to the docks where they'll be waiting. Good luck." He kicked his lead horse up, and the other followed as scavenger rioters began to close in. I did not see what happened to our driver, but thought I heard Tom and Tim racing away, dragging the remnants of their traces, the rioters in pursuit.

From here on, we would be on foot.

Giddy was barking orders like a military sergeant, getting the children and helpers from both wagons together.

"Make sure we have everyone, Gil, and bring up the rear," I told my friend. Gil was a field nurse, not an officer. "Let's go." I nodded at Giddy. He was my sergeant.

"Stay together and keep up," one of the older boys ordered the children. "We got to run like the Devil himself was behind us. This is for our lives, so no whining or complaining. If you skin your knee, you get up and keep running. If someone beside you gets hurt, you help them, but you keep running."

"What if we can't run?" a girl challenged him haughtily.

"Then, Lila Jean, what happens to you will be up to those men," the boy chucked his head toward the rioters. Her body was already maturing. She had a pretty face; light skin, "good" hair, facts she had probably been leveraging for special treatment her whole life. The boy was letting her know that that was not going to work for her today. Looking like a ripe peach ready to be plucked would only ensure the most brutal treatment women experienced in war. Lila Jean paled, thrusting out her jaw.

"I hate you, Hermes Jackson." She flounced past him.

I highly doubted it.

The mob was getting closer. "Let's go, Hermes." I smiled encouragement.

And so, we ran, the orphaned children and I, sure-footed as the deer of their country, a country that would not claim them as its own, or recognize their achievements or promise, as sure and swift as the gazelles of the continent of their ancestors. And I ran too, pretending I was their leader, knowing I was not, and that neither my skin nor my spirit could grant me that place. It was Hermes who led them, encouraging them to run as he did, free and strong, calling them by name, knowing the words each child needed to hear to be reminded of their pride, their resilience, and how strong and mighty were their hearts.

I watched this boy, only a few years younger than myself, but already so much wiser. The dignity of his bearing set him apart, as if he wore the headdress of a prince of that bright, dark content from which his ancestors were stolen. Hermes' grace inspired me. His bravery humbled me. I thought of my infant half-brother and hoped he could become the kind of man Hermes Jackson was.

When a younger boy faltered, Hermes swooped him up, not carrying him in his arms but enfolding him within his strength of spirit.

Lila Jean saw it—felt it, searching and finding something akin to Hermes' leadership within herself, calling on it to urge the children on around her.

No, she did not hate Hermes Jackson. She did not hate him at all.

Giddy was a steady rudder, Gil a long, enduring keel, but Hermes, running through the streets of New York, was magnificent.

We made the final turn onto Grand Street when, once again, hunters found us.

For a moment, they did not know what to make of this herd of children led by this leggy gazelle of a man-child racing free through Lower Manhattan, but the base nature of despair's bitterness could not admire strange beauty it did not understand. It could only try to crush it.

There weren't many rioters here. Not enough to stop us, but sacrifices would be made. I scanned the runners who would come within their grasp.

Not one of them, I vowed. *Not one.*

"Run, my little brothers and sisters. Run and do not stop. Run until your heart breaks." I would do anything to see them on their way…anything, knowing if I did not, my life would be worth nothing to me or anyone else.

A hungry predator reached out to take the child passing closest to him. An invisible spirit, I catapulted myself at the predator. Knocking him into his friends, they fell like bowling pins on a green. The child sailed by, then another, and two more before their would-be assailants got back onto their feet. Confusion slowed their decision-making. They did not know what hit them and blamed each other. I stood in their midst, wound tight, waiting, and when they returned their attention to the children, I spun, striking out, pushing, punching, and kicking at the rioter's legs so they buckled, creating even greater chaos. Once again, the rioters' tempers flared, and they turned on each other. More children sailed past.

I joined the tail end of the group.

We could smell the river's wet banks, the coal and wood of the smokestacks of boats and barges.

Smearing the rain-soaked air, when Idabelle, in her charcoal gray dress, floated out from a side street, a dark center among the light petals of the littles in their white clothes. No longer primly starched, their hair had escaped the tight braids and taut ribbons their caretakers used to confine its wild nature. Freed, it made dark halos around their little heads.

Wallack's company people trailed into the street behind Ida, each carrying a child or two. With shouts of joy and released relief, our children merged with Ida's group, hugs and hands pairing hearts between older and younger children who, abandoned by their blood families, had forged families of choice. The older children's pace slowed as they enfolded the younger into the safety of the herd.

Ida saw Gil first, then Giddy, her face focused forward in fear as she searched and did not find me.

I am still invisible.

I did not care if anyone saw me change. Ida needed to see me, and I needed to be seen. I relaxed into the physical, she found me, her face washed clean in relief.

"We were stopped a few blocks back by a barricade," she told me as I drew closer. "The other wagons were far enough back that they could detour onto side streets, but we were too close and had to abandon the wagon. I see you have met Hermes." Her eyes were warm with affection; her face lit from within. I had never seen her like this at Drake House or Wallack's, and I realized that the prim, controlled, young woman I was familiar with was not Idabelle. This was.

She had Tootie in her arms, and I reached over and took the little girl. Tootie's chubby arms wrapped tight around my neck.

"Where were you, Captain? Tootie could not see you anywhere."

"I am here, Tootie." I hugged her to me.

She laid her soft, fuzzy-down head on my shoulder as Ida and I joined the stream of children rippling and running, babbling and bubbling, to the dock, their joy irrepressible.

"We made it, Cousin, and 'the west yet glimmers with some streaks of day'." Ida smiled.

Most of the wagons were at the dock when we arrived, the children loaded onto the barge. With bargemen working on the docks between the children and any mob that might come, it was a place of relative safety, but there were still some groups unaccounted for, and all were determined; no one would be left behind.

Giddy, Gil, and others of the company's stagehands paced the dock, venturing up the streets to check for the last drays.

As soon as they arrived, the bargemen unwrapped the heavy ropes that tied the vessel to the dock and cast off.

It moved slowly over the water, away from Manhattan.

Ida and I sat close, watching the city skyline take shape against the falling evening. It stopped raining, the rain washing the soot from the air, but it did not put out the fires. New York was burning. From the barge, we could see the bright blazes, furious in their consuming purpose, a denunciation of treatment by man against man in the city's silhouette.

"You look different here with them, Ida," I said. "You look happy."

"I belong and I have a purpose."

"You belong at Drake house."

"I have a place, but I do not belong," she disagreed.

"Of course, you do. You are a Drake."

"According to Bernie, I am hired help."

"You are more to her than that. You must know that."

"I don't. She's never said it."

"Not in words maybe but…"

"But that's what matters to her, Kit: words. She knows a lot of them, how to use them, how to twist them, stab and cut with them, and when to withhold them. She is a master of words. It is her calling and her passion. But she can't manage to say the words that will tell her child that they are hers. Bernie's regard for me is based on my ability to anticipate her needs. Burke is her confidante. Dweetie is—well,

Dweetie. Everyone loves her, and she exists only to help them, asking nothing in return, but I am not Dweetie. I have expectations: respect, honesty. I will never have those things at Drake House. With the children, I know who I am. With Bernie, all I can think about is what I am not, and I don't like the person that makes me. I don't want to live my life being told that I am less than."

"You're not."

"But that is what Bernie's refusal to acknowledge me makes me feel like, that I am not good enough to be her daughter because I am black."

I wanted to confess my own half-bred status, but it was not the time. I did not want to dilute or alter Idabelle's honesty.

"We are a complicated family, we Drakes," I said instead, feeling bad that she was bearing her soul and I was withholding. "The work we do requires difficult choices. Choices most other families do not have to make."

"Families make difficult choices for their children all the time," Ida disagreed. It's just that, as children, we don't see them or understand them. That comes later. You make excuses for the family's failings too easily, Kit," she scolded me. "I've seen you with Tootie and Isaac, and the other children. You would never have abandoned them."

"But I did. I left them in a place with other people, where I thought they would be safe, while I went out into the city to try and find a way to make things better for them. And when we were attacked, I left them again to fight the bastards."

"You fought? Like, you actually hit people with your fists? Kit Drake!" Ida laughed.

I shook my hand. "I don't know what I was thinking. A dozen lessons with Weaver did not make me a fighter, but in that moment, all that mattered was that the children were protected and safe, even if I would never live to see them get on that barge. My mother sent me to Manon's. Bernie left you with the Washingtons because our mothers wanted us to have better childhoods than they believed they could give us, and they could not let the world go as it was without doing something to make it better for us. We did not understand that because we were children. But I think, Ida, that we have judged them unfairly."

She took my injured hand, holding it gently, examining it. "You are the best of them, you know." I was too embarrassed to reply. "Will you stay with us?"

We watched the water, the burning city, the smoke-filled night falling.

"I can't. You will be safe now, but I need to let Bernie know I'm alright—that we are alright. And then there's the theater to be protected."

"Well, you'll know where to find me, Cousin." She kissed me on the cheek.

Act Four, Scene Nine: Drake House, July 14th, Day Two of the Draft Riots.

I stayed the night on Blackwell's Island, helping settle the children into the foyer beneath the asylum's rotunda entry and curved staircase. In the morning, the asylum staff would move patients around to find other spaces for the children until the rioting was quelled, and a new place was found to house them. But the violence on Manhattan spread to Staten Island, Jersey, and some towns in New England, clearly taking on the character of race riots.

"We are without a place to house the children," Doctor Smith shared after sending word to his board members that the staff and children were safe. "The orphanage building is a complete loss."

"You can rebuild," Ida responded.

"Not at the old location. The chairman claims the property has become too valuable. The land will be sold and the funds used to keep us solvent in the face of this disaster."

When the Colored Children's Asylum was built, the site was in the countryside, well outside the city, but with the city's growth North of Union Square, an orphanage for children of color amongst the toney houses did not suit the new neighbors.

I asked the operator of the boat who brought in supplies for Blackwell's Asylum if those of us who wished might ride back to Manhattan with him, and he agreed. Giddy, Gil, and the Wallack's people, who were not staying to help with the children, parted with me. At the docks, they struck out for the theater while I began the long walk to Drake House through the changed cityscape.

Makeshift encampments and barricades of scavenged furniture and scorched timbers from burned-out buildings segmented the grid of New York's streets. Invisible, I passed by, a numbness protecting my raw nerves. It was not that I did not see the broken windows and doors of looted houses, or the trash and rubble of people's lives littering the streets, but my mind avoided attaching meaning to these skeletal remains of tragedy.

The familiar squeak of the little iron gate outside Drake House poked at my heart. I resisted thinking of Bernie's as "home", but in the months since I arrived, it had become that. Though Wallack's still held first place in my heart, I felt a sense of homecoming now.

I was halfway up the front steps when Dweetie threw the door open and launched into me, engulfing me in a cloud of flour and spices.

"Master Kit! You are all right." She pulled away, examining me. "You are all right, yes?"

"Yes. I am fine, Dweetie. I am just very tired."

"And Idabelle?" Bernie stood on the porch above, a wax figurine looking as if she were about to melt.

"Ida is fine as well, Aunt. We were together until just a few hours ago. We took the orphan children to…"

"Blackwell's Island," Bernie finished the sentence for me. "And you think they will be safe there among the insane? She can't possibly be safe in a place like that. You should have brought her home with you."

"Ida and two hundred and thirty-three children? Drake House is not that big, and Ida was not going to leave them. It was her choice to make," I replied firmly.

Bernie sniffed arrogantly, expressing her dislike for being corrected. "It seems you are more like your mother every day."

"Perhaps because you keep making the same mistakes," I countered, my temper short. "If you keep taking the same action, Aunt, you cannot expect a different outcome."

"Well, I am glad you are safe. I think." She spun on her fancy heeled boots and went back inside. With Dweetie's arm wrapped around mine, we climbed the stairs. Burke appeared in the open space Bernie just vacated.

"Look, Mister Burke, Master Kit has returned, and Miss Idabelle is also safe," Dweetie sang out, her kind nature effulgent and irrepressible.

"That is good news, Begam Dweetie. Welcome home, Master Kit," Burke's words were so smooth and unemotional I might have been returning from a pleasure trip.

"I am grateful to be here, Burke." I clasped the man's hand fervently, prepared to force past the cool, polite exterior to honest emotions. "And grateful for all your many kindnesses to a boy who did not deserve half of what you have done for him." Facing death makes a person look at relationships differently, and I was not going to feign polite indifference when that was not what I felt. Burke was surprised but not displeased.

"Oh, for God's sakes, get in the house and close the damned door," Bernie growled, reappearing on the porch. "The entire neighborhood will be watching your little scene like it's a cheap matinee melodrama."

I laughed, enjoying the familiarity of my aunt's crankiness. "I do not think you have seen a cheap matinee in your life, Aunt."

"I have."

"I remain unconvinced," I teased her.

"Insufferable boy."

"It's a family trait." I thought I detected a hint of a smile from her.

Other Wallack's company members began to appear from throughout the house, stagehands mostly, and all but one, male. There were only a handful, but they arrived during the early hours of the riots, their homes inaccessible or uninhabitable.

"They have been helping us keep an eye on the property," Weaver informed me, his handshake and eye contact letting me know that, despite his early doubts, he was relieved I returned unharmed.

"I must thank you for the fighting lessons," I told him. "I recently had cause to use them, but you neglected the part about how much it hurts you when you punch someone else."

Weaver laughed. "Some things must be experienced for the lesson to be remembered."

"What about our other friends, Aunt? The Bees: Charlotte, Charles Stratton, Pfaff, and the Ada's? Have you heard from them?"

"Charles gathered as many as he could the first day and took them on his steamship to his house in the Thimble Islands. About now, they will be recovering from hangovers following the first twelve hours of the house party Lavinia and Charles will make of the event."

"Mister Stratton tried to get your aunt to go with them," Dweetie told me. "But she would not leave without you and Miss Idabelle.

"I wish you had gone, Aunt, but I understand why you did not, and I appreciate it. Ida is fine, though, truly. Now, please excuse me, it has been a very long few days, and I need to lie down for just a few moments."

"I have food," Dweetie offered. "Good food. You must eat."

"Thank you, Begam Dweetie, but right now I do not have the energy to chew. Let me just close my eyes for a few minutes, then I will be able to properly appreciate your delicious food."

I went upstairs and lay down on the bed, closing my eyes, and that was the last thing I remembered.

When I woke, it was still evening, and Spin was sitting at the end of my bed.

"What did I miss?"

"Not much. Just the end of the world."

I guffawed. "In a few hours. That was fast."

"You've been asleep all day. It is now what, for you, would have been tomorrow night."

This was not good news. Kay would be very upset, and who knew how things had evolved within the city over a whole day.

"And where have you been while the city was being pulled down around us?" I asked.

"Helping Bernie read the Weavings. She looked for you."

"And?

Spin rolled his eyes. "She didn't find you. She doesn't know what to look for."

"You could have shown her."

Spin conjured an apple and took a bite. "And have her blame me for anything that goes wrong? No, thank you."

"I could have used your help out there," I suggested.

"Lord Toranado does not like me to interfere."

"Lord Toranado: the tall fellow on the steps at Missus Tyler's? And who is he exactly?"

Spin looked flustered. "Lord Toranado is only himself."

"But what is your relationship to him, Spin?" I knew he could not lie to me now that I asked the question directly.

"We belong to the same family of fey; a tribe of spirits," Spin hedged. I recalled Undergrove calling him "the Blue Duke".

"And you owe this Toranado fealty?"

"Loyalty. Such connections are much more nuanced among my people. I am not a slave, but I support Toranado and therefore accede to his requests."

"So, you must do what he says."

"No, I *choose* to, in most cases."

"But not all," I deduced.

Spin nodded. "Not all."

"And what has that to do with The Agreement?"

He looked troubled. "As I told you in Virginia, it exists. Our families uphold the oaths."

"You have told me the early history of the Agreement; now tell me about its demise." Spin raised an eyebrow. Did he realize I knew he had to answer if I asked in the right way?

"It has not ended."

"No, but you said before, the Drakes agreed to certain actions, and as I understand it, when Manon and Bernie started up their 'workings', they were the first in generations to do so. Wasn't that a problem according to the Agreement?"

"It could have been, if we challenged the contract. But we did not." Spin tossed his apple core aside, and it disappeared. "Over time, the Drake blood naturally became diluted: more human, less fey. There were generations when your ancestors ignored their abilities, hiding them from both the public and their descendants, not passing on what they knew about using their talents. We could not force the family to act, particularly when none of them seemed to have talents. There was no point in investing time and attention in such individuals, so we just went on, and they did the same.

"But when Manon and Bernie began to do 'workings' it renewed fey attention," I surmised.

"And I was assigned to remain near and guide them," Spin confirmed my suspicions.

"Because of The Weaving. Because Bernie is a Weaver."

"Yes," Spin acquiesced. "As your mother grew up, it was clear she had significant talents—abilities that had been in remission in the Drake line for generations. She was special. I tried to explain this to Lord Toranado, but it was not until he met her that he understood.

"You introduced them, and then my mother fell in love with him."

Spin shrugged. "He is the Lord Toranado. Any to whom he turns his attention and smiles upon falls in love with him; men, women, sprites, fairies. It is expected."

"You introduced them, and my mother fell in love with him. That must have been painful."

"You persist in thinking of my relationship with your mother like a dime novel romance, Kit. It is not like that between us. I already told you what Leonie and I have is beyond fleeting emotions and carnal desire. Toranado may have made love to her, but I had the part of Leonara that was precious: her affection and her loyalty. If Toranado and I stood side by side and she was told she must choose between us, she would choose me. Our souls overlap, like close sisters and brothers. She trusts me."

I suddenly went very still inside, hearing nothing after Spin's declaration that Toranado made love to my mother. In the deepest recesses of my most secret thoughts, I wondered, then quickly buried the question, but I was troubled by it since seeing Toranado on the steps of Gardiner House. There had been a shattering recognition between us—a connection where I saw myself in the fey lord's face. When Wood declared I was not Johnathan Becket's son, my mind tried on the possibilities of who might be my father, once again raising the possibility that I was not entirely human.

This was dangerous territory. What did Spin know about Toranado and my mother?

He looked me in the eyes. "I know everything. I was there."

"Ew." I made a face. "That's disgusting."

"Not literally, while they were fucking everything up, I was living in London with Bernie, as was Leonie."

"You were there, and you let this happen?" I did not disguise the accusation in the question.

"Your aunt and I were on tour. When we returned, Leonara announced her engagement to…"

"Jack Becket."

"Yes, to Jack Becket."

He had said too much. Kit Becket of puzzles had put the pieces together.

"Charming, powerful, irresistible, Jack Becket, who was *not* Jack Becket because he was Lord Toranado." Spin did not disabuse me of my hypothesis. "And where was the real Becket?"

Spin pulled at his collar and looked around the room. "Traveling."

I was relieved he had not said "enchanted and locked in a closet."

"Did my mother know the real Becket before they were engaged?" I demanded.

"They met at parties, but then Becket went off somewhere, and Lord Toranado stepped in."

"Which was when she fell in love with 'Jack'." And why she never understood how Johnathan Becket could have been such a bastard, and she did not see it." I felt...so much. "He hurt her, you know, my mother. You claim you care for her, Spin. How could you have stood by and done nothing? You should have told her--tried to warn her—something!"

"I did, and Bernie, who knew nothing about Jack Becket's real identity, tried as well. But your mother was in love. My Lord Toranado can be very appealing, but he does not like me to…"

"Interfere. Yes, I remember."

"And by then Leonie was with child, so, even though Becket seemed different, she felt she had to marry him. It is the sort of thing you humans do in this age. It is expected."

This was what Undergrove and Wood were dangling. My father was not dead, because I was not Johnathan Becket's son. I was Lord Toranado's.

As Charlie Stratton would say: Fuck.

"So, you and I are related," I tweaked the tail of the tiger. "Shall I call you cousin?"

Spin scowled. "If you do, I will cut your dick off."

Downstairs, the Wallack's folk had eaten and were minding their posts, assigned positions throughout the property from which they could see trouble coming before it got here and give warning. Those not on duty were asleep in the basement or the barn, playing cards, or talking and drinking from Charlie Pfaff's legendary cellar, which he had generously divided between Bernie's and Stratton's houses in the Thimble Islands. But though the world seemed unchanged to others, it was changed for me.

I hardly knew what to think or feel.

Bernie was in her library at her writing desk with the door open just enough to say if you really need to talk to me, I am here, but if it's not important, leave me be.

I knocked.

"Aunt, may I have a few moments?"

"Ah, Kit. You are awake." She set aside the paper she was reading. She stopped wearing any hint of cosmetics, keeping her hair simple, braided, and pinned up in back. Gone were the corsets and crinolines worn for the purpose of maintaining her place in society. Society in New York was broken; its pieces burned to ash. A simple cotton dress with enough petticoats beneath it to keep the fabric from scandalously outlining her legs was enough.

"I am sorry to have slept so long."

"You needed the rest."

There was an awkward silence while I tried to find the words I needed to say.

"How well did you know my father before he and my mother were engaged?" I began finally.

"Enough not to like him. I met him once. He was 'Johnathan' then," she spoke the name with an offensively arrogant, annoyingly nasal, upper-crust British accent. "He only allowed himself to be called 'Jack' by Leonie, and then only in the beginning of their courtship. What is this about, Kit?"

"Toranado."

My aunt's color rose. I had not known if she would recognize the name, but she certainly did.

"You cannot believe a word that comes out of that creature's mouth. He is a liar and a trickster."

She began a story about two people who fell in love, despite social norms that broke backs and hearts. Shackled by the duties and responsibilities of their public personas, the lovers found spaces and times to close the doors on prejudice and have the courage to love.

I knew it was Bernie and Ira Aldridge Senior's story, and I knew how it ended. Responsibilities and careers won, and while Ira was preparing to walk down the aisle with someone else, Bernie realized she was with child.

Toranado offered to help her, promising she could bear the child and he could make it so no one would question its legitimacy or parentage.

"But when Idabelle was born, he took the baby from me," Bernie's story went on. "I cried and pleaded with him to no avail. "You said I could have this child!" I reminded him of his promise.

"And you have." He was heartless, entirely unmoved by my tears and a mother's anguish. "I did not say you could raise it. You have responsibilities, Lady Drake—responsibilities to me, and to the Agreement. I have given you what you asked for; no one will question the child's parentage, or your part in its birth. That is what you bargained for.' And he disappeared, taking Ida with him.

"It was Spin who located my baby, placed with a family in the United States, and told me where she was. I moved here and befriended the Washingtons, and when Idabelle was old enough, I approached the family and offered to train her as my lady's maid. I just wanted to have her near me—to be a part of her life."

It was a tragic story, but something else began tickling my mind. "Before, you asked if Mother was with Toranado. Why?"

"Leonara was always a shiny thing, and Toranado likes shiny things, so when she disappeared, naturally, I wondered."

"Mother is no longer at any risk from Toranado."

"We are always at risk from Toranado," Bernie declared. "He is fey, and they think and choose differently than we humans. They are always trying to weasel around their obligations."

"The Agreement, what do you know about it?" I asked. "I mean specifically what is in it? What do the words say?"

Bernie blinked. "I don't know. I don't remember," she admitted.

"You and Manon were just girls when Spin showed up. You would not have thought of demanding to see the Agreement, but it is a contract. It would define, not only each family's responsibilities, but the boundaries they must adhere to, fey and human alike. Sir Francis knew the document would bind his descendants for generations. He would not have allowed all the benefits to be on the fey side."

"Sir Francis was ambitious. He wanted money and power—everything Toranado promised him. And he got it. I do not think he gave a moment's thought to the generations to come."

"Where is the Agreement?" I asked.

"The original? Oh, heavens. Who knows? It was a gruesome thing, written on some kind of hide, or skin, or God knows what. They used blood for the ink, or so it went. An aging aunt told Manon and me the story one Christmas Eve when we were little. Before we were doing workings. It was just a story to us then." Her brows drew together in thought. "There was a copy, though. Look in that chest the Lowdon's sent. There is a brass box. It has a false bottom. Manon had a copy that Spin gave her. She kept it there.

"It would seem invisibility is not your only talent," she mused. "You see the way things should fit together and how they might come apart, due to some weakness. Perhaps you can apply that to something other than mechanical inventions. Interesting, that you have these abilities, when there have been so few male Weavers over the centuries."

"I am not like most other men," I confessed.

"I never thought you were." She smiled warmly. "You have always been yourself, and no one, except your father, ever tried to make you into something else."

I wondered if I should tell her Johnathan Becket was not my father. I wondered if I should confess who I thought it was.

"Spin has been with you a very long time, Aunt, but we should not forget his first loyalty is to Lord Toranado and the fey. As you say, they have their own agenda."

"Spin is family," Bernie defended the little blue man.

"He is Toranado's vassal," I reminded her. Thunder clouds began building in Bernie's gray eyes. "I need to tell you something, Aunt, and you will not like it." I had her attention. "I believe it is possible that Lord Toranado is my father."

Bernie's face went white. "Explain this, nephew."

By the time I told my story, suppositions and all, to Bernie, then Burke, the night was well and fully aged. They waited while I retrieved the document in the false bottom of the brass chest upstairs, half expecting the Blue Duke to appear and argue with me about what

I was doing. When I returned, I found Bernie's and Burke's patience soothed by a bottle of Charlie Pfaff's fine Cognac.

I handed the document from the brass box to Bernie. Her hand shook as she scanned it.

"This part: Toranado and his kin are forbidden any use of enchantment to manipulate Sir Francis's family and descendants," she read the sentence aloud.

"Spin mentioned something about this when he told me the fey were unable to force your ancestors to continue to teach the next generation when they became embarrassed by their connection with the fey."

"He knew," Bernie muttered, holding the document in her hand. "All along, Spin knew about Becket and Toranado, and Leonie." She tossed the paper onto the table. "Next time I see the demon, I am going to choke his little blue neck. Is he here?"

"I do not see him." It was rare that he was not near Bernie, but Toranado's demands came before his duty to protect the Weaver. "Spin learned of Becket and my mother's engagement when you did, Aunt," I defended the little blue man. "He tried to get Mother to break the engagement to Becket, as you did, but she wouldn't listen."

"He did not tell us everything," Bernie's anger simmered.

"No," I admitted. "He did not. And that is what has me questioning: why? The issue, as I see it, is whether or not Toranado's pretense of being Jack Becket counts as a 'manipulative enchantment' as stated in the Agreement."

"Of course it does! He was lying to her their entire courtship, pretending to be someone he was not. Leonie deserved better," Bernie said darkly.

"She was in love with him," I reminded my aunt.

"She was—to the point she refused to see reason," Bernie recalled with a sigh. She studied me, as she had before, but this time she was not looking for the same things. Her statement, *"Not a drop of Becket in you,"* was more prophetic than she realized—anyone except the Blue Duke. "This affects you more than any of us, Kit. How are you feeling? Are you alright with all of this?"

"The man who abused me was not my father." There was relief there, and as Spin said, the pieces of my heritage were already present. What I made of them and who I became was up to me.

Act Four, Scene Ten: Streets of New York, July 15[th,] Day Three of the Draft Riots

The city was sticky and fetid after the summer rain, the stink and ash of burning buildings a weight in the dirty air. Embers fell, a night-sky show of fire-stars, ash falling like dark summer snowflakes. Like snow, it coated the cobbles and paving stones, smothering New York's exuberance. Afraid to breathe, afraid to admit it was still alive, the city retreated into itself. But even hiding, its heart still beats. New York knew how to survive. It had been here before.

I might have felt a lot of things. I should have felt something, but my feelings were worn thin, ironed flat, then cast aside.

New York was shut down; thousands like me scratched together a dinner of longing for invisibility with a side of fear, and were headed for their beds, afraid to light a candle. Our young country, declared naïve by older, more experienced countries that had already passed the growth marks of being embarrassed by their leaders and the persecutions they allowed or encouraged, was devouring its vital organs; the body's heart eating its liver.

And all I could think about was that I was half-fey.

It explained a lot. Had Johnathan Becket suspected and resented me because I was not his blood? Had people I met shied away because they sensed some undefined otherness about me?

There was no one who could advise me from a commonality of experience; no one in whom I could confide. This was the kind of secret that walked beside you your entire life, and you never shared. It would be the guiding Truth that defined my path, and every relationship I hoped for, but that I could never confess: "this is why". It would remain an immutable shadow, misunderstood, unspoken.

I had drawn the protective cloak of invisibility around me and held pain to my chest, identifying myself by those things; weaknesses—excuses to watch life instead of participating, telling myself that if I was not seen, I would not be judged and found wanting.

Hamlet famously voiced his dilemma as *"to be or not to be."* My own words were: "To do or not do, for if you do not, you will be not."

But being seen by others is not the only definition of existence. I could walk through the streets of New York entirely invisible and be wildly alive.

Whatever others thought about me--however much they might wish that people like me did not exist, however much they wanted to ignore or destroy me, I existed.

What was expected of me in return for this existence would be an ongoing negotiation between my conscience, character, and a God I did not believe in.

It was hard for a science-minded person to believe in God or Fate, or anything proclaimed sentient that we are taught affects human lives, but in difficult times when one feels the need for succor beyond human capacity, it is practically impossible not to believe in something. We seem designed for such a belief, or at least our Western culture is, because God is everywhere, responsible for everything good.

"God is on our side," whichever side that is. People wished you God's blessings as a stand-in for good fortune.

But that same omnipotent God was somehow not to blame for the bad things that happened: war, dead boy-soldiers, rape, murder, the mad chaos of riots where humans acted like the demons we claimed our God would protect us from.

God was responsible for abundance, but not poverty. All that was bad was of the Devil, the opposite of God, the work of devilish minions, or just human beings letting loose their ugly side.

Maybe if people accepted responsibility for their own actions, all excuses aside for how we put ourselves together after the lottery of our birth is finished with us, they would not need a God or a Devil to explain their choices and how those choices built the world we live in.

From Washington Square Park, I traveled Northeast in a zigzag, trying to get an idea of where rioters were active and the state the city was in since I had last seen it. There was a large barricade near the Union Steam Works Rifle Factory on Second Avenue below Twenty Third, and a smaller one near the Metropolitan Police Station on Bond between Mulberry and Elizabeth, but the swaths of orange that colored the night sky were scattered across Manhattan.

The city felt paused, waiting for what came next. The rain that dampened the first bursts of the rioters' anger did not put out the embers of bitterness burning in their hearts. If they had been able to find reason in their minds, they might replay the worst moments of what they had seen and done and vow to stop and do no more. If they could find their conscience amid the rubble, they might try to catch a breath and save remorse from drowning in their chests. But chances of either seemed slim.

A family spurted out of a side street, furtively heading west toward the Hudson. I followed at a distance. They came within blocks of an encampment, and I branched off to run silent interference and distract any sentries who might see them and decide to harass their progress. Nearing the camp, I saw by the light of the campfires that activity was low. Men wrapped in blankets, or their own arms, were hugging the security of the fires, their moods sullen. Many of the rioters would have returned to their tenements and slept in their beds when the rain came. They could travel at will. The city was theirs. But some remained here. Were they afraid to face their loved ones after what they had done, afraid of the demons they unleashed within themselves? Maybe there was hope.

I wondered if news of the riots reached Washington, and if there were soldiers somewhere tromping through the mud trying to get to us, to save the city.

A bit further into the camp, I caught sight of an elegant, black carriage--not a burning or battered one without a team to pull it, but an unmolested vehicle pulled by strange-looking horse-like beasts.

Undergrove's carriage. I moved more cautiously. I was invisible to humans, but not to Undergrove. He had not always taken Wood's side when it came to the Drakes, seemingly because of some connection between him and Lord Toranado, but not understanding the why of it, I dared not count on his loyalty. The fey's alliances were malleable at best.

Passing a few tents and hovels stacked to create a shelter from the rain, I spied the brute standing behind Wood, who was talking to a brawny bruiser. The rioter nodded, and Wood handed the man some bills of exchange, then turned back to the carriage.

Undergrove looked my way, and I stepped back behind the cover of the furniture barricade, remaining hidden until the carriage left the encampment, rattling off into the city.

Wood was not only enabling the rioters by refusing to declare Martial Law, he was conspiring with them. My jaw set hard.

And the fey were taking sides.

The cry of a small child drew my and others' attention to the street I had just left, where the family was trying to make their way West. I hurried to catch up.

Hanging back, I watched them reach the shoreline, beaded by refugees seeking to cross the river.

The Hudson was studded with boats gathering up these hopeful evacuees and ferrying them to Staten Island. I watched the family I had followed load into a boat and start across the choppy water, hoping they would make it safely and there would be shelter for them on the other side.

Behind me, to the East and South, I heard shouting. Emboldened by invisibility, I defied instinct and headed toward it.

A dozen rioters were attacking a Protestant parsonage. Four men worked at battering down the front door while four more split off, going around the block to the back of the house, where the yard and carriage house would be. The glass windows were already broken out, and torches lit. The house's fate was clear. I was resigned to the loss of yet another family's home, telling myself it was not of such consequence as long as the inhabitants were safe. The house bore no signs of life.

Then my eye was caught by a pale girlish face moving into the frame of an upper-story attic window. It was joined by another, quite like the first. With bravery that belied the expectations of gender or age, the two girls opened the small window and were planning to crawl out onto the roof. Silent as night-mice and dressed in petticoats and patent, they squeezed their slender bodies through the window's frame, then tiptoed their shiny patents cautiously along a narrow, horizontal edge beneath it to a decorative corbel that could be used as a step. Scrabbling over the lip of the short, mansard roof, they disappeared onto the flat beyond.

Where were they going? I asked myself.

Away. Just away. To anywhere else but where they were, this place, their home, where their nightmare began. Where were their parents? I wondered. Where were their parishioners? In two days of violence, had no one missed two young girls?

And where *should* they go? Where was it safe for them?

They needed to go to the Hudson to meet the boats. The way the blocks were laid out, there were only two directions they could go before they would be forced to climb down to the street and take their chances meeting their attackers, or others like them; East, or West.

"West." I imagined placing the word on an ember falling toward them. *"Turn West, toward the river."*

I hurried to the end of the row of brownstones, looking, as they would be, for a way to get off the roof and not be visible to their attackers. The open western side of the house was clean. I raced to the Southeast side. The garden and yard in the back had one sturdy shade tree, its branches close enough to the house that they would hold small girls if those girls were brave enough to trust to the tree's strength and their own.

I could see the girl's heads and shoulders above the roofline. They were close together, the taller one peering over the side.

"The tree. Go to the tree." The eldest sister was looking at the tree but was not accepting it as an exit route.

A boom announced the torch fire found fuel and was taking hold inside. Soon there would be more light, more panic, more activity.

I made myself visible. "The tree!" I called the children. "You must climb down the tree." The littler girl shook her head, then buried it in her older sister's shoulder. The older sister bit her lip and shook her head as well. "You have to do it. It is the only way," I shouted. The elder sister stroked her little sister's hair, whispering to her, but the younger one still shook her head, no. The elder girl's face crumpled in despair. The younger girl would not risk the climb, and the older one would not leave her. They would hunker down on the roof together, the fire would spread, and either the mob would find them when they began screaming, or the fire would.

I lunged forward, my hands grasping for the top of the back brick wall, pushing and pulling until I made the top. Running along the wall, I leaped for an overhanging branch, swung my legs up, and shimmied to the bole of the tree. Using the intersections of the inner branches, I climbed until I was at a level with the roof, then around the side where the girls could see me.

"I am here to help. Climb to me," I encouraged them. The younger girl's eyes were as round and bright as full moons, her face as pale and white. Her older sister was once again whispering encouragements, but the smaller girl just clung tighter. "Can you climb down?" I asked the older girl.

"Not without her."

"If I can get her to let me carry her down, can you climb down?" I repeated my plan. She nodded. "My name is Kit, Kit Drake, like the famous actress Lady Drake? You may have heard of my aunt?" For God fearing Christian girls, being related to an actress might not have been a plus, but all I could hope was that their father was a worldly pastor. "What are your names?"

"Constance," the older girl said. "And Cora," she glanced at her sister.

"I am pleased to meet you, Miss Constance, and Miss Cora, though I must say the circumstances are less than pleasant. We need to get you off this roof and away from here. Do you understand?" Constance nodded. "Cora, you can't stay here on the roof. It's not safe. Do you understand?" Cora turned her face to me, then hid it again in her sister's shoulder. "Cora, listen to me, please. I know a place where kind people will take you and your sister to safety. Three blocks over, at the river, people are waiting in boats to take frightened children and their families to the other side, where they will be safe." I hoped that was true. I could see that Cora was listening. She stopped shaking. "But you cannot stay here. Do you understand, Cora?" Cora turned her head and nodded, frowning. "Good. Now, you are going to have to climb down." Cora shook her head violently, her full-moon eyes flooding.

"I can't," her tiny voice was a toad's croak.

"Okay. Have you ever been carried piggyback?" Cora nodded, almost smiling. "I will come up and carry you down piggyback." Cora looked at Constance. "Constance will come too, but she is a big girl. She can climb down the tree herself."

"I'm a big girl." Cora let go of her sister.

"Of course you are," I agreed, motioning Constance to come to the tree. "Go, Constance," I whispered, "before she gets scared again."

Constance hurried to the edge and looked down. Unbuckling her shoes, she tossed them down onto the far side of the wall. Her stockings followed. Taking a deep breath, she climbed over the roof's edge, crouched, then flattened herself against the tree branch. Arms and legs wrapped around it; she shimmied over its rough bark and the small twig-branches sticking up like little flags. They caught at her dress and skin, tearing them, but she kept on.

"Constance!" Cora shrieked.

"She's not leaving you. *We're* not leaving you." I turned and crouched down. "Climb onto my back." Her arms clasped my neck with the killing strength of an octopus, and I had to pry them from around my throat, resettling them around my chest and shoulders. "Ready? Let's go." She snuggled her face into my back. I imagined her eyes shut tight. "It's going to be fine, Cora. You're doing really well. Don't worry, I'm an excellent tree climber," I lied. "With years of experience." My arms and legs were shaking, my hands sweaty. I placed them carefully, making certain each hold was secure before moving to the next.

I am a Drake, I reminded myself. *And a fey lord's son. I cannot be killed while climbing a tree.* I did not know if that was true, but it is what I told myself—this new self that I was. *I have powers I don't even know about—powers I have never used. I can climb down a fucking tree.* I kept talking to myself.

And before I knew it, I had. Constance was waiting for us on the wall. I let Cora slip to the top of the wall, making sure she was steady before I joined them.

"I'll go down ahead and catch you," I said, reminding myself I was no mere mortal before leaping to the pavement. Once the girls were safely down, Constance gathered her shoes and socks, and we ran toward the river.

Among the many smaller boats was a larger steamship yacht at anchor in the channel; its dinghy was taking on passengers destined for the safety of its decks.

"Come on, all of you. It's a large ship," Charles Stratton was directing the hopeful evacuees. "We will get all of you aboard before we head across, but the dinghy can only take ten at a time, so some of you will have to wait for the next load." A family of five was next in line, and that was too many for the count of this trip. "Don't worry,"

Charles told the family. "We'll come right back, and you will be first on board for the next trip."

"Do you have room for two small strays?" I stepped forward with my charges.

"Kit!" Stratton leaped the short space between the dinghy and the dock to embrace me. "I am so glad to see you. And you brought new friends."

"I picked them up along the way," I explained.

"Just the two of them?" he asked, leaving the question about their parents unspoken.

"Just them," I confirmed.

"Climb in, girls, there's food and hot drinks on the ship, and my wife, Lavinia, will fuss over you until you are as cozy as if you were at your own aunties." He helped the girls step into the dinghy. "Go," he commanded the rower.

"Aren't you coming, Kit?" Cora demanded, having found her voice.

"I can't right now, Cora. Other children may need piggybacks and a way off a rooftop. I will come find you later, though, and make sure you are all right."

"Don't worry, Missus Stratton will take care of them," Charles promised as the dinghy pulled away. "Everyone else, just be patient and stay quiet. We don't want to draw attention. The boat will be right back."

I turned to him. "I don't need to ask what you are doing here. The evidence is right in front of me. This is wonderful, Charles."

"We had to do something. We got most of The Bees out—those who were willing and had not already left the city, but it isn't nearly enough just rescuing your friends, is it?"

"No," I agreed.

"Damn stubborn Bernie wouldn't let me rescue her."

"My aunt is not the sort of person who often requires rescuing."

"And why are you out here, and not with her where it's safe, I presume?"

"I'm on what the Australian Aboriginals call 'a walkabout'. Traversing the dangerous terrain of the world to test my stuff and find my spirit's true path."

"Bullshit. And Bernie let you out of your padded cell?"

"She couldn't stop me. On walkabout, I have the power of invisibility. I'm going to the Nicholas Hotel again to see if our illustrious leaders have finally drunk enough alcohol to find their balls and done something about restoring order to our fine city, and if they haven't, to badger them into it. What do you think of my chances?"

"They're shit."

"That's what I thought, but I've got to try."

"I can help raise the odds." Charles turned to his man helping dockside. "You all know what to do. When the yacht is at capacity, the captain will steam over to the other side and let them all off. Make sure you count yourself in that last load. Don't stand here waiting on the docks."

"What are you doing?" I asked him.

"I'm going to help you twist arms, Kit."

"It's dangerous in the city, Charles."

"Nonsense. You think you have the power of invisibility on your walk-about, but no one is more invisible than a dwarf," Charles announced, striding confidently away from the dock and into the city.

Act Four, Scene Eleven: The Nicholas Hotel, NYC, July 15th, Day Three of the Draft Riots

The card player's retreat was unchanged except for the smell, which had multiplied from mildly unpleasant to choking anyone who was not already inured to the fumes. The scents of unwashed old men, strong cigars, alcohol, anxious sweat, fatigue, and high nerves made me gag.

"Where is the bourbon?" Stratton called out as he strutted into the room. "I heard there was a game here, and bourbon and cigars could be had for the price of a round of cards." He had an imperious nature for a short man. No one stopped him, and I kept close on his heels. The room was more crowded than before, but not only by men who joined the games. Two more stood nearby. It felt like we just interrupted a conversation that everyone was glad to have ended.

"Stratton!" Charles was greeted eagerly. "I hope you brought your money along with that smart mouth. We could use some fresh blood. Seymour has been winning since he got here on Tuesday."

"What day is it?" someone asked.

"Wednesday," a beleaguered aid replied. What was it like for these assistants to great men to stand by and watch the world crack and crumble while their bosses idled the days away, drinking and gambling? I was very glad I was not one of them and was not required to be polished at University, then humbled into seeking a "good" position with some unethical politician or businessman.

"Plenty of fresh blood out on the streets, gentlemen," Charles pointed out as he circled the table to find an empty seat and climbed up. "Maybe you should open a window and take a look at what's left of your city before it burns down. It stinks in here." He made a face, waving his hand in the air. "What are you smoking, skunks?"

"The mob is nearly done with their little snit," someone declared. "They'll be headed home to sleep off the whiskey soon."

"They can't afford to miss more than two days of work."

"It's three days now," Charles informed them."

The man looked up at the window. "Ah, so it is. When did that happen?"

"The sun comes up every day, Alexander. You just aren't usually out of bed to see it," Charles quipped.

"If you're here to scold us, you can go home, Charlie. We'll do without your money."

"And your judgment."

"You know, James Hammond says the problem isn't slavery, it's that every government needs a lowest class beneath the aristocracy, and New England has insisted on empowering a working class and telling them that they are all equal."

Charles snorted. "James Hammond is a rapist. He even raped his own niece."

"That doesn't make him a liar," the man argued. "When my grandaddy was running the plantation back in the late seventeen-hundreds, Virginia had twice as many people as New York. Ten years ago, New York had three times the population of Virginia."

"And Virginia's still whooping your ass." The men laughed.

"The problem is, they believe that now they have people and more votes, they can tell us what to do."

"That is the way Democracy works," Charles said, sorting his cards.

Opdyke glanced up from his hand and saw me. "You again, Drake. Couldn't get what you wanted from Wood, so you had to find another grown-up? Try Templeton-Strong over there. He's in your jelly belly camp."

"Yeah, Strong loves Ol' Abe. Just loves him."

"Lincoln is our elected President and deserves our respect. He is the best and wisest man I have ever known," Strong stated earnestly. "But what I love is our country and the Democratic principles it stands for."

"I'll respect his Yankee ass when he minds his own business and stops trying to ruin the country," a planter I recognized from luncheons with Bernie replied. There was general agreement from those at the table.

"Eventually, they'll stop playing soldier in Gettysburg and figure out they need to send troops down here to do something. Meanwhile, the rowdies will have let off some steam and the blacks will have been put back in their place, and everything's fine and good."

"Have they asked for help yet?" I asked Templeton-Strong, indicating New York's Governor Seymour and the Mayor, George Opdyke.

Strong's gesture, indicating a reply lacked clarity. "Whatever word they sent, no one is taking them seriously because they have not indicated that the situation is serious. After all, it would make them look bad, and several of them are entertaining runs for some office or other. They absolutely refuse to declare Martial Law, which would make Washington realize there is a problem."

"So, no one knows how bad it is."

"If it's not from a New York official, it doesn't count. They have to admit there's a problem, and they won't."

Lincoln declared the suspension of law in the United States. What did he think was going to happen? If the president can silence and ignore our laws, why would the people continue to follow them?" Governor Seymour declared.

Opdyke jumped in. "The question has been answered right here in the streets of New York. This is not New York's failure. It is Lincoln's." He sounded like he was rehearsing an election speech.

"Is Opdyke running next term?" I asked.

"He is planning on running for president," Templeton-Strong said. "He and Lincoln had a tiff, and Opdyke resented the way he was treated."

"He wasn't arrested," I said hotly. "I think he was treated better than he deserved."

"This is a waste of time. They are never going to do anything." Strong stomped out. With a quick glance at Charles Stratton, I followed.

"Mister Templeton-Strong," I trotted along down the carpeted hallway at his side. His strides were very long. "I know you don't know me, but please, allow me to introduce myself."

"Another time, son."

I refused to accept being brushed aside. "Excuse me for being impertinent, Sir, but my name is Christopher Drake…"

"A friend of Charlie Stratton's. Yes, I saw you come in."

"And a friend of Walt Whitman's," I countered, hoping it might mean something. "I am Lady Bernadette Drake's nephew and acquainted with the family of Secretary of State Seward. My aunt and I stayed with them in Washington only last month." Templeton-Strong stopped. "President Lincoln dropped by after dinner," I added, hoping to seal my bona fides.

"Aside from citing your family connections, what are you trying to tell me, Mister Drake?"

"I believe if we can send a telegram to Secretary Seward in my Aunt's name, he will pay attention and tell the President."

Charles Stratton joined us, quite out of breath.

"Lady Drake has been working on a benefit project for the soldiers' hospitals, George," Charles explained. "Her visit is fresh in their minds, and she is a person of credibility and distinction. Seward won't just brush her concerns aside, and he's sure to bring them up to Lincoln. I can send a second telegram as well, so the call for help comes from more than one credible source and doesn't look like we're playing politics. Lavinia and I were guests at the White House just last February. This will work, George. It's social, not political. We can sidestep the appearance of it being an inappropriate ploy to create dissension designed to make New York's leadership look bad."

"New York's leadership doesn't need help looking bad," Templeton-Strong commented. He paused, thinking. "The rioters have cut the telegraph wires."

"I guarantee you they have been repaired in at least one of the offices along Newspaper Row," Charles promised.

Templeton-Strong shook his head. "The rioters hit the Row pretty hard."

"And I heard the newspapermen fought back, "Charles countered. "The fucking Times had Gatling guns."

"The Tribune took a scorching." Templeton-Strong was thinking about it, but not ready to give in yet.

"Barnum's Museum is practically across the street," Charles reminded him. "And P.T. told me this morning that while he was drinking his morning coffee, he watched a marvelous high wire act by two fellows who repaired that line. Horace Greeley is not going to be without information coming in or going out during events like this: a riot over the draft in New York City, Gettysburg with more dead than they can count, and Vicksburg falling. This week has been a newspaperman's dream. Greeley has a vested interest in keeping those lines open, George. They," he indicated the smoke-filled room we just left, "do not."

"All right. Let's try it." The three of us began to walk South.

"It's strange," Templeton-Strong mused, "When newspaper circulation expanded to include most cities and towns across North America, people suddenly came face to face with other people's opinions. But they didn't become more interested in what others thought; they dug in their heels and refused to listen to anyone else. Suddenly, we were a country of spoiled children who thought anyone who was not in our group was the enemy."

"Henry Adams once defined politics as 'organized hatred'," Charles added.

Templeton-Strong chuckled. "I wish I could say I thought he was wrong."

By dawn, we had sent two telegrams: one to Seward and one to Lincoln. Now, all we could do was wait.

Act Four, Scene Twelve: Wallack's, July 16th, Day Four of the Draft Riots

Leaving the Tribune building, Charles and I shared the way with Mister Templeton-Strong, passing The Times building, whole and untouched. How a newspaper got Gatling guns was a mystery. Perhaps the Times had a Weaver in their circle.

It was dawn, a time when New York streets were deserted except here on Newspaper Row. The city had been under siege for days, but bundles of freshly printed copy was being loaded onto wagons for delivery to ships, trains, and barges. Though newspapermen might not expect to sell papers in the deserted city, life as usual went on in the rest of the country, and folk had come to expect their news. Information was the new addiction.

Near Niblo's Garden and the Metropolitan, we shook hands with Templton-Strong and parted ways.

"You look as if you could use some sleep," Charles said, glancing sideways at me.

"I slept yesterday, or the day before. I'm not sure anymore."

Charles chuckled. "I should get back to the Hudson and my ship. Captain Swan will be trolling the river, searching the banks for me. He won't dare return to the Thimbles without me and face Lavinia's wrath."

We continued to walk together, knowing our ways would part soon.

"You're thinking very loudly, Kit. What about?"

"If I'm thinking so loudly, you should know."

"Well, if you were another sort of young man, I would guess you were thinking about a girl, but since you are not, it would seem logical to simply switch the gender and suppose you are thinking about a boy, but once again, your character stymies me, and that does not seem to fit. The look on your face is too serious for dreamy or lustful thoughts."

"I am thinking of my parentage," I shared.

Charles frowned. "Has it been called to question?"

"Apparently, the manner of my conception is rather akin to legends of old."

"A legendary conception? That's quite a leap for a lad who felt invisible only a few months ago."

"It is rather like the Arthurian legends, with me as the baby Arthur, my father not being who I was told he is, nor who anyone else thought he was. It calls everything into question. Like my whole life has been a lie."

Charles smirked. "All seventeen years of it."

"Almost eighteen," I corrected him.

"My apologies, almost eighteen. An important difference."

"It will be when I get there."

"You expect an inheritance from this new father?"

"I expect nothing."

"And what about the one who acted as Merlin in your fable?"

"He knew everything, of course," I affirmed.

"And never said anything.

"No." We kept walking up Broadway, keeping our eyes open for signs of rioters, though my mind was admittedly focused on the personal matters under discussion. "It seems my Merlin had to keep the manner of my conception secret because if he didn't…"

"It might topple the kingdom?" Charles finished for me.

"In a manner of speaking." I raised both eyebrows, considering this possibility. "I had not thought about it that way, but it is possible that if the circumstances surrounding my conception were revealed, it would void a contract between two great families…

"Montague's and Capulet's? Very Shakespearean," Stratton was enjoying himself.

"No, they are not enemies. They are allies, unless of course…

"The contract has been broken," Stratton again finished.

I nodded. "It is no small thing, Charles. This contract has been in place since the seventeenth century."

"Some activity by your esteemed ancestor, Sir Francis?" Charles deciphered. I nodded again. "Shit. That is serious. So, this broken agreement involves Bernie as well?"

"It does." The echo of our footsteps bouncing off the buildings that rose like cliffs around us was a hollow, brittle percussion, announcing our progress like a hammer cracking an egg's shell.

"Do you understand the consequences of breaking the contract?" Charles asked.

"Not at all."

"What about this shadowy father figure? Might he be of some help?"

"Unlikely. If I am right, he is the reason it is broken."

Charles looked confused. "I thought *you* were the reason it was broken."

"I am the result of its breaking, but he's the one who did it."

"I understand how the act of fathering works," Charles said acerbically. "Men seldom consider the outcome of their lust. What do you know of this man, Kit?"

"Hardly anything, except that my mother fell in love with him while he was pretending to be someone else, then, after she was with child, he abandoned her to a bad marriage."

"A rotter then. How very Greek Myth. Was his name Zeus?"

"No, but it might be an alias."

"I hate him already, and we haven't even met."

"Me neither. My only comfort is that he cannot be worse than the man I thought was my father."

"Becket."

"Yes."

"Are you likely to be pulling a sword from a stone soon?"

I laughed. "Why? Do you have one?"

Act Four, Scene Twelve

"Not on me, but I know people--people who make marvelous props and stage items."

"A fake would be of no use, Charles. Anyone can pull a prop sword from a fake stone."

"It would take magic to do it any other way, Kit."

"It would," I agreed. "Do you believe in magic, Charles?"

"I do: blessings, curses—particularly curses. I believe the gods and fairies enjoy making jokes of human lives." He indicated his short stature.

"It only takes a kiss to make you into a prince," I teased.

"Lavinia kissed me. I am *her* prince." He smiled fondly at the thought of his wife. "That is good enough for me."

We walked along in silence. Charles seemed to have forgotten the notion of leaving me and heading out on his own.

"I don't need a sword and a stone. I am not interested in being a king," I shared.

"Then what are you looking for from this Zeus-father?"

"I don't know." It was the truth and the crux of my dilemma. "That's what I'm thinking about."

"You are a complicated young man, Kit Drake. It would be much simpler if you would just think about boys."

"I'm not sure that's true," I replied.

Approaching Bleeker Street, a large group of rioters forced us to detour off Broadway and take to the less-traveled streets East to avoid the encampment at Mulberry and Elizabeth. Finding it dangerous to continue North or West until we were well beyond the encampment and its patrol areas, we continued to Styvesant before turning North, making me think about Mamie and Styvie. I hoped they were okay, but being old Knickerbocker blood, they were probably at the Styvesant's beach-shore mansion in Rhode Island. For the truly wealthy, the riots in the city would be a distant thunderclap, less than an inconvenience unless their townhouses were looted and burned.

Despite Charles and my efforts to avoid the rioters tracking us, a few dogs caught our scent; sheepdogs, apparently, as we quickly became the sheep, herded into parts of the city we had not planned on visiting. Soon, nothing was familiar except the ever-present smoke and ash.

"We need to find a place to hide," I suggested as the sound of our pursuers grew more boisterous.

"If we hide, we can be cornered," Charles objected.

I could have become invisible, but I could not leave Charles to the mob.

A street sign that had not been removed and repurposed as a weapon of destruction told us our location.

"There's another barricade and encampment up ahead," I warned Charles. "We need to swerve West."

We began to run, quickly finding ourselves in an area where black tradesmen had businesses and homes. The riot burned hot here; the entire block was destroyed. A black man's body hung from a nearby tree, his clothes and skin burned away. A woman's body was curled at his feet. Bloodied and beaten, flies buzzed over her corpse.

Empty of all understanding, all I could do was stare at the grisly scene. I felt sick. Heironymous Undergrove was right. However righteous they claimed to be, humans had a streak of irretrievable evil that no religion could remove, and no love could tame.

"This cannot be. We have to do something," I muttered.

"'More needs *he* the divine than a physician'," Charles quoted. He began tugging on my arm, trying to get me in motion. "We can't stay here, Kit. These men are beyond shame or compassion. I am a dwarf. There will be no consequence for my murder, and you will be punished for being with me." He turned to me for agreement, then froze. "Kit? Kit! Where are you?"

He could not see me. I had become invisible. With only seconds to decide what to do, I realized that, despite the danger to himself, if he did not see me, Charles would stay here and search for me, and the mob would find him. I forced my fear to fade and allowed visibility to return to my form.

"I am right here," I said.

Charles blinked, then frowned, his jaw slack. "I think we need to talk more about this legendary birth of yours," he said carefully.

"Later. We need to go." I gave him no time to question me further. With our pursuers hard on our heels, we made our way to Wallack's.

I threw myself against the stage door, grateful when Giddy opened it.

"Kit and…Mister Stratton? Hurry, come in," he urged us. "We've been fending off waves of rioters since late last night," he announced, not without some pride. "Your aunt just arrived, Kit. She's been looking for you. She's in Wardrobe with Maggie and Gil. Ginny got caught by the mob." He shook his head in answer to my silent question. "They were not kind."

Shouting sounded on the other side of the door, followed by booted feet pounding up the platform's stairs, then the rioters began applying something harder than fists to the door.

"Have more company folk come?" I asked Giddy.

"They've been trickling in for days."

"I'll go fetch more men," I offered.

Giddy shook his head. "When they attack like this, they hit all the entrances at once to spread us thin. Grab Gil and anyone you see that doesn't already have a station, and come back. We'll hold them off as long as we can."

"With what?"

Giddy raised his hand, and I saw a wooden sword. "What we have: prop swords and sticks."

"And that's the plan?"

"Ask Wixx. He and the old sailors are the only ones who've seen any real fighting experience. The rest of us only know stage fighting, and then no one is actually trying to kill you." Giddy was trying to put on a brave face, but he was scared. From the shadows behind him, his grandfather, Old Gideon, came forward. "Grandad came to help," Young Giddy said, his fear of my disapproval at his grandfather's presence fighting with his pride that the old man had shown up.

I held out my hand to the older Gideon. "Thank you for coming, Gideon. It is good of you."

"I was a member of this company for over a decade, and I trod the boards with William when we were only Walking Gentlemen. We were sitting together in a pub when he decided to start his own company and build his first theater. I'll not see that legacy destroyed by a bunch of bitter bullies who never built anything in their lives."

"Good man, Ol' Gid." Stratton pumped Old Gideon's hand. "When this is behind us, I hope you will let me buy you a drink."

"You know I will," Old Giddy replied, grinning.

"We can tell these young ones stories about when I played Puck and you played Bottom and that idiot Fitz-Royale stepped on Bernie's train and tore off the whole back of her dress." Stratton and old Giddy had a good laugh at the memory.

"Her ladyship's bum was hanging out for all the stagehands to see." Old Giddy wiped tears of laughter from his eyes. "Oh, that was a show. The crew had the best seats in the house that night." Old Giddy winked at his grandson. He grabbed up a prop spear leaning on the wall beside the door, then slapped Young Giddy on the back so hard the youngster stumbled forward and had to catch himself against the door. For a moment, the thumping on the other side paused. "What do you think we're doing, lads? Sending you a love letter in Morse Code?" Old Giddy shouted at them. "Get away from this feckin' door before we come out and knock your heads together!" Those on our side of the door broke into grins. Old Gideon might not be much of an actor, but he was no coward. You had to be brave to live your life onstage without talent.

Leaving to find Bernie, I was passing the stage when the pool of yellow lantern light around the ghost light caught my eye. Standing within the circle of light on the floorboards was a tall, regal man, dressed like a lord of old. Light and shadow illuminated his face from below like the footlights of old. His head, covered in the long romantic curls of a medieval knight, he turned in my direction, our gazes meeting. Everything else in the theater faded. There was only him.

"Lord Toranado." I bowed low enough to show respect, but not low enough to make myself servile. "It is fascinating to meet you."

"Is it?"

"I have been hearing much about you, our families' common history, your friendship with my mother."

"And you are incensed and going to challenge me to a duel over her honor." He sighed, looking bored.

"No," I replied. "You did not rape her."

"Certainly not." He appeared genuinely offended at the suggestion that he might have done such a thing. "Leonara was a willing participant in our affair. We were quite taken with each other."

"You did misrepresent yourself, however," I pointed out. "She thought you were her husband."

Toranado dismissed this. "She was unmarried at the time."

"As you say, she had a choice, and she chose you. There is a problem here, but that is not it." I stopped short of accusing the fey lord of breaking the Agreements. He knew what he had done, and so did I. "I never much liked the father I had," I sidestepped this larger issue and returned our introduction to a more personal level.

Toranado sniffed. "I doubt you will like me any better."

"I like you better already, simply because you are not him," I cheerfully disagreed. "You know, when my mother married Johnathan Becket, she thought she was marrying you. She was never in love with him. It was always you she loved."

"It happens." The fey lord looked into the distance, pretending to be annoyed by this trivial talk about human emotions.

Zeus, I thought. My life had been cut and pasted from a Greek tragedy, but when I claimed my mother had always loved him and only him, I saw a flicker of something deeper.

"Did you never think of her, My Lord?" I knew the moment I said it that I was asking him to reveal too much, but a fleeting expression of remorse showed me my arrow had hit its mark.

"The only thing more annoying than an infant human is the woman who is constantly required to suckle it," Toranado wrapped himself in immutable arrogance. "A mother has no room for anyone else. Certainly not her lord." He looked me over. "But you are growing up to be passingly interesting."

"Thank you, Father." A fleeting wince crossed his face. "Should I call you that?"

"I do not expect you to call me at all." The fey lord frowned. "I will not answer."

"So, like Becket. Nothing has changed."

Toranado's offense was instant. "I am nothing like that man."

"Self-centered, arrogant, impatient with the perceived faults of others... You seem very much alike to me. I am glad to have met you, though. It is helpful to have an understanding of where one has come from and, in my case, to finally understand my parents' unfathomable marriage. Meeting you solves the mystery of how my beautiful, intelligent mother could ever have fallen in love with such a boorish bastard as Johnathan Becket. She didn't."

"Yes." Toranado's lips twitched in an almost smile. He was susceptible to flattery. Another thing he and Johnathan Becket had in common. "Leonara was not like other women of her time. She was fresh and curious, with a brilliant mind, and she cared so deeply about everything. She reminded me of someone I loved once--someone very dear to me whose life was stolen from me."

"What happened?"

"La Dulce' was a Weaver. You understand Weavers?"

"Yes. Like my aunt, Lady Bernadette Drake."

"Of course." Toranado frowned, remembering the greater familial connections I had. "It was the Spanish Inquisition. The Grand Inquisitor caught La Dulce', tortured and killed her. Then he became pope. Pope Pius the Fifth," the fey lord sneered.

"And you loved her, this human woman, La Dulce'?"

"She was my Queen. I had given her immortality, but being long-lived can not save you from death if your torturers are determined enough."

"That must have been very painful," I hoped kindness and compassion would earn me more of the story that was connected somehow to my own.

"I thought for a time that Leonara…." He did not finish the sentence. "I thought that perhaps being near her… She had such great passion. I thought I might regain some part of what I had lost with the death of La Dulce'. But then Becket returned to London, and Leonara looked at him with the love she had promised was mine: kissing him, making love to him. How could she not see that he was not me?"

"You were wearing his guise. How was she to know if you did not tell her?" I asked.

"I should not have *had* to tell her," Toranado proclaimed with disdain. "She should have just *known*." It was the answer of a spoiled child in a bad temper.

"You blame her for not loving you enough, but she married Becket because she loved you so much that even though he seemed different and she worried she was making a mistake, she would not abandon her promise to you. She was certain the man she had fallen in love with was still there, somewhere. She refused to give up on Lord Toranado," I informed him, waiting to be struck down with a lightning bolt or turned into a toad. "You have been telling yourself that you punished Leonara for loving another, but you punished her for being loyal to you."

Toranado did not like being wrong. He liked having it pointed out to him even less.

"Do you intend to become a philosopher?" he retreated from any honest emotion.

"A theatrician."

"Same thing, or so they fancy." Toranado turned to Kindle, who had arrived during this conversation and now sat primly observing us, its tiny kitty paws touching like bookends. "He will leave you someday, you know," the fey lord informed the spirit-cat. "Because, though being half fey, he will live longer than a human, he is also half-mortal, and therefore someday he will die. While you," he pointed to Kindle, "are pure spirit, fated to live as long as the energies that created you do. Do not invest too much in this human," he warned Kindle, smiling coldly. "They always disappoint."

A scream coming from the dressing rooms below stabbed through our discourse.

"That's Bernie!" I took off at a run.

There was a thunderous crack as the stage door was breached. Kindle stumbled and shook its head. I froze, pulled by my loyalties.

"Go. The company are at their posts, they will fight them off, and a building is much stronger than an aging woman's body," Kay assured me.

"Bernie!" I shouted as I stumbled down the stairs, catapulting through the tunnels of the theater's lower hallways.

"Kit!" Her answering scream was muffled--cut short. It did not come from the dressing rooms. I spun to retrace my steps.

Two men blocked the stairway. With a screech, claws out, teeth barred, Kindle leaped onto the bald pate of the larger of them. Fighting the cat clinging by its claws to the tight skin of his head, the man lost his balance and tumbled down the stairs, forcing me to jump up and brace myself on both walls. He rolled down between my legs like water tumbling beneath an arched bridge. Kindle had taken a tumble, but they regained their feet and stood, back arched, hissing at the second man. He kicked out at the cat, hard leather and soft stomach coming into painful contact.

"Kindle!" I called out. The cat's body tumbled down the stairs as Kay, in spirit form, exited it.

Still suspended halfway up the stairs, I swung my legs toward Kindle's assailant, landing a hard kick in his chest. I was a Zeus-pretender's son. I hoped this questionable honor was accompanied by Herculean powers.

It was not.

The man stumbled back, but caught himself, raising his cudgel to strike me. I did not have a god's strength, but I had other abilities. I became invisible, my struggle to regain my own footing now occurring in face-saving secrecy. Being unseen gave me the advantage I needed. Remembering how painful it was to punch someone and how long my hand remained useless afterward, I decided against giving the man an invisible punch; instead, I charged his midsection like an angry bull. He could hardly have prepared for something he could not see, and my efforts were rewarded by him staggering back then, looking around him in feral fear.

"What happened to ya'? Where did you go, ya' damned Yank bastard?"

Bernie's scream repeated, and my attacker scrambled down the stairs. Picking up Kindle's limp body, he held it dangling before him.

"Ya' care about this scrawny devil?" It was a ridiculous gambit, the man holding a limp cat as if it were a Viking's shield. The only reason it was not funny was because it was Kindle, and if there was any hope, the little cat was still alive... "Come and get it." The man bounded up the stairs, down the hall, then up more stairs, one flight, two...

He was headed for the flybridge.

I could hear other fights going on throughout the theater. The rioters were inside. Whether Kindle's cat form would survive this brutal treatment, I could not say, and now the theater building itself was in jeopardy. I prayed to the theater gods that our side was winning.

Where was Spin? *With Bernie.* He would have been close to her when she was attacked. To overcome her loyal protector, Bernie's attackers would have needed fey help. *Undergrove.*

"Lord Toranado, you said not to call on you, so you may refuse to hear me now." I spoke to Toranado as I raced up the stairs to the flybridge, taking the steps two at a time. *"But I beg you to help us. The Weaver is in danger. Wood and Undergrove and their allies want to use her abilities for their own purposes, and if she will not help them, they will kill her, like the Pope who murdered your love, La Dulce'. This is what the ignorant do: destroy the bright beings of the world."* I thought about what I read in the Agreements. This was the moment to leverage the knowledge that he had broken them. *"You owe the Drakes your protection, Lord. It is in the Agreements. I have read them. I know the promises you made. If you want the contract to remain in place, show good faith and uphold it now."*

My pleas made, now, all I could do was hope.

The man I pursued came to the intersection where he had to make a choice. Left would take him up more stairs and to the roof. Right would take him to the flybridge above the stage. Out of breath from the strain of climbing, he chose the right.

Foolish man. He had cornered himself. Realizing too late that the flybridge system of catwalks was limited, closed on every side except the several-story open space of the house, he turned to face me.

"There are only two ways down," I informed him, an invisible voice in the darkness. He looked down at the stage floor far below.

Wixx and some of the crew were fighting rioters, while others were trying to douse the fire that the attackers set in the stage wing's curtains.

"You can come through me, or go over the edge," I strengthened the idea that he was dealing with an incorporeal spirit, but it was a stupid challenge. He could not see me, but going through me, though requiring a disbelief in ghostly abilities, was still the better option. He found a third. Tossing Kindle's body aside, he leaped from the catwalk, grabbing a rigging rope in the theater's fly system. "Kindle!" I cried out as the cat fell to the stage floor. Gil saw Kindle land, as did the other stagehands who were nearby, and he knelt beside the theater cat before looking up and seeing me.

What was one small cat's life in the midst of everything we were about to lose? Except, what Gil saw was me, and we were friends. Kindle belonged to our company, and to me. Gil gently gathered the little cat's body and left the stage, disappearing into some part of the theater I could not see.

Young Giddy arrived a moment after Gil did. "Grandad!" he shouted as he ran toward the fly system controls. The ceiling near the apex of the theater was filling with smoke, the fire reaching the top of the drapes and licking at the ropes that held the flybridge suspended.

Skidding down the hemp rope, my assailant lost his grip, his body thunking against the stage floor. His hands were blistered, his ankle injured, but he was down. The flames consuming the curtains on both sides of the stage framed the scene like a set for Dante's *Inferno*. The crew were calling out to each other to drop the curtain. Young Giddy pulled up a rigging rope manned by his grandfather and raced to cut the curtain's attachment, dropping it with a whoosh and a cloud of smoke. The crew set to dousing the flames with buckets of water. My would-be assailant looked up into the flybridge, grinning an overconfident challenge, but I was not where he expected me to be. This was my world, and Young Giddy and I had played among these ropes many an afternoon. I knew just how to ride a weighted rope down and land with the panache of a pirate.

I made myself visible. The man's face fell faster than he had come down the rigging rope. His furtive eyes took in his situation. Company members swarmed the stage, a bucket brigade lined up from the back to the front of the house. Heavy steam laden with soot hissed from the charcoal piles of stage drapes, filling the theater with a dark fog, but the rioters were gone; injured, dead, or just given up. Cast and crew were looking around with wet eyes and streaked cheeks. They had won.

But I had not. My battle was not over.

"Kit!" Bernie was being dragged along the edge of the stage by two thugs. They stopped center stage, and Undergrove joined them, mumbling words; an enchantment, or a spell, preparing to magic my aunt away. Spin was at Bernie's side, anger rolling off him as she glared at Undergrove. Why was he not stopping this? Why did Undergrove have his men bring Bernie to the edge of the stage rather than just exiting the theater? He must realize that the Wallack's cast and crew would be set against him, and though only human, they just faced down a mob and saved their beloved theater, their confidence palpable. Waves of power rippled through the air around them. But Undergrove brought Bernie here. I did not understand the rules of their world and what bounds fettered them, but I remembered something Spin told me once: *The mouth is a threshold between thought and speech. This is why we chant a spell. It creates a door that allows magic to travel from one point to another. The edge of a stage is also a threshold."* The edge of the stage... Undergrove was using the stage's edge and his chanting to create a door. I looked again at Spin, shocked and disturbed to see him helpless. If he could have stopped Undergrove, he would already have done it.

"Young Drake," Undergrove noticed me. Freezing the rest of the company, he now ignored them. "You are just in time for the finale."

"Let my aunt go, Heironymous," I growled. "You know who I am. You know who my family is. It would be unwise to cross Lord Toranado."

"Toranado has no interest in you, Little Fox. He has sired hundreds--thousands of bastards over the centuries. After he sated his desire, he never paid any attention to any of them. No, the once mighty lord is a shell of who he was, brought down by an ill-fated love. Human prejudices are so easily manipulated, and human bodies so easily extinguished. Toranado has lost all interest in mortals and their world. Here in your world, echoes haunt him. In the fey world, it is so much easier to forget La Dulce's dying screams. Perhaps if your mother had been less independent and more interested in decorating the arm of a fey lord, she might have rescued him from his grief, but she did not, and he is lost."

"Spin, can you speak to Bernie?" I addressed the Blue Duke mentally. Spin subtly lowered his eyes, indicating he could not. *"Kay, can you hear me? I need your help. Bernie is in trouble. Listen, and do as I direct you—as if these were cues, and I am the Technical Director."* The Ghost light flickered twice. *"Release the bolts on the trapdoor."*

"Aunt, you look uncomfortable there so close to the edge," I addressed Bernie. "She has always had a fear of falling," I informed the thugs holding her arms. "But in the theater, we must face our fears. Still, if you gentlemen would allow her to just shift a little toward Center Stage, she would feel much safer, and perhaps she would not faint on you."

Bernie stared down the thugs and, holding her head at its most regal angle, stepped toward Center Stage.

"Spin, there is a trapdoor in the stage floor two steps upstage. Wait for my diversion, then use it as a True Door," I emphasized the word door, hoping he would understand.

"Blackout!" I shouted to Kay. The ghost light flared, crackled, and went dark. Undergrove stopped chanting. Disoriented, Bernie's guards loosened their grip. She stepped onto the trapdoor, and she and Spin disappeared.

A loud laugh rang through the theater. I turned. There was a tall presence behind me.

Undergrove lowered his head, his body curving like a crescent moon in servility.

"You have lost your prize, Heironymous," Toranado strolled forward. Undergrove's face was murderous, his lips twitching. "And more than that, you have lost the game. Tell your mistress I look forward to our next contest, and let her know the Fox's Kit has my attention. He is no pawn."

Undergrove swallowed his anger, bowed lower, then vanished.

"Well done, my son." Toranado turned and smiled at me, then disappeared. A second later, the company began to move, restored to life. Mister Lester was walking through the house.

"I don't know what just happened here, but I am thinking that I probably don't want to," he said as he came up the stairs onto the stage.

"That is wise." Maggie chuckled, stepping forward. Her skirts were wet and charred, her face sooty, but when she turned and winked at me, all I saw was a beautiful soul. "If there is one thing theater teaches us, it is that it is best not to explain the magic."

"Maggie…Kindle?" I asked, afraid to give my fears voice.

"Kindle and her kitten are resting in Wardrobe," Maggie replied. "She is badly injured, Kit, but one of her kits looks like it will make it; a strong, scrappy little black thing it is."

"The cat is a *she*?" Young Giddy harrumphed. "That explains a lot."

"Yeah, like why she never liked you, Gid," Darragh teased his friend.

Down in Wardrobe, Gil and Ginny sat beside Kindle's battered body. Ginny was pale, her frailty shredded like thin paper. Maggie must have found her a peasant costume, because her own clothes were too damaged, and after what happened to her, wearing them would be like wearing a nightmare. Looking out for someone else seemed to have done her some good.

"I am so sorry, Kit," she touched my arm gently, calling me by name for the first time.

"Oh, Kin, look at you," my whisper, too, was shredded. Hearing my voice, the little cat tried to rise, but it was too weak, and it sank back onto the green paisley shawl Maggie had curled up to make a bed. Ginny made room, and I knelt beside the cat, reaching out my hand so Kindle would not have to move to reach me. One small black kitten was squirming across the shawl seeking a teat. The other was not moving. Gil picked it up and stepped away, taking it with him.

Kindle looked up at me, pain, love, and trust all there in her gold eyes.

"My brave, good girl." My hand stroked her dark fur as tears stroked my cheeks. "Hold on, love," I encouraged her as she closed her eyes, a shudder riffling her fur.

"It is too hard," Kay spoke to me. *"Everything is broken, and the pain is unbearable. I have stayed in her body long enough so she could birth her kits and say goodbye. I owe her that.*

I was there beside Kindle as her coal black kitten filled its belly, the tiny mouth covered in milk. I was there as it snuggled into the half-moon circle of its mother's tummy between the broken legs. I was there when my friend breathed her last, Maggie's arms around my shoulders as I wept.

Act Four, Scene Thirteen: Pfaff's, July 17th

Dark and humid as the giant throat Pfaff's hidden entrance conjured in my mind, my footsteps made cautious clicks as they struck the cement steps. When I came here on my first night in New York City, I imagined a monster living beneath New York's pavement. Now I know the monsters were human beings stalking difference by their scent. Being different was not allowed in the United States of the mid-nineteenth century. Difference suggested some value of less, and more, fraught with underpinnings of resentment and fear. Greatness was suspect; success resented. Weakness was unforgivable and possibly contagious. The myth of homogeneity was the wealthy's goal for the masses. Supreme wealth and power over culture was their dream. They would pay to have history written as they wished it to be and sweep aside inconvenient truths.

The pub's heavy wooden door gave readily to my touch. Neither lock nor bolt had slowed the city's determined rioters. Papa Pfaff had not even bothered, leaving it as a hiding place for any patron who might find themselves in need. I imagined the gentlemanly Gerald and his young lover, James, holding each other tightly, listening for the stampede of rioters, hoping to hide their lives beneath the ground like the fey hid beneath the Tors of Britain. But there was no one here now, only the ghostly echoes of memories that would fade from aging minds, their significance ignored by history.

For me, Pfaff's had been a place of firsts, awakening a longing to belong, to join the Bohemian parade of passion to sculpt a better world, brave women and men who had the courage to be themselves and embraced others who did the same miraculously finding each other in this new kingdom of commerce, hissing steam engines, and the bright heat of smelting foundries.

What was humanity getting with this mad rush to mechanize the world? Workers were still poor, children still hungry. A few men were acquiring wealth that would elevate their family names for generations, but they were building it on the backs of destitute immigrants unable to make a living wage. The wrongness of it was in my bones, but though I was different, I was not poor. It was hubris to think I could give these people's woes a voice, but saying nothing and doing less was a coward's option. If you saw something and felt compelled to draw attention to it, was it not incumbent on you to do that for the health of your soul? I understood the Wide-Awake movement, young people demanding that old, tired men and their entrenched ways, their policies made in support of their own wealth, needed to become a thing of the past.

The pub had evidence of Pfaff's hurried exit. Though he had removed the gems of his curated cellar to Charles' and Bernie's, lesser vintages and brands were left on the shelves, dusty after only five days. Such a fragile thing is a moment in time. Would Pfaff and his patrons return? Would the pub ever be the same? I was about to leave when I sensed another presence in the room.

"Hello, Merlin," I greeted Spin.

"You know I am not he," the blue man replied.

"And I am no Arthur, and will never be king, despite my birth."

"A prince of theater, perhaps," Spin suggested.

"Perhaps. You must admit there is a similarity in the events surrounding my conception, however."

"A fanciful one, but yes." Spin gave me a rueful smile. "Your aunt had a caller before I left. A captain of the Union Army sent to thank her for her telegram apprising Secretary Seward about the true situation with the riots here in the city. The President asked him to look in on her and make certain she was safe and had everything she needed. She was most surprised to discover that she had sent such a telegram."

"Someone had to make sure Lincoln knew what was really happening here," I confessed.

"She covered gracefully."

"As expected."

"So, are we good, you and I?" he asked.

"If you mean, do I understand why you acted as you did? I do, and we are. You protected Bernie as was required of you, even though your heart wished to take you somewhere else. That's rather noble for a ne'er-do-well spirit like yourself. I suspect you have been hanging around The Bees too long."

"I expect that is true," Spin admitted. "Leonie always understood where my first responsibility was. The sacrifices inherent in what we do are as quietly epic as the outcomes. Few see them. No one extols them. They are endured, and we go on, for the stakes are always high, and individual human lives are specks of dust swept aside by the winds of time."

"You will be remembered no more than we," I assured him.

"I have no interest in being remembered. But human greatness? It draws fey attention like bees to flowers. The stories that the "Gods" must be responsible for any singular talent in a human being is a lie created by jealous fey—one which, over time, both humans and the fey have fallen prey to. The feral fey, as opposed to a tribe like our own, who have interacted with humans for hundreds and thousands of years, are of an ethereal nature, which makes them susceptible to their own constructs and fantasies and easily distracted by the thought-worlds they create. This can often be seen when a fey builds misguided ideas around a human they become enamored of, making that human seem more than they truly are. When the veneer of these fantasies begins to peel, as it inevitably does, the fey feels betrayed. The human is always blamed. Feys commonly say that humans always disappoint, as if the human deceived *them,* and they had no part in the fall of their golden idol. An example is Bottom as seen by Titania. Though Bottom is an ass, the fairy queen thinks him beautiful. I am quite convinced that Will Shakespeare had some insight into fey nature."

I frowned, my brows knitting. "You are 'convinced', or you know?" I prodded.

"I only admit to knowing the chap," Spin demurred. "But it is a common flaw among our kind, one that those of us who are more grounded openly acknowledge. Because of our commitment to guarding Weavers, my tribe's thinking reflects the influence of human thought and culture. More so than feral fey," he explained. "We have seen the effects of human doings and understand that our worlds do not truly function separately. There is a connection. The Agreement ties our purpose to that connection." He paused, musing privately before continuing.

"Leonie had a positive effect on Toranado. She returned a liveliness and interest in the world that he had lost with La Dulce's death, and I believed that through Leonie, Toranado was finding himself again. It was naïve. Leonie's role was not a Weaver's. She did not sit in a room and play with futures. She took direct action. She was committed to that and to being a mother. Toranado is abhorrently selfish of the attention of his amors."

"Like Becket."

"There were similarities," Spin agreed. "Which supported Leonie's belief that her husband and lover were one and the same."

"And you did not disabuse her of that belief." I did not mean it as a conviction of Spin's decisions, but as a statement of what had occurred.

"By the time I understood what Toranado was doing, it was too late. Not only had Leonie accepted Becket's proposal, but she was pregnant by Toranado, with you." I could see that the memory of his complicity pained him.

"Do you think she suspected?" I mused.

"Sometimes I did. Sometimes…." Spin shrugged.

"So, what about the Agreement?" I asked. "Where are we now?"

Spin wriggled uncomfortably. "I have done what I could to preserve it. Perhaps more than I should have, but it is too late to change my actions or their consequences. Those decisions are in the past. In her way, Leonie protected it as well, experiencing a bright moment of great promise, then making her peace with quiet enduring. The outcome of their affection was not what any of us hoped, but she did get you." Spin smiled, his sharp little teeth making it less comforting than it might have been on a more human face. "I do not think she regrets her choice or feels wronged. But whether the Agreement stands or is voided now is up to the two of you, it would seem."

"My mother has a forgiving nature."

"She does. And you, Kit? Would you make a claim against my lord?"

"Toranado did not lie to me, and he was not the one who abused me."

"No, but Johnathan Becket would not have had the opportunity to misuse you if…"

"There are many ifs in a life, my fey friend. If we are to live our days blaming people, based on the outcomes that might have been, what a bitter existence we would be left to endure. It is enough for me to deal with events as they *did* happen, not as they *might* have."

"The Drake Saga: a Greek tragedy." Spin chuckled.

"What pleases the audience most at the end of a tragedy is that at the curtain call, everyone is alive."

"Thank God for the curtain call," Spin hailed the theater tradition. "Where would we be without it?

Act Five, Scene One: *MacBeth* Fundraiser, Grover's National Theater, Washington D.C., September 1863

On a crisp September Sunday, Wallack's Company, plus and minus a few members, arrived at Grover's National Theater in Washington, D.C., and began to move in.

Drays brought the sets from the train station, and stagehands fell to setting them up, ordering them as they would be revealed during the production. The towers, having no artistic uniqueness, were recreated by Wixx and an advanced crew, using local lumber. The many contraptions used to create lighting effects were now settled in wooden crates at the base of those towers, while adaptations and changes to the lighting plot were explored.

The city was reviving after the long, hot summer, not only by the cooler weather of autumn but by news of the Union's nearly bloodless victory at Cumberland Gap. Still, the most common description of the "Rail splitter", Abraham Lincoln, was that he overstepped his role and treated the presidency as if it were a dictatorship. Many Americans saw Lincoln as an embarrassment who was ruining the country.

They did not know him.

This attack by the social elite, who resented Lincoln being "common", was a symptom of their disgust and mistrust of difference. How could an honest man with a poet's heart and a storyteller's talent possibly fit in among Washington City's swarm of self-important socialites?

In the weeks after the Draft Riots, nearly a quarter of New York City's black citizens closed their businesses and sold their homes to move somewhere safer. Idabelle confided in me that she would be one of them. When Ida announced her intention to Bernie, my aunt vowed she would move anywhere Ida wished, if only Bernie could go with her daughter, a relationship both finally openly acknowledged.

New York's grateful leaders eagerly agreed to have Tammany Hall run future draft lotteries. William "Boss" Tweed declared his organization would pay the three-hundred-dollar fee for any man who wanted his name removed. The loyalty strings attached to the offer were understood, and many of the city's new citizens found positions within city government.

I was just happy to be off hiatus and back at work. Of all the terrible things that came from the riots, the closeness of Wallack's Company was the most precious. Their theater cat's sacrifice gained mythical status, and Kindle's surviving kitten, Shadow, whom Kay now inhabited, was a favorite among the company's members. Unlike her mother, Shadow liked many of the company members and encouraged their affection.

Edwin Booth, who would make his debut as the lead in *MacBeth* in the D.C. fundraiser, was running lines with Bernie onstage, discussing his idea of playing the title role as less brutish and more a man manipulated by his ambitious wife--Bernie's Lady MacBeth--as the sets and lights evolved around them.

From my tower, I had a sliver-view of the street through the open theater doors, and some motion there drew my attention to Mary Hall's carriage driving up. Walt Whitman stepped out, turning back to offer a hand to a petite ginger-haired woman.

Mother. My soul flooded out of my body.

"Mother!" I called out, leaping down multiple ladder rungs to land on the boards.

Bernie and Mister Booth stopped in the middle of their discussion, watching as I jumped off the edge of the stage into my mother's arms; safe…seen…loved.

"Kit," my name on her lips was a prayer, and we clung to each other, our bodies shaking with the strength of emotions, our shared tears wetting each other's cheeks. "Kit. Oh, my Kit. My boy," she murmured, turning her face into my hair and taking a whiff.

"I knew you would come," I whispered back, my words muffled by the heavy silk material of her dress. It did not fit well and looked borrowed. I suspected Mary Hall had a hand in dressing my mother for this reunion. I doubted my mother was in a position to purchase a fashionable gown for some years.

"I am sorry it took so long. Too long," Mother apologized.

The entire theater stopped to witness our reunion, which meant when Wixx returned to the stage, nothing was getting done.

"No one's on break," he scolded. "Get to work. We have a show to put on." He looked around and saw what had stolen everyone's attention. Seeing me in this strange woman's embrace and perhaps noting some family resemblance, he made a reasonable assumption. "You must be Leonara Becket, Kit's mother?" His manner was familiar and a bit rough. "Welcome back." My mother dried her wet cheeks with a kerchief. "Please excuse us, though, Missus Becket, we are moving in a show and have limited time." He gave me a look that said I had a few minutes, then I needed to get back to work.

My mother held me at arm's length and took a good, long look at me. "The eternally 'old' boy has become a young man."

Spin stood at the edge of the stage, invisible to all but my mother and me, the expression on his face bright, pained, regretful, and joyous; all human emotions he learned living alongside us, all of them laid bare in this moment.

"We have missed you," I told Mother quietly, "Spin, and I, and Bernie, and the others."

"And I have missed all of you, but I am here now." She directed the last part of this to the little blue man.

"I know what you did," she spoke sub-vocally to Spin.

"The Natives captured him. Becket was going to die. It was only a matter of how painful it would be and how long it would take. I controlled the where and when, so he would suffer less. That is all."

"He was the father of my child." Spin remained silent, just looking at her, waiting for her to reveal that she knew he was not.

"We should talk about that."

"And so much more," she finished. *"You know I cannot forgive you."* I was uncertain which of Spin's transgressions she was referring to.

"I'm not asking," Spin declared. *"Johnathan Becket did not deserve mercy, but I did not wish you to keep worrying and putting yourself in danger unnecessarily."*

"And you made sure he was dead?" Leonie asked, her eyes welling.

"I did. He will never bother you or your family again." My mother considered this before answering.

"Thank you." Later, they would work out where their choices led them, as old friends do, after a long time apart. Moving her eyes from Spin to Bernie, my mother greeted our aunt. "Hello, Bernie."

"You look well, Leonara." Bernie's words were careful, correct, but her face was a collision of emotions.

"I am well," Mother replied. I licked my dry lips and tasted the tension in the air. "You look marvelous, Bernie. It could have been only days ago that we last spoke."

"But it was not. Time may sand down an old woman's temper, and soften her sharp tongue, Leonara, but her memories and regrets remain sharp."

"Is that an apology?" Mother's laugh flummoxed Bernie, who did not know what to make of it.

"No…I mean, yes; it should have been anyway."

"You owe me no apology, Aunt. We are family."

Bernie looked relieved. "Yes, we are." She looked at me, her smile broadening. "And what a family we are. Trusting us with your son has been a great gift."

"He is very special," my mother agreed.

"You have no idea," Bernie retorted.

"I think I might." My mother placed an arm around my shoulder and pulled me in toward her.

Bernie turned her gaze to Walt and nodded her silent thanks for whatever part he played in this reunion.

"I am very glad to see you, Leonie, but there is a lot that still needs doing before curtain tomorrow night. I hope we can talk later?" Bernie turned back to her rehearsal with Mister Booth.

"I don't want to leave you, but I have things that must be done as well," I apologized. "I work the stage right tower."

Mother smiled. "Walt told me."

"You will stay? You won't go away again?" I asked, my voice pleading as if I were a much younger person than I wished to appear to be.

"Bernie and I need to talk, but if she agrees, I intend to return with you to New York when you go. There are just some things I must explain first."

"Good. I am looking forward to meeting my little brother," I said, hoping to relieve any anxiety she was holding on that account. "But don't expect Spin to hold him or any of that. He doesn't like babies."

"No, he does not. I remember, but you seem to have won him over."

"It may only be a détente, who knows?" My mother hugged me again.

"I have missed so much, but I cannot wait for you and your brother to meet." Her eyes shone. "I will be at the show tomorrow night." She squeezed my arm. "And we will talk afterward."

Walt winked and smiled at me as he turned to follow her through the house, back to the carriage.

The house was full opening night. With names like Bernadette Drake, Edwin Booth, and Gilbert Collmeyer, how could it not be? The lighting effects were not as magical as at Wallack's, a tribute to the Wallack family's decisions when rebuilding the theater in the new uptown space and the use of limelight, but the D.C. audience was not as sophisticated as New York audiences and did not know the difference. Caught up in the performance, unencumbered by the rips of stage magic that accompany oafish sets, cumbersome set changes, and poor, unimaginative lighting, they were suitably moved.

I was acutely aware of my mother's attention as I climbed proudly to my perch and thought about how much harder it must be to be on the stage, having the sense of every move scrutinized, but just then, Fanny Seward entered the Lincoln family box, waving at me, and taking my attention away from my self-consciousness. Fanny's parents, Mister and Missus Seward followed, Charles Stratton and his wife as they entered, rounding out the presidential party.

It was good to see friendly faces, and I wished Kay could be here. It almost felt like a betrayal to work in another theater, but she had matured past such jealous feelings. Since sacrificing her cat body for me and giving birth, the theater spirit's nature had become rather motherly, I, being one of her large family of children-charges.

Act Five, Scene One

I located my mother sitting with Walt and Miss Mary in a box opposite the one decorated to indicate the President would occupy it.

In the box beside the President's a single occupant sat, tall and slender, dark, with romantically long, curling hair. I knew him by the tilt of his head, the angle of his chin, the charisma he exuded. Toranado had come as himself, and everyone was looking at him, fascinated, wondering… He looked at no one but my mother. Like the other women seated in the house, Mother's eyes were drawn to him. Unlike them, they did not remain. He was a handsome stranger. She did not know him. In truth, she never had. What did he feel when he looked at her now? Did he finally understand he lost her because of his mistake, or was he too proud and fey to admit it? I felt some satisfaction thinking he felt at least a twinge of regret.

Movement in a box several down from Toranado's drew my eyes to a party of politicians entering. The party included New York Congressman Fernando Wood. Heironymous Undergrove was nowhere to be seen. My eyes met Wood's, and his narrowed. Undergrove had abandoned Wood. The politician was once again just a small, petty man with ambitions above his abilities and no magical allies.

The President and Missus Lincoln entered, and the audience applauded as they took their seats. Lincoln caught my eye and saluted me, and I smiled shyly, giving a nod that was more of a bow to acknowledge the great man, aware, again, that my mother was watching. We both had stories to tell. I suspected it would take years to tell them all.

My two worlds were meeting here tonight: theater and the subterfuge of politics, and I thought about the lifetimes of Drakes before me who had taken risks and made sacrifices to form the world I inhabited and would continue to inhabit for more years than most of my peers. I wondered what Bernie was seeing in her Weavings, but I would not ask, content with what I knew now, in this moment, and with the people for whom I bore affection and were sharing it with me.

I had a good view of the President from my perch, and when I was able to steal a moment from my duties, I watched his face as he was pulled and held in the embrace of the performance.

Was Edwin's more thoughtful MacBeth precipitated on the actor's suppositions of Lincoln's experiences in his fateful role as president during a civil war? Had Booth read into the Bard's thoughts on revenge and ambition an echo of Lincoln's difficulties in Washington, trying to form a cohesive coalition of spatting generals and vengeful politicians seeking to replace him? What hand had taken part in the choosing of this play for this time? Gettysburg had lost more men in four days of battle than the modern world could claim had ever died in a war before, and in a month, the president would address the nation at the dedication of the battle site as a National Memorial. I knew Bernie was key in choosing *MacBeth* and that the reasons behind it had been stated as financial convenience, but had there been some other, greater purpose?

"Will all great Neptune's ocean wash this blood clean from my hand?" MacBeth asked early in the play, the line an echo of every leader who has sent soldiers into battle. When Booth spoke, the question, did it spark the same query in our president's breast, making him reconsider his decision to embark on a war because he believed our young country had to survive, even if its young men did not? Did our tall friend also feel a lump when MacBeth confessed that he could not speak the word "amen," his confidence in the rightness of his actions undermined by his fears that what he had done could not be justified and was wrong in the eyes of God and men?

"Let grief convert to anger," Malcolm declares in Act Four, and yet where does such violent vengeance lead a country that is ultimately fighting itself?

"Stars, hide your fires. Let not light see my black and deep desires," the witch's words wrung our country's kind leader's heart. I could see it on his face.

"Give sorrow words, the grief that does not speak knits up the o'erwrought heart and bids it break." I knew that after all he had endured, Abraham Lincoln's heart was broken even before the gruesome tragedy of Gettysburg. The crevice-creek wrinkles of the man's craggy face filled with tears, reflecting the theater lights.

"My soul is too much charged with the blood of thine already," MacBeth warded off MacDuff. Lincoln heard other ghosts. When he spoke at Gettysburg, what would he say?

Toranado was gone before the curtain call began. What he took from the performance, I could not say. I could not read the fey lord's face, but I read the human faces in the audience, and for them the magic had worked.

Walt's gaze found me on my tower.

"This was art," I heard him say silently, nodding to me.

After the final curtain came down, the audience lingered in the lobby and on the street outside, uncertain how to leave, where to go, still feeling the expansion of performing arts swelling in their breasts. It was a benefit, and Bernie would play the role of her public stage persona until the last guest with a pocketbook left the building.

The President stood in the lobby, everything else shrinking in his tall, sedate presence.

"Lady Drake," he took her small hand. "All the perfumes of Arabia are not needed to sweeten this little hand," he altered Lady MacBeth's line to his purpose, raising it to his lips in uncommonly princely fashion. "Thank you for this. I do not remember when I was so moved by a theatrical production. Please do not ask me for any favor, as it would be most unfair. After this brilliant performance, I fear I could deny you nothing." He bowed to her. Beside him, Missus Lincoln cleared her throat, looking like a hen whose feathers were out of placc.

"I would ask nothing of you, Mister President, but that you take great care of yourself," Bernie charged him. "The world is filled with dangers these days, even more so for you than for the rest of us." She leaned in and whispered, "A dark future stalks you. I will do all I can to thwart it, but it may not be enough. Be vigilant and do not make light of your life."

Lincoln laughed. "I hope that is not a prophecy, Lady Drake."

"I hope so, too." Bernie squeezed his hand before letting it go.

Act Five, Scene Two: Epilogue: An End to it all.

Our years were marked in rehearsals and shows, ideas that failed and those that flamed into life for brief, bright moments on the stage. The theater art's evolution to include plays that explored subjects of societal importance was slow, but gradually audiences and the art matured as did Kay and I, striving with each new production to give voice to the whispers of humanity's inner heart and bring them to the stage.

I finally had my first kiss. As far as I know, Charlie Stratton had nothing to do with arranging it, but to maintain some self-respect, I never asked.

Billy Bunson, the shop boy at Hanson's Store, was like me, inexperienced, recognizing only a mutual attraction, but uncertain what, if anything, could be done about it. Fingers fumbled with buttons and flaps with no conscious goal but feeling flesh touch flesh, which, when it happened, was a revelation. Afterward, we were too embarrassed to look each other in the eyes; nevertheless, we fumbled through the process twice more before Billy disappeared from Hansen's.

I never saw him again.

In November 1864, Wallack's, Barnum's Museum, and eight other establishments survived an election day arson attempt. The first fire, set at the Metropolitan Hotel, was discovered soon after it was set, and fearing they would be caught, the conspirators abandoned the project. The Copperheads fled to Canada. Copperhead sympathizer, Congressman Fernando Wood, and William "Boss" Tweed declared they were appalled, and New York would not tolerate threats to their city.

Gil Collmeyer grew from a spring stallion to a mature champion, and I remained his friend. He and Ginny married, but not to each other. She wed a merchant she did not deserve, and Gil married an actress he did. I stood as his best man.

On April 9, 1865, Robert E. Lee surrendered to General Grant at Appomattox Courthouse, marking the end of the war between the states.

President Lincoln asked the Union States to reach out to their Southern brothers, forgive them, and ask for their forgiveness, so everyone could focus on rebuilding our nation, leaving acrimony out of the mortar mix of Reconstruction. The Northern states felt peace was upon us and reconciliation at hand. We were naive and did not understand the depth of resentment and anger still smoldering in so many hearts.

The celebrations had barely died down on April fifteenth when William Seward was attacked while at his house in Lafayette Park. He was recovering from a recent carriage accident, and he and his wife had declined the Lincoln's invitation to attend Laura Keene's Company's performance of *Our American Cousin* at Ford's Theater. Accompanied by his tutor, Tad Lincoln chose to attend *Aladin* at Grover's National Theater that night instead of going with his parents to Ford's.

As an established actor, considered a rising star by John T. Ford, a Confederate sympathizer, John Wilkes Booth was well known at both Ford's and Grovers theaters and had purchased tickets to both plays.

It should not have been a surprise when Abraham Lincoln was assassinated. He had survived five attempts before John Wilkes Booth's attack at Ford's.

As Ford's Theater was shut down and its stagehands and actors arrested, word spread quickly through the theater community across the nation. Stunned, beyond their feelings of loss, lurked a fear about what John Wilkes' involvement might mean for theater in America. Throughout the country, theaters across the nation sat empty. The only theater in the news was Ford's, the only actor was John Wilkes Booth.

The stagehands, support people, and actors working at Ford's that night, including those in Laura Keene's touring company, were arrested, imprisoned, and interrogated at length. Some remained in custody for months. Some never recovered. Many never worked in the theater again.

Lester Wallack was heard to declare: "Theater will rise again. It always does."

Devastated by his brother's actions, Edwin Booth left the stage, certain the country would never forgive him, declaring, "I am retired. No one will ever want to see me perform again." Charlie Stratton brought Booth to his home in the Thimble Islands, out of the public eye, to help his friend recover.

When Walt Whitman's heart bled the poetic words "Captain, my captain," onto the page, I wept alone in my room at Drake house, remembering that fateful Thread in the Weave that Bernie had worked so hard to alter.

"How will we go forward now?' People asked, dabbing their eyes. A country that complained about Lincoln's common folksiness and reviled him, now shrouded their windows with black bunting, lining the streets and train tracks that bore his coffin on a last farewell across the country as he was returned to the woods of Illinois, his death drawing the country together in a way his life never had.

Emerson's eulogy of Lincoln eloquently expressed the nation's grief for a man they did not value as much as he deserved during his life, and were trying to absolve themselves of the guilt by elevating him to near sainthood in death, when it would not have mattered to him. Lincoln's sole desire for any legacy had been to bring his country back together, but the manner of his death and the politics of the man who held the gun imbued in Northern hearts a desire for revenge that shattered that wish.

With Lincoln's passing, the presidency fell from the shoulders of a sincere, if flawed, man, being hailed as a great hero and martyr, to a confused, indecisive Southern gentleman. Standing in the shadow of the giant Lincoln had rendered Johnson's efforts at Reconstruction inadequate. He had neither the character nor the will to stop the wreck and rape of resources that became the Reconstruction.

Three months after Lincoln's death, Ford reopened his theater with *The Octoroon*. The opening was accompanied by death and arson threats.

In 1866, eighteen months after his brother assassinated Abraham Lincoln, Edwin Booth returned to the stage playing the title role in *Hamlet* to glowing reviews, but though he continued to enjoy a successful career, in the public mind, the Wilkes name could not shed the association with what the younger Booth had done.

It is natural to wonder how Abraham Lincoln's death altered our country's path; how, with his compassionate leadership, Reconstruction might have been kinder, the country's healing better tended, but how it might have been different and in what ways, even a Weaver cannot know with certainty.

But this is not Abraham Lincoln's story. It is mine, and my future may be revealed.

E.F. Winters

Epilogue: Port of Los Angeles, 1919

A career in theater has been good to me. I found and lost human loves, but the defining relationship of my life remained the deep bond between Kay and me. But Kay's spirit was bound to the Wallack's building. Renamed the Star after the company moved further uptown, the building was torn down in 1901.

Kay lived there for forty years. What happens to a theatre's spirit after the building is gone? You can't move it in a box or a cage. It is a wild thing. But you can carry it in your heart, thinking of it whenever you see a ghost light pushing back at the darkness.

The actors and stagehands, production people, and designers who passed through Wallack's Company and the many others I worked with across the country became my family.

Bernie passed peacefully in her London townhouse. Spin, Burke, Dweetie, and Idabelle, her husband and children, were present, and Ira Aldridge Senior held her hand.

My mother and little brother lived with me at Drake House until Ade was grown and he began a life of his own, outside the theater. Leonie, Spin, and I continued to live together until she passed away at our home in the Hudson River Valley. Her many secrets died with her.

By the end of World War One, I had had my fill of intrigues, politics, and wars, and informed my colleagues I was retiring. All I wanted to do was sit on a beach and watch the waves chase each other.

Bernie told me once that "sometimes the persona we have been playing outlives its usefulness and we must take on another." I thought about her words a good deal as I contemplated ending my work on the world's political stage. I still had many good years, but I could not live them as Kit Drake without awkward explanations about my age. I needed to leave that name behind.

As Spin and I stepped off the boat onto a sun-drenched dock in the Port of Los Angeles, a porter approached me and a fellow passenger, a fascinating fellow who introduced himself as D.W. Griffith. We spent many hours of our voyage discussing the

Epilogue

challenges and innovations of lighting and how they were affecting this new entertainment field called movies.

"Where shall I have your luggage delivered Mister Griffith?" the porter asked my friend.

"The Hollywood Hotel," Griffith replied. He turned to me. "And what about you, Chris? Where will you land for your next adventure?" I squinted into the bright new day.

"Which way is Hollywood?" I grinned. "I hear they are doing fascinating things with machinery and light there, and the world is always in need of more light and magic."

A note from the author:

Years of casual reading about history have affected this work of fiction. In the beginning, I was uncertain in what time period to place my story, which led to more research before I could begin writing. I grew up in the theatre and have a long love affair with it and its denizens. Kit's love reflects my own.

Once I chose the Civil War era, pieces fell into place; the Bees and Pfaff's among them. This was one of the situations where I had a piece I thought was my own fiction that turned out to be historical fact. I do love research. It became a challenge to keep the rich, compelling history in its lane and not allow it to overwhelm the story. Any errors, unintentional or made for dramatic purposes, are solely my own, with apologies to real historians. If you are interested in knowing more about the period, I encourage you to take your own dive down the rabbit hole. It is quite a journey and remains pertinent if only for perspective.

I would like to thank my Beta Readers, S. Batty, A. Hutchinson, and L. Oslund, for the gift of their time and catching inconsistencies or pieces that required clarification. As always, my greatest gratitude goes to my editor, book, compiler, and partner in everything, J, for his patience when I shatter the silence of his morning chai time by sharing "out loud" what's happening with my characters as they reveal themselves. His career in technical theater informed my understanding of the important role of the stalwarts behind the scenes. They are vital to every production and each performance. If you are one of these stalwarts, thank you.

Bibliography

Cushman, Charlotte, and ALEXANDER NEMEROV. "A Stone's Throw." *Acting in the Night: Macbeth and the Places of the Civil War*, 1st ed., University of California Press, 2010, pp. 7–58. *JSTOR*, http://www.jstor.org/stable/10.1525/j.ctt1pp5nj.4. Accessed 25 Apr. 2024.

"We are Lincoln Men" (Abraham Lincoln and his Friends) by David Herbert Donald Pub: Simon and Schuster, NY, NY, copyright 2003 David Herbert Donald

"Wide Awake" (the forgotten Force that elected Lincoln and spurred the Civil War) by Jon Grinspan, pub: Bloomsbury Publishing Ny. NY copyright The Smithsonian Institute 2024

"The Bowery" (the strange history of new York's Oldest Street) by Stephen Paul Devillo published by Skyhorse Publishing copyright Stephen Paul Devillo 2019

"Gilded Lives, Fatal Voyage (The Titanic's First Class Passengers and their world) by Hugh Brewster Published in the U.S. by Broadway Paperbacks an imprint of Crown Publishing Group a division of Random House, Inc.

"The Gilded Age" published by: Captivating History copyright 2020 (no author listed)

"A Season of Splendor" (The court of Mrs. Astor in the Gilded Age) by Greg King published by John Wiley and Sons, inc. Hoboken New Jersey copyright 2009 Greg king

"Indigenous Continent" Pekka Hamalainen published as a Liveright paperback 2023 a division of W.W> Norton and Co. Inc. NY, NY

"The Dawn of Everything" (a new human history of humanity) David Graeber and David Wengrow copyright 2021 originally published in 2021 by Allen Lane, Great Britain published in the United States in 2021 by Farrar, Straus, and Giroux first paperback edition 2023

"American Nations" (A history of the Eleven Rival Regional Cultures of north America) by Colin Woodward, published by Penguin Books an imprint of Penguin Random house LLC copyright 2011 and 2022 Collin Woodward

"The Complete Works of William Shakespeare" edited by W.G. Calrk and W. Aldis Wright published by Nelson Doubleday Inc. Garden City NY

http://www.essentialcivilwarcurriculum.com
Backstage at the Lincoln Assassination: Thomas A Bogar author copyright 2013. Published in the United States by Regenery History
Washington, DC

Abraham Lincoln Papers, 1774-1948: Library of Congress

Life of Abraham Lincoln Timeline: Bill of Rights Institute

We are Lincoln Men: David Herbert Donald author. Simon and Schuster NY, NY. 2004

Indigenous Continent: Pekka Hamalainen author. Liveright Publishing Corporation a division of W.W. Norton Company NY, NY. 2022

American Nations: Colin Woodward author. Penguin Books Random House 2011

The Dawn of Everything: David Graeber and David Wengrow authors. Picador NY, NY, 2021

Backstage at the Lincoln Assassination: Thomas Bogart author
Boundarystones.weta.org, 2013

Scientific American (SCIAM), https://www.scientificamerican.com/.Author Gayoung Lee, Warfare History Network